The Things We Do To Our Friends

'One of the best suspense debuts I've read . . . Darwent's
prose is like a fine, dark silk shivering on your skin'
Julia Heaberlin, author of *We Are All the Same in the Dark*

'Compelling, twisty and surprising, with an
intriguing and complex heroine'
Phoebe Wynne, author of *Madam*

'Very, very good. Menacing and suspenseful with
drippings of Donna Tartt. Such a treat!'
Victoria Selman, author of *Blood for Blood*

'Dark and compulsive, it will have you
turning the pages late into the night'
Sarah Bonner, author of *Her Perfect Twin*

'A stunning debut. A deliciously dark story of toxic
friendship that made me gasp on several occasions'
Nikki Smith, author of *Look What You Made Me Do*

'Power, privilege and the most toxic of friendships.
All set against the stunning backdrop of Edinburgh'
Carys Jones, author of *The List*

'What a debut!! Sinister, compelling, utterly
spellbinding. I couldn't put it down!'
Vikki Patis, author of *Girl, Lost*

'An immersive, surprising, impressive debut. Draw the curtains, put on a bit of Lana Del Ray and sink into the creepy-delicate-deliciousness of this novel'
Niamh Hargan, author of *Twelve Days In May*

'Dark academia and twisted friendships in gothic Edinburgh – what more could you want? One for fans of *The Secret History* and all things deliciously dark'
Cailean Steed, author of *HOME*

'Razor sharp prose and an atmosphere sizzling with tension and intrigue . . . a deeply compelling story of friendships turned rotten'
Rosemary Hennigan, author of *The Truth Will Out*

'Satisfyingly dark, cleverly plotted and pleasingly (Donna) Tarttish. Looking forward to seeing what Heather Darwent does next!'
Emma Flint, author of *Little Deaths*

'Like nothing you've read before! A menacing and marvellous portrayal of power, friendship and belonging'
Lauren North, author of *Safe at Home*

ABOUT THE AUTHOR

Heather Darwent is based just outside of Edinburgh. Originally from Yorkshire, she came to Scotland to study History of Art at the University of Edinburgh, like her character Clare, and ended up never quite leaving. When she's not writing, you'll find her reading chaotic non-fiction about Silicon Valley and swimming in the sea . . . or being unbearably boring in conversation about swimming in the sea. *The Things We Do To Our Friends* is her debut novel.

The Things We Do To Our Friends

HEATHER DARWENT

VIKING
an imprint of
PENGUIN BOOKS

VIKING

UK | USA | Canada | Ireland | Australia
India | New Zealand | South Africa

Viking is part of the Penguin Random House group of companies
whose addresses can be found at global.penguinrandomhouse.com.

First published 2023
001

Copyright © Heather Darwent, 2023

The moral right of the author has been asserted

Set in 12.5/15.25pt Dante MT Std
Typeset by Jouve (UK), Milton Keynes
Printed and bound in Great Britain by Clays Ltd, Elcograf S.p.A.

The authorized representative in the EEA is Penguin Random House Ireland,
Morrison Chambers, 32 Nassau Street, Dublin D02 YH68

A CIP catalogue record for this book is available from the British Library

HARDBACK ISBN: 978–0–241–53882–1
TRADE PAPERBACK ISBN: 978–0–241–53883–8

www.greenpenguin.co.uk

For D

France

Three girls dance in front of him.

One of them has set up an old stereo, and tinny music blares, blocking out the sound of the cicadas that sing relentlessly at this time in the evening.

The garden looked beautiful when he first arrived, extending back to meet an old farmhouse where delicate vines stroke the white walls. There is grass that feels comforting – a damp rug under his feet. But things are not right, and the smell is a little aggravating. It makes his nose itch and his eyes water. When he focuses, the place looks like it has been left to become wild, and the fruits loaded on the trees are overripe. The garden has the heavy, sweet smell of the monkey enclosure at a zoo.

He struggles to concentrate on his girls, because of the sun on his face, perhaps, but it's enough to summon the tangled beginning of an urgent lust, deep in his gut. Two of them hold hands high above their heads to create an arc and the third shimmies and then dives under. There is a screech of excitement as she does so.

He remembers that kind of frenzied joy. When he was their age, summer seemed to go on forever. He would get up to all sorts of things, unsupervised. Now, these months are oppressive, caked to his life like dry mud on a car. Summer means foreigners clogging the roads, children everywhere and the slog of work. Supplier events, tastings, factory rounds: in this part of the country, none of it stops because of the heat. It all becomes more tiring the older you get, and each summer is more difficult to tolerate than the last. An itch on the sole of his left foot. A gurgle, and a cranky, more than irritable, bowel.

Each shadow of physical discomfort is worse in the evening heat, but these girls know none of the pain that comes with age. The girls are life itself, and things seem easy for them. They are too young to feel a pinch near the hips or the pull in the lower back as their bodies contort to the music.

They certainly hadn't a care in the world earlier in the day. He'd seen them outside the shop on the bench in the car park, waiting for a lift that hadn't come. When he picked them up, he could barely tell them apart. In that delicious way, the girls were preferable in a collection, a flick of hair, a flash of a smile. Tumbling in confidently, like it was their right to be taken to wherever they pleased. Their grimy knees up, pushing against the back of the seats in front with no consideration for the upholstery, something he would never have let his daughters do, and the smell as they'd chewed on strawberry-flavoured gum – a horrible habit – and chatted away to each other, ignoring him.

Now, hours later, he sees how different the girls are as they peel away from each other in the garden. That stack of limbs jumbled together in his car has parted to make way for three separate identities, and it seems fitting that he gives each of them a name.

There's the one who's tall and blonde and the most classically beautiful, with straight white teeth and a face that is perfectly symmetrical. She's bruised all over her tanned shins, but not in the way that you'd associate with abuse. A healthy, monied type of injury that he imagines might be from playing a gruelling game of lacrosse or falling in a photogenic pile when skiing. Each limb looks taut, her calves clearly defined and ripples of muscles in her forearms. He can tell she's the one in charge, as she issues directions to the others. He'll call her Blondie.

There's the one who has black hair braided into a complex arrangement and then pinned high on her head. He can see her shoulders, and he notices that they're sullied with a thread of sunburn. Braid will do for her. Staring at Braid, he feels a pang in his loins for that dark hair, those dark eyes, and an idle thought that he might like to slit her throat, to slice across the neck where the sunburn marks it and cut her head away. He imagines hacking at her to separate her sweet face from the unsightly mess of those bodily scars inflicted by the cruel sun.

The final one in the trio looks like a child dressed up as a belly dancer. Her body still has that lovely, almost dripping layer of fat that jiggles as she moves, and she appears to be swaddled in a full-length velvet floral gown. She blows him a kiss, and her eyelid dips into a theatrical wink. He nods back, acknowledging her but declining to invite her further. There'll be plenty of time for that later. He'll call her Winky.

The sun is so low in the sky. A scarlet flare that bleeds more across the horizon every time he treats himself to a long blink. The brightness sears his eyeballs when his eyes are shut, forcing him to reopen them and refocus. He assesses the situation. He's sitting at the centre. The star of the show, a treasured guest. He tips his head back and breathes in, realizing how deeply, deeply thirsty he is. The thirst is crunchy in the back of his throat; dry air hurts his nostrils. Everywhere, his skin seems tight and parched, like every drop of moisture has been sucked out.

A grubby metal tube lies on the table next to him. He recognizes it. There are many tubes that are very similar at work. He shakes his head in wonder, and beads of sweat run off his face and down on to his suit. Yes, he's still in his suit.

Could that be true? The tube is from the farms? Perhaps. Perhaps not. Suddenly, it's important. What detail! What sensitive *curation* of the experience.

It explains things, in some part, but the whole picture won't quite form properly.

He tries to nod for water.

Winky ignores the gesture, but she saunters over and pours

a glass for herself from the pitcher on the table. She takes a deep glug and slams it back down. The other two have stopped dancing, and the mood has changed. The music is louder. Some kind of horrible rock music and he can't escape it. Something is happening; the sense of relaxation has disappeared.

Everything changes.

Braid and Winky have gone now, and it's just Blondie. He sits straight and tugs at the handcuffs around his wrists, tentatively pushing his ankles apart to test the restraints there. They're far too tight to budge. Blondie unfolds a white cotton napkin and lays it out in front of him.

Winky and Braid emerge from the house, and Braid has an enormous platter. It's antique silver, far too big for her, like she's in a school play. She lifts the top off the platter and reveals a dish, holding it under his nose with glee. A deep bowl of mushroom risotto, the rice hot and steaming. The aroma of stock and fresh porcini.

Winky picks up the serving spoon. She shoves it into his mouth while Braid secures him for the feed – her fingers dig into his gums. They ignore the fact that the food is escaping and spilling down his front. He barely has a moment to think; all he can taste is mealy rice.

Blondie is laughing quite madly.

No, he wants to shout out, *not me*, but there will be no words to phrase an impassioned plea to the girls.

The mushrooms become warmed slugs and they stick in his throat, but there's no time to chew, so he gulps, hoping to push the chunks down. The next course is a ratatouille served by Winky, and again, she feeds him, spooning the food into his mouth, forcing it down. She does so alone and the other two watch. Then corn, fried in butter and laced with herbs, ripped from the cob and forced down his gullet. He pulls at his wrists, but there's no point.

He can only measure time by the food that arrives.

Vegetable stews, creamy cauliflower gratin, a yolk-yellow soufflé, then pasta coated in cheap American cheese that you use to top burgers on a barbecue and should never, ever be used in a pasta dish.

They manoeuvre the implements with ease, ramming the courses down. The metal of the spoon is painful against his palate, like a dental instrument, and then, later, further and deeper into his throat.

He is choking.

The food congeals, turns to grey glue as night falls. His body convulses and the music plays on.

PART I

I.

Edinburgh

I've decided to look back and make some kind of sense of it all, and the initial idea of starting to put the pieces together in one place was because Tabitha's mother asked me to write it all down so she had something of Tabitha's – a tangible record of her life for the extended family – but I couldn't quite bring myself to cobble together a fictional account where we were normal students who did normal things, so I ended up giving her a vague excuse, and she didn't ask again. But the idea wouldn't die down once she'd brought it up, and I thought, why not? Why shouldn't I go back over what happened for my own purposes?

Then the question was, where does the tale begin, and although there are other places that may seem more logical, September 2005 feels right.

My arrival.

How very dramatic that sounds! But it felt dramatic at the time.

September is a month that has a special anticipation associated with it. As the leaves turn and the nights darken. The first time you open a book, cracking the spine and smoothing down the pages so they can't spring back up.

It's a month that means fresh beginnings, and that only happens a few times in life, when the slate is wiped clean and the story is ready for you to begin and tell it how you wish. The first day of a job when you're cautious and rule-abiding, or with a new partner when you share appealing parts of yourself to test the reaction. At university, it is even more of an opportunity. Nobody knows who you are; there are no expectations or preconceptions. How you answer each question and how you position yourself is entirely up to you. But it needs to begin somewhere, and for me it was Edinburgh, at Waverley Station.

I was ready to move, so desperate to leave Hull for good, but it was hard not to feel a little discouraged when I stepped off the train and strode out into the city. I was expecting post-summer blustery days with the warmth still in the air, but the weather was particularly bad that year. I thought of my granny and what she'd say in that scornful tone: 'It's just a few hours away, Clare. I don't know why you expected it to be so *different.*'

How grey the Old Town was. It was magnificent, but there was an underlying sense of squalor below it all. Steps led to alleys, weaving with possibility, where you could just as easily find a grand square as you could a dead end and a seagull gnawing on scraps of cold chips. I remember the magnitude of scale when I walked along to Queen Street and stared down to the New Town. The views went all the way to the Firth of Forth, a glimpse of water, but the winds were quick and soon a dampish fog obscured it all, like a bundle of laundry pulled dripping from the washing machine, then pinned up. I ignored the weather. I was determined to stay optimistic about the whole thing.

Enough wandering. I had a map printed, tucked in my bag, showing where I was staying. My new home was under a mile away, so I decided to walk. It was a battle through the streets alone with two suitcases, which contained everything I owned, and on the way I encountered a group of confused tourists. They blocked the entire road and craned their heads to take pictures of St Giles' Cathedral with bulky cameras hanging from their necks. Then there were the other students who bumbled alongside harried commuters. What a mix of people to get lost in!

I was a bubble of nervous energy, and I could have screamed out loud, right there in the middle of the street, but I held it in.

2.

Everyone was starting a new life in that first week and there were structures to help us, because we were still children, untethered from our parents with no idea of how to live. There were social activities, stilted mixers and society nights, but during those early days, I struggled to fit in with the people I met.

We'd speak. They'd ask me questions and listen to my responses intently, almost running them through a checklist in their heads to see if I was like them. State school or private? Funny, a joker? Pretty? Boyfriend (yawn) back at home? Horsey? Medic? Sporty? Then there would be a pause, and I'd see their eyes dart behind me, looking for the next person to suss out, because it was hard to place me in a category. I didn't make jokes because I don't like them, and I often laughed too late or too quickly in the group – a forced, chaotic giggle even to my own ears. The conversations always petered out.

It was a clear case of not fitting in, and I was out of practice when it came to socializing with people my own age, so I told stories alone in my room, testing them on myself in front of the mirror – light anecdotes and stilted introductions that I tried to pull off breezily, but they sounded rehearsed, of course, my voice awkward and tense.

I felt observed in those first weeks. It sounds paranoid to say so, but it's true. I felt eyes on me when I walked and would look back over my shoulder, but I saw nothing of note. I thought of what my granny would have said if I'd voiced my concerns: 'You're in Edinburgh! Why would anyone be interested in what you're doing? For heaven's sake . . .' And she'd have been right because not much happened at the start. The days were heavy with administration, form after form, and I brandished my chewed biro for each one. *Sign here, sign here, now just here where we've put the 'x' for you. Do you have a GP? Where's that accent from? Would you like to pay extra for the insurance, or set up a direct debit, perhaps? Just a quick picture of you for this card. No, no, don't worry about reading the terms and conditions, nothing important there.*

There was a wave of dull paperwork. I made decisions when prompted, but after a while I stopped caring. I put my name down for lectures: An Introduction to Dutch Art; Garden Design of the Eighteenth Century. With little thought, I signed away my whole year on an impressive-sounding title, my name, today's date, and it felt like I was 'getting things done', whizzing through the days in a blur, buying books and batteries and extension cords.

The memories that come back sharper and sweeter are when I think of the bar. That tight knot of anticipation high in my chest as I turned up for my first shift, the slosh of amber triple sec and tequila when I learned how to make a margarita, squeezing fresh limes into glasses as the juice stung where the skin around my nails was broken, leaving my hands red and raw. The bar was where it all began for me. First with Finn and then, later, with them.

Finn was a sign that things might go my way. He came about because of my more significant problem: money. A distinct lack of it. That was easily solved. I decided I'd work in a bar and that would be an answer to some of my problems. A job would give me a task to do and a way for people to understand me – I'd be a girl who works in a bar, who pours drinks and stays out too late. Perhaps I'd make friends with art students covered in tattoos and Australians with deep tans. It seemed like a good plan.

I'd heard about a place in passing that was looking for staff. It was hidden away down an alleyway in the Grassmarket, squeezed in between sandwich shops and newsagents, so you could walk past and barely notice it was there. I pushed open the glass doors, even though it seemed like the place was closed, and made eye contact with a tall man in a checked shirt who froze behind the bar when he saw me as if I was an intruder. He had an ice bucket in hand and his brow was furrowed.

'Can I help you?' he asked in a tone that wasn't friendly but wasn't unfriendly. I took a deep breath and broke into a smile, one that hurt my cheeks it stretched so far. I hoped I was being inviting; I hoped my smile said, *I'm easy and happy*, but the skin felt too tight at the sides of my mouth and it probably looked more like a grimace.

The man smiled back at me. It reached his eyes and small crinkles came out around them. I asked him about the job, and he wiped his hand down the side of his jeans and took my CV. He had a soft Scottish accent that I liked straight away. I gave the flesh of my tongue a sharp bite to remind myself how to draw out my vowels and clip my syllables. I'd watched television for hours each day in Hull to smooth out my accent.

He asked me what experience I had.

'Not much,' I conceded. 'But I'm a quick learner.'

'OK.' He raised an eyebrow and grinned. It seemed a little suggestive, but not seedy. I tried to work out his age, which I decided was around late twenties.

'So, no experience with cocktails? I mean, we're a cocktail bar, which, to be honest, is a total pain. Endless mojitos, crushing ice for hours, all that kind of thing. We can teach you all that, of course.'

'No, no cocktails.' I kept it short. There was no point in mentioning I didn't think I'd ever drunk a cocktail before either.

'OK.'

He seemed to be a man of OKs. And I didn't mind that.

A moment of silence, but it wasn't too uncomfortable. He looked at my CV again, which was a jumble. I didn't quite know what to do, so I tapped my foot while I waited.

'Well, we're pretty informal here. We'd start with a trial shift, which I'm happy to do if that suits you?'

'Great, when?'

'Saturday at seven. There's no uniform or anything. We'll have you in for an hour or so and see how you get on; if it works out, then we have shifts available in the evenings, so it fits most of you around your lectures.' He lumped me in with 'most of you'.

'Amazing,' I blurted out, then felt as if I'd overreacted. I hadn't got the job; I'd just been invited for a trial which I didn't think would be paid, but it was a start. I was about to leave, and then I circled back. 'Sorry, what was your name?'

'I'm Finn. I manage this place,' he said.

'I'm Clare.'

'I know. It says here.' He held up my CV, deadpan. 'Also, one last thing, *Clare*. We have a lot of students working here, but if you're going to fuck off back to London or something for three weeks at Christmas and for reading week then that's not going to work.' The sentence ended in a low snarl, but he wasn't angry at me, I could tell. He wasn't unkind.

'No, I'm not going to do that,' I said.

And it was true, I wasn't.

I couldn't.

3.

Tiny baby steps, but I was proud of how I'd done. I'd been more relaxed for some reason and, as a result, I thought I'd come across well. The hard lump that had been living in my throat, threatening to explode upwards into tears or a scream, had faded. If I could do two shifts a week, that would be enough for food out, for drinks and a social life, even for a laptop, so I didn't have to type my essays up at the library. I could go back to Hull for maybe just a few days at Christmas; it would give me an excuse to return to Edinburgh sooner. That day, I walked back slowly, and I was deep into prematurely planning out the logistics of my new life when I arrived at the flat.

It had been disappointing when I'd stepped inside on that first cold day to meet my flatmates. I'd expected something grander, showing its history in every nook and cranny. I wanted high ceilings. A room with a little wooden desk full of knots set up against a huge, shuttered window that looked out on to the city's rooftops. But I was probably imagining some collegiate fiction from tales of Oxford or Cambridge, and, really, I should've been grateful.

Compared to the house back in Hull, the place was spacious, but still, there were too many cramped corridors and boxy cupboards filled with half-empty bottles of bleach and dusty fire extinguishers.

Dark, student accommodation purpose-built in the seventies, where the windows in each room looked straight out on to the walls of the opposite buildings, and the kitchen floor was stained lino that never felt properly clean. The furniture was basic, each piece chipped from years of use: some institutional-looking armchairs in a line against the wall like a waiting room and a plastic table bolted to the floor in case someone inconceivably decided to steal it.

The flat may have been disappointing, but the city wasn't. Edinburgh was a demanding host; she didn't welcome you in with open arms. I was living in the centre of the Old Town, in a glossy theme park. Gothic Edinburgh sanitized for tourists, moulded and photographed for piles of cheap brochures with big bubble letters in red, screaming: 'Haunted Ghost Tour/ Frights guaranteed/Free entry/Spanish+French translation'.

I ignored the somewhat tawdry surface of my new home, because if I burrowed a little further down, it suited me well. It was a city made to explore on foot. Walking down steep wynds to discover a graveyard or a tiny pub or shop full of tartan tat. The buildings became more and more crooked as they soared upwards, haphazardly leaning against each other, cutting the sky into fragmented shapes in the hashed-together Old Town. Spires knotted against guttered roofs to form a dark tangle.

I liked that the people weren't intrusive in the slightest. Perhaps they were used to the transient nature of all the visitors, but even if I went to the same cafe every day, I knew I'd be greeted by a blank stare.

Right from the beginning, I spent most of my time out of that flat. But, sadly, sometimes I needed to return, and with that came my flatmates.

That day, after my first visit to the bar, I came back to find the living room damp with steam. It smelt of pasta with an undertone of plastic and something dairy-ish. Ashley's head sprang up from the table, away from her notes. A gooey meal sat in a bowl next to her. The whole thing had a tangy edge, as though it was 'about to turn', as my granny would have said.

'Clare!' she exclaimed. Her hair was scraped back into a

knot, and she was wearing a loose pair of pyjamas, with a stained tea towel slung inexplicably over her shoulder.

'How's it going?' I asked.

'Good, good. Just catching up!' she replied. There was a floral binder laid out on the table with notes highlighted in different colours. She studied geology, and the allure of the subject so far seemed to be the invitation to colour in rock formations. I had no idea what she was writing; lectures had started only a few days ago and nothing had happened yet.

As if reading my thoughts, she continued, 'Just bits and bobs, you know how it is when you're not on top of things. I don't want to fall behind in the first week. That would stress me out, and the term *is* only ten weeks long.'

I nodded. I knew that, but ten weeks felt like a lifetime.

Ashley was from some village in Staffordshire from which she'd appeared two weeks ago alongside very nervous-looking parents. For some reason, the dog had accompanied them for Ashley's send-off, and it had wandered around our cramped flat searching for an Aga to curl up against, looking uncomfortable, before finally settling for a clandestine piss in the corner.

'Where have you been?' she asked.

'Out. I got a job, actually.'

'A job!' she exclaimed, her voice going high, delighted and fearful for me all at once.

'Yes, I need to work.'

'Oh, good for you! There's so much on, I can't even imagine getting a job now, but that's brilliant. Well done, you.'

'I need one. I can't afford to be here if I'm not working.' I pulled out a bottle of wine from the fridge; I didn't bother to offer Ashley a glass.

She blushed. 'Totally, well that's exciting. Where's your job?'

'A bar. It's a trial shift so we'll have to see how it goes.'

'Soooooo exciting,' Ashley repeated, and she leaned in, keen to hear more. 'Do you know when you'll be working? Will they let you choose your shifts around your lectures? What are the other people like?'

I explained that I didn't know anyone, and it was just a trial, and there was nothing more to say on the matter. Scooping up my things, I went to my room at the far end of the flat, leaving Ashley to her frenzied highlighting.

I dived under the covers to get warm. My room didn't have any other seating options.

The wine was to celebrate. I unscrewed the bottle and took a long glug before pouring half of it into the mug by the side of my bed. I felt the tension leave my shoulders and my neck.

When I said that I'd struggled to find friends, it may have been a little pickiness on my part. After all, it was essential that I found people who would help me become who I wanted to be. It wasn't Ashley's fault. Ashley was nice and pleasant, and she'd done everything right to get here. Good grades. Hockey club. Clarinet lessons, sleepovers and her parents driving her to a French tutor in the neighbouring village. The structure of it all, the perfect predictability – she depressed me.

There she was, 300 miles away from home. She could be wild, she could be crazy and change herself, but she seemed unsure of quite what to do.

Her upbringing was so different from mine, which wasn't the problem – everyone's upbringing was going to be different from mine – but when I'd met Ashley and her earnest counterpart, our other flatmate, Georgia (whom we rarely saw as her entire life seemed focused around competing with, socializing amongst and talking about the university swim team), I'd known they weren't for me, even though they were so eager for us all to be friends because it would be nice and tidy.

I knew why I was so keen to avoid them. With Ashley, it was a desperation that seeped like blood from an open wound. The thought of other people seeing that same neediness in me made me shudder. I understood it well. I'd been on the other side, and I'd been somewhat clingy myself, so I wasn't entirely unsympathetic. But the sympathy wasn't enough. However much I tried to be nice and easy and rational, Ashley made my skin crawl, irritation rising almost instantly as soon as I started speaking to her. I did everything I could to avoid being drawn into her schedule of cosy nights in, watching comedy box sets from a laptop positioned on a chair.

Living there was about becoming someone else – and I needed the right people around me for that.

I wasn't sure who I would become. A sketch of an idea existed in my head, but it swayed from one thing to another. I knew that it could be easily adjusted based on who I met. With my wine in hand, my mind was free to wander, and when I dared think about it more, it felt comforting and yet hurt to even imagine, like poking at a raw cut in the side of your mouth with your tongue.

4.

There was so much rain, but they arrived perfectly dry for some reason that was never made clear.

A thunderstorm, and in the morning, before it started, outside smelt like damp clothes. The air was too thick when I walked to work, and then the weather broke quite suddenly. Rain fell in soft, fat tears. Inside the bar it sounded relentless, hammering against the roof like a succession of drumbeats, and I could see from out of the window that the cobbles were pitted with inky pools of water. Black cabs sped by and caused mini tidal waves to gush on to the pavements outside the entrance.

I recognized them from our very first lecture together. A girl. She was pale and tall, with blonde hair pulled off her face and tied up high on her head, so it bounced against her back in a treacly pile of neat curls. I wanted to reach out and touch them.

Alongside her, there was a smaller girl with round cheeks, dark plaits down her back and big brown eyes. When she smiled, her hand jumped up to cover her teeth, even though they seemed very normal to me. It gave her a self-consciousness in those moments, like a child, but her default expression was a twitchy scowl.

Then two boys, on the skinny and awkward cusp of manhood – still youngish-looking, each with chins that melted into thick necks (Finn called boys like these Chinless Wonders and laughed under his breath at his own wit). They were both dressed in mint-green chinos and crisp shirts, and they took their seats at a booth by the door. I went to get my orders pad, and Finn raised an eyebrow.

'Let them come over,' he said. It was just the two of us working that night, and the place was empty, so it felt natural to go to them and take their order. Plus, I *wanted* to; I felt drawn to them. Finn was just being difficult because they were young and loud.

I knew how to manage him. 'No, I recognize them.'

'Your pals?' Finn asked.

I was still working on the words I used, the way I spoke, and I liked it when he used the word 'pal', but when I'd tried to use it, the term hadn't quite hung right and I'd made a mental note to avoid it.

'No, just some people from my course.'

I went over to the booth to take the order.

The blonde girl beamed at me. 'Vodka martinis for us all,' she chirped, throwing her hands in the air. She sounded a little like the Queen to me, but tinnier and more frantic. Hands back down, nails tapping on the table, and then suddenly she stopped and just stared at me with a bright smile.

'No problem. How would you like them?' I asked.

'Dirty.' One of the boys jumped in, very pleased with himself. They both sniggered and the girl with the dark hair rolled her eyes.

'Ignore him – he's an idiot,' the dark-haired girl said. 'Actually, can I have a vodka soda, please, with fresh lime.' She stressed the 'fresh' with a pained but confiding expression as if I would agree with the necessity of real lime over cordial. Cordial! Imagine!

I walked back to the bar. Finn snatched the drinks order from me and made them. He barely hid his annoyance as the boys shouted over each other to tell their stories.

The blonde girl watched him make hers intently.

Then, I carried over the drinks with care. I couldn't risk spilling a drop with this table.

The blonde girl offered a hand, not to help but to shake. It was thrust at me floppily.

'I'm Tabitha,' she said. 'And this is Imogen.'

I nodded, holding the tray, showing I couldn't shake a hand.

'I've seen you around. You're History of Art, like us?' Imogen asked warily.

'Yes, I'm Clare,' I said.

'History of Art, eh? Learn about a few paintings before someone puts a ring on it?' one of the boys in the booth barked, falling into the middle of the table in a fit of honking laughter, and the other cackled back at him.

Tabitha stared at the boys with loathing.

'Shut the fuck up, you moron.' She enunciated every word, speaking with a confidence I'd never seen in anyone our age before, and stared in a way I adored, so much steely disdain. He looked quite shocked and he laughed a little uneasily.

She turned back to me, her face open and warm. 'Yum, yum, yum. Thanks for the drinks, Clare. You should stay, have one with us if you can?'

The comment was such an indication of who she was, where she was from. Surely, she'd never had a job in her life? To me it was obvious that I wouldn't be able to do this.

'I can't. I have to get back to work, but thanks,' I said.

Tabitha picked up her martini and sipped it, smacking her lips together while she watched me. 'OK, but we'll see you in lectures next week?' she asked.

All first-year History of Art students were required to take some core introductory lectures. The idea of being in them now I'd properly met this girl, Tabitha, sent a small buzz through my body.

'Definitely,' I said.

I walked away from them, and I knew they were looking at me, but it wasn't unpleasant. I started cleaning glasses along the back bar.

'A nice bunch,' Finn said. His tone indicated the opposite.

'I don't know them. They're just in my lectures.'

'London boarding school kids. We get them in here all the time.'

'I guess so,' I replied. I kept glancing over to them as they laughed and drank, the two girls scoffing at something the boys had said, and I was filled with a deep, almost painful longing.

I wanted to sit with them. Feel the sketch I'd made, the sketch of who I could become forming, filling out like them; their easy confidence with each other felt remarkable.

Finn watched me watching, but he said nothing.

At the end of the night, one of the boys asked for the bill. Even though the balance was well over a hundred pounds, he barely glanced at it. He just pulled out his card and paid.

'We'll see you around, Clare,' Tabitha said, extricating herself firmly from the boy's grip as soon as I'd handed him the receipt.

Finn shook his head. 'Too much money.'

The girls stalked out into the rain as if the clouds would part around them. The boys followed, pushing and shoving, trying to knock each other over.

Looking back, I sometimes feel bad about what I did to one of those boys. But at the time it was as unavoidable as getting wet when you go outside on a rainy night.

5.

We'd be friends.

I was oddly certain, based on small things. They'd smiled, and the smiles seemed real, with no indication that I was too quiet or too loud or too 'not like them' even though it was clear I was nothing like them. They were the right fit, but I didn't want to let myself get carried away and go too hard too soon; however, it was also important not to reach the point where too much time had elapsed, and I hadn't found my group. I imagined if that happened then a foul smell would radiate from me – much like Ashley's pasta dishes – and people would wonder why I didn't know anyone. What was wrong with me that no one wanted to be my friend? I was so much better with people around me. I just needed to be patient. They were who I was supposed to meet, but there was no sense in pushing it, and I knew from experience to build our friendship at the right pace, starting with the foundations, brick on brick, to create a solid base. I would have to wait, and we'd circle around each other to see if we fitted and to make sure it was right for all of us.

The lectures took place in a hall that seemed, on first inspection, too grand for us lowly first years. A lavish, oversized dome with a mural of lazing figures, their bodies plump and softly winged. It felt like staring into the heavens, but down on ground level, it was nothing special. Wood, dust and stale breath. No one else was interested in the ceiling, but I sat on my own and often looked up as somewhere to divert my attention, so I didn't stare at the rest of the class. Everyone else was bleary-eyed most of the time, taking out pens and pencils in a syrupy state of hungover lethargy.

Tabitha and Imogen sat at the back with their feet up, pushing them against the chairs in front of them. First, I'd hear Tabitha's excessive squeal once or twice: *To the back!* And then they would race like naughty schoolgirls to create a private nest. Bags in a messy ring around them, spilling out their things everywhere (so confident!), marking their territory to ward off anyone else who might dare try to sit with them.

I got in the habit of looking for them in each lecture. Peering to the back of the darkened room and waiting until my eyes adjusted, until I saw them, a pile of legs and notes and coats. On one particularly brave day, I hovered near them, and then on another I actually sat to the left of Imogen. Sometimes I wouldn't sit close to them, but I hoped they'd notice my absence.

And then, one day, Tabitha moved a bag so I could sit in the seat next to her, and finally they started chatting with me.

'Clare! From the bar!' Tabitha crowed, bringing me into the fold.

Oh, the rich joy of Tabitha. She brought a chaotic energy to every conversation, constantly moving in a way I'd only seen in adverts. You could almost imagine her waking up to the beep of an alarm, arms over her head in an exaggerated stretch, pulling the curtains open to the tune of a jingle (the jazzy twang of a commercial for a Swedish brand of shower gel) and getting ready for a new day all in thirty seconds. She had an airbrushed quality suited to a model or an actress, someone you watched as opposed to someone you interacted with. This was emphasized by the presence of Imogen, who was pretty enough and always put together neatly, but who had an underlying unpleasantness. She didn't smile much and, when she did, she always covered her mouth with her hand, the way she had that first night, as if she was embarrassed by her teeth. A constant snarl was ready to bubble up under her hand. Early on there was a niggling guilty thought that maybe it was why

Tabitha hung out with Imogen. The contrast made her shine brighter.

They didn't attend anywhere near all of the lectures, and they were in different tutorial groups from me, but things were changing, I was sure of it, and I sensed they gained a certain enjoyment from having me around. One time I saw them waving to me to come over. When I sat, I felt Tabitha's arm pulling me into her.

'Sit closer, Clare; you're my favourite.'

I felt the sting as Imogen pouted at the remark, hiding behind her notepad. They were always scribbling something, sometimes their own notes – Tabitha's were meandering and unintelligible afterwards while Imogen's were tidy and comprehensive – and sometimes notes to each other or me.

Then they put their notes to one side to paint their nails on their laps, with the bottles spread out on the desks. One nail deep red, one pearly pink, one the sickly green of an unripe banana and so on, until their fingers became jewels when they moved their hands. So unlike the others in our year, who were always texting with glazed-over expressions, in a world of their own – Tabitha and Imogen barely used phones.

I remember something that happened, and it was a little odd. Tabitha had been talking about the lecturer for the entire time. She chatted away about how she was surprised by how attractive he was, and she claimed she was going to give him her number at the end of the lecture and see what happened.

I was shocked, mainly because he seemed . . . old. He must have been about fifty. It came so out of the blue that I didn't think she could be serious about it, but she wrote her number out with a flourish.

'Just a bit of fun!' Tabitha said. 'You do like fun, don't you?' she said to me, suddenly very serious as if we were discussing a fatal medical condition.

I agreed.

Of course I liked fun.

Nothing came of it. The whole thing felt like a bit of a test, and the idea seemed to tail off.

Our discussions never touched on anything serious. They were the back-and-forth kind of conversations that you have to pass the time. Imogen's face was often flooded with impatient displeasure, and I wanted to ask her straight out: What would make you happy? What do I have to do to please you?

Generally, she stayed on the offence with lots of brisk (bordering on rude) questions as if she was interviewing me:

Do you think it will get warmer . . . ever?

How long for you to walk here? Where do you live?

Do you have all the books? Why not, Clare?

When she'd finished a round of inquisition, her own tirade of complaints began. She was tired and she hated the food here – hated haggis, which she seemed to cook frequently for some reason – and the weather, and the lectures, which were too easy, and the hills, which were too steep . . . Eventually, Tabitha would quieten her with an abrupt technique – she would cut her off by starting an unrelated anecdote about a friend or a friend of a friend. It could begin as a light, comedic tale of the slapstick variety, and then it might morph quite rapidly into an awful tragedy – usually a gruesome medical kind – followed by a neat resolution, all delivered in the same upbeat tone.

We listened to Tabitha; both of us did. One of us sat on either side, and the two of them required very little from me, apart from to watch. I took pleasure in balancing out our threesome, even though Imogen and I had got off on the wrong foot. I think I had imagined that Imogen and Tabitha were an impenetrable duo when I'd seen them in the bar, *best friends forever*, but I realized soon enough that for all their easiness, sharing tampons and tissues, squabbling and singing, Imogen was more of a reluctant follower, and the two of them weren't on equal footing at all. There was space for me, an unbiased observer at that point, with none of their presumed history or alliances. Immune to their bickering, but already with my own prescribed traits.

Oh, Clare can only take notes if she's laid all her pens out in front of her just so, Tabitha would trill, and I would look down to notice that was true, and every pen was lined up to choose from. Had I always been that way? I hoped I hadn't picked up the habit from Ashley. *Clare is deviously good at remembering dates*, she would declare, based on absolutely no evidence. Sometimes she said it while doing an impression of me, for some reason, and a shiver ran down my spine. She was an eerily good mimic. *Clare has to have a coffee. Otherwise she can't function*, she announced every time I arrived, regardless of whether I had a coffee in my hand or not. And, more and more, I found myself leaning into my new traits.

Yes, perhaps I could remember dates better than the average person. The more I played into it, the more I saw it was true, and I needed a coffee to get me through the day. As though it had always been the case.

When lectures ended, I didn't know where they went. Quick smiles, and then off in a flash, rushing away from me, which made me concerned about the sour smell of my solitude. Neither of them ever asked me about my plans. Even if they had, I would have lied to give my life some colour.

So much time alone. No one should spend that much time without the company of others.

Sometimes I smoked on the bench near the library for a while and looked out for them around the campus, but I wasn't a committed smoker – I wasn't a committed anything yet – it was just something to do to break up the day. Eventually, I'd end up going back to the flat, which hadn't improved. In the afternoons I'd switch between how to make cocktails, reciting the measures for daiquiris and cosmopolitans in my head over and over again, then trying to memorize the names and dates of Dutch paintings for light relief.

Sometimes I spent evenings with Georgia after her swim meets, her swimming costume slung quite territorially on the radiator producing chlorinated steam, or I watched TV with Ashley when she insisted on some bonding time.

They were poor substitutes for Tabitha.

I wasn't into make-up, but one day I managed to track down a lipstick just like Tabitha's, after searching in various department stores, scanning the samples laid out from the hundreds on offer. I didn't recognize the brand she used, the one I'd seen in lectures with its angular silver logo, but I found the same colour in the end. An *unnatural* colour – an apricot hue but with a greyish sheen to it.

After I'd bought it, I hurried home. Refused to let the shop assistant put it on me in public – she had wanted to try it out on me, but she didn't understand that the whole thing needed to be private, that the act of application was important and . . . ceremonial.

I pulled the top off the lipstick carefully, put it on in front of the mirror in my room and assessed the effect.

The colour was too bright. It jarred with my skin, and I was all red at the top of my cheeks and my forehead, instead of softly flushed. The lipstick hadn't made me look like Tabitha, and however hard I tried to paint it on straight, I couldn't even apply it in the way she did. Her trademark – she always reached into her bag and put it on without a mirror, as instinctively as scratching an itch. I grinned and I looked awful.

A gash of oily orange with that grey tint, like a slab of dead fish.

How pathetic of me to even try. How unbearably, unforgivably *needy* I was.

I wrapped it up in toilet roll, so it resembled some secret bleeding thing, and threw it in the bin.

That day I smashed a mirror with my hand in a single unguarded moment. Didn't bother to wrap the glass up with the care I'd shown the lipstick, just put the shards straight in the bin. If I cut myself, or if Ashley and Georgia did, then so be it.

They heard my strangled scream of frustration, my flatmates did, but they didn't say a word.

6.

I thought about Tabitha and Imogen often, about what they did outside of the hours we spent together. Again and again, they disappeared after the lecture finished. I was almost beginning to lose hope until, one day, it happened.

'This is so boring I could *die*.' Tabitha turned to me.

She was drawing. She drew often and came up with surprisingly good little sketches, though she tended to revel in adding her own brutal flair. Idly copying Rembrandt's gloomy self-portrait from the lecture slides, adding pins that stabbed through the starched ruff around his neck.

'We only ever see you in lectures, Clare, and it's just not good enough. You should come round for dinner.' She leaned over her ruled pad and grabbed my arm (she was always clawing at me to get my attention, bending in, her arms around my shoulders or pushing me to one side; cold hands on mine, and the bone of her shoulder blade pressed up close). Abandoning her picture, she scribbled an address on a piece torn from her notebook.

'Tonight. Is that too soon? You're not working, are you?' She treated the job at the bar with an over-the-top respect.

I shook my head. A wrong move could lead to her taking the invitation back.

'Great, we'll see you there at seven,' she said.

'OK, will it just be us three?'

'Oh God, no,' Tabitha squawked. 'You must be sick of the sight of us, especially Imogen – she's such a fucking downer. Samuel will be there too, and Ava.'

Imogen rolled her eyes. Something she did so frequently, it meant very little.

It was the first I'd heard of Ava or Samuel. There had been no further mention of the two boys from the bar, who I guessed were minor players. Still, I was glad the group was larger. That would work better for me.

'Imogen's a great cook,' Tabitha said, throwing her a titbit, and Imogen nodded semi-modestly. Placated.

We didn't discuss it any further, and I went back to annotating slides and listening to our professor talk about the genesis of Fauvism.

Tabitha ignored him and doodled a love heart on her notepad next to her hacked Rembrandt. This sketch was not to be – his face had dissolved in a nest of biro scrawl. She speared it with an arrow and spent the rest of the lecture gouging a dark rain shower on either side, stabbing her pen so hard at the paper that the ink stained through to the desk.

7.

My stomach heaved as I waited, a sick feeling that wasn't unpleasant. There was no unmarked doorbell like most of the other student flats, instead there was an engraved plaque with her surname, so I knew where to ring. She buzzed me in, and I found myself in a tiled entrance, the floor patterned with colours from an auction room – deep ruby reds and snooker table greens. A circular staircase curved up away from me.

We were right in the centre of the New Town, just off Dundas Street. I knew the area because, during my first weekends in Edinburgh, I had walked those streets often in the evenings if I had an hour or two to spare between lectures and work. It was nothing like the Old Town, where swarms of tourists blocked the roads and the buildings looked as if they might, at any point, topple into the crowded streets like creaking old dominoes. Where Tabitha lived seemed a world away. This part of the city was so quiet. Similarly hilly, but much more orderly, with spacious, tree-lined streets. So many sweeping crescents framed by lengths of spindly wrought-iron fences that protected gated gardens – always locked to keep out the public. At twilight, drawing rooms were lit up for display with barely a soul in them; instead, the glowing lamps were a statement of wealth projected outwards – a show of shallow benevolence for the masses. Later, the monied owners pulled across the tall shutters and quietly closed off their homes to the world as night drew in.

I climbed the stairs, up to the highest flat in the building, where Tabitha opened the door, her cheeks flushed. Warm heat rushed out and hit me in the face. I handed her a bunch of lilies dyed orange and a bottle of Pinot Noir – a far more expensive bottle than I'd usually buy.

'Come in, come in,' Tabitha said, grinning. 'It's a total madhouse here, so forgive us!' She sounded unapologetic as she ditched the wine and the flowers on the table – a rustic oak affair sitting centre stage in a large kitchen with gleaming silver appliances.

I regretted my decision – I could see the flowers would look garish, like the slash of a child's crayon drawing, against the russet carpet. Later, I would discover that the present guaranteed to make Tabitha's eyes light up was far easier and cheaper to procure – a simple scratch card was the way to her heart.

'I'm so excited for you to meet everyone. I'll give you a tour of the flat.' Her hands firmly on my arm.

We made our way down the corridor, and she spoke as we walked. 'So Immy is here. And Ava, who lives with us. She's lovely, but she won't show it, so don't worry about her. Samuel's here too, of course, but he's probably hiding – he's an absolute sweetheart as well. He'll like you – you'll see.'

To the end of the hall where there were three doors for three bedrooms, each closed. She didn't offer to show me them and they didn't seem part of the tour; instead, she pulled me into the drawing room.

The space almost perfectly matched my romantic dream of what a drawing room should look like. This was the jewel of a Georgian tenement building, with windows set in severe symmetry and brocade curtains opened on to the glittering street lamps below.

It was the lighting that got to me. In my flat, there was one glaring overhead bulb that was always on, bright and ruthless and buzzing. Here, there was no central light but lamps of varying sizes; candles and uplighters on the portraits gave the room a fuzzy radiance. And a fire, an actual fire! I stopped myself from running up and warming my hands. I noted there was no TV, which didn't surprise me at all. There were pictures everywhere, though, framed paintings and photographs, so I hardly got a chance to look closely, but there was one that caught my eye. A much younger Tabitha, gap-toothed and standing outside a big house that looked like it was somewhere hot, all blue skies, long grasses around her ankles.

'Here's Samuel,' Tabitha said.

He sat at the window with his laptop open, focused intently on the screen. As I entered, he slammed it shut and rose to greet me. I saw how broad he was. More man than boy.

'Well, hello, Clare from the lecture hall. I've heard so much about you. I'm Sam.'

That was how he introduced himself, but I never called him Sam after that; none of us did. It was always Samuel or Sammy.

Tall and handsome with a shock of curly red hair. It was a bold type of beauty that suggested a level of maintenance. The result of expensive orthodontics from an early age and a good diet. He wore a formal shirt and trousers, and his clothes were carefully ironed in a way I'd not seen much amongst the general student population. I thought back to the two boys in the bar. I'd already forgotten their faces, but I remembered their braying laughs as they pawed at Tabitha and Imogen. Samuel was different from those boys.

The girl who I guessed to be Ava sat to one side, away from the windows, next to the fire, curled up like a cat on an overstuffed armchair that looked about a hundred years old with stuffing seeping out from its sides. I couldn't imagine being so relaxed.

She gave me a small nod and stretched out so I could see how tall she was, all legs and knees and elbows sheathed in a fussy assortment of leather and denim with lots of buckles.

'Clare, nice to meet you.'

An American accent but with something else mixed in that I couldn't place. The way she constructed the sentence sounded very formal, like a governess or an army sergeant. I felt my teeth instinctively draw down on my lips, testing my own pronunciation.

Imogen rushed in, pushing a glass of wine into my hand, fussing over me in full hosting mode with a frilly red apron tied around her waist. She had unfurled a little, which suited her, her hair falling in her face as she pushed it out of the way.

'Oh, hello, Clare,' she said, far happier than I'd ever seen her in our lectures together, almost as if she'd briefly forgotten that she didn't like me much at all. 'Do come through and we'll eat.'

8.

We ate in the kitchen, and Tabitha sat at the head of the table. Imogen produced a stodgy aubergine Parmigiana.

'No haggis, Immy? Booo!' Tabitha declared, sticking her tongue out at no one in particular.

'Not everyone likes offal,' Imogen said, dishing out her meal like a dinner lady, piling it on to our plates in huge portions without any other side dishes.

Finn laughed a lot when I told him later about Tabitha's fixation with serving haggis. 'Of course they eat haggis, Clare. Cultural tourists, all of them do it. A four-year anthropological study of the *locals*. I bet they don't eat jellied eels when they pop back to London every weekend, though,' he said scornfully. I smiled at his haughty explanation. It made sense that Tabitha would consider eating haggis all the time as *a charming thing to do*.

Imogen had served Samuel first, clearing his cutlery to make room and making sure he had a napkin, then blushing like a proud housewife.

He ignored her and wolfed it down. I stored the quiet imbalance in that interaction to ponder on later.

They all chattered about nothing much, mostly ignoring me. Questions bubbled up in my head, but I pushed them down.

'So how do you all know each other?' I asked finally. It was the polite thing to say.

'Oh, school, down south. And then we came here together.' Tabitha took a long sip of wine from her glass and when she'd finished her lips were stained with it, her lipstick rubbed away.

'Samuel and I . . .' She let the words curl around her tongue. 'Well, we really have known each other forever, haven't we?'

Samuel grinned. 'It's a funny story.'

I smiled encouragingly even though I've always hated it when people say that. Surely it's up to me to decide if it's funny or not?

Tabitha laughed. 'Oh, doooo tell!' she pleaded.

He shook his head. 'I don't know, love. Does our new friend want to hear that?'

'Go on,' she urged.

He seemed to delight in her attention and, after a bit more back-and-forth that was bordering on tedious, he turned to me. 'Our mothers were in hospital together, Clare. In a private hospital in Bahrain. Anyway, there we were, and the nurses were a fucking shitshow, cooing over us non-stop, you know.' He flashed a conspiratorial grin at Tabitha. 'They wrapped us up in swaddling, and we were swapped about, and in the end we were handed back over, and they discharged my mother and Tabitha's. Anyway, old Minta, Tabs' ma, gets home, opens up the swaddling and there's a fucking cock there.' He paused for dramatic effect, face deadpan, little finger raised.

Tabitha wheezed at the other side of the table, and Imogen and Ava laughed obligingly.

'So, she calls up the hospital, and she's screaming at them in English, and they're shouting back in Arabic. Probably thinks her little princess has been sold to some sheikh or something, and they end up calling my mother, who's so out of it on Prozac she's barely even noticed her new baby boy is, in fact, a girl! Anyway, no one wants to go back to the hospital, and both of our fathers were working pretty much non-stop, so Tabs' ma ends up calling mine, and they meet up at some compound in Manama and "exchange".' He raised an eyebrow, his eyes locked with Tabitha's. 'Then they both realize they know virtually no one, and they're absolutely crap at the whole expat thing, although Tabs' ma was a little better than mine at society life. And then it was happy ever after and we basically grew up together before we came back to the UK, didn't we, Tabs?'

I had no idea what to say so I just nodded and tried not to show my horror at the tale.

Tabitha had reverted to a more serious pout. 'Well told, Sammy. We had a brilliant time up to a point. Once I was back in the UK, it wasn't so great, Clare, for me anyway – family stuff.'

I nodded. I understood *family stuff*, but I found myself wanting to break eye contact. It was all a little intense. 'I'm sorry,' I said.

'No, no, it's fine. But we moved around a bit. Then I was away at school, but Samuel and I stayed close – we ended up at the same school much later. I helped him out of some tricky spots!'

Samuel's face was made smooth by the candles, like a polished stone, and I couldn't quite read his expression.

'And Ava?' I asked.

'Ah yes, Ava and I met at school too.'

Ava paused before she spoke, and I could tell she was considering how much to say. 'I came over when I was thirteen. I'm originally from Russia. Via the US. A bit of everything. Do you smoke, Clare?' She changed the subject with no subtlety. Something Tabitha did too, I had noticed.

I nodded.

Tabitha twisted a tendril of hair around one finger and we all looked at her. 'Immy and I will come too,' she said.

I noted an exhausted-looking Imogen, hot from cooking and serving and faffing around, and saw she'd gone from relaxed to tattered.

'Why don't you sort out pudding?' Ava replied.

Tabitha and Ava stared at each other. A silent pull and push of power. I could tell that they were in charge, Tabitha loud and braying and Ava a quieter strength just under the surface.

Tabitha bowed her head, as if excusing Ava from the table.

'Come outside with me to smoke. It's so hot in here,' Ava said. That was the way she spoke, in swift directives issued calmly, making it hard to work out whether there was even a choice to follow them.

We left the flat in silence and stood on the pavement. Wordlessly, she handed me a lit cigarette, the taste of smoke mixing with the smell of bonfire already in the air. It gave me a chance to examine her. She had long dark hair, a little like Imogen, but that was where the similarities between them ended. Ava was all harsh lines. She was also shiny like she'd been covered with a thin veneer of plastic everywhere: coated lips and a strangely lacquered ponytail on the top of her head. Not a look I'd seen before, but I liked it.

She lit her own cigarette and leaned back against the sandstone.

'It's not true,' she said.

'What do you mean?' I asked.

'That story, about her and Samuel.'

'Really?'

'No. I've heard many versions of Tabitha meets Samuel over the years. Cruise ships, abductions, heists . . . Shameless, really. Who knows how they actually met; it was before my time. Those two just like to see how people respond. It's play.'

'Why, though?' I asked. Although the story had seemed over the top and exaggerated for effect, it hadn't occurred to me that it might not be true.

'Why not? I mean, the story always ends the same. Best friends, some deep connection forged through some awful or fantastic drama, so what does it matter where it begins? The end is the only thing that matters, don't you think?'

I shrugged. 'That's a bit odd, but I guess it doesn't really make much of a difference to me.'

'No, it doesn't, and I would say be careful, but there's

absolutely no point. Whatever happens with Tabitha, it just happens, and you have to go along with it. You're also her type.'

'Her type?'

'Yup, her type.'

I found this even more remarkable.

Ava burst out laughing, but laughing didn't suit her face, and it surprised me. 'You know, pretty in a wild kind of way,' she said. 'That's all I meant – someone she'd want around. You look terrified. There's really no need to be at all. Here. This.' She gestured up to the flat above us with the end of her cigarette. 'In there, them, us, it's everything you've ever wanted, and you're going to love it. I promise. I'll look after you.'

It was a big statement, but I already felt comfortable enough around Ava to want to force myself to trust it.

She winked (this, again, didn't suit her and seemed forced) and threw her cigarette on to the ground with mine.

9.

I had assumed we'd avoid discussing anything too personal at that first dinner party.

This was based on my interactions with Georgia and Ashley, who would stare passively at the TV for hours and then review the programme with analytical detail. Then, with other students I'd met, the chat was all about music, the latest band, or else the endless dissection of relationships and friendships to forensic levels. Who'd said what to who; who was being unfair; petty household disputes involving stolen cooking oil that built up to become grave feuds.

It was like they were opting out of being young, which was fine by me. It was a relief, as I wouldn't have understood the cultural references, but there was no talk of bands or TV or anything like that. Once I'd jumped through the awkward introductions as they tested me out, what we spoke about extensively, almost without a break, was money.

Money should have been a difficult topic, but over the course of that first evening I saw that it wasn't awkward at all. I'd never spoken about money before with friends too much because there had always been imbalances.

I had expected them to be closed off or awkward. It was clear they all had varying amounts and sources of money, which I'd come to understand in time; none of them had part-time jobs as far as I could tell. Sitting in that grand flat in one of the priciest parts of the city, there was no shame or apology to the discussion.

Tabitha took the lead and the rest followed. She bemoaned how expensive running the place was. At this, she gave Imogen a winning smile. Oh, how Imogen *glowered*. I learned that instead of being rented like most student flats, the place belonged to Tabitha's father, which now seemed obvious given all the antiques. He'd bought it for her to live in with friends while she studied and she charged Imogen and Ava a very steep rent.

Later, we ate tablet, with coffee served formally in cups with saucers, and whisky afterwards, sloshing in our cups, so the liquor mixed with the coffee grinds and became bitter and lukewarm. Tabitha pointed out some of her favourite pieces and how much they were worth. The old chair Ava had been sitting on had cost so much that, when she told me, I choked on my whisky, and then hid it with a cough.

'Not that I'd sell it at the moment, Clare!' Tabitha exclaimed, wide-eyed. 'But don't spill anything on it.'

I put my cup down, making a mental note to use a coaster next time.

The chair was assessed by the group with a bland detachment. They cared very little for the actual object. Ava declared the designer at some point and Tabitha just scrunched her nose and started to talk about how Lebanese wine was a shrewd investment.

One of the things I had looked at and assumed to be expensive – an oil painting of a colonel, his face wrinkled and the effect heightened by the age-induced cracks of the paint – turned out to be basically worthless, or at least to them because they weren't sentimental about possessions in the slightest.

'Charity shop find from home.' Samuel winked. 'The chap had the thing propped up by the side of the road one day, and I asked if I could buy it. Cost about a tenner or something, nabbed it for Tabs' eighteenth.'

Looking back now, so many years later, I notice people of my age often drift into the monotony of discussing property prices. I don't think I quite appreciated at the time how rare it was to sit around at eighteen or nineteen and discuss such matters with keen interest, but they included me in it, so it didn't feel as strange. They drew me in without any kind of test, and I listened quietly as they chattered away.

'When I'm older, I hope I'll have a cool mil' to spend on somewhere decent. Maybe here, or some ramshackle old castle up in the Highlands,' said Samuel.

'Oh, of course you will, darling,' Tabitha exclaimed. 'You just get so much for your money up north.' She finished with a smooth purr.

I didn't ask what 'north' meant, as I'd quickly learned from our lectures together that anything above London was 'the north'.

Maybe I should have felt uncomfortable at how the conversation developed, but it hummed along, and I didn't interject much. I just listened as it floated around me like the comfort of a warm bath. It didn't niggle being on the outside. It was pretentious, but not irritating. Right from that first night, I never thought that they considered me poor, or not like them, and that was before I knew more detail about their individual circumstances.

Later, Ava produced a ladder, and we climbed through a hatch up to the top of the building so we could look out and see the familiar landmarks from the rooftop, all lit up. Samuel pulled out a joint and we smoked it. It could have been the weed but by the end of that night I was happy in a way that had such an unexpected lightness to it. It was the simple delight of spending time with people I felt such a strong pull towards, of learning more about them and watching the way they spoke to each other – I inhaled the details. Those wrenching waves deep inside my gut that had been there for a while had gone.

It was like we were pretending to be grown-ups with clip-on earrings. Playing at holding a dinner party and talking about money like it was a game of Monopoly.

Then, at the end of the night, Tabitha led me out of the

drawing room and into the corridor where there was a large print in a cheap-looking plastic frame that I hadn't noticed when I'd come in.

'My favourite,' she said, when she saw I'd seen it.

'Klimt,' I said, recognizing the style immediately. Rudimentary art history. The woman with her long body framed in scratchy fragments of gold. So decorative; an almost armoured dress that slipped to the sides and showed a lengthy, moon-coloured stretch of flesh from blurred clavicle to belly button. A rosy breast.

Not *The Kiss* – the picture that so many students our age had as a print on their walls. A different painting.

'Klimt, yes, of course,' she said. 'His picture of Judith – do you know the story?'

'No.'

She spoke with adoration. 'The story's been done a million times in art, but this is Klimt's version. My favourite version. Judith, a strong, quite frankly vicious widow enters the tent of Holofernes,' she said, then sighed. 'And what a woman she was – *look* at her! He finds her intoxicating, beautiful; it's easy for her to get into his tent, exactly where she wants him. They fuck. He's wasted; he passes out and she . . .'

Tabitha drew a finger across her lovely throat.

And it was only then that I looked away from the gaze of the formidable Judith and to the side of the artwork. It was partially cut off, so you hardly noticed until you looked properly. I realized Tabitha's gesture had been quite literal. In the painting, the decapitated head of a man. Cast in shadows under Judith's arm. Her hand on top of the man's head gripping at his hair, her face triumphant but relaxed.

Then Tabitha reached out and I wasn't sure what she was going to do, but when she let her middle finger run along the skin of my throat very slowly, as if it was only the two of us in the flat, it seemed perfectly natural. When she was almost at the point of reaching to the back of my neck, she pulled away as if nothing had happened and said brightly, 'That plastic frame's vile, isn't it? One day I'll sort it out. Give her the proper one she deserves.'

And if ever there was a warning sign, that was it, but I just stared on at Judith's beautiful dress.

IO.

After that night, they all came into the bar often to see me, and Finn was vocal in his scorn. 'Those girls, there's something off about them. They're . . . mean. I'm being serious. Like sharks, like a shoal of sharks.'

I looked it up on the computer in the office later.

'A shark is a shiver, not a shoal. A shiver of sharks,' I said.

He laughed loudly. 'Yes, that's exactly what they fucking are, a shiver.'

He gnashed his teeth together to make the point.

The Shiver. That's what I called them from that point onwards. When I told Tabitha, she *adored* it. Her impression of a shark swimming around me in her flat, with her fin made from two hands clasped high above her head, was so over the top I was glad she hadn't performed it in public.

Finn was a good, calming contrast. Kind eyes. Easy.

The story of Finn and me doesn't involve grand romance. It happened one night when we were talking after closing time, although not about anything in particular. We drank expensive wine, dregs left over from a tasting earlier in the day, inches of Malbec, tart sips of Soave, swilling it, and we ended up becoming very, very drunk, and his mouth was on mine. The two of us as one pressed up against the bar, his hand up my skirt, clawing at me with a hunger I hadn't seen in him before.

'Clare just gets on with it,' Finn said to the rest of them. 'She doesn't moan or complain that there's too much cleaning up to do, or that she's tired.' He was right – I didn't complain much. My lack of any objection to the job they paid me to do seemed to have inspired Finn's attraction to me.

It certainly wasn't based on our conversations. Finn was prone to long stories about his summer childhood in Shetland or detailed rants about trying to return something or other to a shop unsuccessfully – *But, Clare, I had the receipt!*

The conversations didn't excite me, but from the beginning I found him calming, like white noise. He was wilfully uncomplicated in my new world, which worked well, as I was having to use all my energy to keep up with Tabitha and the rest of them to justify my place in the group.

The main surprise was that whatever we had together didn't fizzle out in those early months when I was navigating so many different things. But once it started, the pattern continued. It revolved around waking up late in the afternoon, hung-over, our mouths dry, and chasing away the night before with coffee and buttered toast.

He didn't care about my course, and he never asked about my background. The evenings we worked together were fun enough, and the job grew easier. I liked the ceremony of it. Endless hours of prep, picking mint leaves off the stem and stacking them away, crushing ice and preparing sugar syrups. Grabbing coats from the lost property to wear home, because who cared whether the owners ever got them back.

I wouldn't have said I was a good cocktail bartender.

'You're slapdash,' Finn said, shaking his head. 'No care for the presentation. Imagine what the customer would think, getting *that*.' He placed his own neat daiquiri on the bar with care. 'There you go.'

I apologized and nodded, practised making them again and again. But he was right. Of course, I didn't want to get fired, but also, I didn't care about the final product. I could hear Finn's voice droning on, talking about the importance of the customer. To me, it was just a drink, and the buzz I got was from throwing the drinks out as fast as I could, challenging myself to remember the quantities, the techniques and garnishes until there was no room for anything else. It was an effective escape – the attention from Finn, from our customers.

At the bar, Finn was the only one I got on with. He had a reputation, which may have caused some ripples. The other bartenders we worked with had told me about him. First with their raised eyebrows when they saw us leaving together and then more explicitly later on, but it didn't matter to me that there were nights when I didn't know where he was. He came in smelling of cloying perfume that wasn't mine, but I didn't mind. Then I would arrive at work and I would feel his finger brushing my arm on shift or his hand grazing over my back, and then he didn't seem so boring, and it was enough to start the whole thing off again. I considered us to be quite casual.

One night I went in to pick up my payslip. It was early, and the door should still have been locked, but it wasn't. I heard two of the girls we worked with talking in the back room. Then a tinkly laugh from one of them.

'Yeah, I know.' I recognized the voice – Kaylie, an Australian who I'd initially thought I could be friends with.

There was a mutter from someone else, and then Kaylie spoke a little louder. 'She seems nice enough, but she's just a bit weird, you know? Like, you say something and she just . . . stares at you gormlessly.'

The other girl said something that I couldn't make out, but I heard my name.

'Yeah, well, we know why *he* likes her,' Kaylie said.

Clearly, we weren't destined to get on.

Kaylie replied again. 'You're right. I'm being harsh. She's fine, I guess, but you wouldn't want to be stuck on a shift alone with her, would you?'

She appeared in the door frame and had the decency to blush a little, but she recovered quickly. 'Oh, hey, Clare. You're not working today, are you?'

'I just came in to get my payslip.'

'Oh, OK. I'll get that for you.' She disappeared into the back room.

Her comments were fair. I probably did stare too often. The groups of girls that we worked with were difficult to navigate, however hard I'd tried to work them out. They were nice enough to my face, but I could never believe that they actually liked me. It was almost a relief to write them off. I felt fine about it because I had Tabitha and Ava, and even Imogen.

Then there was Samuel.

II.

After our first meeting, I saw Samuel more and more and I learned about his personal eccentricities. The character he played was a dapper English gentleman, and there were things he prided himself on. He opened doors and did things in the right way. It was important to wear the right clothes, and he always greeted people properly with two kisses or a handshake depending on the occasion and their background. He knew people worth knowing; he made sure to tell you about them often – *Oh, Catherine, yes, of course I can put you in touch with her.*

Early on, I could see that his entire existence revolved around a slow accumulation of favours: of gathering them up, paying them back and fostering calculated goodwill. He even carved up his day with an actual diary with appointments in it (he was far more ingrained in general student life than the rest of them). And he was always in his car.

The car was notable. It wasn't practical to drive in Edinburgh as a student – there was no parking; everything was mostly close enough to walk – but Samuel paid no attention to the inconvenience. He drove to the bar all the time – he said he liked the car because it gave him *more access*. He'd chat with me intensely about disconnected topics: *Did I know anyone with contacts in Brazil? How much was my jacket? Had I tried Caribbean food?* And then he'd be off again, tapping his keys against the bar top for the entire conversation like a possessed metronome.

This wasn't a problem in the early evening, but at night the way he was with me seemed different. The first time he appeared, on a quiet Tuesday shift, he knocked hard on the door, which we'd locked when we'd closed to the customers. It was late, past one, and the lights were turned up as we cleaned hurriedly, keen to get home. Finn clucked with irritation and went over to the window. He peered through the glass, mouthing *go away*, but I could see Samuel, in a smart overcoat, jabbing his finger at me, his car parked haphazardly on the street with disregard for the rules.

'Oh, it's my friend – you remember? Can we let him in?' I asked Finn.

Looking annoyed about the whole thing, Finn opened the door, and Samuel stormed in, rubbing his hands together in glee. Seeing them together, they couldn't have been more different. Samuel was a collection of sharp lines drawn with a ruler, and then there was Finn, all crumpled like an empty crisp packet.

For a second, Samuel looked a little uncomfortable, as if he wasn't sure what to do once he'd achieved the goal of getting into the bar, but he composed himself.

'I was just in the area and I thought you'd like a lift home?' he asked me.

Finn and I both stared at him, surprised.

'Thanks, but I'm fine,' I said. I lived a ten-minute walk away from the bar; there was no need for a lift which would take as long.

'Come on, Clare,' he said brightly. His words had an edge to them. He wouldn't break eye contact, and I knew there was no simple way out. The three of us stood there. Awkward, but I also felt a buzz. There's something affirming about two men fighting over you even if you're unsure about your feelings for either. I was flattered.

I looked over at Finn. I could tell what he was going to say, as always. He'd let me go.

'I'll finish up here then,' Finn said. He went back to cleaning down the bar top and ignored both of us.

Samuel grinned triumphantly, and we went out into the cold night towards his car. When we got in, I turned to him and spoke more rudely than I'd intended. 'Why are you here?'

He whistled, ignoring my tone. Turned the key so the engine grunted.

'No need to shout! I was out and about, and I thought you'd appreciate it.'

I pushed back with my feet, so that I sank further into the leather seat of the car. I wasn't scared, the word seems too much. But there was a harshness to his smile – the way it turned down at the sides made me on edge when it was just the two of us.

We were off, away from the bar and down the Grassmarket. We could reset this.

'Nice wheels,' I said.

He nodded proudly, and I knew it was a good conversation starter.

'Thank you! She's a little unreliable, but I just love driving around this city and seeing what's going on. Everyone says Edinburgh's a nightmare to drive in but look at her now.'

I looked out of the window. The streets were dark, but at this time of night, in this area, it was busy. Hens and stags milling around after closing time, trying to make their way back to their hotels and hostels. A messy fight looked to be taking place outside one of the strip clubs. Pubs were lit up with fake lanterns.

I didn't mind it, but I also liked it even later when it was quieter, in the few hours when the nightlife died away and before the commuters rattled around outside their office buildings, when it was almost impossible to imagine people in the city, and the buildings and hills took centre stage. You could look towards the shadow of Arthur's Seat. You could think of hot lava spilling like it would have done, millions of years ago.

'This is when I drive around, think about things, you know. Unravel the day,' he said.

He had a point. In the car, at that moment, it was peaceful.

'I was going to take you straight home, but it's not that late. I can drive us around a bit if you like?'

I shrugged. I didn't feel particularly comfortable in the car, but I wasn't tired.

Samuel was quiet; the indicator clicked; the gears changed. He spoke, and when he did, I could tell that he'd been mulling it over.

'You're not like Tabitha, you know,' he remarked.

'What do you mean?'

'She could never lie there, just enjoying the company. With Tabitha, she'd be sitting there prattling away or trying to entertain me or shock me or something. She can never just . . . be.'

I nodded.

'I'm not saying it's a bad thing!' His voice rose slightly. 'Don't say anything to her.' He sounded nervous.

'I won't say anything,' I reassured him. I enjoyed being a confidante. 'I know what you mean. It's a show, isn't it?'

He laughed, a deep belly laugh that petered into a chuckle. He was delighted. 'A show! Yes, I've never quite thought of it like that, but that's a good way of putting it, Clare. It's always a show. Although that makes it sound like it's all fun and games.'

'Isn't it?' The mood seemed to have changed. My lower back felt tight, and I was aware of the sweat stains under my armpits. I was sick of this cryptic conversation. I didn't quite trust him.

'Oh yes, of course it is. The most fun you've had in your life,' he said.

And then – a flick of the steering wheel.

Sudden and so jarring. I screamed, certain that we were going to swerve into oncoming traffic, because we went so far over on the wrong side. My neck jerked back painfully, and I pulled my hands up to my face.

'What was that?' I asked as we moved back into our lane as quickly as we'd left.

'What?' he said, driving on like nothing had happened.

'You could have killed us!'

He'd done it to shock me. For attention. I was familiar with the urge to shock but I hadn't expected something like that from Samuel.

It was a strange thing, but even as I shouted at him, I experienced an enjoyable rush of adrenaline. I was sure that he saw it in that moment, and I didn't want him to, didn't want him to have any kind of power over me. I just wanted to get back.

'I told you.' He grinned, but there was something shark-like about it, all teeth and no joy. 'All the fun. You're fine.'

And with that he looped back on himself to take me to my flat. I thanked him for the ride, and he drove off into the night, circling the city, looking for things or people to observe.

12.

I felt we were better than the other students from the start, even before I knew how much Tabitha had planned for us.

To be clear, the other people studying our course weren't uninteresting by general standards. In fact, many people would have probably considered them to be quirky, but I've always been picky about my friends. Several years before we started, a certain prince you'll have heard of had gone to St Andrews to study History of Art, and the course had soared in popularity everywhere. The result was a steady influx of attractive, rich students. A cohort full of them, with braying laughs and expensive handbags in stiff leather. One Tuesday, everyone wore a beret for some reason (even Tabitha and Imogen). I never found out how they all decided on this, and I sat, beret-less, and pretended I didn't mind.

The other first years tried to be unique, but they weren't, or at least to me they weren't. Once you saw past the expensive clothes, they were quite dull, huddled together talking about printer cartridges or essay word counts, regurgitating their parents' political opinions in neat soundbites to try and pass them off as their own. Worst of all, they were interested in things like student elections. Tabitha compared the bunch of them to the fatty section around a pork chop (a light dig at Imogen's cooking, I think). *You have to cut away with a knife to get to the meat, and there's always more of it than you expect.* I wasn't quite sure if we were the meat, but we were better than them.

It was exciting, to be on the right side, but at the beginning I was always on edge, never knowing quite what to say, so invariably I was quiet in the corner. Meek Clare. I just didn't want to mess it all up, for them to see parts of me I hid away. For them to reject me.

The conversation was invariably focused on money if Tabitha was around – how much things cost, how much people made – and then if things slowed down or became unbearably mundane, she would do something out of the blue, like a child playing up for attention. We were in a lecture once, and I was wearing a completely forgettable top, and she looked at me for a moment, pointed at my top and hers, then said, 'Swap?'

I was confused by why she'd want to swap, but before I could even protest, she put her coat on and then shimmied out of her blouse like a snake shedding skin. I saw the flash of soft flesh just under the lace edge of her bra, and the most perfect oval of a bruise sitting there. A mottled purple kiss situated on the high crest of her ribcage. Squirming, she hooked her blouse under one arm and then proffered it to me, a scrap of fabric hanging on the end of one finger. And I took a deep breath and tried to ignore the other students around us who were starting to stare, as I pulled my top off, awkwardly cloaking myself with my jacket. Felt a rush of excitement that made me dizzy.

I passed it to her, and she pulled it on.

'Ta-da!' she exclaimed, tearing her own coat away to show me. She looked good.

Things like that, all the time, meant that whenever the pace slowed, I knew she wouldn't let it stay sluggish for long.

I kept her top and I slept with it next to me, on my pillow, because it smelt of her. Of sweat and musk and sugar sweets and artificial lemons.

We didn't integrate with the rest of the student body much. I felt people's eyes on us – of course they watched us, why wouldn't they when we did things like swap clothes in public and talk loudly – but I never felt too embarrassed. I was happy and, most importantly, I didn't do anything bad. That only happened once during my first year in Edinburgh.

It's the sense of being wronged. When I think that someone has mistreated me, it's not something I can forget and move on from. It was manageable at that point because I had worked hard not to let things affect me like they used to. I could rein it all back in with my carefully formulated tricks. There was no one to punish any more.

There were a few times in that first term when I'd sit in the flat at 9 p.m., too early to go to bed but late enough to feel the pull of whatever was going on outside. The walls closing in on me became too much. I would need to go out into the city, on to the streets, to stay alive.

There was one night.

One night when I dressed up, which I liked to do occasionally as it was out of character. Pointy shoes and a short, short skirt because it made me feel like someone else.

When I walked out of the door, I was sure I was hallucinating. Everyone was in costumes, their faces too bright with big broad clown grins on plastic masks. There was a doughy sumo wrestler in a blow-up suit, his arm wrapped around a girl dressed as some kind of sexed-up cat in a leotard with scrappy whiskers painted on her cheeks.

The two of them were already stumbling, and she shrieked, holding on to him to stop herself falling.

Of course, I realized it was Halloween, and I weaved through the busy streets, clotted with partygoers, to a club where I could lose myself, alone in a crowd packed together. I danced for hours that night, until I was sweaty, screaming to the music, and my arms ached and my throat hurt. As I left the club, I was still in my own world. I was deep in the Edinburgh night, snaking through the streets with the bass still moving through me, looking for the parts where nobody was to continue my walk and decompress.

I saw a group of men or boys ahead of me, staggering down the road.

Their voices echoed in the alley. First years like me, I guessed by the excitement levels. You could tell they were incredibly drunk from the way they kept pushing each other, hardly able to keep together in a group. Then, somehow, the pack fractured, ambling off into the night to cause havoc separately as the boys branched down different streets, blessing the world with the sound of their deep, rumbling goodbyes.

Not all of them, though. One boy lagged behind the rest. He kept walking slower and slower in front of me, waiting, I think, for us to meet and walk side by side.

I was close to home, and I was alert; I didn't want to be cautious. I felt electric coming out of the club. The bite in the air. It made me jangly – a word my parents always used about me when they thought I was behaving a little too boisterously.

Just me and the boy; he stopped and leaned against a wall then set his pace to mine as I passed.

Clever of him.

I recognized him. I'd seen him the first time I'd met Tabitha and Imogen – he'd paid the bill at the bar. Chinless Wonder.

I avoided eye contact, but he'd already seen me, and I could tell he was interested in a confused way. A drunken narrowing of the eyes, a hunger behind them that betrayed his intentions.

'Hey, you,' he said, too loudly for how close he was to me. So confident that I'd want to speak to him. 'I know you.'

'I don't think so,' I replied.

'No, I do. From that bar, right?' Amiable now and slurring.

I wanted to get away from him, but I didn't feel especially nervous about his closeness, more that I was irritated by his lack of fear.

How *relaxed* he was.

And how different this was for him than it was for me or for any girl alone at night. To never be thinking of soft footsteps behind him. Certainly, no sense of danger. Even at three in the morning, where the line between the dead and living fades. Tourist trickery in the day becomes real in the dark, with a cold gust and candles snuffed by spirits' breaths. The sudden sense of the maze of vaults below where screams echo. The dead are near in the city when night falls. They press against you, but I think it's the living who come for you.

Just the two of us in a dim alley.

She had it coming to her, walking alone in that short skirt so late – the beginning of every story you hear when that kind of thing happens.

This is not that story.

I felt anger swell in my chest and I sped up, but he met my pace. He came closer, swerved without subtlety into me, and he touched my arm. It was too much.

I pulled away.

It did not deter him.

'I. Know. You,' he said, smiling gormlessly. He really was quite drunk. Not a threat but certainly blocking my way.

'You need to back off,' I said as calmly as I could.

'Hey, don't freak out!' He held up his hands in a conciliatory gesture, but it was short-lived. He was testing me, because he moved in closer again and I could smell him. Dried sweat and sweet aftershave.

'This could be something nice,' he said, which could have meant a lot of different things.

Such a lack of hesitancy. An absolute certainty that everything would go his way. Now, I could ignore it and smile, let the rage grow and then recede, like a wave that rises then falls, before the waters turn still. Back then, that kind of control wasn't possible.

I wasn't able to let him leave.

If someone had shouted out one of my names in the street

and pulled me back, it wouldn't have worked. I was set on my course and when the boy came towards me again, jerkily this time, like he might fall over, I pushed him and he stumbled, lost his footing and fell to the ground. It was all happening in sharp focus and the world was brighter than I wanted, but I was alive, buzzing. It was a feeling I recognized well.

I kicked him hard. A rush of satisfaction as the spike of my heel grazed his arm where his sleeve was rolled up, and then in a split second I pinned the arm to the floor. A drawing pin skewering paper. He tried to wrench it away, so I pushed down. His flesh was pliable, almost plasticky and inflatable, like the sumo wrestler I'd seen earlier.

He howled, and the sound rang through the quiet streets. I pulled back at the loudness of it. I hadn't broken his skin; it would bruise, though. The anger and that hot fizz of energy had retreated.

Soft waves lapping.

The boy wheezed. He didn't seem that aggravated, but he looked like he'd sobered up a bit. He was speaking, I think, but he was incoherent to me, his words more of an indistinguishable bleat against the ringing in my ears. It was cold, but my body didn't register the sensation any more, just calmness. The adrenaline faded away, along with that loss of bodily function, as if I was in a dream or a video game.

Was I scared of the repercussions? I don't think so – I had hurt him in a way that would heal. It was rare for me to be confident about things back then, but in that instance I was quite sure he wouldn't go to the police because that would make him question what had happened, make him wonder how he'd touched me.

I took both shoes off, so my bare feet slapped against the cobbles as I walked the short distance home. A feeling of weightlessness, like I was gliding above the streets, and I crept back into the flat.

A few hours later I woke up to a gentle knock on my door as Ashley offered me a cup of tea. I thought she hadn't noticed my discarded shoes and dirt from my feet on the floor until she shuddered.

'I hate Halloween,' she said, putting my tea down next to my bed. 'What did you dress as?'

I groaned, pulled up the covers over my head, and she tutted, shutting my door behind her.

13.

The Shiver began to peel off from each other and seek me out individually as the term went on.

Despite the way that night had ended, things were fine between me and Samuel. I found him brash and over-the-top at times, but the car thing hadn't scared me. If anything, the whole episode was intriguing. I thought perhaps he had been testing me to see how I'd react and after it happened we somehow seemed easier around each other.

I also suspected he might be interested in something more than friendship, and I didn't entirely shut the notion down because I liked the attention. Better to leave it in a blurred place of possibility. So our nights continued, and he picked me up regularly without notice.

Finn was irritable about it, huffing and puffing when he saw him. But the visits were nice, and they were innocent enough.

Full admission into Tabitha's circle meant I was invited round to the flat more. For breakfast, she played hostess, serving up badly cooked eggs Benedict around her messy kitchen table. She never cooked them for long enough, so the whites always had the consistency of phlegm.

Oh just dig in, Clare, don't be precious! she would say.

We never discussed normal things; we were trapped in a world of storytelling, in a universe where we were the centre of it all. Loud, dramatic tales from Tabitha, where she told me she was descended from royalty, name dropping so heavily that I nearly laughed out loud, or she asked me to skim over an essay she'd written like she was doing me a favour by allowing me to read it. Then there were business ideas from her too, involving importing French wine from near her mother's house, and she mentioned something about selling organs that I was almost sure was a joke. All these things were still surface level. I think I only started to really understand them because of Servants' Christmas.

Tabitha announced it, and I had no idea what it was, but Imogen and Samuel exchanged a knowing glance, a rare show of Samuel acknowledging Imogen – he tended to ignore her however hard she tried to get his attention. The look between them made me think this wasn't a new thing and also that it wasn't optional. The premise was that we wouldn't give out presents and waste money on gifts for each other, but we would each perform services. And it couldn't just be an IOU (*how slovenly*, Tabitha said), everyone's gift needed to be a tailored treat for the recipient. The other odd thing about Servants' Christmas was that gifts could be given in private – if anything, this was encouraged. Initially, I was dreading it; I wasn't used to such things – when I was a child we celebrated the occasion simply, with a meal on Christmas Eve.

Servants' Christmas felt like something they all knew how to navigate, something they'd done before. I decided to wait and see what my gifts were before organizing anything myself, and as December began, slowly, my 'gifts' started to appear.

From Ava I received a vigorous massage. If she'd told me I was going to have a massage for an hour, I would have been anxious, but instead, one day when I was round at their flat, she just emerged and wordlessly pulled me into a room. I lay there as she pummelled each muscle into submission, signalling she'd finished by giving me a light tap on the rump to send me on my way like a show pony. It was pleasant enough, but it hadn't felt tailored to me. I later learned that each of us got the same thing apart from Tabitha, who refused to discuss any of it with us. Finn had shuddered when I'd told him about the massage. 'That girl is *too* weird.'

Samuel took me out in the car, of course, for a day in Perth-shire. 'Sounds like a date,' Finn had remarked caustically.

I followed Samuel into a forest that smelt of pine needles, where I could hear running water, and it was very damp in the air. Then he called me over and picked up a mushroom. Held it up to where the light came in through the trees and turned his hair to fire.

'This,' he said excitedly. 'Winter chanterelle!'

He tried to pass the grimy thing to me. I shook my head and he shrugged, unperturbed, gave it a cursory clean with his thumb, and then he popped it in his mouth.

A few seconds passed. The light in the forest changed as clouds moved over us.

He collapsed, shuddering, gasping for breath.

I observed him.

After a moment or two, he composed himself and got up. Giving me a strange look, he brushed the soil off his trousers. 'Just a wheeze, they *are* actually chanterelles. Thought you might have been a bit more worried about me,' he said in a hearty tone that didn't quite ring true as he nudged me with his shoulder.

I shrugged and we kept moving through the woods, picking up mushrooms as we went.

I'd been dreading Imogen's gift. She'd warmed up to me a bit, but she was still territorial when it came to Tabitha. I don't think she thought I deserved to be part of it – part of them – I hadn't earned it. She invited herself round to my flat on one of those brutal days in early December when all you want to do is stay in bed.

She scrunched up her nose when I let her in.

'Now I see why you're always round ours,' she said.

There was a welcome consistency in her frankness. I couldn't bear the thought of Tabitha waltzing around my tiny, grubby flat, saying, 'Oh, it's *lovely* here.' I would have to grin and agree or grimace and protest.

Imogen's gift turned out to be nice and practical. She arrived with something called a lint roller, shoe polish and an industrial-looking steamer. With matronly vigour, she set upon my entire wardrobe, throwing away old pieces I'd had for years and scrubbing my boots until they gleamed.

I helped her a little, and I wondered if Imogen and I could find a way to become friends. I didn't crave it exactly, but I thought the time would arise naturally and we could establish a deeper relationship. When she came round that day, the possibility of a connection felt close. She sang songs under her breath as she worked away, enjoying being bossy and restoring order. She seemed lighter that afternoon away from the rest of them.

'Isn't that better,' she said happily as we both looked at my streamlined wardrobe.

'This was so kind of you, thank you,' I said. It really was a very useful gift, and I was touched.

'No problem.'

As we folded the last pieces in a companionable silence, I felt I could ask her the question I'd wanted to, maybe a way for us to become a little closer and find common ground.

'Tabitha hasn't got me anything yet. I wonder, has she done something for you?'

She froze midway through folding a shirt and tore round to face me. 'What on earth do you mean?' All of a sudden, her face was screwed up in rage.

'I didn't mean anything!' I said.

'Why are you even asking?' she said. I could tell she was trying to slow her breathing and calm down.

I stumbled to explain. 'I just wondered because she hasn't done anything for me! It's fine – if you don't want to tell me, you don't want to tell me. It's not a big deal. We don't have to make a thing out of it.' I put both hands up in defence.

She seemed to have worn herself out. She was still upset, but I could tell it was over, and there would be no more sorting of my wardrobe. My opportunity had gone.

'I need to leave,' she said, picking up her bag and wrestling with the steamer. There was no goodbye.

14.

For them, I agonized for hours. All their gifts to me had involved so much one-on-one time – it had been a lot to navigate.

In the end, I broke the rules and turned up at Tabitha's flat laden with bottles, banishing them all to the kitchen to wait. Then, I welcomed them into the drawing room where I'd made cocktails, a carefully selected recipe for each of them.

I'd practised at work, buying all the spirits and liquors I'd need, which had cost far more than I could afford.

For Samuel, a perfect Manhattan with aged bourbon.

For Imogen, a piña colada made with fresh coconut milk and served garishly in half a coconut shell (in retrospect, I'm not sure why I chose something so kitsch for someone so unplayful, but I put an undue amount of effort into it because whatever I'd said to upset her, I wanted to make it up to her).

For Ava, a spicy Bloody Mary filled to the brim with a grizzled chunk of salty chorizo and slithers of celery, then topped with a floating glug of thin red wine.

And finally, for Tabitha, a classic champagne cocktail. The brown sugar cube in the bottom of the glass seeped upwards in a fizzy cloud when I handed it over to her, and the muddy effect made me think of a Victorian tonic brewed for the infirm.

They stood around the drawing room sipping them – although Tabitha barely touched hers – lauding my inventiveness. Still, there was a flatness to the evening that I couldn't quite put my finger on. I was sure there were shared looks that I wasn't a part of.

Samuel didn't even take a sip, and for some reason it seemed like a test that I'd tried so earnestly to pass but had ended up failing.

I came back into the room later when Imogen and Tabitha had gone, abandoning the evening to try on dresses in Tabitha's room.

Ava was still there, throwing back the dregs of her last Bloody Mary, lying out on the floor next to the window. It was something I'd often seen her do, something I imagined a child might do. She looked out so she could people watch, staying low down so they couldn't see her if they stared up and peered in.

'Hello, Clare,' she said when she saw me. So formal.

I lay down by her, both of us on our fronts with our hips and stomachs pressed against the floorboards. Our shoulders rubbed against each other as we stared out, watching heads bobbing along below.

'I'm not sure I quite did it right,' I said.

'Oh, I don't know about that. Mine's amazing. Reminds me of parties in Malibu; we'd make these by the pool although they were nowhere near as good as this. The ice would always melt, and there was never enough salt. Or enough vodka.'

'Gazpacho,' I commented.

'I guess. I know, it sounds disgusting now, doesn't it?' she said. 'Still, it was pretty great at the time.' She sucked at the straw noisily and put the empty glass to one side.

It was very, very unusual for Ava to talk about being in the US. She treated it as a place that didn't quite belong to her but that she acknowledged occasionally. Her accent had a touch of those tiny crescendos that I recognized from American TV shows, when everything sounds like a question, and I'd heard her mutter something scathingly incomprehensible like 'valley girl' about a fellow American student on her course.

'Horseradish or something in it?' she asked.

'Just mustard. I'm not sure Tabitha liked hers – or the whole idea, really,' I admitted.

'Ahhh, Tabitha.' She said it like she was recalling a particularly moreish meal. 'The thing is, you didn't make it about her. It was so . . . what's the right word –' she clicked her fingers when she found it – 'egalitarian. She doesn't like that so much. Now, if you'd made one of those champagne towers for her, that would have been a different story. But what you'll come to see is that she's the star.'

'How do you always know what to do with her?'

'It'll come. Remember, when I met Tabitha, I'd moved around so much. First from Russia to LA, then to England when I was thirteen for school; I was so scared. I didn't know anyone, and I arrived at this school in the middle of nowhere. I felt like I'd been exiled. I didn't look the same as everyone else; I've always dressed . . . in an unusual way. My parents *despaired* of me. They wanted me to look tidy and sensible, to wear plaid. They probably would have loved it if I'd have looked like you.'

I stayed quiet. I hadn't been a particularly good child.

She continued. 'Anyway, school was so cliquey, and I was totally alone. If anything, it was worse than in LA, which I didn't think would be possible. They all had these plummy English accents, like Tabitha, I guess. My parents didn't care if I was happy or not, to be honest.'

'What do your parents do?' I asked. It felt good to share like this, even if I wasn't volunteering anything.

'They have various business interests.'

A clear shut-down on the topic.

'It's a different life,' she continued. 'I just had nothing in common with anyone. I'd never fitted in in the States and I didn't fit in in England either. But then I met Tabitha and straight away she took me under her wing and involved me in everything, just like that. She *made* me fit in. There was no need for anything else or anyone else. She swept me up as if it was the easiest thing in the world. Same with Imogen and Samuel. You know what it's like,' she finished.

I did.

'She just wants to feel special. She is special,' she said.

We lay there for a minute or so, surveying the people who passed below us.

'Also, she might have been a bit annoyed about Samuel,' she added.

I hadn't picked up on much closeness between Ava and Samuel. She was too impassive; he was too excitable. They were polite enough but wary of each other.

'What about him?' I asked.

'He doesn't drink.'

'What?' I exclaimed, louder than I usually would with any of them. 'I hadn't noticed!'

'Hasn't touched it for years.'

'So, what's the story there?'

'When Tabitha and Samuel were growing up, he had some issues. It was all a long time ago. When he was younger, he would get so drunk, start these fights – he was actually in trouble with the police. Do you not see?'

'See what?'

'There's something . . . a little off sometimes about him.'

I thought of Samuel. So big and towering, but I couldn't really imagine him in a physical fight. Then I remembered his almost cruel smile as he'd veered across the road for fun.

Ava continued. 'Tabitha was always so protective of him. She was basically a lifeline – no-nonsense, no sympathy really. She helped him get into this crazy expensive rehab programme for young people with drinking problems. Anyone who said anything about him, she was on at them, like, properly. You can imagine . . .'

I could imagine. Tabitha, like a lioness protecting her cubs.

'Anyway, he cut it all out,' she finished.

Was I so wrapped up in myself that I didn't notice anyone else, or did he hide it in a way that meant you saw what you wanted to see? I thought of him with his cocktail, promptly put to one side. The nights we'd spent together, hadn't he been drinking like the rest of us?

I must have looked worried, because she placated me. 'Oh, don't worry about it. You couldn't have known. That would be a lot to ask – he carries a glass of wine around all the time as a prop. Anyway, it's done now.' She yawned and started playing with the ends of my hair sleepily. The lines between my body and hers so blurred.

'Are you thinking about her?' she asked quite suddenly. 'She expects a lot. But it's worth it.'

I nodded to agree with her.

'I'm serious,' she said. 'Without Tabitha, I don't know where I'd be. She has so much planned for us, honestly.'

'What does she have planned?' I asked. Tabitha hadn't mentioned anything solid to me, not at that point.

'You'll see,' Ava said, sweeping the question away smoothly.

And then we fell into silence, and I felt like I needed to say something positive after she'd divulged so much to me. That was how I was back then, always rooting around and working out what to do.

'I hope she appreciates you,' I said. It seemed like the right thing to say.

She gave me a very kind look. 'Of course she does. Now don't worry about this whole thing. You did great, and we just love having you around, Clare. You must know that.'

I stood up and went to leave, but she called after me. 'Clare, one more thing.'

I turned back to face her as she got up from the floor and dusted herself off.

'There's another reason you couldn't have got it right with the drink tonight,' she explained. 'Anything made behind her back – she doesn't trust it.'

15.

Looking back, so much of what I savoured was scraped from offhand comments. Savage little bites of knowledge delivered by each shark with a gossipy ease.

A memory of an illicit expedition to get belly-button piercings solicited from Ava. A mention of Imogen's parents' holiday home in the 'tacky part' of the Algarve from Tabitha.

Ava's never quite mastered sarcasm. A light little dig from Samuel.

Samuel's parking tickets are becoming . . . obscene. Ava flicked through them in disgust – he frequently dumped them in a chunky stack on Tabitha's kitchen table, and I wondered who paid them. Just another strange thread of reliance that I didn't quite understand.

It seems pathetic to say so, but oh, how I adored it! Their snipes and their petty revelations were so addictive, and I always left wanting just a bit more, especially when it related to Tabitha. I couldn't stay away from them. They were a drug that builds in effectiveness as it accumulates in the bloodstream.

But then, as soon as they let me in, the doors shut again and again. There was the sense that I was on the outside and I wasn't quite privy to what was going on. Even from the beginning, there were many projects that I heard about and felt I was slightly involved with, but not fully.

They varied in intensity, popping up, sizzling for a while with a frenetic urgency that consumed us all, then cooled again just as quickly. Thematically, they were varied. Tabitha had a bizarre notion of creating an underground supper club, serving shark fin and bird's nest soups. She pushed for the creation of a specialist student matchmaking scheme – English students seeking Scottish landowners. A lot was wrong with all these ideas. Often they had a commercially astute element to them – usually misguided – but the concepts were never fully formed.

On a windy night, I saw Ava and Tabitha together, both so tall and both wrapped up in coats and scarves. If it had crossed my mind before that Ava was part of some kind of mob family, then seeing her pacing around in white fur made it seem even more believable, and how *strident* they were! They took up the whole pavement, and other people walking down the street knew to move around them and let them pass as they stalked through the city. I wondered where they were going and what they were doing. Still, the curious thing was that they saw me, but they didn't stop. Ava gave a curt nod of the head as if I was a casual acquaintance.

I was quite hurt, of course, but I didn't blame them. It did make me question what they did when I wasn't there and how close we actually were. Did they have other friends like me? But then I forced myself to remember it was fine. I had a life around them, my job and Finn, and they seemed to respect that. Friendships worth having were built slowly.

Then there was university. Academically, I was unremarkable through a lack of effort. My first set of exams could have gone better, but I didn't think I'd failed. I also wasn't sure History of Art was for me, but I wasn't overly concerned. After all, Tabitha often talked about our 'big plans', how we were destined for more exciting things.

'Just you wait. You, Clare, are made for great things, things other people are too scared to do. Just like us,' she would say out of the blue, and when I listened to her, I was delighted, and I couldn't help but believe that there was something on the horizon for us all.

I had picked up more bar shifts in those funny quiet weeks

up until the middle of December when the main quadrant of the university was a ghost town, but the restaurants and bars were packed with tourists darting around in a frenzy, throwing money at souvenirs and cups of mulled wine.

The rest of them left sharpish. Ava disappeared without fanfare a few weeks before Christmas. She set off for a night flight to LAX, under duress from her parents, I guessed. I imagined her skulking around tree-lined boulevards looking out of place and pining for us.

Tabitha, Samuel and Imogen all took the train back to London. They chose to take the London King's Cross departure from Waverley ten days before Christmas, which was packed with students. About a quarter of the way into the journey, I'd been told, it turned into a party as the passengers wandered up and down the aisles, and the tables got stickier and stickier with spilt drinks.

There was one particular train that was infamous – the 15.17 departure – and while Tabitha and Samuel and Imogen were so scathing about our fellow students, they seemed to prefer to board it, then judge from afar – retreating to the quiet carriage where I'm sure they managed to be resolutely unquiet.

I went back to Hull just a few days before Christmas. I stayed with my granny, and she came to meet me at the station as I knew she would, though I'd told her not to bother. She looked steely and grim, even when smiling. No knitted cardigans or soft perm like a grandmother from a picture book. Sinewy arms and legs, and a mismatched tracksuit because vanity was highly discouraged. She'd always found my mother to be very vain.

She had a cigarette in her mouth as usual, and she wrapped me up in a tight hug, so my nose pressed into the top of her head, and I smelt the familiar scent of old smoke mixed with bleach.

'Clare?' she said as if she was trying the name out. It sat there uneasily. She'd always felt odd about my name. 'Come on,' she said into my shoulder as she pulled away from the hug.

We walked back to her house, and I almost had to rush to keep up with her. She kept her head down. I immediately thought it was because she didn't want anyone to see us and to ask questions.

It was a two-up two-down on an estate. The street wasn't well kept, and bits of rubbish were scattered along the side of the road as usual, but the house itself had a fresh green door that looked like it had been painted since I'd left in September.

She opened the door, and I followed her in, dumping my suitcase at the bottom of the stairs.

'Tea?' she asked, and I nodded. Her dog wandered in from the kitchen and started yapping at my feet. It had never liked me. I refused to acknowledge its name – one inspired by a dead soap opera character. I gave the dog a quick stroke, and grease passed off its fur on to my hand, which I wiped on the side of my trousers. It felt grimy even though the room itself was spotlessly clean. My granny's face did it. When she looked at me, she couldn't hide what she was thinking, every thought she had about me was there for me to take, and I wanted to pick up something from the table and hurl it at her.

We sat across from each other.

'So, I've not heard from you much, which, I take it, is a good thing. How is it?' she asked.

'It's fine, I'm enjoying it.' As I said the words aloud, I realized they were true.

'And you've made friends?'

'Yes.' I didn't feel the need to explain any further.

She blew on her tea, deep in thought. 'I just worry about you. Up there. All alone.'

'I'm not alone at all. I worry about you here on *your* own.'

She gave me a small smile. 'You know me – I just get on with it. Nothing much changes around here.'

'Didn't bother with a tree this year?' I asked. There wasn't that much space for a tree, but I wanted one. For some reason it was very important at that moment that we had one.

But she shook her head. 'I didn't see the point.'

I nursed my cup of tea in my hands to keep warm. Sitting there felt wrong. It was the kind of space where you were always moving around through corridors, trying to get out. My granny was always up and down. She could never settle, especially not when I was there. I couldn't imagine my father as a child in this house, running around. I knew he'd grown up here, but it was impossible to actually picture him because it didn't seem set up for children at all, all hard, shiny surfaces. Every time I came down the stairs, I scraped my shins on the banister or bashed my head against the ceiling. The house seemed like it was growing smaller and smaller, the walls creeping inwards on me, until one day the whole place would crush me.

I made the mistake of mentioning this suspicion to my mother once after visiting as a child, and she replied that I was probably just getting fatter.

We sipped our tea.

'I haven't got you anything yet. I didn't know what you'd want,' she said after a while. 'We can go and choose something tomorrow if you like. If there's something you need.'

'There's nothing I need.'

'You're OK for money?'

'I'm fine. I got a job.'

'Ah, good on you,' she grinned. There was nothing that impressed her more than quiet self-sufficiency. Nothing showy, just earning and doing. 'I'll be working every day apart from Christmas. Need the hours this time of year,' she said. She worked in the supermarket around the corner and had done for as long as I could remember.

'Do you want me to pick up some decorations at all?' I asked.

She looked at me, her brow furrowed. 'I wouldn't bother, love. It's just me and you, not worth spending your hard-earned cash. But it's up to yourself – your money.' She picked up the remote control and turned the television on. The bark of a talk show was a neat signal for the end of our catch-up. We sat there watching it and drinking our tea, and then I went up to my room with my suitcase.

After that, we had a few quiet days together. I'd bought her a bottle of cheap rum that I knew she'd like, and she drank it with Coke and no ice on Christmas Eve as a treat. She didn't end up buying me anything, and on Christmas Day we ordered an Indian takeaway from around the corner, a set meal for one as it's enough for two, and ate in front of the television.

On my last day, she walked me back to the station and wrapped me up in a hug that was too tight. I hugged her back.

'Look after yourself,' she said. The words trailed with a tremor at the end.

16.

It was a while before I received Tabitha's gift.

After Christmas, we hunkered down for more exams, revising slide after slide, remembering dates and titles and movements. A blur of tutorials held in the galleries that kept me distracted. Then she invited me to hers early on a sunny Saturday afternoon in February. I wasn't sure she'd remember to expect me, or if she'd even be in, but I arrived and she was there as promised. She opened the door and straight away it was all wide-eyed joy at my arrival, and she spoke very fast, even for her. She ushered me to the kitchen table and gestured to a seat, then she sat opposite me, her foot tapping away. The other two didn't seem to be in.

'Coffee?' she asked warmly. She already had a cup in front of her.

I declined. I'd seen the coffee she and Imogen drank. Tar-like shots of the stuff, so strong it made your eyes water and your head ache for the rest of the day.

'So, I have something planned today, my gift to you, for Christmas,' she said.

I'd assumed she'd forgotten.

'You didn't think I'd forgotten, did you? You did! Of course I didn't. So, no offence, but I think we should do something about your hair.'

Hair was, in a way, how I'd first noticed them. When I met Tabitha she was radiant and coiffed, and one of my initial thoughts was how similar our hair was in its simplest state. But mine was wild, and Tabitha had a controlled mane with subtle tawny highlights. It tumbled in corkscrew curls, smelling of sweet coconut if you got close enough, or else she pinned strands up in extravagant pineapples on her head.

Her dedication invited compliments: *Oh, I love your hair. How do you get it so long? What products do you use to make it so shiny?* Tabitha was always distrustful of people who didn't comment on her hair.

I was taken aback, but I tried not to show it; I'd never done anything much with my hair, and my hand automatically reached to the bun on top of my head that I'd tied up as an afterthought. I forced myself to bring my hands down and place them on the table in front of me, just like Tabitha.

She'd stopped tapping away. She just sat there, watching me. This was her way of moving that aimed to disorientate. She alternated between a restless vigour as she rushed around the flat madly, gesticulating as she told a story, opening a window then dipping into a downward dog, all while the tale pattered away. But then she was able to switch to a meditative stillness, observing you coolly with a blankness that made you fill in the gaps in conversation. I'd once read that mirroring someone's body language is an ordinary occurrence that creates a tight bond. It had never come naturally to me and Tabitha; when she froze, erect and proud like a Greek sculpture, I fidgeted or picked at the skin around my nails until it bled and dry pieces came off between my fingers.

'I haven't had it cut in forever,' I said, choosing my words carefully. Not a straight yes or no.

'I know, darling, and it's . . . a look. But you have the most fantastic hair. You should make the most of it.' Her hand was in mine, gripping tightly.

I wanted to ask why? Who was this for? We never went anywhere or did anything much.

'I'm not sure if it's something I want to do,' I said. I thought she'd be angry, but she just smiled and stood up. Her back to me, she looked out of the window to the gardens that surrounded the flat. It was a cloudless day if you looked up, past the shadows from the buildings. I remember it was the kind of day that makes you believe you can take on the world.

She spoke again, although I couldn't see her expression. 'I understand. I'm crazy protective about my hair too. There are only a few places I'd go and generally I wouldn't go in Edinburgh. But it just so happens that I've found this fantastic guy, Rand, and you'd be able to get it done today.'

'Today!' I spluttered.

She spun back to face me, and her smile was huge. 'I know, right, the stars align.' She sat back down. 'Look, just let me do this for you as a treat.' Her voice had become a high whine. She settled, waiting for me to give in.

'I guess. If you think it would be a good idea . . .' I said.

'It's the best idea ever.' She was up, gathering her things. 'We'll go now.'

Her enthusiasm was infectious, and I'd warmed up to the idea without even quite realizing. I was wondering what I'd go for. A rich russet colour perhaps, or a dark wavy bob that would swing around my neck.

When I recall what happened with the haircut, it seems odd how easily I went along with it, but you must understand, finding Tabitha and the rest of them hadn't changed things entirely for me. I still woke up some mornings wanting to claw the skin off my face when I looked in the mirror. I would sit there and practise a natural-looking grin, or I'd frown and see the furrows in my brow. But being with them made me feel like I was part of something. I craved them when I wasn't there with them. When I saw them look towards each other and share secret glances, I was desperate to be involved. When I heard someone talking about them, I felt almost drunk on the sense of superiority that came with being who we were.

We were so special. And there she was, offering to turn me into the best version of myself. It wasn't something I could turn down.

17.

We were whisked in a cab down into the guts of Leith, right at the shore and then along the seafront. Tabitha had chatted away on the journey, so I hadn't noticed the streets change, as smart Georgian townhouses made way for tower blocks. *All so grey*, she said, and she was right. But it was funny how grey could speak of a tasteful refinement in some places, and in other parts, like here, the colour was resolutely bleak. Not a colour so much as a wash-out, like everything had been watered down. We saw a warehouse, then a car park, then flats, then nothing, then repeated: warehouse, car park, flats. Finally, we arrived in a suburb I didn't recognize, where the air had an aftertaste of fish. The place didn't look like much from the out-side. Semi-derelict on first inspection, with graffiti lining the walls. It was so rare to be somewhere with Tabitha that wasn't lovely. She looked out of place, her nose wrinkled in distaste, and it made me think it had to be something good that had dragged us here.

I hadn't been to the hairdresser's much in the past, but even in my limited experience, this was like no hairdresser I'd ever visited. We went in and a man I assumed was Rand appeared from nowhere and took us down a long set of stairs. We ended up in a basement with no windows, and there were no other customers there, just a few chairs with large circular mirrors facing them. He offered me a glass of champagne, which I declined, and soon I was the centre of a frenzy of tinfoil and dye as four or more people assembled around me until I was lightheaded with the flurry of attention.

Later, Tabitha sat next to me, fussing away.

'You look peaky – are you OK?' she asked, putting her hand to my forehead.

'I don't feel great,' I said.

The next thing just popped out. 'Talk to me? Tell me a story?' I said. At that moment, I just wanted to let my head fall back on the chair and hear something soothing that would take my mind off my headache.

It was the bleach, I think – bleach reminded me too much of my granny, reminded me of being a child.

'Poor you. But I'll take your mind off things, of course I will,' she said.

'Tell me about your family?' I asked.

Tabitha didn't talk about her family much, just as I'd hardly mentioned mine, but they were contained in the objects she surrounded herself with. The armoire that belonged to her great-grandmother. The fountain pen with the missing lid gifted to her for her eighteenth. Links certainly, links to royalty (ancestors everywhere and anywhere; she wasn't a snob about lineage – Sweden, Latvia, Chile and Ireland), but few real stories of a closer family.

'My family?' she said in a sing-song voice, but she didn't sound surprised. 'OK, Claaaaaaare.'

I lay back into the soft leather of the chair. It felt oddly similar to being in Samuel's car, deceptively safe.

Her story began. 'When I was sixteen, I came home from school, just for the weekend. That was unusual. I didn't come home much in those first years. I didn't tell anyone because I wanted it to be a surprise, and I thought it would be nice to see them all. In my head I imagined this full weekend, bursting with wholesome activities like long country walks and roast dinners that take all day to cook, but I was being silly, it wasn't like that with my family – we didn't do those kind of things.'

I nodded away as she spoke. I understood.

'I'm an only child, but that particular weekend I thought

things would be different. While I was away at school, I imagined all these things happened at home, so if I showed up without telling anyone, I could just join in this family life going on without me.' She laughed. 'I know, I know, it sounds crazy now I tell the story.'

This was textbook Tabitha. I didn't need to say anything, and she just imagined my response and slotted it in.

She continued. 'Anyway, I get the train then a taxi from the station and I walk into the house in Hampstead, and it's quiet in that middle-of-the-day kind of way, which I wasn't too surprised at. Ma could have been out walking the dogs, so I went upstairs to drop my bag, and I saw him at the window of his study – Pa.

'He was standing with his back to the door, and he was kissing this woman, with his hands all over her. Grabbing her. Although she wasn't a woman, she was a fucking girl, only a few years older than me, in this incredibly trashy suit thing, and she saw me, and she just giggled.' Tabitha's face was red and scrunched up now. 'Anyway, Pa turns round, and you can tell he's been thrown; he's shaken, but he recovers. He comes to the door and just pushes it gently to a close, right in my face.'

'So, what did you do?'

'I took my case, and I went to my room to unpack,' she said simply.

'But what happened after that?'

'Oh, after that, they were done. He left. He took nearly everything – the house, all the money was so tied up and hidden. It led to Ma having a breakdown. The whole thing was wretched, really. She never recovered. She gets these terrible pains in her feet and legs. She got to keep France, but it was bittersweet. He essentially exiled her there because the house would never sell, so she'd never be able to afford to come back to London. Ma had no idea. She hadn't suspected a thing, so she wasn't prepared. She hadn't worked in years, and she was utterly unemployable.'

'Did you tell your mother?' I asked. Facing the mirror, I felt confident enough to ask her this.

'No. I didn't need to. Once I'd seen them, it was all over. It was like he couldn't carry on once I knew.'

'Do you wish you hadn't walked in?'

She looked at me – or maybe herself – kindly. Her face was next to mine in the mirror, and our reflections stared back at us.

'I hate the way it unfolded because it meant Ma was always on the back foot. But you have to understand that him cheating, that part was inevitable. He's had a string of girlfriends over the last few years, all very temporary and nubile. But if she'd had a better understanding of what was going on, she wouldn't have been left with so little after so long. If I regret anything, it's that we didn't get the exit we deserved.'

I mulled this over. I thought of the beautiful flat. Tabitha didn't seem to be doing too badly when it came to 'an exit' in my opinion.

'So, what happened after that?' I asked.

'Nothing at all.' Just like that, the sing-song voice was gone. 'I went back to school; they got divorced; I came here. He bought the flat because it's a good investment, so it made sense at the time.'

'Are you still in touch?' I asked.

'We've not always got on well. I can't be around his new girlfriends, they're too young. Anyway, you didn't ask for a happy story, did you?' She gave my shoulder a half-hearted squeeze and rose. 'He'll want to dry your hair now.'

And he did want to dry it. He stepped back, and we assessed the results, with Tabitha next to me.

We were two golden twins.

In my head, the conversation was almost there, gently presenting itself, where I'd said what I wanted or who I wanted to look like, and he'd done it for me. But that wasn't what happened. Rand and I hadn't said one word, so presumably Tabitha had planned it all.

There had always been a resemblance between me and Tabitha, but now we were more alike than ever. I was primped and shiny, tamed like a pet.

She picked up a strand of my hair like it belonged to her. 'What do you think?'

I was exhausted, but she seemed so happy, and she'd done something I wouldn't have been able to afford to do. I should have been thankful, and I tried to remind myself of that, but my head was pounding. Pulling away from her, I got up, shaking off the grogginess. There was no plan, I just wanted to get out of the weird basement room on my own, and then her arm was on mine, steering me to the door alongside her. She must have paid but I didn't see her do it.

'Let's go back to mine for a while. You don't seem yourself,' she said.

So, we went back in a cab, waves of nausea moving through my body.

'I'm not feeling good,' I said as we walked up the stairs to her flat.

The flat was quiet, and I wondered where Ava and Imogen were.

'I think you should go for a lie-down,' she suggested.

I moved to go to one of the bedrooms, drawn like a magnet to those three closed doors, but she directed me into the drawing room. She pointed to the sofa. I hoped she wouldn't shut the door – the thought of being locked in a room caused my stomach to flip – and she didn't, she left it ajar and sauntered away into the kitchen.

I lay down, and when I pressed my nose against the cushions, I could smell dust and bleach and burnt sugar blended with her sharp citric scent.

18.

When I woke up, I had no idea what the time was. The room was pitch-black and the air was flowing and cold, as if there was a draught somewhere. Silent in a way that felt heavy and made me sure there wasn't anyone else around. I called out their names and no one answered. The scissors from the hairdresser were lying next to me on the floor. Perhaps Tabitha had slipped them down the side of her dress, doing it on a whim to enjoy cold steel against her thigh.

Someone had put a blanket over me; I pushed it off and got up unsteadily. Still full of sleep, I walked out into the corridor and to the front door. Stood in the wide hallway where the post was always piled up by the door, bills alongside cards and brochures and bank statements – *our precious kindling*, Tabitha called it, and she had been known to use anything in sight to light a fire.

One of Tabitha's essays, ripped from the manila envelope, was strewn on the floor. I picked it up and flicked through. Looping scrawl on the last page stated: 'Big improvement – much more cohesive.'

I put the essay down, back on the floor where it seemed to live, and, warming up to my exploration, I went down to the far end of the corridor. There were three bedrooms. The doors were unmarked and I wasn't clear on which one belonged to who.

All three doors were shut. I called out their names again, but no one answered.

Was it so late that everyone was sleeping? I pushed open the first bedroom door, thinking that maybe I'd find one of them there.

I recognized that the room belonged to Ava without knowing quite how. White walls and a bed carefully made with a beautiful spread that changed almost imperceptibly, thread by thread, from the lightest, airiest blue to a deep navy flecked with gold. There was nothing on the floor or the walls.

I opened her wardrobe, and her shoes were lined up, the shirts ironed, and some of her more extravagant clothes hung neatly.

The second bedroom was Imogen's – the same layout and nothing too fancy. Like Ava's room, it was tidy, with to-do lists pinned up and some books from our course reading list on the shelf in alphabetical order. Photos – far too many of Samuel. Not a shrine to Samuel, that would be too extreme for Imogen, but certainly a curated collection.

The third and final bedroom was Tabitha's. Three doors. There's a symmetry to three. Three craves comparison in every fairy tale. You can't help but line them up: two that are not quite right and, always, miraculously, one that is a perfect fit.

First Ava. Then Imogen. But as soon as I walked in, it felt like Tabitha's was the room I wanted to curl up in, to lie in the mess of it all.

The space was homely. Even though it was the same size as the other two, there was a lot more furniture squeezed in, with a sofa to one side and a laptop on it, open. Her belongings were everywhere and her clothes looked as if they'd leaked from her wardrobe, forming a silky puddle. One wall was lined with books of varying literary tastes, from bound erotica to a selection of paperback crime novels.

There was a towering set of drawers, the top one partially opened, and on display there were many, many framed photographs of Tabitha. Of Ava and Tabitha together, and of a spaniel looking happy with itself in a field, its coat covered in mud. In my head I slotted myself into the picture, imagined Tabitha's arm looped around my waist.

I opened the drawer a little further. It was full of lingerie. The second was filled with soft knitwear that looked expensive, and I ran my fingers over the pieces, held a cardigan up against myself. Lots of the items still had labels on, and some even had plastic security tags attached. I paused for a moment. This would look bad if she walked in and I was going through her things, but I'd got this far. How could I ignore the third drawer?

The third and final drawer in the third and final room, and it was clearly being used as a dumping ground. There was very little order. Pens and staplers and tape cohabited with batteries and a chequebook. Then bills, notepads and a whole wedge of files. Letters referencing setting up a business account and some printed tables that looked like budgets. What was Tabitha up to? She was obsessed with us doing something, and I knew she had her sights set on a scheme of some sort, but I wondered why she hadn't mentioned anything if she actually had an idea of what it might be.

Under the accounts there were more photos. Folded pictures alongside larger, professional prints of a younger Tabitha.

Tabitha and what could only have been Samuel as babies in a cafe.

Tabitha on a dappled pony, both dotted with red rosettes, their hair in matching plaits.

Tabitha with her head twisted violently, looking back over one shoulder in a puffy prom dress with a corset top. So many photos. I moved some aside and froze when I saw them.

Photos of me.

In one, I was smoking a cigarette outside the library. In another, I was walking towards the bar on the way to work. Another showed me outside the lecture theatre, waiting to go in. The pictures must have dated back to close to the beginning of the term.

They'd been watching me.

19.

Looking back on it all now – the dinners, the strong coffees, the drawn-out conversations about nothing memorable – they all merge into one nondescript but nevertheless pleasant assortment of things we did to pass the time. I can recall them all, but there's a certain intensity when it comes to my memory of the pictures. It's so easy to transport myself back there. Holding those photographs in one hand and running my fingers over the print where the shot wasn't quite in focus, so I was all blurred. The matt texture of the paper and the raised seam in the centre from the fold.

I should have been shocked. I should have been appalled by the invasion of privacy. And I could tell you that. I could say how *affronted* I was that they'd stalked me, and how unnerving it was. The Shiver had been spying on me, after all. Working out what I did and where I went.

I could reform the narrative, because now, after so long, I can pull out the parts I like into the brightness and send the aspects I don't want to share back into the shade. But there's really no point in doing that. As far as I can, I'd rather be honest and say that I was rather proud when I saw those photos. They cared about me and wanted to befriend me. I was flattered that they thought I was special. I was tempted to take one for myself to keep, but of course I didn't.

Now, when I think about my own work these days, I wouldn't bother taking pictures in that way because it's too time-consuming, but those pictures captured something. I was made bleaker by the camera, a dirty sadness like I hadn't washed for days. The slippery oil slick of my hair scraped back from my head. My clothes looked rumpled as if I was on the verge of unravelling and I was fixated by the red of my eyes. It was shocking how unhinged I looked. I know it's just the effect that flash has – it picks up the raw connective tissue in the back of the socket, something that's vaguely unsettling in itself – but it also gave the photos a look of something demonic. A feral creature roaming the streets.

I hadn't realized how close I was to some kind of awful precipice, how terribly lonely I had been right at the start, and they'd pulled me away from that state of desperation and welcomed me into their world.

20.

Spring in Edinburgh was then, and is now, marked by the change in the cherry blossom trees. In winter, you'd hardly notice them. They're bare, all stripped bark and unremarkable branches, then in April they come back to life. Overnight they transform and turn pink and frothy like a strawberry milkshake, forming a flashy canopy down the Meadows, a large grassed area near the university. I walked down those long pathways that sliced the lawns in half. I wasn't going anywhere in particular, just towards the south of the city to see the pink at each side of my peripheral vision turn my world rose-tinted.

I'd mentioned to Imogen that I enjoyed walking through the Meadows and she'd looked at me, quite shocked. She told me that last year a man had laid tripwires along those narrow paths, and when dusk fell, he would lurk nearby, waiting as long as it took until finally a young woman on her own would stumble, and then he'd grab her, so fast she'd barely know what was happening. She told me it had happened time and time again, and he'd never been caught because his method was so effective. She wanted to scare me.

After that, I couldn't see those paths in quite the same way. I imagined the thin knots of threaded barbed wire; the moonlight bouncing off them. I pictured a woman strolling through on a balmy night, her jumper tied around her waist, falling to the ground before she even knew what was happening. The trees shielding whatever came next.

Who knows if it was the truth? From then on, I took a different route back through the streets away from the greenery of the city, but even so, spring means the pink of the cherry blossom to me to this day. And even now, if I don't see them, I know they are there, and that spring has come.

I'd settled into a routine. I didn't have to think about what the week had in store for me any more, or what I'd do each day. I had my shifts, I had my friends, and I had Finn. He was a good outlet. He prevented me from being too intense with the others, from caring too much. It was good to have people that I didn't mind about impressing at all.

Those months passed quickly. I was invited to dinner parties again, and they all took a similar format. Not fancy, but I looked forward to them, although the nervous clench of my entire body every time I rang Tabitha's doorbell never quite left.

The one thing that edged closer and closer was France. I knew they were planning on going to France – to Tabitha's house – over Reading Week. They seemed to have visited a lot when they were at school and this year they were keen to resurrect the tradition. Imogen talked constantly whenever I was around about the new swimwear she was planning to buy. It wasn't subtle – it was petty – her attempt to make her position stronger by trying to diminish mine. By mid-April they'd skirted around the topic for long enough that I was sick of it. The thought of going made me feel ill, but the idea of being excluded was painful too.

Finally, it happened. I had arrived early for my shift at work and Ava was sitting at the bar, her coat flung over a stool. The remains of a Bloody Mary sat in front of her. She'd picked out all the garnishes – a few glistening olives and gherkins, a piece of celery, a boiled half quail's egg on a cocktail stick – and laid them on one side of her glass. A puddle of red juice had formed, and it reminded me of a cat bringing in prey and laying out the heart for its owner. At least she seemed to have been reminded of her fondness for the drink, and I congratulated myself for that. She was talking to Finn, or rather he was talking at her, stilted and nervous, and as I approached, they fell silent.

'Clare!' she greeted me.

Finn gave me a sharp look and then turned his back to us.

'What are you doing here?' I asked her, almost forgetting myself and being unusually direct.

'I've just been catching up on some work at the library and I thought a nightcap would help.'

This made little sense, as it was only half past five in the evening. The muscles in my neck tightened as they always did when my two worlds came together. Finn, whose behaviour I could always predict in any given circumstance, and Ava, who seemed to know what I'd do before I even knew myself.

It felt like a worrying clash, but I forced myself to relax. She was my friend. I should have been glad to see her.

I moved round to the other side of the bar, so we were separated by wood.

'Why are you really here?' It was just with Ava I could be that confident.

'We want you to come to France with us.'

'France?' I feigned surprise.

'A week with all of us over Reading Week. It'll be amazing – sun, sea – well, not much sea in central France. Samuel . . .' She trailed off and gave me an exaggerated wink.

'Why would I care about Samuel?'

'Oh, whatever,' she shrugged as if she had no interest in discussing it any further.

I knew they thought there might be something between Samuel and me. I glanced along the bar to where Finn was busying himself and doing his best to ignore the whole thing.

'Won't you want to go back to the US?'

'Don't worry about me. I might go back for a few days. I'll fly from Bordeaux, I guess.'

I didn't show it, but inwardly I noted the remarkable cost

that would be incurred by her spontaneous travel planning, and how little she seemed to care.

'OK. I mean, it sounds great. Why didn't Tabitha ask me, though? It's her house.'

Ava finished the dregs of her drink and put it to one side. 'She just wanted me to do it. But it won't be all lying in the sun. There's a project she wants to begin – something for all of us. France will be a perfect place for us to talk to you about it.'

So that was why we were going to France. I nodded; I was used to the projects, and surely it was linked to the documents I'd found in Tabitha's drawer, all the different business ideas whirling in the background. But now, I learned, there was something else underway too.

'This one is a change. In scope,' she said.

'Any clues?'

'You'll find out when you find out and don't worry, Tabitha will sort your ticket. All you need to do is turn up at the airport.'

I didn't reply, let the scenario play in my head, and then I blurted out, 'Why me?'

Ava tipped her head to one side. 'Explain?' she said.

'Why did you choose to be friends with me?'

I hoped I wasn't showing that I'd found the photographs.

I could tell Finn was pretending not to listen in the corner with his back to us.

She looked calm, unreadable, giving nothing away. I could almost see her brain working.

'You overthink things – but I think it's because you see it like us, or like her anyway,' she said with a sigh.

'What do you mean?'

She smiled and pulled me over, so we looked out on to the street in front of the bar. 'Look out and tell me the first thing you see,' she said, and I did. I stared out of the window, aware that she was completely focused on me and on what I was looking at.

I saw a woman wrapped up in a floor-length black coat with an enormous greyhound pulling at the lead. 'Well, there's a woman in a coa–' I started.

She cut me off with a laugh. It was always odd when Ava laughed, but this time it was quite natural, just at her own delight in being right.

'Yup.' She patted my arm. 'That's why.'

'Why what?'

'Because you're just like Tabitha. You want to see the beauty and the glamour, the buildings, the food, the people who have far too much money. Houses that take your breath away, dramatic liaisons and secrets; things to be spectacular. I don't think either of you even see the rubbish on the pavement or the workmen. The electricity bills, council tax, the cogs of life, the shitty bits, all the unglamorous parts. I see all that, but the two of you, I think you view the world in the same entirely unrealistic way.' She paused for effect. 'Or maybe it's nothing like that and you're just a misfit like the rest of us. Anyway, enough heart-to-hearts for today.'

She was right in a way. Tabitha and I did see the world selectively most of the time. It wasn't something that I necessarily considered a flaw or a talent.

She threw Finn the largest, fakest smile I'd ever seen and left.

'So friendly, your friends,' Finn remarked, scooping up Ava's discards in one hand. The gherkins were stained and bean-shaped, like feline kidneys, and he flicked them in the bin.

'I know they can be cold sometimes,' I said carefully.

'Cold? They treat me like a servant, but for some reason, they've deemed you good enough to associate with.'

'I don't think they quite treat you like a servant. I'm sorry you feel that way.' I used what I thought was my most conciliatory tone.

'*I'm sorry you feel that way.* Quit the counselling bullshit.

I couldn't care less. I just think you need to be careful who you spend your time with. There's something creepy about them.'

'They're interesting; they're fun to be with. And they chose me. They want me to be their friend.'

'Why? What if they only like you because you're pretty?'

I laughed at that.

Redness entered his cheeks and he turned away from me. This was what I liked about Finn. I didn't find much of what he said very interesting most of the time, but there was a hesitant sweetness to him that came out occasionally. Compliments that I didn't think I needed.

'Is that right?' I said.

'Oh, shut up, you know you're pretty,' he said. 'In all serious- ness, it's strange. They never come in together, it's all just "popping in" to see you, or one of them randomly turns up on some pretence. They look at the menu, at how much stuff costs, even though they're clearly all loaded. That guy Samuel looks like he's going to a funeral every time I see him, and that girl, Ada, is it? She dresses like a dominatrix. It's fucking weird.'

I ignored his dig at Ava. 'He just likes to look smart! I get your point, though. I'll be careful, I promise. Give me the diary – I need a week off.'

'Students, always with the holidays.' But he laughed, bared his teeth in our shared understanding of a shark, and walked away.

I was thinking of Ava. It was one of the first times I'd seen her in action as she spun plates and juggled everything for Tabitha like it was the easiest thing in the world.

21.

On a chilly April afternoon, we gathered in the New Town. A motley crew, skulking with an assortment of luggage – waiting for Tabitha.

Ava counted bags of tobacco into her case, the leather she usually wore swapped out for ripped dungarees. Imogen looked demure in a printed summer dress and an oversized straw hat that she kept batting at irritably as it flopped about in the wind.

Samuel was very dapper in pressed chinos and a pair of sunglasses on his head – with a noticeable artificial orange tinge to his skin.

Finally, Tabitha emerged from the front door, locking it up and presenting herself to us for mass adoration – pared-back like an off-duty Parisian model in a white cotton shift dress and faded espadrilles, her bare legs skeletal and surprisingly hairy, like furry cocktail sticks.

'You look nice,' Samuel said to her as she twirled round in front of us.

Imogen's face darkened, but she didn't quite dare to scowl openly at Tabitha; instead, she rolled her eyes at me, then almost immediately looked away, regretting the slip and the show of closeness. Things were better between the two of us, though. Imogen and I seemed to have reached an undeclared and silent truce since I'd upset her before Christmas, even though I still didn't understand what I'd done.

'Clare!' Tabitha hugged me and then pulled back and squeezed her arms around herself. 'Always so bloody cold here, even in April. The weather looks fantastic at Ma's, it's going to be an absolute blast. Did Ava tell you what we have planned?'

'She mentioned a project,' I replied.

'*Un projet*, yes. We can discuss it all there. Is that all you're bringing? You can put things in the hold, you know.' She was laden with bags and she tossed one of them in Imogen's direction. I just had a single canvas holdall.

I was jangly, my feet tapping, trying to keep it all together, and I saw Ava give me a quizzical look, an eyebrow raised as if to say, 'Calm down.'

Tabitha didn't notice, and then we were off.

I couldn't sleep or eat on the flight. I was sick to my stomach, sitting there on the plane. The others ignored me, oblivious to my nerves. I imagined how horrified my granny would be at me doing this, and what she would have said if I'd told her. Fear slithered up my throat, so I swallowed hard and long to push it down. I couldn't help but think of my parents, of what they might be doing or what they'd say about my trip.

But there was only so long I could stay at the edge, all jittery and alert, before my body refused to participate and I crashed – dread was too exhausting. As we walked out of the airport in Limoges to hail a taxi, I smelt that musty rush of foreignness. The smell of a country when you don't live there. I finally let go, felt the muscles in my back and shoulders relax, because we'd arrived and there was nothing more I could do.

We were all tired and tetchy in the taxi, barely talking as we wound round country roads, our bodies sweaty and pushed together too closely. I didn't speak to the taxi driver as Tabitha and Imogen battled away, trying to engage him in jumbled French; I cringed at their bad accents and had to hold back to stop myself from jumping in. Tried to stay calm.

Each time we turned a corner, I felt like it couldn't possibly be any further, surely not, but it was, and then it was dark and the road had turned into a dirt track.

After what seemed like hours, the house came into view, and Tabitha let out a deep sigh of contentment. The sigh of someone coming home.

At first it looked imposing – a huge, white country house. It changed as we got closer, and it was clear the grandeur resided in the sheer size of the place. On closer inspection, I noted the peeling facade and windows boarded up – a crumbling ruin, not the palace I had imagined it to be.

Tabitha rang the bell and a woman who was unmistakably her mother opened the door. Bone-thin to the point of nothing, her hair a greying nest of rats' tails, she was bundled up in a soup of creased linen; her trailing circular skirt billowed and touched the floor. She reached for a pair of horn-rimmed glasses from a chain around her neck, and I saw the flash from a chunky diamond ring hanging off the skinniest of fingers.

'Ahh, darling Tabby. Come in, come in.' Long vowels, just like Tabitha. The words were a little slurred, and she stood back to let us into the house. Samuel pushed in front of the rest of us, forgetting his usual politeness and embracing her in a hug. I thought of the fond way he'd talked about her during our midnight car journeys, her dazzling beauty when he was a child, although I took everything Samuel said with a pinch of salt. It must have been strange for him, seeing her like that, but if it was, he didn't show it in the slightest.

'Minta, thank you so much for having us. We've been looking forward to this holiday,' he declared loudly, more of a show for me than an actual exchange.

She didn't move aside, and we all stood in the first room that led off from the entrance vestibule. It was cluttered with what looked like a whole club's worth of tennis rackets. A dining room at one point, perhaps, but the space had become something else, dominated by an enormous desk with stacks of yellowing paper piled up high. Boxes and newspapers covered the floor, obscuring a rug that looked like the one in Tabitha's flat back in Edinburgh. Dust and dirt had settled on flagstones beneath, and two huge white cats basked near an unplugged storage heater, oblivious to the chaos of it all. I remembered Tabitha's words: *the house in France would never sell.*

In that disorderly room, a lump rose in my throat, and I thought that if I spoke, I might cry. What were we doing? What was *I* doing in such a strange house with people I'd only known for a few months, in France of all places? It felt almost a peculiar betrayal of Ava not to warn me, to tell me what it was going to be like and what I was walking into, so I would know what to expect and how to react. But the two of them seemed happy enough, Imogen and Ava. They offered Minta big kisses on the cheek, plying her with cashmere socks and gin. Tabitha gave her mother a small hug, enclosing her gently as if she might break.

'Ma, this is Clare.' She gestured for me to come forward. 'Remember, I've told you all about her.'

'Yes, yes. Clare. Lovely to meet you, darling.' She placed a hand on my arm; a light touch. 'Welcome. It's so good to have you this year – these reprobates are desperate for some new blood. How was the journey?'

'Fine,' Tabitha replied.

'Well, I'm sure you can sort yourself out. I'll be in my bedroom if you need anything, but please do keep it down and don't disturb the boys, Tabitha.'

She said Tabitha's name pointedly as she waved a hand in the direction of the cats, which made me wonder how she had disturbed them in the past. One of them stared at Tabitha malevolently and started to thump its tail on the floor in an erratic beat. Tabitha gave the animal a haughty glance, her mother an eye-roll, and then turned to me.

'The cats are affronted by the mess; it puts them in a bad mood and who can blame them. Come on, Clare. You're up here.' It was the only time during the trip she would reference the state of the place. She took my hand and led me up to a small, hot room, high in the eaves of the house.

'Goodnight,' she said, even though it was early. Her lips touched my cheek, and she gave me a swift hug to end the evening.

In my room, far away from where the rest of them were staying, I decided I needed some ammunition to sleep, so I tip-toed down the stairs to the bathroom where I opened the cabinet to see some English medicines. Diazepam, some kind of beta blocker and amitriptyline. A treasure chest of drugs that sat alongside various old-fashioned tonic bottles and remedies with cryptic names and instructions like *Cat's sage* and *For deep sleep – take* only *on full moon*, written in handwriting very similar to Tabitha's.

I remembered Tabitha's description of her mother's pains and hesitated for a second over the sleeping tablet for the full moon. Internally, I congratulated myself for resisting checking if there was a full moon outside before I swallowed. It tasted of cinnamon and bark. I pocketed two diazepam as a back-up and headed back to bed.

The bedroom I was staying in appeared to be poised on the brink of crumbling to the floor. Dark damp started from the skirting boards and rose in an ombre haze that looked like a faddish paint effect. It had covered the bottom third of one wall. There was a window to the side of the room which would have looked out over the garden but appeared to have been hastily boarded up. I pulled back the sheets, which were almost slimy to the touch.

The mould. It has always had an effect on me ever since I was a child. I remember it in my mother's room, seeping up the walls, and whenever she scrubbed it away it came back, or at least she claimed it did. That dank smell like stale water and mushrooms and earth. She told me it filled her lungs and consumed her thoughts.

That night it was like she was with me. With each breath, I imagined inhaling the spores.

Would the crumbling walls collapse to the floor if I stopped watching? At that point, the combination of sickness and sweatiness and a thickening fatigue from the day made it almost impossible to stay awake. Despite the strange feeling that everything might fall down – the room, my life, every story or lie I'd ever told – despite it all, my eyelids felt heavy and, in the end, sleep came.

22.

Back in Edinburgh, whenever I wasn't with them, when I was at work or in my flat, I imagined them together laughing, with their shared – potentially invented – stories and histories, in a circle that maybe I would never be fully part of. The first two terms had been a lot of work, and I saw it as my probation. I didn't speak much because my phrasing always seemed off. I didn't want to say anything that would open me up to questions, and I was careful not to be too loud. I lived on the edges for a while, and they let me stay there. They never asked me much, and they let me exist without pushing me. I knew not to try too hard – not to challenge things. It would be unwise to let them see how I could be in certain situations. I hadn't become angry at anyone for a while, hadn't experienced that change I used to feel as blackness took over. My moods had settled.

I was self-conscious all the time back then. That hot embarrassment and that certainty they are all waiting for you to mess up? It's only with age that you see it's mostly in your head, and that you're not that special – the thudding epiphany that most people are far too preoccupied with their own lives to care about yours.

But on that holiday, it wasn't paranoia. I was not *imagining* the intense focus on me. I felt it strongly. Felt everyone clawing at me. I wasn't an outsider any more, instead I was the centre of the whole thing, and they were all orbiting around me in a way I'd never experienced before.

It began from that first morning, when I got up, and I could see in the thin morning light that the house looked out on to a vast and glorious garden. Wild and untamed, it stretched far

past the main buildings, dotted with trees and long grass filled with wild flowers. The garden seemed to flaunt its lack of maintenance with ease in a way that worked – the same showy, unapologetic nature that Tabitha applied to everything she did. The house, however, was as bleak as the night before, even on a bright spring day. A selection of bedrooms peeled off at unplanned intervals like roots, and I wasn't sure where the others slept, but I got the sense they had their usual rooms, decided long ago in previous visits. So much *stuff*: rubbish and trinkets and chairs and bin bags of old clothes. In one room, a jumble of musical instruments including a cello, which looked to have been set up for practice one day, with sheet music open on a stand, and then abandoned for years. A sad vignette of better times.

Stepping out there on that first morning, I realized I didn't know what we'd *do* while we were there.

What do you do on holiday? It requires effort, a decision on how the day should unfold, and it had been years since I'd been on one.

There was no studying to do. We'd had a busy few weeks in the lead-up to the break; Ava and Samuel studied law and had been holed up with an intensive revision schedule. Imogen, Tabitha and I had studied sporadically, often together. I can grudgingly admit now, after so long, that Imogen had a natural flair for the subject. Not much seemed to please her, but art was her thing. When she wrote about paintings, they came to life. She fawned over them lovingly, poring over every brushstroke, each historical detail analysed, even though the style of painting she always went for bored me to tears. She liked landscapes. Tidy landscapes with a tree to the side, perhaps even a wandering shepherd. She could write about those forever, and although it really wasn't to my taste, I could appreciate that her essays were thoroughly researched, insightful even. Unlike mine, which were usually rushed off after a shift at the bar, and worlds

away from Tabitha's, which were mostly unintelligible. I'd read a particular first draft of Tabitha's shortly after we'd become friends, and it had resembled a typed-up stream of conscious-ness with no referencing or footnotes. The actual artworks were only mentioned in the first and final sentences, bookending a dreamy piece that bounced from magazine self-help to song lyrics to her thoughts on food critics to a long tangent on medical bias. She usually managed to shoehorn in at least a few sen-tences about her beloved Klimt, regardless of the topic. Perhaps in a scholar's careful hands, Tabitha's unusual approach could have been a sign of genius, but, unfortunately, she wasn't hard-working or skilled at writing. There was no mistaking that Tabitha's essays were offbeat in the wrong way. She muddled through, though I wasn't sure how.

Soon, it became apparent there was no need to make any decisions. I saw them all on that first morning, lazing around on blankets, and understood that, in the light of day, we could escape the house and spend our days in the garden.

I decided not to go out yet and started on the washing-up instead, to gain some points with Tabitha and Minta. The hoarding hadn't quite crept to the kitchen, and it was tidier than the rest of the house. The first thing I saw when I went to the sink was Minta's ring, carefully placed next to the soap. I guessed that she'd removed it to wash up then wandered off, and I picked it up between two fingers. I marvelled at the light that splintered off the large diamond.

Then, Samuel was there, behind me, pushing into my side with his hip. 'Want a hand drying?' he asked.

'Sure.'

His eyes went to the ring. 'What are you doing with that?' he asked.

'Nothing!' I nearly dropped it to the floor. 'Honestly, I just found it here.'

He looked at me out of the corner of his eye and then

laughed. He grabbed a tea towel, flicked it at me, and began vigorously drying a bowl, a line of sweat forming at his hairline. 'I believe you! As a seasoned liar myself, I know when someone just can't help but tell the truth! Never fear.' He put the bowl down and reached out to take the ring from my hands. 'Even if you were going to pinch that thing, it's a fake. Look.' He brushed his finger over the band to show where the gold had rubbed away, tapped at the diamond. 'Costume jewellery, I think they call it. You didn't think it was real, did you, Clarey? She sold all the good stuff years ago.' Carelessly, he tossed the ring back to the side of the sink. His mouth dipped at the edges cruelly.

His hair was wet, and he looked as sleek as a gingery otter. I felt an unexpected jolt of something there, a pang of longing, hot and liquid, that I'd never experienced with him before.

I wanted to reach out and grab him, but I made myself hold back. Hold back from kissing him very hard and fast and deep to taste the salt and the sun on him. To surprise him. It was a sudden, delicious impulse, something just for me, and he was unaware, although he must have seen something in my face.

'You OK, Clarey?' he said. That mean smile again.

'I'm fine.'

The moment had passed.

How strange! I'd never quite found Samuel attractive. In that moment, though, seeing him, there was something between us.

It was like Ava had said, and she always seemed to know best. Knowing what I'd do and how I'd react before I even felt like I knew myself.

And so it progressed for the next few days.

Their attention on me, it spread like a virus. I saw them looking at each other for a beat too long – silent messages passing between them. Each time I moved, Imogen was clucking around me, making me drink more water in case I suffered from dehydration, prioritizing me above Samuel and Tabitha for once.

We went to buy food – Tabitha enjoyed shoplifting, and she dragged me along with her. We took old, rusty bikes, and Tabitha picked up various tarts and quiches to pay for. I watched as she covertly slipped extra pastries into her bag.

Back at the house, Ava certainly seemed present all the time in a firmer way, next to me with a smile or a nod to comfort me as if I might run away at any point.

The first few days were lazy, playful even.

Most of the time we lay outside in the garden – yes, it was warm enough even in April to lie out in the sun. There was a small pond at the bottom of the lawn that looked idyllic, and I remember Samuel jumped in one day. A mistake, as it was freezing cold and full of swampish matter, and he came out looking dirty and irritated. And then Tabitha was there, shrieking and chasing Samuel with sunscreen, squirting him in a climactic finale that made me think something was there between them, something brewing perhaps. Then Tabitha came up to me and wrapped her arms around me, and the rest of them joined her, embracing me and clawing at me as if they were taking something, but it felt so good.

Finally, Tabitha flung herself down on the grass next to me and placed a cold hand on my stomach, then squeezed her body up against mine.

'I'm so, so glad you came, Clare. Why don't you rest up, have a nap? Dinner tonight – we'll talk about *le projet*?'

The project. I wished she'd stop calling it that in her terribly over-the-top French accent.

23.

As instructed, I had a long nap. In general, rest was difficult to get – I had become more and more convinced that I was ingesting the mould in the room, but when I'd asked Tabitha, she'd brushed the whole thing off. *What are you talking about! There's only a speckle of it!*

The sound of laughter woke me. They must have been down on the terrace, and I heard a wild shriek. Bottles clinked. Something smashed and there were low coos and the sound of sweeping. I could have lain there for a while longer and listened, but then the screech of chair legs against stone and a surge of curiosity forced me up, and I climbed out of bed to watch from above as they walked over to the back of the garden. Tabitha peered up at my bedroom, squinting, searching for me. It was time to join them.

Downstairs, I weaved through a path that had been cleared from mess down the main artery of the house as a route from place to place. Stepping outside into the evening, it was still, and hot even though the sun had set. In the darkness, the grime on Minta's house had faded away and the overgrown grass was romantic instead of chaotic, pressed close against the outbuildings around the house.

They sat at a long table under the trees covered with what looked like a floral bed sheet. There were tiny glass bottles, each filled with a single wild flower. Runny cheese and bread on a thick board. As I approached, Tabitha filled her glass so it overflowed and red drips soaked into the tablecloth. She wiped them in a juddering stroke with her index finger and then she sucked on it, long and hard. She beckoned for me to sit.

There she was, in prime position at the centre of the table, with Imogen next to her. At that moment I was struck, not for the first time, by just how disagreeable Imogen looked, with her mouth pursed tightly. Samuel observed me and his expression was impossible to read. Then Ava approached from inside the house, carrying a huge dish, steam rising from it. It was filled with risotto. It felt repulsive. *I* felt repulsive, but there was nothing I could do apart from sit there and wait.

When Ava served it, she gave us huge portions, far, far bigger than we could possibly eat in one sitting. Dishing it out, then bringing over more bottles of wine for the table.

Finally, she sat down too.

Tabitha poured me a glass, handed it to me, and then she began. 'I'll jump right in. I have an idea. I'd like to ask you a question first. How much do you make at the bar?'

She was drunk, I could tell, speaking so loudly. I didn't respond. Tabitha didn't get messy like this, not usually.

'Come on! Humour me? We're all friends and we should be able to speak about money! They always say there's three things you don't talk about, sex, religion and politics, don't they?' She leaned forward. I could see she wasn't wearing a bra and I averted my eyes.

'It's not true, though, is it?' she continued. 'We could talk about those all night, who's fucking who, who supports who, and we'd die of boredom – nobody would care. But money . . . money is different.'

I glanced at the others. Imogen looked like she was about to pass out. Samuel gave undue focus to the plate in front of him.

'It's just a part-time job. It's minimum wage,' I said.

'I thought so. And have you thought about what you'll do when you graduate?'

In all honesty, I'd thought about it a lot. About them – never about myself. My personal trajectory seemed to trail off as much as I hoped it would stay close to theirs, but their futures were easier to imagine, the fabric of their lives still woven together with weddings and reunions and dinners. Often as I lay in bed at night trying to sleep, my brain and body still wired from my shift, I'd think of them. Ava would be back in the US, in a white-walled office. In a black suit and bonier with age. The fixer for some huge conglomerate, perhaps doing something not entirely legal. For Imogen, something to match her scrappy perseverance. I'd always imagined her as a high-end estate agent, flustered in a tight skirt, tumbling out of her SUV with a million sets of keys to show clients some crumbling heap in the Home Counties. In the evenings, she'd return to her own tidy country house, thinking it vastly superior to the ones she showed all day. Samuel was in a boardroom, playing an undetermined role, in a smart suit. Not wearing a tie – he would regard that as a little gauche – his expensive shirt straining to hide the gut that would grow as he reached his thirties, eyes glazing over a complicated pie chart, instead choosing to dazzle his audience with a wolfish grin and an outlandish anecdote.

Sometimes, when we lay in bed, Finn asked what I was thinking about and my thoughts would come to a halt, because of course there was no way to describe these odd trips into a predicted future. I knew what Finn would have said: *You're obsessed with them all, but they're not like you, not like us, and they'll drop you in a heartbeat.*

I never told him.

These futures played out in my mind like exaggerated sketches; university never felt like it was the place for them. They didn't participate in any of it enough. I got the sense that they were all waiting for the next part of the journey.

My thoughts about their lives weren't set in stone. I'd seen Minta bumble from room to room, grunting as she bent down to coo over a cat. Observing us with a polite, detached confusion, like she wasn't quite sure why we were in her house.

From the moment I'd arrived, it had become clear that Tabitha's future was far less certain. There probably wasn't a massive pot of family money to dip into, no safety net.

I tried to focus on them all as they sat in a line in front of me, my head aching.

'I haven't thought that much about it,' I said.

'Well, we've never talked much about it, have we?' she said. 'Although we haven't discussed it, I have a plan that's very much coming together, and it involves you. I don't want to faff around with anything, Clare. I'd rather just take you through everything honestly, and then we can eat and digest it – the food and the idea.' She sounded stern.

With all the time we'd spent together, I didn't know her like the rest of them knew her, but I was beginning to get there. She didn't want the flow of a conversation – she rarely did. Instead, our glorious dictator was handing me the script for reference so I could follow, with enter stage right clearly marked for her, our leading actress, as she took her position.

We, the audience, waited for the drunken performance to begin.

24.

'So here it is. I've told you about my father. You know what he did to us, and it was awful. And now you're here in France. I was desperate for you to come, you know, almost to the point that I was actually too scared to ask you myself!' She was rushing through this bit, then she stopped and chuckled to herself. 'That's why I asked Ava to see if you'd be up for it. Anyway, I have something planned for us. It relates to what he did to us, and the whole thing made me think about how I'm going to make sure that I'm financially independent. And how you can be too. How we can do something together!'

The wording didn't sound like Tabitha; it was gabbled, but still it flowed in a semi-logical way. This had been rehearsed. This was a pitch, and I wondered if the wine was because she was nervous.

She continued. 'What I've always wanted is to do something I care about – which probably comes as a shock to you, but I care a lot, and I want you all to be involved.' She swept her hands across the table to show her benevolent inclusion, nearly knocking over her glass.

'I want to create a business, something we can do now and grow, one that we'll all work on. The premise is simple, Clare. We'll have specific clients, some of which our Business Development Director has already started to look into.'

She gave Samuel an affectionate wink, more, it seemed, for my sake so I could identify him as Business Development Director than for him, as he looked away from her, a little embarrassed.

'And we'll fulfil a service to those clients. The service is simple. These are women just like my mother. Women who are in a marriage where it's almost certain they are going to be completely screwed over, and we help them.'

She wanted me to ask. I couldn't help it. 'How will we help them?'

'By putting them in control. The women will get the chance to create their own narrative because we'll be weeding out those men who are going to cheat, and we'll do it using a term I hate, but I'll use it for clarity – honey trapping.'

I wondered where she was going with this.

'The rest of them have known about it for a while,' she said as if Samuel and Ava and Imogen weren't even there and it was just me and her. 'We've been exploring logistics and client acquisition. We need to find women who this will work for, and we need to do it discreetly, of course. I plan for it to become a premium service. So, we have Samuel, who's been instrumental in setting up the bones of the thing, stitching it all together. We needed capital and he did an excellent job in securing that, some from Ava's family.'

I looked to Ava. Not even a ripple of a smile or acknowledgement.

'Ava has been in charge of the purse strings as well as sorting out the website –' Tabitha started.

I interrupted. 'You have a website for this?' I'd never really seen them use the internet much.

Tabitha looked at me, so still, suddenly clear-headed. 'Of course! I'll show it to you tonight if you want. Ava and Samuel have been working hard forging those connections in London and in Scotland.'

It was like she was speaking in a language I'd never heard her even touch the edges of, but it was all coming out of her mouth as if she'd been using it for years: *client acquisition, forging connections.*

She continued. 'When it comes to those on the ground, that

would be me and you mostly, with Imogen doing the research. We need to have you for this.'

'We'd be going out, finding . . . sleeping with them?' I asked.

She stared at me, wide-eyed. 'Oh, we don't have to sleep with them, Clare, although I'm not sure why that would bother you so much. It's just about getting the evidence. Let's focus on you. You're perfect. Samuel was entranced the moment he met you, weren't you?'

Drunk Tabitha was largely the same as sober Tabitha, only nastier, and I was embarrassed at Samuel's response – a faint blush crept up his cheeks, he ducked his head.

'And then there was Finn . . .' she continued.

'There still is Finn,' I corrected her.

'Oh, yes, I know. He's besotted! We all know that.'

I imagined them buzzing around the bar like flies.

'And what if I don't want to?' I asked.

I was transported back to her flat before we went to get my haircut. There was the to-and-fro, the gentle battle before I did what she always knew I would.

Her tongue was purple and her eyes glittered. She replied, 'I think it's something you need to think about first. I want to give you time to really consider it. Do dig in.'

She started to shovel the risotto into her mouth. I looked at the cheese, oozing in the heat. I knew I needed to be alone for a minute. I stood up and very shakily went to the toilet inside, where I sat, gathering my thoughts. When I came out, Ava was there looking at me, hip cocked.

'What are you doing? Are you OK?' she asked with mild concern.

'I'm fine, but this idea . . . Why has Tabitha got so fixated on this?'

Even as I said the words, I realized I wasn't entirely against the idea at all. It was more a surge of something strong and unexpected that felt like jealousy because they hadn't included me in the planning.

'The idea's fine; doing it's another matter. But you should be aware that she knows about you. About what happened in . . . Périgueux, is it?' She gave me an apologetic smile. 'I mean, I wouldn't bring it up with her if I were you,' she continued. 'It does mean she has a bit of an upper hand knowing about your past and all . . . Look, I'm desperate for a pee. Move out the way?' she asked, crossing her legs.

A quick shard of panic ran through me, so hot and sharp that I nearly yelped like a yappy dog right then and there, nearly pushed her away to stop her from seeing straight through me.

I contained myself. Became hard and icy in the face of her terrible words.

She knew about Périgueux.

25.

I like the name Clare, you see, but it has not always been my name.

They seemed to know that. In fact, they seemed to know all about what happened to me when I was sixteen. I assumed they knew that my father is British and my mother is French, and that I had lived in Périgueux my whole life, until I moved to England.

I left because we punished a man one night, me and my friends, Adrienne and Dina. We'd met him down by the lake, and then things happened. We made him pay in a way that was messy and long.

Most of my memories of that night are tacky in my mind. The fizz of the champagne, sour and warm. Then the earthy taste of mushrooms on the wood of the spoon after we stirred them with butter and garlic.

Fingers red and sticky like licked sweeties.

Later, there was screaming.

After it happened, I went to stay permanently with my grandmother in Hull – a town I hated immediately and one where I knew no one. They told me it wasn't a good idea for me to go back to France – not now and not ever. They told me they'd moved, then when I asked where, they were vague. I finished up my studies via a correspondence course. Even though my English had always been fluent, I picked up idioms methodically. It's raining cats and dogs. Kill two birds with one stone. My granny had always said I was more English than French.

So began a year of immersion. Of listening to the radio,

practising what the presenter said again and again until my accent was flawless. A year of trying to catch up on popular TV shows, films, jokes. A year of cooking beans on toast and reading crime procedural novels bought from charity shops to test my knowledge of the culture. Waiting for life to begin, applying to universities, thinking about the person I was going to be. Walking the streets at night when they were quiet even though those streets were too rough for it to be advisable.

My parents cut me off and made it clear that they'd done their bit. They'd got me that far and even helped me afterwards in clearing up the mess I'd made. So much time wasted in courtrooms and the shame of it all. They called it *the episode*.

They were rid of me, and they would prefer it stayed that way.

We managed to get my name changed and I became Clare.

Clare – I'd chosen it because it was so different from my birth name, which was long and crackled with consonants. 'Clare' forced my mouth into a semblance of a smile when I said it, and then it ran over my tongue, short and sweet. Every time the word came out of my mouth at the beginning, I thought of *des éclairs au chocolat* and how we used to eat them at the expensive school we went to, built over the ruins. We would lick the chocolate slowly off the top and then the cream and finally the light choux pastry, throwing the greasy wax paper to the floor for someone else to pick up.

Tears came to my eyes, tears that I couldn't help, and I blinked them back, of course, because I didn't want to show Ava anything. The lump in my throat was like a ball of barbed wire that I couldn't swallow away. My jaw clenched hard. If I spoke, I'd cry or scream or do both. I managed to control it, but I was so angry at her for dragging it up.

Everything I'd constructed – everything I'd worked *so hard on*, for so long – torn away. I could hardly believe Tabitha's betrayal, that she'd dug into my past, refusing to leave it be, poking at something they wouldn't understand, even if they thought they had the facts. They couldn't just let it lie.

But there was something else too. A sick kind of relief that it was out in the open.

I forced myself to analyse the evening, pick apart the ending. When it came to what Ava had done, there was no reason to tear me down so casually like that, her legs crossed, her face blandly apologetic as if she'd stepped on my toe. It became clear to me that they saw it as a business decision. So very strategic of Ava to bring it up in that moment, showing me in an instant that Tabitha planned to hold those unfortunate events over me.

26.

We didn't have any kind of dramatic showdown that night. I needed time to think, and it took all my effort to hold everything in, but I managed it. Walked away from Ava without a word and went to bed. A restless night's sleep followed, and I woke to the taste of iron where I'd bitten through the skin at the side of my mouth.

The next day I got up early. The dew was still sitting on the grass as we lay out in the garden. Tabitha and me. Alone, side by side, both with sunglasses on, and with coffee brewed too strongly and served black. Water and stale croissants from yesterday's bakery run sat between us. The others hadn't surfaced yet, and we'd chosen the bottom of the garden, basking next to the pond as the temperature rose. I could smell the scent that always reminds me of France to this day – the smell of dusty heat. A foul stench rose from the water as well, and it hung in the air because there was no wind to whisk it away.

Under a scrap of a bikini, Tabitha was a slick of white paint, like she'd never seen a minute of the sun. In contrast, my skin started to tan straight away, but we still looked alike. No one could deny that. Tall and blonde. She was focused on youthful preservation and proceeded to coat every inch of herself in a thick layer of sunscreen. When she had finished, she went to retrieve a laptop from inside the house.

I didn't know if I should bring it up. Ava had said not to, but I wanted to, badly. To try to somehow explain what had happened and give her some kind of assurance that I wasn't a criminal.

I nearly did, very nearly asked her what she knew, how much

she thought she knew, but the words wouldn't come. Where would I have begun? I needed it to stay hidden, and if I mentioned the past, we could never come back from it. It would linger. There would be questions.

Luckily, there wasn't much need for me to speak. She wanted to set the agenda. She showed me some mock-ups of a website. It was far more professional than I'd expected – artful graphics – but no company name and almost no information.

'We don't want to say too much. Word of mouth is better, really, and we have a great network in London. We have a client in mind, so we'll try to meet her when we're ready, in a few months.'

I nodded, eyes closed as the sun shone down so I could see the blood in my eyelids. I wondered what she knew about what had happened, how she'd discovered it. She would have had to have known someone; this wasn't just a case of digging about on the internet, she would have needed contacts with access. But, at the same time, I suspected she could have done it, especially as her mother lived here.

I forced myself to concentrate. 'How will that work?' I asked.

'Very straightforward! We'll meet her, see what she requires, scope it out and agree on a fee.' She grinned, rolling over on the grass to face me. 'We need to transform ourselves – well, whichever of us she thinks will work best, she'll know exactly how to play it. It's all about our characters. We'll become a character each time.'

'Surely if we're adapting to become whatever these men want, that's . . . cheating the system?'

It was odd: because of what she knew of Périgueux, we were freer with each other and my sentences were easier, less laboured.

'Oh, the system – so now you think there's a system!' She laughed. 'It isn't fair, Clare. Who said it was going to be fair?

None of life is fair. I don't think it's *fair* that I'm essentially being cut off after university.'

I hadn't known this, but it made sense. I stored the information away for later.

Then her hand was pressed against my neck. Tabitha touched in a way that was so natural, like you were an extension of her.

'We might as well try it. What do we have to lose?' she said.

'What about Imogen?' I asked.

'What about her?'

'I thought she was going to be involved too?'

Tabitha raised an eyebrow. 'Perhaps. We'll be flexible. I'm not sure she's cut out for it, but you're like me. You know how to be glorious – like a peacock or a hawk! Imogen's just . . . Imogen, isn't she?'

Was there ever a more scathing assessment?

'I don't know if I'm anything like you,' I said.

'Oh, don't be ridiculous, of course you are. Have you seen how similar we look? Apart from the tan.'

'Is this what the haircut was about?' I asked. It seemed so obvious.

She looked amused. 'That was a treat because I wanted you to feel good about yourself and I thought it might loosen you up a little! We met you, and we liked you, but I was interested to see how far you'd go.' She switched from earnest to soft. 'I know last night was a shock, but I didn't know how else to do it. The rest of us have all been working on this for so long, I wanted to position the whole concept to you in the right way.'

'So, you trapped me somewhere I couldn't get away and did it then.'

She threw her head back and laughed. 'You're right. I suppose I did. Anyway, look at this.' She handed me a piece of paper, carefully folded, with a breakdown of figures.

'This is what I expect you to earn in our first year,' she said. It was a lot.

'More than you thought?' she asked.

I considered how to respond. At that moment, Samuel emerged from the house.

'Morning, ladies, you're up early.' He stretched, letting out an over-the-top groan as his back arched.

'Samuel!' said Tabitha. 'Brilliant timing. Clare, you've seen our website that's in progress – but Samuel and I have been working on another one all year that I think you might find fun.' She pushed her sunglasses up on to her head and handed him the laptop.

He took it and clicked around a bit, then he turned the screen towards me. I peered closer; it was hard to see in the sun. I could just about make out red fabric against a pale back-drop. Artful photography stylized with exaggerated shadows, but it wasn't completely terrible.

I began to read out the accompanying text: 'Red satin slip, worn by a twenty-year-old physics student. While she's wrap-ping her head around the Schrödinger equation, Elodie often wears this barely-there slip. She's been known to get –'

'Hot and sweaty in passionate frustration as she rips it off blah blah blah.' Samuel finished my sentence. 'I wrote it. Not one of my best, I'm more partial to the humanities ones, but we'll probably get £300 for that. Not bad for something I found on Tabby's bedroom floor, eh?' He sounded impossibly smug, and in that second, I felt an overwhelming urge to give him a good hard slap.

'I threw it away. It had a hole,' Tabitha added very solemnly.

'Yes,' said Samuel. 'A revelatory hole at the hip bone, so just a hint of flesh emerges, titillating a banker in Swindon, no doubt.' He sighed and flashed a smile at me. He was enjoying this part of it, I could tell.

Tabitha swatted at him. 'Oh, stop it. Honestly, I'm glad that you looked at that one, some of the other ones are *sordid*!'

She clearly loved sordid.

Samuel parked himself next to me. 'It has good margins and there's a real market for it,' he explained. 'The photography's a work in progress. The descriptions are easier, pretty straightforward to construct. You just need to read a bit of erotica and steal the good parts, because most of it's dross. I see it as an upmarket forum, no bidding or anything, we think that's distasteful, plus discretion and all that.'

'All of it's up for debate,' Tabitha chipped in. 'Our customers are surprisingly lax about their contact details, which makes their occupations lovely and easy to track. We thought it might be worth discussing blackmail further down the line.' She grinned, and I must have looked horrified because she changed tack and moved to a more comforting tone.

'I'm obviously joking! We're not committing a crime here, it's not nearly so black and white as that.'

Funnily enough, I hadn't even considered any legal implications, I think because Tabitha was such a force of nature that acting outside of the law seemed quite natural with her protection.

She reached out and slammed the screen shut before I could see any more. 'In all seriousness, the reason I showed you is that we've been playing about with these bits for the last year and the progression has been fine, but it's also been a way to get necessary funds for our main project. Now you can see that we're totally committed. We'll keep Perfect Pieces running but this just shows we can do it, run something and make it work because talk is talk – what matters is the delivery. What I'm saying, in a roundabout way, is that we're prepared.'

'Perfect Pieces?' I repeated. The phrase sounded grubby.

'Yes, in retrospect the name is a bit naff, isn't it . . . Imogen came up with it.'

I imagined Imogen mulling it over for days and finally coming up with such an awful name, then presenting it to Ava and

Tabitha, who would probably be laughing at her behind her back, but would let her have it – a nugget of goodwill.

'OK.' There was a pause. The two of them watched me, gauging my reaction.

'What's the matter, Clare?' she asked. 'Are you just upset because we didn't include you from the start?'

Oh, she was good. She read people, and she knew exactly when they were pulling away and when she was losing them. She had all the tricks to reel them back in. And she was right. With all of this, there was a huge element of being apart from it all. Left out in the cold while The Shiver schemed and plotted. I struggled to separate it logically from the unexpected nature of the work. Still, the longer I considered it, the work didn't even seem that shocking. I thought of the photographs I'd found of myself. They'd clearly had me in their sights.

She squeezed my hand. 'I trust you. I'm showing you everything. If you're in, you're all in.' She pushed her sunglasses back down over her nose and lay back in the sun to mark the conversation as over.

After the pitch, they let me be. They didn't push or cajole or even bring it up again. Tabitha just waited for the week to pan out and, at the end of it, when we sat down to tear baguettes open and eat them with stubby little bottles of beer as a final picnicking feast, I said yes. I would join them.

We hashed out the details. We'd get ready and start in the summer, limiting our activities to Scotland, which Tabitha assured me would be easy. I would keep up my bar job and, most importantly, no one would know. Absolute discretion always.

In my head, I tried to justify it – Tabitha knew about what had happened to me back in Périgueux, what I'd done, so surely I didn't have much choice but to do what she wanted me to.

I couldn't let those events get out, not after all the time that had passed. Who knew what she'd do if I declined?

And even now, after so long, I remember just how good it was to have her convince me. She wooed me, and there was the sweet rumble of pleasure of being connected to them all in a way that felt unbreakable.

27.

Years later, I went to Paris with my husband.

I think he planned the trip in the main so that he could talk about it with his colleagues and friends afterwards. It wouldn't have been my top choice – I do not like to speak French.

'I took her to Paris,' I imagined him saying, like I was a travel accessory, as if he'd stowed me away, unpacked me from bubble wrap to show me off, then taken me back in his hand luggage. All in a long weekend.

The trip was fine. We went in August when all the Parisians left the city for the countryside, so the streets were quiet, but it still smelt of bodies crammed together in the heat, the musk of people living and working and moving, of the smoke of engines and cars and restaurant grills late into the night. He spent a lot of time flicking between apps on his phone, unable to settle. I enjoyed long afternoon naps in the hotel and steak served blue.

Before we went to bed, we opened the window to air the room, and we could hear the roar of scooters speeding around the city, the sound of people laughing and probably enjoying their summer more than we were.

On the final day, we sat in an overpriced cafe by the Canal Saint-Martin. When we ordered, my language skills impressed my husband. Another thing I suspected he might have boasted about to his friends.

We drank expensive orange juice and picked at pastries, our suitcases piled up next to us getting under the waiter's feet, as we tried to pass the time before we needed to get our flight. We were at that funny bit at the end of a holiday where you wish you could press fast forward and be back at home in your own bed. Using up the last of our euros and chatting about nothing much. Then he brought up Tabitha.

'She was your closest friend?' he asked mildly, out of the blue, interrupting the flow of discussion about when we should set off for the airport.

He didn't know the full extent of what had happened, of course, but he knew that I visited Tabitha regularly. It was a ritual that he couldn't or wouldn't take part in. I wasn't quite sure which, as we'd never discussed everything that had happened properly. He also knew I was the only person who went to see her where she was, locked away from us all forever.

I sipped my orange juice. It had cost an extortionate amount – ten euros – and it was sickly sweet. Concentrated, not fresh. Paris was a con.

I hadn't thought of her for a while. It took a significant amount of energy to actually focus and properly think back to how Tabitha had been.

'More like family by the end,' I replied.

'Ah,' he said knowingly. 'Like a sister?'

Funny how he thought he had some deep understanding of sisterhood.

I thought of the days when she'd nursed me. 'More like a mother, I think.'

'A mother,' he repeated, long and slow, and he looked at me with pity. 'I'm sorry,' he said. He reached out and wrapped his hand around mine. I dug my nails in, but not so much that he'd pull away. He liked it.

I tried to smile. 'It's fine. We should go.'

PART 2

28.

The building came into view slowly as we approached by car. Foliage had hidden it from the road, and then, as we moved closer, the leaves peeled away to reveal a single storey.

To me, it was more sculpture than house, as I took in the slithers of red brick and delicate steel window frames with a tarnished patina, then floor-to-ceiling glass and the trickle of a manicured lawn that threw off green reflections, giving the bottom half of the house the look of a dank pond, shadowy even though it was a bright July day. Low and flat like an air hangar rising from underwater. I could smell the salt in the air from the sea, but it wasn't fresh and bracing, it was too briny for that.

Just Ava, Tabitha and me. We'd travelled in a taxi to the address, which was about an hour away from Edinburgh, playing Tabitha's favourite game the whole way there. Oysters or caviar, steak or chicken? She liked us to plan our hypothetical deathbed meals for fun.

We were due at 2 p.m. – the right kind of time to meet someone for a proper appointment. A small sign obscured by trees and grasses pronounced our destination: 'Storl House'. The taxi driver let out a low whistle.

'Fancy place, girls. I've picked up a few people here – apparently, it's a real cracker.'

'Isn't it just,' Ava said smoothly.

There's much to say about the Landores and everything that happened with them, but it all started with Mrs Landore when she greeted us at the door of her glass house.

The tight 'o' her mouth made wasn't good or bad, just

surprised, I think, that we'd actually showed up. She could have been in her mid-forties, tall and boyish with hardly a pinch of fat on her, and she dressed in a way that I identified as discreetly expensive: a mesh of tasteful neutrals, beige layered on blush, finished with a light shawl of taupe, and a full face of understated make-up. A limp handshake, limper even than Tabitha's, as if it was a great effort to move her fingers over mine, and then she gestured for us to follow her. She glided through her house, barely touching the floor and making me aware of my own heavy footsteps.

From the entrance corridor, she led us into a cavernous open-plan kitchen and dining room. Instead of offering us coffee or tea like we were equals, she gave each of us a glass of tap water.

'Come in, girls, do sit.'

We followed her into what looked like a conservatory where plump armchairs beckoned. I realized it wasn't a proper conservatory, it was a severe cube of an extension with light flooding in at every corner and virtually no other furniture apart from the chairs.

I could see there was a sheer drop at the side of the house – we were teetering on the edge. If you peered right up to the glass and down you could see a man-made cliff, but moulded and textured to give it a rough sea-beaten appearance. There was another glass cube below and in it a kidney-shaped swimming pool, then beyond was the sea: a drab sheet of grey.

Tabitha inhaled the place. She was in awe, barely able to hide her delight.

We took our seats. Tabitha and I sat facing Mrs Landore and Ava stood slightly away from us, like she wasn't quite part of it. There was a small pause as Mrs Landore tapped her foot. I glanced to my side where Tabitha sat next to me, absolutely motionless and smiling until the foot-tapping petered out.

'Thanks for coming. I don't even know why I agreed to this. I just called you and then it happened. I'm not sure I want to go into it . . .' Mrs Landore trailed off.

I waited for Tabitha to begin, to ask her about her husband, what he did, who he was, what she wanted from this, but she didn't do any of that. She just kept smiling – that smile I knew so well, so open and warm, it lit up her whole face, inviting you to dive right in and tell her everything. Then she spoke. 'Mrs Landore, this really is such a beautiful house.'

Eve Landore smiled back.

I disagreed silently in my head. Not beautiful, it was too bare for that – like an empty gallery built on a hill with no soft edges. The place was jaw-dropping, a house no one could walk into without commenting upon.

'Thank you so much. The house really does mean a lot to me. We bought it years ago, back when this area wasn't even that popular. Honestly, the prices were a lot cheaper back then.' She shrugged, and Tabitha nodded encouragingly.

She continued. 'We put every penny into buying it, and you should have seen it! It was basically derelict, although it's an excellent example from the architect. We lived here so happily at first that we didn't mind because it was the first thing we'd ever owned together.

'Of course, Tom had such confidence. He had it all mapped out – how much he'd earn, his savings, that kind of thing. He was in it for the long haul, so he understood the finances, but I had the vision. I studied architecture, so this house was a real find.'

She stood up and walked towards the water, looking out, away from us.

'Sometimes you see dolphins out there.' She pointed to the sea, hopefully.

We all turned to look at the choppy waves.

There were no dolphins.

'How lovely! It must have been a lot of work for you?' Tabitha said.

'Oh yes, so much work. I didn't go back to my job after the boys went to school. I put everything into this house. I project-managed the entire renovation over the years. Every room. Every single purchase.

'It didn't feel like work because I enjoyed it so much. As you can imagine, it's a labour of love finding that period piece, going to auction houses to track down the right chair from the era, one that I knew would pull it all together. Oh no, it never felt like work.'

I liked the way she spoke. A lilting voice, just slightly animated. Any nerves melted away when she started to talk about the house.

'I mean, when you love something, it doesn't, does it?' Tabitha said vigorously. What exactly did Tabitha *love*, I wondered?

'No, it doesn't,' she agreed. 'And we were in various interior magazines, which was nice, something Tom would boast about. He insists on having them out on the table for people to see, which is so silly really. The house has been used for film-sets, which has been quite lucrative for us, something Tom didn't want – he thought it was disruptive for the boys, but I pushed, and it was great, really exciting.'

'I can see this place being in a film,' said Tabitha.

'Yes, it's been in a few, although they bring all their own paraphernalia in, to stage it. Once you see the end result with all the effects and staging, you hardly recognize it.'

Tabitha nodded politely. 'So, what about now? Is it done?'

A change in expression as Eve Landore looked at Tabitha as if she was seeing her clearly for the first time and had decided that she was a child who didn't know how anything worked. 'Oh, my dear, it's never *done*. You can't finish a house like this! The upkeep alone . . . the major work's been completed, of course, although I still have lots of plans. It's different now, though, with Tom.'

'How so?'

'How he is with me, with the house . . .'

'I'm sorry to hear that. In what way?' Tabitha asked.

I thought Mrs Landore would clam up, but she started ticking off things on her fingers. 'Oh, he's working all the time. All the things we want to do are too expensive. The place is a money pit, we should never have bought it; whatever we've put in, we'll never get back – he's always going on about that even though we've never even discussed selling it. Everything's so much harder, and now I wonder what he's doing. Things haven't been right with us for a while. It's also made me think about the house. The boys don't live here full time any more, but it's still their home.

'We've invested more and more over the years, especially when the house started to work for us as a set. It seemed like the right thing to do. People come, and they all say the same thing – they walk in and they can't believe it. Everyone thinks we're sitting on this massive pile of money, and it just isn't true. There isn't much else. This is our only asset.'

'That makes total sense.'

'It doesn't. None of this does. But I want to know what he would do.'

'Absolutely,' Tabitha said.

'That's the top priority,' Mrs Landore continued. 'Then the second is the house. I need to think about the house.' Her voice, which had been so level, had taken on a shrillness, a new side to her. I could picture her screeching at someone for placing something on the clean countertops or traipsing over the marble floor in muddy boots. I almost felt sorry for the occupants, living in this glass cage.

'I understand completely,' Tabitha said.

But how could she?

Ava piped up. 'Mrs Landore, this has been so instructive. Now, I know you and I have discussed the details, so you understand what we can do for you. We don't need to go into all that unless you have any questions.' Ava sounded like the lawyer she was training to become.

Eve Landore shook her head. 'I don't.' And after staring at Tabitha the whole time, she ripped her gaze away to look reluctantly at me.

'You, I think.'

Me.

I could feel Tabitha willing me not to speak and I just tried the smile I'd seen her do many times – gracious and open. It came out as more of a grimace and Mrs Landore turned away from me as if she suddenly found me disgusting.

'Thank you,' said Tabitha. 'I don't think there's anything further to talk about. We'll leave you to enjoy your day. It was very nice to meet you.'

Tabitha was so excruciatingly formal with her.

Walking back up the driveway, she was ecstatic. 'It's ideal. We need to suss out Tom, but, Clare, you were fantastic.' She beamed at me and did a little girlish jump. Ava quickly pulled at her arm to stop her as it was likely Mrs Landore could still see us from inside.

'I didn't do anything!' I said.

'I know, and it went exactly how I imagined it would go. Just do the same next time.'

The whole thing had seemed clumsy and awkward to me.

'I have all the material,' said Ava.

'Material?' I asked.

'Yup, and as you'll be doing it, Imogen will discuss how we'll run it with you both.'

'It'll be fine!' Tabitha trilled.

I soon learned that would always be her mantra, smoothing over our worries.

The Landores were where it all began, and in that first meeting, if I repelled Mrs Landore, then there was also something about her that made me recoil too. As if her frosty sadness was contagious and would brand me in some painful and permanent way.

29.

To go back though. Back to before we met Mrs Landore, before we'd looked out of the window for dolphins that weren't there and communicated with clunky eye contact as we tried not to speak over each other and been our *most sincere and businesslike*, before all of that, we'd had months of preparation. Starting in May when exams tailed off, we decided we'd stay in Edinburgh. Ava, Tabitha and me.

I moved between Finn's tiny studio flat – where I was a partially welcome guest, as long as I didn't talk about the group too much and focused on him – and Tabitha's grand flat. Georgia and Ashley were keen for me to move in with them that coming September, which felt like an easy option as there was no room for me with The Shiver, but for the time being, before the new term, I was happy to crash on Tabitha's sofa in the drawing room where we never closed the curtains, so the light flooded in each morning, waking me up.

I'd potter around before everyone got up and dream of living there with them.

Imogen was always in and out. She maintained a lot of hobbies that kept her busy, like the recorder (I'd yet to meet any other willing recorder players over the age of ten) and hockey, which she did, but rarely mentioned. I knew why: Tabitha was ever so scathing of anything that didn't directly impact the plans.

'Imogen craves a distraction,' Tabitha said coldly of it all. And I think she was right. It suited Imogen to stay involved and leech moodily off the excitement, but she also seemed to be hedging her bets with other things to fill her time.

Which made sense, as she was never quite able to ascend the ranks.

Samuel went back to London often, to a flurry of balls and parties and excursions that we knew very little of. That was fine; it was permitted because it was networking, and it all helped the grand cause. He wrote the most excruciating copy for Perfect Pieces, reading the descriptions out to us in the evenings and making Imogen in particular wince (she winced but didn't move away – she'd never forfeit an opportunity to listen to Samuel), but I could tell he was enjoying his position managing it.

'You'll come down?' he'd suggested to me hopefully one night before he left. I shook my head. I didn't offer an excuse, and he didn't push any further or take offence. I wondered if he might come back with a girlfriend after that long summer – a London summer with real heat for weeks, and warm flesh on the Tube. When I imagined it, I always based it on memories that I didn't have – I'd hardly been to London – but in my head he was alongside all his friends from school: days at the races, long evenings in tuxes with too much to drink, too many drugs, and a girl kissing him. A girl with no face – I couldn't picture what she'd be like. I also wondered how I'd feel if that happened. Would I be jealous?

There were many other jobs we could have done if we'd been so inclined. I was still working at the bar, but the rest of them could have easily found work. We could have taught English to all the international students who poured into the city over the summer by bus. We could have taken internships at PR agencies and banks – dressing in cheap, wrinkled suits to make coffee all day for over-caffeinated men and women in their more expensive wrinkled suits. Working all summer for a single line on our future CVs to show we were *keen and employable*.

We didn't do any of it because we had bigger and better

plans. I'd thought there would be more laziness involved, imagined scorching days where we'd have barbecues at Inverleith Park or sit outside bars with pints of lager growing warm in our hands, but the summer didn't work out that way. As May seeped into a windy, strangely dreich June, the heat never came, and we spent lots of time in the flat. I remember the sound of our bare feet on the floorboards, handstands up against the wall and classical music floating through the rooms. And plotting – so much planning and discussion.

30.

Firstly, we needed to work out how to be around the wives and with this we improved over the summer.

As laboured and awkward as our exchange with Mrs Landore had seemed at the time, the conversation was a dramatic improvement compared to our early encounters when Samuel set us up with some friends of friends who were interested in what we were doing. Afterwards, one of them had phoned Samuel and firmly declined the offer. Because of Tabitha.

'That girl, she's far too much.'

I was taken aback. I'd spent so long trying to not be too much, to talk slower, be nicer and meeker and calmer and not to stare. Never to be angry because no one likes that. The rules didn't exist for Tabitha, and the idea of her being too much was impossible for me to comprehend. Tabitha had her quirks, but she wasn't too much for me. She was everything.

Samuel told me and then immediately regretted it. He begged me not to tell any of the others.

'She didn't like Tabitha?' I was incredulous.

'She didn't *understand* her like we do,' he replied, shutting down the conversation.

So, we adapted.

Ava would feature more prominently in some cases; her voice was low and she calmed people. An accent you couldn't quite identify that made her sound a little more mature – *international and probably quite rich*. She worked well as a steering force. A safe pair of hands.

Tabitha, although intense and too much for long periods, dazzled in small doses, so her role was pared back. She was vital, though, because she added a dynamism to the whole thing that worked in our favour. I saw the way Mrs Landore had assessed her – she couldn't believe that someone so young could be so assured. Then me, quiet and set to the side. The one they so often chose.

It was a balancing act.

We worked on our playbook, and Edinburgh served us well for that. The students had mostly gone, but the city bulged at the seams with visitors to practise on. A dropped pen; a shy request for directions. We tried all the tricks and carefully built up a profile of what worked and what didn't. We re-assessed and we learned, or *iterated* as Tabitha said, because she'd been buried in books about entrepreneurship for the entire summer.

Under it all, there was the fundamental fact that we were so youthful. We could dress up and act and say what we thought people should say, but none of that meant we understood rela-tionships. None of us had ever really been in a long-term relationship, excluding Finn from the equation because I still didn't count it as anything serious. Tabitha and Ava were scath-ing of boyfriends, and of men in general.

What do men want?

We pondered.

'They like to be listened to,' Tabitha stated.

Ava and I exchanged a look. Tabitha's listening skills left something to be desired.

'I saw it with my father,' Tabitha continued. 'He'd come home from work exhausted and desperate to talk about his day, but his relationship with my mother had become so logis-tical. She'd ask him if he'd take the bins out. He'd ask her what was for dinner. She'd tell him he needed to sort out the house insurance. They're the conversations I remember. So . . . *yawn*. Relentless,' she finished, with her own theatrical yawn.

There wasn't much similarity when I thought of my parents

and their glacial alliance against me – whispers in the corridor that faded into nothing when I entered the room, their bedroom door closed, always. I could recall opening it and feeling my mother's hand on my wrist, nails digging in, and her hissing, 'Knock.'

Tabitha was right, though. Listening was the key. For our first few clients, we listened to their problems, we made them think we understood. We practised and we got better at it. I was a good listener. Less awkward than I'd been at the beginning, when I first moved to Edinburgh, because I understood my role better.

A clean start, and the focus was the present. Over that summer The Shiver never asked me about my background, and I appreciated that they never dragged Périgueux to the surface.

Often when you decide not to think about things, it's impossible. But my own past, everything I'd buried, didn't cross my mind much. Our world blinded me with its ambition, its increasing brightness, and it was easy to avoid examining any of it closely.

31.

When I was young, we would go clothes shopping in Bordeaux. My mother dragged me around, pulled me into dark shops with oiled wood floors where you had to ring a bell to enter. Even at the time, it was old-fashioned. I was forced into starched dresses, garments pulled over my head roughly, cutting into me at the armpits or the waist and never quite fitting. Those items were wrong when I was seven, more suitable for a child much younger. Then I was older, and there was no money for clothes, although I craved what Adrienne and Dina wore – flared jeans and brand-new pedal pushers. Wanted to fit in with them and look the part. Perhaps if we'd had money when I was a teenager, I would have grown to love shopping, but there was no point – better to see fashion as unimportant and take a lofty stance against consumerism.

That wasn't to say I didn't notice it, though; I wasn't interested in it for myself, but I drank it all in when it came to my friends, and with Tabitha and Ava, their clothes were a constant source of fascination. They both wore dresses a lot. Tabitha chose slippery little pieces that draped on her, or skimmed her body like a second skin in some places. Her obsession with Klimt was easy to see – necklines often fell in a deep V to reveal the bones of her chest. Lots of gold too.

Ava was not a painting or an ornament. She had all the clean lines of a brutalist building that was mid construction, as her dresses were structurally complex in the vein of scaffolding. Leather cut with net and fabrics I'd never even seen before that rippled or creased. There was always a tie or a place where the material was cut out, forcing her to fiddle with it. I'm sure this was on purpose. It drew the eye to her neck as she readjusted a bow or a zip. It made me want to reach out and touch her, and often I did because all of us felt our way around each other with touch. Where one of us ended and the other began – the boundaries were barely there any more.

Clothes were essential to the project, and I'd thought Ava would be guiding that part of it, but she was indifferent. For the Landores, Imogen was in charge. She loved the act of shopping; her capacity for rooting around for the perfect items seemed endless. So I went over to their flat to prepare for Tom Landore. Predictably, Imogen had been called in to perform some type of makeover. She'd bought a range of clothes: a pink silk slip, lace underwear, a designer leather handbag that I knew cost more than a month of my rent.

We always converged in Tabitha's room. I was never in there alone, though, only when she was there too, and that day I sat on the bed. Imogen stood in front of me, her expression filled with judgement.

Tabitha moved into a variety of yoga poses by the window.

'Landore will go for you. You look enough like one of those magazine models. You just need to smarten up a bit,' Imogen said, holding up the long slip with delicate straps against herself and then tossing it over towards me.

'Underwear?' I asked. 'I think I just need a swimsuit.'

'Oh, I know he won't see it. That's just a little something. To get you in the mood.'

Imogen sounded hateful about the mood. I picked up the slip. It was an intense pink. I put it to one side, mentally noting that Samuel would appreciate it for Perfect Pieces.

'Breathtaking!' Tabitha called over.

'I'm not sure,' I said.

Imogen's eyes widened. 'Well, well. Clare finally comes out of her shell and objects to something! I knew you would eventually.' She sounded triumphant, and a little nasty.

I met her eye. 'What else do you know about them?' I asked.

'About who?' she asked innocently.

'The Landores,' I replied.

She just pursed her lips and called for Tabitha to come over.

'We're starting?' Tabitha asked, snuggling up on the bed close to me and stroking my elbow.

I turned to her. 'How did you find Mrs Landore?' I asked.

'Oh, you don't need to bother thinking about that!' she said breezily.

'I want to know, though.'

'Okayyy.' She stretched the word as if she was humouring a small child. 'Through Samuel. She's a close family friend.'

'And he's OK with this?'

'Of *course* he is!' Tabitha turned to face me, her expression so very serious. 'He approached her; he just told her what we do and how we could help her protect herself.'

We both lay back on the bed and Imogen stood in front of us to present, clearly enjoying her new involvement. She always did like the research side of it all.

'Chop chop, Immy,' Tabitha said fondly.

Imogen gave her a small smile.

'You're always so fucking slow with everything,' Tabitha continued.

Imogen's face fell for a second, but she recovered quickly and began. 'Tom Landore seems like a bit of a dick. He's not Eton or anything, but he did go to Oxford – PPE, as you'd expect. Moved up here to work for a bank and they bought that weird glass place. It's not all in the house. He's made a ton – not that she'll see any of that.'

'You know how much money he has?' I asked.

'I have elements of his accounts. Enough for these purposes,' she replied, closing down the conversation. I wondered if it linked to Perfect Pieces, then I pushed the thought from my mind. Part of this was the pact I made with myself early on. I would never search on the internet for any information about them, ever. Doing so brought what we were doing to life too much and reminded me that these people were real. I'd only ever seen a few photographs of him, formal ones in the house. I remembered one of him standing, suit on, one hand on his wife's shoulder as she sat below him.

That snapshot, alongside anything else I could glean from Imogen, would be enough.

'Clever girl,' Tabitha said to Imogen, and I could see Imogen melt a little, even offering a tentative smile – never completely immune to Tabitha's charms and forgiving her for earlier.

Imogen hummed a song and Tabitha joined in tunelessly, pulling Imogen into an ungainly waltz around the room. I didn't recognize it. A song or hymn from when they were younger perhaps. Although they didn't mention school much, sometimes their history together leaked through into the present. Long sleepovers, midnight feasts and pillow fights – as innocent as anything. Imogen enjoyed it; she mellowed in Tabitha's arms.

Then Tabitha turned her attention to me, came so close I could smell beyond her skin to something sourer.

She pulled my hair back, running her hands through the roots and smoothing it out at the ends. Like an animal grooming her offspring, purposeful instead of gentle.

'We're going to make you into everything he wants, and then it's up to him. In this whole thing he absolutely has agency. You understand that, don't you? You'll be amazing.'

Her words were rushed. Her eyes were bright.

I wondered if she was almost jealous, like she wanted to do this herself. I basked in the praise and adoration as she dressed me up like a doll.

32.

We can't help gathering information on our friends. Everyone does it. Even if we don't think we're storing it all away, we do it instinctively.

Back then, I didn't really notice some of the things that perhaps would have helped me more. At first, I was so focused on myself and how I was coming across to them. However, the more time we spent together over a long and tepid summer, certain facts became apparent.

As I've said, there were no boyfriends or girlfriends on the scene. No mentions of the more attractive people in our tutorials or classes, and no staggering home drained and hung-over in the morning, still in the clothes from the night before. After a year, that seemed a little unusual, but if you looked closer, it became more explainable.

There was Ava's methodical productivity. Ava tried to pare back certain aspects of herself, but it was the chinks in her armour that were so appealing to me. Like her dismissal of anything American on a surface level, then, deep down, an almost childish love of those wrapped sugary sweets. Candy canes that came out around October and were sucked on deep into January. Bright pink Jell-O set in lumpish shapes that made your mouth hurt it was so sugary. She was private to a fault, quietly and almost intellectually interested in fashion *but not shopping*. She organized everything with efficiency. When she laughed or smiled it was like her face wasn't quite used to it and the muscles took a while longer to move those expressions into place.

Imogen and Samuel were less focused on it all. The inner

circle just about, but beyond that they had their own lives. Imogen's favourite thing to do, when she wasn't preoccupied with Tabitha, was fuss over Samuel: she laughed at his jokes for too long; she always asked him where he'd been, who he'd been with. It was the saddest little crush, and the more he batted her off with barely a thought, the more she rushed around after him. She obeyed Tabitha, of course, and there was a fondness, but also a sneering hostility. In return, Tabitha treated her like an annoying younger sister. It was a brittle kind of intimacy.

With Samuel and me, whatever we were together, it had become easier. I'd started to think his feelings had never really existed, not really. He just liked to flirt, to shock me because I was newer to the group. He would throw out playful remarks to see if anything came back, but he was never particularly bothered if it didn't.

The crushes that underpinned the group were never fully in focus because the business was the nucleus of it all – they just existed in the background. Everyone was held together with bonds made stronger by juicy infatuations that waxed and waned. We played and we dressed up and we flirted with each other almost as something to do. And I was happy about it, I think. At the time, at least. As much as I loved it when it was just Tabitha and Ava and me, as a larger group we were safer. A three is always so difficult.

And what about me?

My commitment to Tabitha wasn't a secret; at some points I thought I'd do anything for her. But my love affair at that time was larger and more expansive. Part of it was Edinburgh, where I could be whoever I wanted to be, walk the streets as an observer. I went to pubs, old-man pubs where the ceilings were low and there was folk music in the evening. I wandered around the Botanic Garden, where I could stand in a towering greenhouse. The city belonged to me: I'd earned it.

And finally, Tabitha. The sun we orbited around; we'd die

without her rays. With Tabitha, if you peeled away all the layers, you could even get past her distrust of men, which surely came from more than just her father's affair. You could go below, deeper, and under it all you found a single-mindedness that I agreed with in the most part. She possessed a unifying belief that we deserved something different, something that would mark us out. She said we could make our own luck, and I believed her.

I collected scraps of information as if I was stockpiling food for a disaster or saving away my pay cheques for an emergency, a natural accumulation.

I hoarded the fragments to use as some kind of currency later, kidding myself that I knew all of their secrets.

33.

The west of Edinburgh wasn't for us. It was too corporate: chain shops and towering office blocks bleeding into cheap sandwich shops, into conference centres, into expensive hotels with gyms and no signs because the people who went to them didn't need the directions.

At one of these gyms, Tom Landore engaged in an extremely thorough, timed stretching routine every Wednesday evening, one I associated with someone who had an unhealthy obsession with injury prevention. Tabitha assured me that this was just an occupational hazard of being old. In her head, erratic behaviour presented by anyone over the age of thirty-five could be explained by them being *very old*.

Afterwards, he enjoyed an aggressive match of squash against another man of a similar age. After forty minutes of sweaty, swearing play, he had a shower for precisely five minutes – icy cold for the final two – then retreated to the sauna for twenty minutes. This was despite the fact he had one at home where he could bask like a fat seal on a rock. After his sauna, he dressed before leaving on the dot at 8 p.m.

All of this came through the filter of Imogen, and who knew how she had quite so much detailed intel. She used the term *fat seal* gleefully as she passed on her biting assessment. I couldn't tell if her disgust was aimed at him or at me.

The first time I met him, he entered and sat down with a nod. I imagined the almost pleasurable soreness in his neck, in his back, the muscles worked right to the brink of exhaustion.

He closed his eyes, moving his neck to one side and then to the other.

I thought he would be leery, panting on me with hot breath, but, of course, it wasn't like that at all. He maintained perfect etiquette in the sauna, following a protocol that I didn't know existed. I'd never been into a spa before. In France I was too young, in Hull I was too poor and in Edinburgh I was too busy.

There was no one else in the sauna, and he gave me a quick smile and sat opposite me at a respectful distance. My hair was tied up tightly in a bun and I wore a plain black one-piece. I didn't look like Eve Landore, that was for sure. Hair stripped back from my face and no make-up. I leaned inwards to the hot coals where a bucket of water sat with a ladle poking from the top.

'Do you mind?' I asked, even though I felt like I was melting almost immediately, because I wasn't used to it.

He opened one eye lazily.

'Absolutely not,' he replied, letting out a deep sigh and relaxing back in the heat.

I poured.

'I like it as hot as possible,' I said, not flirtatiously, just factually. Also a lie.

'Me too.' His eyes were closed again. 'Pump out all the toxins.'

He grunted and tried to tuck his foot under his inner thigh. Tabitha would have known the proper name for this silly-looking stretch.

I tried not to make a face. Men always seemed so confident about stretching anywhere, positions that I would never contort myself into in public.

'Yes.' I cocked my head to the side. A gesture stolen from Tabitha. 'What have you been playing?'

'Oh, just a friendly game of squash.'

'Well, I hope you won.'

He opened both eyes now. He seemed to want to converse.

'Indeed, I did.' In future conversations, I would always ask him, and he would always say he won, which wasn't true.

'Enjoy your sauna.'

I left, making sure to close the door firmly.

And that was it. The first time I met Tom Landore. For him, it was probably an entirely forgettable experience, one he'd had many times before – a girl, a few words and nothing more. The challenge for me was to make it more.

I showered and met Tabitha and Ava outside, where we walked together.

The next time I was there again in the sauna he gave me a nod of acknowledgement. I introduced myself and so did he.

'Looks like you really do like the heat,' he commented.

And so, Tom Landore and I began.

34.

The things I learned about Tom Landore over the coming weeks rose like steam from the coals, the words teased out in the dim sauna. A very hot and clammy form of therapy.

He hated his job. It was boring and his colleagues didn't appreciate him. His underlings were lazy or rude; they didn't follow the simplest of directions. His boss was a nightmare; she asked far too much of him and she didn't appreciate him either – if anything, she took the credit for his ideas and passed them off as her own. His wife was always so distracted; she didn't care about anything apart from the house and the children (surely there were other things in life, deeper things to care about?). The children had somehow turned out to be very expensive and they expected so much. Everything had been so easy for them and he wondered if he'd been too soft? The schools he'd sent them away to had made them grasp for more – for ski lessons and ugly, expensive trainers. He didn't know if he liked what they'd become but felt guilty to say it, to even think it, because it was probably his fault. He couldn't believe he was saying it to me, a stranger. He blushed deeply when he called me a stranger. He was at the age where he was starting to understand that there were some things he wouldn't ever do, things he didn't even necessarily want to do, oddly creative ambitions like becoming an actor, but still, it was upsetting that these thoughts, these possibilities, were no longer viable. It wasn't pessimistic to say it was too late, it was just realistic, and he wasn't sure when that had happened, the day when things had changed. *These aren't things you can talk about. They're not things anyone talks about.*

The information that Tom Landore learned about me was limited, of course. He knew I was young. He knew I lived nearby, but he didn't know exactly where. He didn't ask, not really, and when he edged towards a question, it was easy for me to divert attention away from myself and back towards his bank of miseries.

His anxieties washed over me as we poured water on the coals, and I listened. I noted that he would stop talking if someone else came into the sauna, and we would sit in a charged silence. When strangers left, he would start to speak again. I listened to it all and I didn't understand, of course. I couldn't understand. The problems were nothing like mine, they were so far from my life or anything I'd ever experienced, but listening was easy. I had become very good at it.

Listening was nodding and agreeing and coaxing the rest of a story out of him. The sheer act allowed him to be the protagonist.

When he leaned in to kiss me, as we stepped out of the sauna and into the spa corridor, I kissed him back. His mouth was surprisingly yielding, his tongue probing then hesitant. It was a kiss that went on for a while, a nice kiss, and I let my damp body press into him.

It lasted until he pulled back and looked at me, and it was like he was seeing me properly for the first time. 'I never do this,' he said. He seemed shaken, and I walked away.

I felt like it had been comparable to a cold shower for him – a shock that had sent him running back to his wife.

A job well done, Tabitha announced. *Nice positioning in the corridor too for the photos.*

As far as I knew, Tabitha wasn't surprised by how the job had gone. From her perspective, we'd done exactly what we'd set out to do, and Tom Landore had responded appropriately. It was simple cause and effect. We had footage from the spa to show Mrs Landore – grainy video from the security cameras. I was impressed by this and had no idea how we'd managed to get it, but Samuel was so well connected that we seemed to be able to get anything we wanted, or at least anything we were willing to pay for. I asked what would happen next. Would I come with them to tell Mrs Landore what had happened?

Tabitha and Ava exchanged a look.

'I don't think that would be for the best . . .' Tabitha said. 'It's probably not in anyone's interest. Think of the emotional state she'll be in. Just me and Ava.'

It was odd, walking back that day after it was over, and I left the spa to go home.

I remember the intense heat of the sauna and the icy cold shower I'd had afterwards. Any vestige of tension – the tightness in my shoulders and the stiffness in my back – had left. My whole body tingled with adrenaline. Every muscle and ligament aligned. Everything was performing at its peak. If I jumped in the air, I knew it was the highest I would ever jump, so I did, right there on the street, ignoring the passers-by.

I felt powerful.

Finn noticed the difference in me that night when I suggested that we meet for a drink. He arrived looking rushed yet happy to see me. I got the impression that he'd moved his schedule around to accommodate the date at the last minute.

He went to get lager and crisps for us from the bar. So sluggish in ordering, so methodical about it all, and usually it calmed me – made me slow down and not rush so much – but I couldn't be calmed that night; I was impatient and the time it took him to reach his seat from the bar was annoying.

'You seem . . . well,' he noted. 'You've been hanging out mainly with them?' he asked, bringing his drink to his lips, and for some reason it was maddening, the way the foam settled on his upper lip and he took forever to wipe it off.

'Mainly,' I said.

'What about those girls you live with? You should hang out with them more. They're nicer. More normal.'

I just sipped my drink and rubbed at the side of my neck as something to do with my hands. It was almost laughable that Finn thought he could dictate what I did.

He continued as if he saw my silence as an invitation to plough on. 'And there are plenty of other posh girls to be friends with. Girls who are less . . . odd.'

How lazy to settle on *odd*! It was so far from how I viewed them all. He didn't understand that they were different. He was too mediocre to comprehend it, but I didn't say anything. Nothing could take the moment away from me.

I did not allow him to probe deeper. Instead, we talked about nothing much. Work, his brother's upcoming stag party. We finished our drinks quickly and, outside the pub, I pushed him up against the wall. In that moment, I had to, and I kissed him hungrily. He pulled me in and bent to fit my body, tasting of beer and oil. Then he took my hands in his and squeezed them so hard it hurt. My roughness thrown back at me, and I enjoyed it. When he pulled away – because he pulled away before I did – he seemed surprised.

'You are doing well, aren't you? Very well indeed.'

It was a moment when I was fully with him, with no thought of anything else, until he started telling me an in-depth story about a traffic jam. Then his voice became calming background noise, which I tuned out of instantly so I could replay the events of the previous few days in my head.

35.

And then, after Tom Landore, we were so confident.

The city was full of visitors for the Festival, and there were other men, of course. Men who I met over the summer as the days got longer and longer, until it stayed light until midnight.

August was busy. I followed a doctor who worked night shifts and turned out to be logistically difficult to pin down, whose movements we tracked obsessively until we found him. I ended up entwined in a drunken grope on a night bus. For him, it was just a few meetings, and a few quick photographs. Easy.

Then there was a man who should have made my skin crawl but, in fact, I thought he was fascinating. He kept spiders in tanks, so many of them in a room, and although at first I had to feign an interest in arachnids, I soon found that I wasn't pretending at all. I liked their soft fuzzy claws pressed all over my hands. We gathered copious amounts of text messages where the conversation veered away from tank maintenance and into more X-rated matters. He sent me things to wear, and I sent pictures back, cutting my face off (I never let my face be photographed clearly for these purposes), just my body swathed in soft black mohair. Spider-like – and was I the spider or was I being eaten by it? Limbs askew and sticking out at strange angles against the soft wool. It was hard to tell. Regardless, it was a particularly nice jumper and I kept it afterwards.

What a joyous summer, to dip into these lives and try them on like fancy dress. And the reward of seeing the pure bliss in Tabitha's face when we got pictures or text messages or anything.

When I tell the story, I'm aware of how it must come

across. It suggests that we were irresistible to any man: ridiculously flirty, so seductive and incredibly attractive. That wasn't quite the case. We had a set of refined procedures and expectations. A flawless setting where each element was calibrated for certain things to take place. The drink would be perfect, something from his past or simply his favourite, the one he always ordered, what chance! That was my favourite drink too! What I wore would be right, it would be what he liked. I sounded right – I was becoming better at changing my voice, not quite as good as Tabitha but I could sense improvement. I acted right, and it was all based on research. The research was always extensive without being intrusive.

There were other factors at play. An uneasy mix of art and science in motion. On the one hand, Tabitha had the intention to set it up as some kind of official-looking corporation. There were meetings and there was talk of appraisals and bonuses. She was keen we logged our hours and we pinned up ideas for marketing on a board – *a PR event, discounts for referrals, more testimonials?!* There was so much discussion at the beginning around the future. So much specificity to some discussions, certainly, but then a definite sense of deliberate ambiguity when it came to the detail of what each job should involve.

'As long as we're managing expectations for the client,' Tabitha would say, and it was all so exciting and new that I never stopped to question further.

I was never fully sure what those expectations were. At the time, I just assumed she meant sleeping with them. That was naive of me. At the same time, it all just felt like one big game. We never thought about it too much. Samuel certainly didn't, he stayed focused on the leads, on schmoozing rich women.

Sometimes, everything got a bit strange. Tabitha had an interest in the occult that, in Imogen's opinion, jarred horribly with the concept of running a functioning, professional business. Despite eschewing our actual course texts, Tabitha

devoured books about witchcraft and mentioned the super-
natural frequently.

'Witches in Scotland were wealthy, you know,' she'd say to
me pointedly, or, 'A witch could make a man impotent.'

'Could she though?' Imogen replied to that one.

'*Could she though*,' Tabitha said, perfectly impersonating
Imogen's whine at first, then exaggerating it into something
louder and squeakier. Imogen scowled, but Tabitha just smiled,
and answered her own question. 'Of course she could!' Back
to her own exuberant shriek.

Tabitha laid out oysters for us and various types of chillies.
Some were curled up and dried out like papery chrysalises,
and some were fresh and smooth-skinned: crumpled, collapsing in on themselves and waxy to the touch. She claimed such
things were aphrodisiacs and that we should try them and
assess our libido in a scientific way, and then we should find
ways to integrate them.

Tabitha was also very interested in the possibility of a love
potion (presumably Imogen would do the actual concocting of
this), but we never moved past the story-book idea of some rose-
scented mixture brewing on a stove, although she had asked me,
casually, how I might feel about retrieving a lock of hair from the
man with the spiders. That one had been a firm 'no', and she
didn't pursue it any further, just shrugged and tapped her nails
up and down my arm so it felt like a swarm of ants.

'I don't understand why you believe in this stuff,' Imogen
whined, reaching to the edge of how much she'd openly contradict Tabitha.

'I'm open-minded about anything that helps us,' Tabitha
replied. You couldn't rile her up about the things she believed
in – her own conviction in herself was sufficient. She froze
Imogen out for a few days after that comment.

Secretly, I quite liked it – the idea of us as witches. Something to bind us, something wicked.

Everyone had been delighted after Tom Landore. They'd passed on the news to Mrs Landore, along with some photographs.

They didn't tell me how she'd responded, and it did make me a little worried. What if he came after me or tracked me down in some way? His wife was going to accuse him of having an affair, and surely his first thought would be how did she know? It was impossible not to dwell on the fact that he must have known. A young girl appears, interested in him, well versed in all his interests. But the more of the work we did, the more I realized that it was almost impossible for the men to conceive that their wives would do such a thing, that they'd be so manipulative or plan something so elaborate.

'Think about it,' Tabitha said. 'These women we deal with, they do everything, organize everything – every part of their family's life. They're thinking, like, ten steps ahead, and their husbands are tragically prone to underestimating them.'

She shook her head as if she was, in fact, sad about the whole unfortunate, unavoidable thing.

'It's beyond catastrophizing, isn't it?' I said to Tabitha as she brushed my hair and curled it neatly, so it looked just like hers. 'Plotting and planning and actually orchestrating something, setting their husbands up to fail, really. Don't you think it's a little paranoid?'

She pursed her lips. 'But they need to protect themselves. This is how we help them do that.'

'So you think that all men cheat?' I asked. How brave I'd become!

She put the hairbrush down at the side of the bed.

'No, of course not.' One of her hands was on my face, edging in closer so that I could see open pores and the hint of a spot. I was static, waiting for her to come even closer. Just as I was wondering what that would be like, if she'd taste sweet like watermelon, or of something tarter, she pulled back.

She picked up the hairbrush again, sweeping it through the curls. 'But I do think people should be tested because it's transactional essentially, isn't it? The whole idea of marriage. I know the vows say "in sickness and in health, for richer or for poorer". But when, say, a man with a decent chunk of money marries a woman who is beautiful and thin and biddable . . . It's an implicit agreement taking place. It's business!'

'I guess,' I said.

'What we're doing is right. We're helping people.'

And in that moment, I nearly said something to her, nearly brought up Périgueux, and she waited, sensing that I was about to speak. But in the end I didn't, and she continued to pull at my hair so hard that I wanted to jerk away.

36.

There were many times it didn't work. Times when they looked at us in horror partway into the whole set-up.

We still got paid, as far as I knew, and secretly I wasn't too concerned when it happened, at least at first. So much of the fun of our scheme was in the getting ready. Blasting music, playing cards, trying on so many different items of clothing and analysing each look forensically to see that it gave the right impression.

I remember an evening with the CEO of a technology company. We went down to London to approach him. He spent almost all his time in the office, but I cornered him at a restaurant bar late at night, somewhere he would go for a solitary drink after a long day. He seemed nice and very lonely. He wore wire-framed glasses and he took them on and off again while he spoke. When he noticed he was doing it, he was embarrassed and forced his hands down on to the top of the bar, thumbing the wood. We talked about nothing in particular. I bought him a drink, and he asked me why I was there. He had a backpack, and when he opened it to take out his wallet, I could see a transparent pencil case filled with sharpened pencils. They were all the same length and there was a white eraser that was worn down uniformly on every side, as if he used it one way, then the other, working round to make sure it never lost its neat, angular shape.

When I leaned into him, he pulled away, shaking his head.

'I'm sorry. I think we've got our wires crossed,' he said simply. It wasn't cruel at all, just direct, and he stood up and walked away. Tabitha was surprised when I reported back.

'How interesting!' she said.

'It is . . . affirming,' I replied.

'Well, I don't think that's quite the right attitude.'

The same flash of disappointment that I'd seen at Servants' Christmas. I wanted to kick myself for my choice of wording, but I also experienced a flurry of understanding. She didn't want to go back to the client with news of innocence. She wanted the men to be guilty, and she wanted the wives to leave them.

More occasional let-downs. A man pulled away, colour flooding his face. He stumbled from me, almost running. It happened, of course it did. Our targets probably thought we were very persistent escorts.

'Well, you kind of are,' Imogen had said, her tone smarmy and low. She wasn't brave enough to say it so that Tabitha could hear. It was directed at me; only I heard it, and it didn't affect me in the slightest.

Tabitha never actually told me much about her jobs, and I suspected her success rate must have been similar to my own. I knew she slept with them if she felt it was necessary – she mentioned it with ease, joking about flustered interactions, performance issues.

When it didn't work, she was incredulous each time.

She interrogated me one afternoon as we lay across a bench in the private gardens next to her flat. She'd pulled out a huge, almost ornamental-looking key, and unlocked it for us.

'Ta-da!' she announced. 'I can't bear how busy it is up at Princes Street Gardens at the moment. This is much better. Anyway, back to what happened. You talked to him about Napoleon for *three hours*?!'

The thought of Tabitha doing anything for three hours without losing interest was unimaginable. Even then I could tell she was poised to get up, her eyes flitting around the gardens at who was there, who we might speak to or use or know. Kicking a shoe off, her foot veined and pointed like a ballerina's.

Some golden-haired children threw a Frisbee to a tired-looking dog, its thick ears drooping to the ground.

'I think he enjoyed the conversation very much,' I said. I sounded terse, defensive – I could hear it in my own voice, and I saw that she heard it too.

'When you put it like that, I can see why it didn't work,' she mused. 'A siege isn't very sensual, is it?' The words seemed accusatory.

'Ah well, that's fine,' she continued. 'We'll do better next time.'

'Next time,' I repeated. Not as a question, just as a statement.

'Yes, next time,' she said, and her tone turned more serious. 'You need to be confident in your own success for next time, Clare.' She sounded rattled.

'It's not that, of course I'll try harder. It's just, it can't go on forever, can it?' I said, faltering.

'What do you mean?' she asked sharply.

'We'll need to get real jobs,' I said, unsure as soon as the words came out of my mouth.

'Real jobs?' Tabitha's hand moved to her chest in over-the-top shock.

'Yes,' I said.

'Like what?'

'I don't know. Work in an office or something?'

'An office! I think we're better than that. Or even if we weren't, there are no jobs for us. What on earth would we be qualified to do? We're learning about paintings and dates. We're completely unemployable.' She stated this proudly. 'I don't think we'll ever have jobs like that.'

'But we can't do this forever?'

'Oh, this is just the beginning. And Perfect Pieces is going well, despite the name. It has the potential to be very interesting. Even if this ends, there'll be something else. There's always something else.'

What she said made sense. Tabitha would never work in an office. How could she? To think of Tabitha in an airless cubicle, or even catching the bus or the train at a set time every day, was impossible. She couldn't take orders from anyone and, in a way, she was right. We weren't employable, and we were going to graduate into a time when it would be hard to find a job.

'Even if we could do this for a long time, don't you ever feel bad about it?' I asked.

'What do you mean?' She looked puzzled.

'The men.'

'Oh, God, no. I don't feel bad for them at all. I know how they are. The comments, the digs, the cheating, the assumption that they're better than us. They think they can get away with anything.'

All of this had been said quite offhandedly, but she sounded more serious when she spoke next. 'What we're doing. It's partly about using our skills, about making things right, but it's more than that. It's about us too, pushing ourselves past the ordinary, into something unimaginably special. However far you think you're able to go, you just go further. That's what it's all about. It's what *life* is about.'

We lay there while the children ran circles until they fell over, dizzy and hysterical. One of them started to cry, but Tabitha didn't seem to notice at all. She was in one of her states of stillness, lying as a dead girl, head thrown too far back over the side of the bench as if her neck had been broken.

37.

A new academic year began in September.

New notepads bought, new courses chosen: modern portraiture for Tabitha and me; more weepy landscapes for Imogen. When it came to non-work-related endeavours, it was important to Tabitha that we tried new things to broaden our horizons. *To stretch ourselves*, she said, and I thought of a body pulled at either end in a tug of war, stretched taut until it reached the breaking point and snapped and splintered into two parts above the hips in a bloody mess.

Tabitha's focus was on things that would help the business long-term.

'Clubs?' Samuel had thrown into the ring. No one asked him what kind of 'clubs' he meant. He had started to mention *girls who weren't part of The Shiver* much more by that point.

'Cookery classes?' Imogen had suggested hopefully.

Tabitha didn't dignify the suggestions with a response, and it was an illusion that we had a say in the whole thing anyway. All other ideas were met with light derision.

She was prone to distraction, always drawn to any shiny scheme, and she did seem to recognize this in herself. She said she needed to stay *focused on cash flow*, which is why she decided that we should have a go at gambling. In a casino. With the money that we'd made over the summer. We'd made a lot, but we wanted more.

What to play? Poker was too fiddly. Roulette was just chance, really, and Tabitha didn't like to bet on chance. We settled on blackjack. It was easy enough to get the hang of and, when we started, she had grand plans involving card counting. She thought we'd be excellent card counters. This was entirely misjudged. We were all predictably hopeless, while staying enthusiastic about playing in general as we sat around at night in the flat, going through round after round. Hitting and standing, and laughing the whole time. The end goal was a casino trip. None of us had been to a casino before.

We only went once, and I think that was always the plan. Sometimes they preferred the elegance of doing things once. Steal a cat from the street for the night, feed it milk, pretend it was ours, just once. Stay up all night on the roof, just once. And then talk about everything endlessly: *the time we skinny-dipped in the North Sea*; *the time we counted cards at the casino*. The memories of events became bigger and brasher, easy group folklore to dip into on demand and slide into conversation.

'It will be like Monaco,' Tabitha said when she told us what she wanted us to do.

'Monaco!' Imogen squealed, her hand to her chest, typically prudish.

'Monaco,' Ava repeated flatly.

And that's how we treated it. Dressed up far too fancily in frocks that fell off our shoulders, floor-length like we were going to a ball, make-up done by Imogen, trowelled on in greasy slicks. Tabitha wore something that was sequined all over, pale blue and unsuitable. Dastardly ice queen meets cruise ship glitterball. And then she kept banging on about Monaco. Anyway, the more she talked, the more we all started to look forward to it.

'There might be some *girls* at the casino,' Samuel said buoyantly, rarely deterred.

When we walked in, it was clear Tabitha was wrong, and the casinos in Edinburgh weren't remotely like our fantasies of Monaco. The one we went to was extremely rundown, and we arrived too early. Apparently, it was at its busiest and most exciting at three a.m. when the clubs emptied out and the overspill gathered drunkenly to throw notes at the croupiers. There was an old red carpet, all crusty and hard with some unknown substance. Bottles of drinks in blue and green served with a straw. The smell of vomit and of aftershave and, absurdly, of hot butter. But the truth of it all was that it didn't matter if the casino was depressing. When she saw what the place looked like, Tabitha just shrugged, pushed her shoulders back and told Imogen to get her a drink.

'She needs the money, you know. I heard her dad won't give her any kind of allowance next year,' Imogen whispered to me before she passed the drinks out. Straight after she said it, she squeaked like a mouse, and her hand went to her mouth at the betrayal of it – and to *me* of all people. Her teeth covered again, retreating away from me.

Interesting.

It was decided that one person should take the chips, play on behalf of us all.

Ava piped up: 'I'm not sure it should be you, Tabitha? Maybe Samuel?' Saying what the rest of us were thinking. Tabitha, a flailing magpie who wouldn't be able to stay focused.

We all thought Tabitha would object. She kind of pursed her lips, looking at Ava as if weighing up what to say, and there was a bit of a stare-off, which I think was more for show than anything else. Tabitha laughed and reached out, pulling Ava towards her, then letting go. She turned to us all, blessing us with her decision.

'Samuel,' she said firmly, as if that had been her idea in the first place.

Samuel could do it. Samuel who could work out VAT in his head and seemed *highly and strategically numerate*, to me at least.

So, Samuel sat there intently, sweat forming on his hairline (a drip of orange – fake tan certainly). He wouldn't want to let us down. He liked to please, of course. We all did.

So much riding on it! A kind of delicious fear, and I could see why people liked gambling.

We watched.

Imogen was looking at him in awe like he was some sort of god. Willing him on so he'd win. It made me quite angry for her, and at her. I wanted her to say something. I wanted her to be bolder about it – to tell him how she felt. That's what Tabitha would have done, or Ava, or even me. We took more than Imogen ever did, greedily, anything we wanted. Imogen never did, and I wonder if it was because she didn't think she deserved to.

Samuel doubled down and we were surprised because he had a five and a seven. The other people around the table looked annoyed. It was bad strategy. He lost the hand, and then he did it again.

A crowd was forming around us now and I had a sinking feeling we'd lose every penny and have to start again from scratch.

Hand after hand, he kept doubling down.

He doubled down on a five and a six, and a face card came up. Twenty-one. He won the hand.

And then the tides turned and he was winning, the next hand and the next, and I couldn't believe I'd ever thought he'd lose – how misguided of me! Things tended to go our way, back then.

I remember after he'd won a few hands, a girl who'd been watching him scuttled up to him with a wide smile, but Tabitha sent her on her way with a loud hiss.

So many shiny plastic chips in red and green, which Tabitha loved. 'Take a picture of me with them,' she said. Snaps of her with dirty casino chips clasped between straight white teeth, fully completing her transformation into cruise ship cabaret star. And then, when we exchanged the chips at the booth, a chunk of money for us, in crisp notes, and she took it without question.

Later, it was busier. The smell of butter became more pronounced, and then everyone seemed to be eating cheese toasties
passed out indiscriminately by the staff to mop up the alcohol.
Thinner, meaner-looking versions of a croque-monsieur.

Ava went up to the booth and paid for a huge pile of chips
without batting an eyelid, an amount that we gasped at, and
she split them amongst us.

'I want us to have fun tonight!' she said lightly.

Imogen refused her chips covertly. 'Who knows where this
is from? Dirty money,' she said and passed them to me under
the table, so Ava didn't see.

Samuel refused too. 'I don't like owing people,' he said.

Ava and Tabitha and I went wild. Ava's money – once con-
verted into chips, nothing could have felt more like Monopoly
money.

It was a power-play in itself – Ava had never been showy
before. For some reason, she had a change of heart that night
and displayed her unlimited funds. To me, she seemed to be
making a point – she didn't have to be in business with us all and
she wanted to demonstrate this to us, display some kind of clout
that wasn't overwhelming, but certainly made a statement.

It was in contrast to Tabitha, who had drawn back from paying for things and who put so much focus on creating revenue
at every turn. Who wasn't getting anything from her parents
any more.

Before much longer, however, it would become apparent to
me that it was never just about the money for Tabitha. It was
important to her, yes, but it wasn't the sole reason. She had
other requirements.

38.

Eventually, I saw Tabitha in action. Glorious, awful action.

'An inbound lead!' she cooed, stroking the top of her laptop to reward it for delivering a lucrative find.

She announced it to us. 'And she's just *lovely*. I've only met her a few times, but we're already so aligned on our vision for it.' Tabitha liked to use words like 'aligned', and often it served to obscure any kind of meaning.

Imogen laid out the details for us, as usual: a large Victorian villa in the suburbs of the city; a house far too big for a family of three; a wife, who'd given up her job as a professional dancer in London. They'd moved to Scotland years ago for his job, which didn't sound especially above board, but the details were vague; some kind of sketchy background in private security.

'He's been cheating on her for years,' Tabitha said, scanning her notes. 'She just wants proof.'

I didn't understand why there wouldn't be emails or text messages, but there wasn't anything. He was talented at maintaining his privacy. Apparently.

'Our surveillance methods won't work because the house is really well protected from stuff like that because of his job. All sorts of things have been set up,' Tabitha mused. 'That's if we want to do it near the house. Which we do.'

She spoke like I knew what these methods were. I didn't. So far, we'd managed to get proof in various ways, as far as I could tell. Friends I didn't know about in places I didn't understand.

'OK, so what's the plan?' I asked. I wasn't sure why she was involving me.

'Nothing elaborate. I would ask Imogen, but I'd prefer you for this,' she said.

Oh, the *buzz* at being chosen, but I couldn't help asking the question: 'Why?'

She was coy. 'I just would.'

'What do you want me to do?' I asked carefully.

'Come and take a few pictures.'

'Of what?'

'Oh, just the usual.' She waved a hand in the air to bat away the question. 'It will be in front of the house, so just some quick snaps.' She clicked a finger down on an imaginary air camera with a wink and leaned in closer to me. 'If anything happens, I just feel that you'll be able to move nice and fast, Clare.'

'Why would I need to move fast? I'll just take some pictures, and then you'll go inside, won't you?' I asked.

'Oh, yes, yes . . . just a precaution.' She nodded, her hand on mine. 'Just make sure you get the pics straight away with the flash on, so I know when you're done.'

'He'll see the flash, won't he?'

'Oh, don't worry about that.'

I was confused. I knew from experience there was no point in pushing, though. I didn't want to be excluded from the whole thing for the sake of curiosity.

I looked to Imogen, who'd been quiet during this erratic briefing. I think Imogen knew that it might not be as simple as Tabitha was making out, but she didn't say a word. She just scrunched up her nose, as if to say, *don't involve me, this one's all on you.*

'Imogen, you have something stuck in your teeth,' Tabitha said sweetly. Imogen turned bright red, rooting about with a nail into her gums.

'Hmmm, looks like there was nothing there at all,' Tabitha said coolly after a moment or two.

Then Imogen was dismissed, and nothing else seemed to be

required from me. For the rest of the afternoon, I sat there on the bed in Tabitha's room. Watching her try on outfits.

She danced around in a tight leather skirt with her legs encased in ribbed woollen tights. She assessed herself in a heavy kilt, and then something huge made of orange chiffon that was almost certainly stolen as it emerged from a bin bag wrapped in tinfoil.

In the end, the outfit she settled on was all in black like a burglar, her hair fanned out on her back in a shock of yellow. A heavy gold watch looped around her skinny wrist.

I sat there in the room, cosy while the wind raged outside, wondering what Tabitha could possibly have planned and savouring the fact that it was something we'd be doing together.

39.

It was a late, dark afternoon. The street lights were just starting to flicker, and they lined the road like tiny fires. Leaves
crunched beneath my feet and smoke hung in the air – it was a
day or so after Bonfire Night. I remember noting that because
the last dribble of fireworks had already started in the distance.
They flared up into a half-hearted display over the boxy flats as
I walked up the street. All of a sudden, the flats gave way to a
blocky row of huge, blackened villas with thick privet hedges
protecting them from the street and vast cars, like tanks ready
for war, lining the pavements.

Most of the houses looked very smart, but some seemed
like they'd been owned by old, hallowed Edinburgh money
(the type of generational wealth that Tabitha was obsessed
with, although she wasn't always fussy – new money was also
fine), and they'd been left over the years to grow shabby around
the edges – a few loose tiles or paint flaking at the door frame.

One residence had a pumpkin still sitting outside from Halloween. It had started to rot, the stringy flesh greying where it
had been cut and the fanged mouth collapsing, so the face
looked like a gummy, drooling animal.

I winced. The hacked-up face reminded me of the unfortunate events of last Halloween. The boy from the bar. An arm
pincered under my heel.

Tabitha and I had agreed on a specific time, and I was early
because I wanted to be prepared and to work out the best
place to lie in wait.

Her instructions were that I'd just need to be nice and close
to the house, on the other side of the street, so that I'd see

them come up to the front door. Once I was there, I hovered behind some bins, trying not to be too self-conscious even though there was no one else around at all. The place was so quiet at that time of day, just before people started coming home from work. I stamped my feet to stay warm, feeling quite relaxed about the whole thing. Tabitha trusted me, and I'd been given an easy job. It was just a case of taking a few photos.

I heard them before I saw them. They came from around the corner, walking towards the house.

I could almost believe that she was amping up her performance for me, becoming louder and louder, more of a caricature of herself. She was laughing vigorously already, then her laugh morphed into a rather frightening high-pitched peal.

In one hand, she had her handbag. I remember thinking for a second that it was odd she'd brought such a large bag with her. She threw her entire body erratically from side to side with gusto, in a way that was very clever because it made her look a little unpredictable and drunk, but I knew she wouldn't be because she so rarely drank much.

I felt a small quiver of fear in my chest. He was large – not fat but extremely muscular. If anything happened, he'd be a tricky opponent. Tabitha, usually the tallest in the room, looked so slight compared to him.

I didn't take my eyes off them for a second. She moved in closer and grabbed his hand in hers, letting it go again, letting him reach back out to her to draw her in. I wondered why he didn't mind her doing this, being so open when anyone could see them together, but I realized when he stumbled forward that *he* was entirely out of it. Maybe more than drunk.

They stood there, outside the house in the driveway, and there was some privacy. Still, I had a perfect line of vision, and I could see both of them, as well as a small, wooden rocking horse in the window that looked like it was moving to and fro.

He was swaying too, next to her, in a suit and a shirt unbuttoned at the neck.

He was very hungry for her – I could see that. He saw what we all saw in Tabitha. Probably found her mildly annoying, yet also irresistible.

There was almost a pause; she had her hand on his arm. She looked out away from him and towards where I stood. Although she couldn't possibly see me, I took it as a sign to take a picture.

Snap.

I took the first shot. Her hand up close on his face, stroking his chin as he leaned in.

Captured – the way he was using his body to close himself around her that gave her the appearance of a china doll, like she might break if he kept bearing down on her. There was so little fat on her, and I thought, as they stood there, what would I do if he grabbed her? If he grabbed her neck hard and she screamed? No one would hear and I'd have to be the one to save her because, of course, I'd go to her rescue. Suddenly I remembered the flash and, cursing, I turned it on.

Snap.

Another picture with her face almost touching his, and then it all happened so quickly.

He looked out into the dark to see where the flash had come from, almost locking eyes with me. I froze, watching Tabitha. I saw that she had a flask in her hand like the ones we brought along to lectures. She held it in front of him, offering it to him, it seemed.

Then she threw the contents of the flask into his face.

The liquid splashed all over him, into his eyes. It looked like water, and for a moment I was confused: why would Tabitha throw water in his face?

A second passed and then the sound he made was long and low and primal, like the howl of an animal caught in a trap. It rang through the quiet streets. I was sure someone would hear, but it was one of those streets where no one ever came out to check on their neighbours. He clawed at his face, rubbing frantically at his eyes, and then he bent at the waist as if the act of standing up had become too much. I thought he might crumble to the ground entirely. Instead, he reached out towards Tabitha, grabbing at air – because she was gone. It was just him and the rocking horse, still swaying in the background.

I hadn't been able to stop staring at him. I'd almost forgotten about her, then seconds later she was next to me as I stood there, frozen, and she tugged hard at my sleeve. She was bright and alert and not drunk in the slightest, clutching her bag to her chest with her other hand. He'd fallen to the ground at this point.

'Come on, quick!' She let go and darted in front of me, taking off at top speed away down the street.

What else could I do?

He was still on the ground and I could have helped him. I willed him to get up, and for a moment I thought I might stay, but I'd be kidding myself if it was out of kindness. It was more from the need to see what on earth she'd done to him.

I followed her instead; of course I did.

40.

We ran south, down identical streets. Quick turns left and right until I lost track of where we'd come from. She was my shining beacon as she threaded from pavement to road. We started to pass people, and she weaved in and out without care. I tried to keep up, pushed myself so I wouldn't lose her, and we were fast in our getaway. Just as I was starting to reach peak exhaustion, she suddenly swerved right off the road. I followed her down steep steps slick with the damp cover of fallen leaves, until she stopped under a shelter.

It was a bridge, I realized that straight away. We were standing on a shaded walkway, one of the long bike paths that wound away from the city centre, next to the Water of Leith. Down in the shadows with a river gushing close by – it felt very far away from the city, where we'd been just seconds ago.

We pressed our backs against the slimy stone of the underside of the bridge, and I slid down to the ground to sit, trying to get my breath back.

She was silent.

'What was that?' I asked her.

'That went well, I think,' she said, panting, ignoring my question. 'Also, I don't think he followed us. We really were quick, weren't we? Ava said you were nice and fast! Did you run in school or something?' She chattered away at me.

I shook my head. 'I don't understand what just happened. What did you do to him?'

'I think you got the pictures, didn't you?' she asked with sudden urgency, ignoring my question.

'Yes.'

'OK. That's good.' She turned to look at me, her face a greenish pearl in our shadowy hiding place. 'I'm sorry I didn't tell you in advance, but I thought it would be smoother that way, and it was quite smooth, wasn't it?'

'Tabitha –' I reached out, gripped at her arm, and then spoke very slowly, like she was a child. 'Was that . . . acid?'

She smiled broadly. 'No, no. I'm glad it came across like that though. That's ever so good.'

'What was it, then?'

'It's this stuff off the internet.' She said the word 'internet' with a turned-up nose.

I was slightly relieved that she hadn't made it herself in some kind of science experiment.

'Anyway, it would have felt like acid to him at the beginning, just searing, all-consuming pain.' She said this as a statement, then continued, as if she was reading it from a book. 'He wouldn't have been able to open his eyes at all. For a second or two, it would have incapacitated him. The pain gives way to feelings that I've read about: he would have thought that his face had been scarred beyond recognition, a life-changing injury. Then, a larger fear – blindness, I think, although that one might come first. It depends how vain he is.'

She took the flask out of her bag and gave it a little shake. Whatever was in there looked harmless enough, like water. It wasn't bubbling or anything.

'How do you know this?' I asked.

'Oh, it's just what I've read.'

'And then what? Will he be OK?'

'Yes, yes, don't fuss. He'll be tons better in a few hours and fine by tomorrow. I discussed it all with the client. We felt it was a nice ending.'

We sat there in silence under the bridge. I didn't know what to say. The setting was almost peaceful. A dog walker approached us and only glanced at us quickly before looking away, which signalled to me that we probably looked unhinged.

Tabitha brushed herself down and stood up. 'Come on. You can come back to ours if you want to have a bit of a rest.'

I shook my head.

'OK, suit yourself,' she said. She held out a hand. 'Camera please?'

I passed it to her.

'Thanks,' she sang, backing away from me. 'Good job today. I know that was a lot, but I just wanted to show you what happens when we go further.'

I went back home and filed away whatever had just happened. I believed her claim that he'd never report us to the police. Still, I felt uneasy about her actions for a few weeks afterwards. Because it had been terrifying and unexpected and risky and, in a way, it reminded me of other events, but there had also been something invigorating about the whole thing. The absolute sense that we were above the law.

I wasn't sure how to feel on balance, but as long as the justification was there, that he deserved it, I could try to forget the strange viciousness in the execution.

41.

The city – dark and cold – was a grumpy old man who'd been freshened up. Old buildings that I considered mine stood with battered window frames and bricks worn away. They were coated in sheets of tiny white lights which made me marvel at how good Christmas was at covering up the cracks.

After lectures, trudging from the Old to the New Town, to visit Tabitha, I peered into each window of the flats to see the trees.

I hadn't paid much attention to them the year before, but that Christmas they mesmerized me. Each room held a towering sculpture of a fir, always by the window so passers-by stopped and stared. Not like any I'd ever seen before: their decorations glinted and the colours matched. They didn't bend and buckle organically like *proper trees*; instead, they were uniformly trimmed and symmetrical. No tatty strings of lights or mismatched decorations, and the branches were coated with frosted quilts of cut glass blown into perfect spheres. There were many cherubs perched atop those trees – fat and ruddy.

Tabitha bought a chunky Norway spruce because she said we'd earned it, and we lugged the great thing up the stairs. Like her neighbours, we decorated it with expensive decorations and old treasures she'd hoarded away.

There was no mention of Servants' Christmas. After last year, this was a relief. She made a big thing out of her shopping, and I remember that she bought present after present for us that year. However, with all that ended up happening, we didn't open the gifts. They sat there for weeks, in gold wrapping paper with floppy bows, and I never did find out what happened to them after Christmas.

I spent more time with Samuel and I enjoyed his company. He often turned up at my flat bleary-eyed on a Saturday morning. He always insisted on coming to me and I later discovered through Imogen (not that she ever really criticized him much, but she was a terrible gossip) that for all Samuel's airs and graces, he lived in an ordinary student house with a bunch of rugby players, which was probably why his car was a useful tool for projecting a more glamorous, nomadic existence.

He always arrived with gifts in his arms: king-sized milky coffees and muffins, alongside a bag of stock to be shipped around the country. The traps had slowed down a little, but Perfect Pieces drummed up even more business in the festive months for some reason.

Lots of lacy knickers that had to be packaged up inventively.

Remember, no returns, Tabitha insisted.

'You're a hard worker!' he said to me (a similar refrain I was used to from Finn) and it was nice to get his praise.

'This is easy,' I said, because it was.

'I like easy,' he said, and I could see this was true – I don't think Samuel wanted peak drama or strange complications. Like Imogen, he was happy just doing it in his spare time for extra money.

He turned serious. 'Remember, though, this is paid work, Clare. You don't owe me. I don't owe you. Equals.'

I was fine with that and we worked well together. We'd draft a story, carefully create a certain stain if necessary, using whatever I had lying around in the flat, or a rip to add heated authenticity. Then we'd sit on my bedroom floor and label them up, popping on a spritz of perfume, adding a handwritten note and a sales receipt, all in companionable silence. It felt very regimented. Uniform packaging. Desire produced by assembly line.

I have such fond memories of those weeks because, despite what happened afterwards, there will always be that slice of life before Christmas when all was perfect, which I can carve out now when I look back. A period that started from the end of November until we went up north mid-December. Sometimes you can reflect on your life and portion away a time when all the moving parts – family, friends, work – that usually grind against each other and compete for attention, suddenly move together in a perfect whir.

I had money – more than I needed from my jobs – to buy whatever I wanted and there was a sense of security in that. The weather was perfect nearly every day: skies so blue and a layer of frost on the buildings each morning.

My living situation was closer to what I'd envisioned when I'd moved to the city. The flat Georgia and Ashley and I had chosen for our second year was much better than the flat from our first year. It was high up and my room was the smallest, a circular space with an old fireplace and creaking floorboards. I even had the wooden desk I'd always wanted, placed next to the window so I could look out on to the street below.

The days became elastic. All I needed to do was shave off an hour of sleep here or there and there were no repercussions, as I had more energy than I ever thought possible. I guzzled the hours greedily. I'd reached an endpoint – one I'd always imagined – where I wasn't even struggling to keep it all together; I didn't get angry or act out.

The problem is, when things are drumming along so nicely, something big always throws them off course.

Ava turned up at my flat in a taxi late at night. She buzzed and buzzed, and Georgia and Ashley came out of their rooms, looking worried.

'Why can't your friends use the phone like normal people?'

Georgia hissed at me sleepily. I shooed them back to bed and went downstairs to meet her.

'We've secured something big and you need to come over now,' she said.

Secured. Like some sort of government contract. I didn't say no. I'd never say no to anything that Tabitha needed.

42.

Shortly afterwards, we sat around on the bed in Tabitha's room. This was always one of my favourite parts of the whole thing. Tabitha speaking and Ava our adjudicator looking after us, usually silently. Imogen scratching away, taking notes and interrupting. Samuel was absent and I wondered where he was, but only for a second, because the briefing began.

A man.

He was wealthy, Tabitha explained, an American called Jack.

When Imogen showed us a picture, Tabitha started running around the room snorting at us wildly, her nose pressed so hard into my ear I had to push her away, and she fell back on the floor cackling in delight: 'He looks like a pig. Like a big fat pig.'

We named him Jack the Pig, or just The Pig. His wife had contacted us from their house out in Palm Springs. I maintained the same stance as that first time – I didn't look him up online. There was no point. At first, I thought I'd just assimilate the information from Imogen. But, for a change, Imogen didn't seem as involved.

The fee structure was different too. Tabitha announced that she and Ava had decided on a hefty price that would relate to whether or not we succeeded, whether we got the evidence of infidelity. That was new.

'I thought we were supposed to be setting up a scenario, not making sure we succeed?' I asked.

Tabitha responded smoothly. 'Absolutely, Clare. See it from the consumer perspective, though. Our clients need to feel that we're motivated. They need to make sure we're trying hard enough, and if there's scope to cheat, we'll find it. All sales jobs have commission, don't they?'

I didn't know. I had never had a real sales job and, as far as I knew, neither had she. She smiled brightly, ironing out the issues like hands over creased sheets.

The weekend itself wasn't like anything we'd done in the past few months. This was the information I obtained from them: we'd be going and staying there, sleeping there, becoming part of the group; there were security cameras around the whole place, apparently, so anything that happened would be captured; the house was in the Highlands – Ava was hazy about the actual address – and then there was the other part of the set-up – we'd be hunting for pheasants.

It was a step up from anything we'd ever done before, and it was all very confusing from the beginning. I was unsure if we would actually attend the shoot. The guest list consisted of men who were travelling from all around the world. No wives invited.

From the beginning, Tabitha was obsessed with Jack the Pig and his acquisitions, which were beyond plentiful – we got a completely unnecessary amount of detail as she called out to us, *Seven bedrooms! An in-home cinema!* He had many properties and aircraft and help for everything. That seemed to be the root of Tabitha's immediate fascination with The Pig – the services money could buy. She often talked about how, if you were that rich, everything would be done for you: a cleaner, a housekeeper, a gardener. The ability to outsource life. It was the ultimate privilege. Imagine if you could pay away your problems, your chores, all the things you've ever hated doing, leaving your day as a blank slate of free time for you to do exactly what you wanted with.

'It's all arranged,' Ava assured me. 'A friend of my cousin went to school with the daughter of the owner; they're more than happy to have us as guests for the weekend so we can learn to shoot.'

'Oh, she's so good at organizing, isn't she?' Tabitha crowed to me, her hand knotted in Ava's hair, twisting until Ava pulled away.

'Do you not think it's odd that all three of us would go?' I asked.

'We all need to go,' Tabitha said. 'Ava connects us to the group just enough, although she'll use a fake name. Without her, none of the set-up makes sense. We both go and we see who he chooses – me or you.'

'Are you sure? It just seems over the top for all three of us to be there.' It was bold for me to question her like that.

She gave me a long stare. Such a Tabitha stare in its intensity, like a steely nanny. It was almost as if she was about to tell me to finish my homework and send me to bed. 'I'm sure. Let's get ready – there's a lot to do.'

Tabitha insisted we put even more effort in than usual, and Ava, normally the voice of reason, obliged. Maroon leggings and musty waxed coats for all of us. For Ava, a merino wool jumper in teal, and for Tabitha, a nude crêpe dress with a hint of shell-pink that rippled through the fabric. A gown with a demure front and then a back that dropped away to reveal each knobble of her spine.

Furs too. One thing we'd encountered early on, a minor stumbling block, was the women who couldn't access the amount of money they'd need without their husbands' attention. This had happened in a few cases, and the result had been bartering in all its forms: a tawny fur with so many undercoats it made you want to dig your fingers deep into the layers; a case of wine from a particularly excellent year in Bordeaux; clusters of fat pearls, strung long. These were things Ava and Tabitha hoarded away to sell, but in this case Tabitha was wrapped up in something quite old, that had apparently come from two hundred chinchillas. Dina and Adrienne would not have approved.

Tabitha was still chatting away. 'It's worth hedging our bets with who attracts his attention,' she explained. 'He's only in the UK for one or two weekends a year, so this may well be the one chance we get.'

I picked out dresses and leggings and boots alongside them. We moved as one, became well versed in things I'd never heard of, from macrobiotic diets to Yoga Nidra. A welcome distraction until we were ready.

43.

First, we had something planned. A night that ended up spilling in many directions, and it came about because Tabitha said
we deserved a Christmas treat. None of us would be leaving
Edinburgh until much later that year.

'Maybe Finn would like to come?' she had suggested in the
days before, so sweetly I could almost believe she genuinely
wanted him there. Of course, I didn't ask Finn. He felt very far
away from what we were doing; whereas before I'd found him
calming, it had reached the point where he just seemed colourless. Time spent with him was wasted.

Anyway, it was just bait for Samuel, who rolled his eyes.
'Ugh, so dull. Really, Tabs. *Finn?!*'

She batted him away, and he stuck his tongue out and pretended to lick her arm.

Just another episode of the Samuel and Tabitha show, but it
was the last time I'd see such an easiness between the two of
them. At the time I just found it a little annoying.

The chosen destination was the private room in a large
Chinese restaurant down a side street, and when we entered
it was busy and hot in that pre-Christmas buzz. I had been
worried Tabitha might wear a kimono to mark the occasion, because she loved doing that kind of thing, the type of
thing that made people grimace – it didn't matter if they
scorned her inaccurate cultural appropriation, so long as
they paid attention. She didn't, though; she looked as lovely
as ever in a dress the deep, bruised colour of aubergines
cooked in the oven for hours until the skin starts to peel
away.

'This is so nice, isn't it!' she cooed as we sat there. 'It's all on me, everyone have whatever you want, and to drink too. Order something fabulous, Ava.'

Ava took charge as usual. Poker-faced, she ordered bottles of red, and far too much food: a swede sculpted into a delicate fan; a whole Peking duck with a glossy rust to its skin, the dark sauce frosted solid, like a meaty, hard-boiled sweet; a heavy dish of something called Szechuan prawns, spiked with spring onion confetti. The fish curled around floating clots of red sauce.

After we'd had a few drinks, we settled into the evening. The chat flowed, even if the mood was a little stilted, and Tabitha rose at the end. She tapped her glass and declared we should open our fortune cookies.

She announced hers to us: 'Like a lion hunting its prey, if you maintain great focus on your quest, you will be triumphant.' She held her hand to her chest and chuckled. 'Brilliant! I think there's something in this. Imogen?'

I was fully expecting Imogen to roll her eyes, but she didn't. It was the first time I'd focused on her that evening. When I looked properly, I could see that the energy had been sapped from her. Hair frizzing at the sides and even more frowning than usual. Cautiously, like something living might jump out, she opened up her cookie and squinted at it angrily like she knew it wasn't going to be in her favour. She read the fortune out to us: 'Your intelligence is an asset to be shared. Seen by all, it will be rewarded appropriately.'

She looked up and crumpled the scrap in her hand. 'I don't believe in any of this.'

'Oh, Imogen, you think I don't recognize your intelligence?' Tabitha replied.

They stared at each other over the hunk of duck in the middle of the table and Imogen looked away first. 'Oh, whatever,' she said huffily.

'Don't sulk!' Tabitha said breezily. 'Everyone open theirs, please! What fun!'

I opened mine.

You will create your own world.

Although I knew you could read just about anything into those cookies, this felt right. I *had* created my own world, the one I had always wanted. I'd never envisaged living like this, of course, but the last few months had been some of the best of my life. I hadn't just slotted in; I had become an important part and everything we'd done I'd help create.

I wondered if she'd make us all read them out, but she didn't, she just raised her glass in the air.

'A toast! To us all.' She tapped her head to each of us in turn.

'Samuel, you've changed so much. Look at you! Compared to school!'

It was condescending and Samuel looked very tired. The Samuel who'd rolled around on the floor licking Tabitha's arm only days ago seemed like a different person.

'And you two.' She lumped Ava and me together for some reason. 'You've both done so much for this. We're doing something to be proud of.'

Nothing for Imogen.

We all raised our glasses dutifully to meet hers. The mood was still stiff and Imogen left after we'd finished the meal. Samuel slunk away from us too. He headed to the adjoining bar, where he could still peer into the private room, and I went over to him.

He was sitting looking miserable with a glass of mineral water in front of him.

'Is Imogen OK?' I asked.

He took a long sip before replying. 'She'll be fine. Always drama isn't there, with girls.'

A silly, sweeping generalization, but he seemed so down I didn't pick him up on it. 'I guess,' I said. 'I think she likes you, though. *Likes* you. You know.'

'Imogen?' he questioned, quite lightly.

'Yes.'

He didn't seem fazed at all. 'No, no, you're misreading it. She's like a little sister to me.'

He shook his head, disregarding the idea, but he was so calm. I could tell he already knew and he just didn't care to examine it. She meant so little to him, he couldn't even be bothered to discuss it with me.

I didn't push him on the subject, and we sat there in silence for a while; Ava and Tabitha were still at the table talking.

'They seem good, don't they?' I said to Samuel.

'Yes. Good,' he nodded.

'And you. You're good?'

He wasn't looking at me much. His eyes kept jumping back to Tabitha at the table, and to his phone as well. 'I'm fine. With Imogen and me, we've all been friends for so long. It's just not as plain sailing as it could be at the moment.'

'Oh. Right.' I was surprised, but I tried not to show it. 'Anything you want to share?' I asked.

'Honestly, it's . . . fine. There are issues that have popped up. I think it's what you have to expect when you're doing hard things.'

I nodded soothingly, hoping he'd reveal a bit more. If there was one part I excelled at, it was the empathetic listener.

'I didn't think so much about what would happen . . . afterwards,' he said finally. His words had been chosen with much caution.

'Afterwards?' I asked.

'Yes,' he said quietly. He was watching Ava and Tabitha, who were coiled into each other at the table, the debris of the meal and so many glasses piled around them. Ava's murmur was so soft that you could barely hear her, and Tabitha's laugh loud and harsh, especially in our private room.

'Anyway, I'm probably just knackered from Perfect Pieces. Fucking exhausting, to be honest.' He threw back his water, grimacing as if the glass was filled with whisky.

Tabitha peered over at us. 'I hope that's not booze, Samuel,' she cried out.

I'd never heard her reference his drinking in public before, and he turned white as a sheet, presumably at the betrayal. Tabitha picking up his past like a rock and throwing it at him like that with abandon. He composed himself, ignored her, and she turned back to her conversation.

'I owe her a lot. Owing people something's the worst,' he said to me quietly as a means of explanation.

'I'm sure you can sort it out with her – it is Tabitha, after all!' I said. I couldn't help but jump to her defence, jump to fuse us back together as a group.

He looked at me very levelly, like he was assessing his options, then in a flash he was up, and he left without even a goodbye to the other two.

I went back to the table where Tabitha and Ava were sitting. Tabitha didn't seem to care at all that he'd gone.

'Clare,' she called out, 'you should have seen Ava when we were at school. She was nothing like she is now. Now, she's a goddess.' And for some reason, this was very funny to Tabitha and her laughter was infectious, and Ava seemed so happy. I think that was one of the only times I saw, without distraction, the joy that existed sometimes between them, which they seemed to extract from each other, and I don't think I was even particularly jealous, because they weren't shutting me out. The Shiver, or at least what was left of them, were generous with me that night.

I don't remember exactly what we talked about, but there were so many stories. Tabitha told us them, ones we'd heard before mixed with new tales, and I listened. She talked about the gymkhana where she'd nearly fallen off – *imagine me on a pony!* – and the prom night when she'd lost her virginity – *so disappointing it's hardly even worth bringing up* – and the stories came to life when I thought back to the photos I'd seen of her that night: the chunky little pony, the frothy prom-night ball gown.

I made the conscious decision to hold back.

Don't be wild.

Don't be loud.

Don't be too much.

No one likes that. It can scare them.

We sat there, empty plates around us and our glasses drained. Shiny wrappers from our fortune cookies glittered on the table like jagged pools. Tabitha put one hand on mine and one on Ava's.

I could tell the evening was on a knife edge where the whole thing could die down and fade out; we could all go home and go to bed, or it could keep going, getting bigger and wilder, and I wasn't surprised when she said it.

'There's somewhere we should go tonight,' Tabitha announced.

'Where?' I asked.

'I have tickets for a ceilidh.'

'A ceilidh?' I vaguely knew what this was from hearing about a reeling society.

'You know. Scottish dancing,' she said. 'It will be good practice for the next job, I think.' She handed me a ticket with a flourish. An old-fashioned ticket with the perforated line to rip down the side.

'I'm not sure I'm dressed for it?' I gestured to my clothes, which were nothing like what Tabitha and Ava were wearing. I wasn't sure what they were wearing was suitable either. Ava was striking in a black satin dress nipped at the waist with rusted silver chains.

'It will be fine.' Tabitha's eternal closing remark, because, in her world, it always would be.

44.

The hall was bigger even than our lecture theatres, and it struck me that we were doing what other people did while we were usually sat plotting in the flat. Going to a ceilidh was how you celebrated things like Christmas, if you were rich and you liked colour and light and music and everything that makes the world feel like there is no darkness. The venue was an explosion of green and red; garlands, tinsel and foliage without restraint.

As soon as we entered, we were in a mass of people and chatter, and it was almost too much to take in. There was a real reindeer looking slightly sweaty, eyes darting nervously as it stood, confined to a fenced-off Winter Wonderland on stage.

There was a miniature ice rink to one side and a huge bar lined with tiny Christmas trees, so the bartenders had to peer through the pine needles to serve the attendees.

I asked Ava how much the tickets had been.

'Expensive. She must have got them for free from someone,' Ava replied a little dreamily, staring at the reindeer. 'I bet they brought it down from the Cairngorms. I wonder if we'll get to stroke him?'

I looked out of place in a simple pair of trousers and a plain shirt, whereas the crowd around us wore kilts and full-skirted dresses. I hadn't expected the night to be so extravagant, but there was no time to dwell on that because the floor cleared and there was an expectant pause before the next song began.

'"The Dashing White Sergeant",' boomed a man standing at the front.

The lady next to me was kind. 'You look lost, come on!' She

pulled me into a group, and then I was in a circle – a tight band of six of us.

Everyone was smiling and laughing. I stood there awkwardly. It was odd; I couldn't believe people danced like this for fun. My discomfort must have shown because the man to the right of me, who held my hand, gave me an encouraging smile and I smiled back. He was in a full kilt and sporran. 'Don't worry, I'll keep you right,' he said.

'Eight steps round and back,' came the instruction from the man at the front (who I now know is the caller), which meant nothing to me, but our little circle spun slowly and I saw the other dancers in our group.

I saw him.

His expression morphed. It went from a kind of friendly recognition to shock, and all the colour drained away in his face. Of course, I recognized him too, it had only been a few months.

Tom Landore, looking well dressed. Maybe a little gaunter than before – I saw that when I got closer.

He was about to say something to me but I whipped away from him, from the whole circle, and he didn't try to stop me in the chaos of that night, a chaos that I hardly noticed until I felt the judgement of his gaze.

The violins screeched. Tens of circles of dancers in a haze of tartan. It looked perfectly structured but, as I was weaving through them, their faces were bright and too wide. It was impossible not to picture them all careening into each other.

I ran from him.

And then Ava and Tabitha were at my side, steering me outside.

The whole thing was all too much. When the cold air hit my face the duck rose up, sweet and rich, the kaleidoscope of colours and the sugary coating on the meat. I was sick on the pavement. No time to get to a bin.

I was purged. The nausea was gone, and Tabitha had her arm around my shoulders.

'Are you OK?' she asked me, concerned.

I went to speak, to mention Tom Landore, but she interrupted. 'You seem better now, probably just that food. It was so rich. That was boring,' she added. 'I have another idea.'

No mention of him.

We must have walked for a mile or so, down busy streets. Tabitha led us to somewhere I'd mentioned before to her, somewhere I liked, and I was touched that she'd remembered.

The graveyard – Greyfriars Kirkyard.

I enjoyed the cemeteries of Edinburgh in general back then. Quiet and well kept. Graves dotted around like observers, just about visible in the dark.

Tabitha begged us to go into the mausoleum, but Ava and I declined.

'I can see why you like it here,' Tabitha said to me. She handed me a hip flask and we stopped for a moment, in the middle where the path wound and all you could see in front, behind and either side were neat lines of gravestones. I could still hear the faint murmur of traffic from the city.

The moon that night was round and bright, and the smell of dirt was a bit stronger than I would have expected, like a freshly dug grave, even though I didn't really think people were buried there any more. The ceilidh was almost forgotten and the Chinese meal seemed like days ago.

I took a sip of Tabitha's whisky; it tasted like barbecued disinfectant, and it made my head spin. I probably didn't need anything more to drink; I was already drunk by then, which wasn't like me.

The two of them stood there, their shadows cast on the path in front of them. Ava was a sharp silhouette, looming.

'I think I should take a picture of you,' I said to them.

'Do you?' said Tabitha.

'You look like witches,' I said.

Tabitha squealed. Of course, it was the best thing I could have said. She came over and grabbed my hand. 'Oh, I fucking *adore* it. Ava and I are ever so wicked,' she sang. 'If we're witches, of course, there are three of us.' She pulled me into a circle.

'Three witches,' I repeated.

'And poor Imogen is our pussycat,' she squawked, her hands on her knees now, laughing at herself. If anyone had seen us, we would have looked mad, or at least disrespectful, because she grabbed us both again and we spun in the graveyard, dancing with the tombstones set around us – a captive, coffined audience.

'This is our night,' Tabitha crowed. 'I can feel it. Can you? What am I, Clare, say it again!'

I could feel something and maybe that's why it happened.

I'm not sure what it was, but I couldn't bring to mind the English word. Even though I'd just said it, something in my brain wouldn't click. It had never happened before that I could remember, and I don't think it's occurred since. The word in English just wouldn't come to me. A block – completely irretrievable.

I said it before I could even properly think it through: '*Une sorcière.*'

Tabitha looked at me curiously.

'I think I heard something,' Ava announced abruptly. 'We should leave, there are wardens around here.'

In my head I thanked Ava for saving me in that moment, shot her a grateful look. Our shared agreement that we didn't talk about my past – they kept my secret for me because they were my friends.

45.

That was the first and only time I ever went to a ceilidh. Now, years later, my husband attends them regularly. Weddings in particular tend to feature them in Scotland.

I choose not to go.

The whole thing felt quite ridiculous at the time: the formality, the sense of misplaced ceremony in a made-up dance, the violence of being flung into the arms of various strangers against the backdrop of awful string music – all in the name of fun. It has only become more repellent to me with age.

I've often thought of that night in the years that have passed. I'd always been so scared that one of the men would see us later, but when it actually happened, it hadn't been too terrible, apart from being sick of course, which nobody saw anyway. It was easy to slip away and pretend it had never happened. I was proud of myself at the time for reacting so well.

I remember Tom Landore's expression. That look of complete disbelief as he saw me and then something else that I didn't think to question.

I could have gone back in. Said something to him to find out exactly what that expression meant. Events could have all worked out differently if I had, and certain things could have been nipped in the bud right there. Then again, everything might have turned out exactly the same, because at that point I don't think anything would have stopped me going to the Highlands.

46.

We set off a few days later. I always used to classify the countryside as one place. The Dales or the Moors, it was all just 'not the city' – some combination of hills and fields that meant little to me. The countryside in England was highly controlled compared to France, where things grew wild in the sun. When I'd stayed with my granny, on the way to her house it was all carefully mown fields that framed the side of the train tracks. A meadow with a pond or a hill with a winding footpath. Everything felt staged, like if you touched it you'd realize it was a painted scene.

Scotland, and this trip in particular, showed me a new kind of geography. The land up close had a sharpness to it, as if someone had taken one of those undulating hills and torn chunks from it, bitten off sections hungrily, stripped it to the bone to reveal craggy rocks and water and marshland. The peaks stretched up away from the road, like we were buried deep in the valleys. I remember the views of a loch that went on for as far as the eye could see, and huge birds soaring over us. Pine trees in the air; the smell of bonfires too, which always reminded me of sitting on Tabitha's roof.

Soon there were no other cars around at all, and Samuel accelerated with glee.

There was none of the dread I'd felt when we'd gone to Minta's house – the only other real group excursion we'd done – but the mood in the car was subdued.

'You know I saw Tom Landore, don't you?' I said after we'd been silent for a long time. I hadn't wanted to make a big thing of it, after all, and despite the fact I thought I'd handled the moment well enough, I also knew I needed to raise what had happened.

Pressed close to me, Tabitha's leg tensed.

'Yes, we saw him too – he was at the ceilidh, wasn't he? You didn't speak to him, did you?' she asked mildly.

'No, I left with you both.'

She knew that, surely.

'Oh, that's good. Best not to talk to anyone when it's all over.' She continued to murmur 'good' to herself, and I saw Samuel try to catch her eye then give up.

Ava was sitting in the front seat, her hair swept up. Straight-backed and giving nothing away. Samuel seemed about to say something, but he didn't manage to quite get the words out, he just swallowed, and the drive continued in a silence that I wrote off as tiredness. We had all been working hard – it was no wonder we were a little fractious.

Eventually, we pulled up to a small coach house set to the side of the road next to large gates. Tabitha perked up and started fidgeting. She'd been staring listlessly out of the window at the scenery up until now, but she came to life when she saw a man come out of the building to greet us.

He asked for our names. We gave them to him – fake, forgettable – and he went back into his little house and pressed something, concealed to his side under a desk, at which point the gates crept open automatically. Amazing how they could be unlocked by the most tentative of family connections. An estate squirrelled away with gates and codes and staff. All you needed was to know the right person, for someone to vouch you were good for it, and the world opened right up. You could take it all, as much as you wanted.

We continued our drive slowly across uneven gravel on a driveway that swept in a gentle curve towards the main house. I heard Tabitha's sharp intake of breath as she took in the views. She grinned conspiratorially at me. I knew she was excited – so was I.

Various expensive-looking cars were peppered untidily across the drive. Whoever was inside, it appeared they'd abandoned them, or valet parking hadn't materialized. One was bright red but the rest looked faded in muted colours – mustards and greens and pale greys: vintage cars. The grounds were clearly expansive, acres and acres of land. Up close, the house was breathtaking, all sombre white stone and rows and rows of little windows. There were turrets and spires that had been tampered with over the years, a hodge-podge of styles added haphazardly. Grand and chaotic.

Samuel pulled up and jumped out to retrieve our bags for us from the boot.

'Are you really going straight back?' I asked. He planned to drive back to Edinburgh and pick us up in a few days' time.

'Things to do, people to see,' he said, handing me my bag.

As he drove away, a group of men emerged from the woods.

47.

My breathing quickened in anticipation as they trudged towards us in a cloud of camouflage. There must have been about ten of them – a hunting party. It was a quick march and they seemed unsurprised to see us. I found it hard to make out their faces, which were obscured by hats and beards, but I could certainly see the long, tan gun cases slung over their shoulders.

As they came closer, they surveyed us in silence, and Tabitha stared back, fascinated by them.

Two groups. Them and us. We were far smaller though, just the three of us.

They were still a fair distance away from us and they watched on for a few more moments.

One of the men waved at us, and then the others followed. I peered at them, trying to work them out. Was The Pig in there? Surely he was? I couldn't decide which one he was, though.

Then, just like that, they swerved and walked past us, round to the back of the house. I thought for a second that Tabitha might follow them, but she didn't. She exhaled loudly and buzzed the doorbell long and hard.

A girl peeked out from the window, the curtains open only a fraction. She seemed to be waiting until she was sure that the men had left. A few more moments passed before she finally opened the door.

She was small and a similar age to us, maybe twenty or a little older. Her face was framed by a boyish crop; colourless lashes made her watery eyes look even paler. It must have seemed odd when we showed up – I was concerned that she may have thought we were wearing fancy-dress costumes because we'd gone overboard with tweed and leather and tartan. I wondered how much she knew about what we were planning to do.

'Hello, I'm Sorcha,' she said, shifting her weight from one leg to the other.

A man emerged from behind her and she introduced him to us as her father; he shook each of our hands warmly. He was older than I would have expected when I saw him close up, and his skin was papery to the touch. The unconcealed delight as he greeted us made me think that we might have been the first friends Sorcha had invited to the house.

I noticed how she hovered around us more than him. It was as if she wanted to be in the group, maybe using us as much as we were using her, because basking in Tabitha's glow was a lovely thing.

'Looks like everyone is just getting back from the hunt,' the man said. 'Sorcha, you should ask Martha to pull together some tea for the girls.'

'Yes. Tea,' she replied shakily. She seemed . . . nervous.

Was she scared of us, I wondered? Perhaps.

We couldn't really refuse tea, and without even glancing towards Ava or me, Tabitha nodded on behalf of the group.

Dragging her feet a little, Sorcha took us into a room that felt miles away, down a long corridor to the back of the house where there was a small, cheap-looking metal table and a clutter of chairs. We found ourselves crammed in tight as it was full of plants – hundreds of them.

I suspected that the initial idea had been to create a lush tropical paradise, but it was far from that. It smelt of dry dirt and something possibly faecal. The plants were dying or dead; they all looked brownish or yellow, and their leaves had crisped and hardened. Towering stalks blocked the glass of the windows, which were crusted with dirt. At one point this would have been a beautiful room, though, you could tell.

'It's an orangery,' Sorcha said tonelessly.

'How nice!' said Tabitha with an admirable enthusiasm that I knew I'd struggle to match if she expected me to speak.

'My father likes to keep it like this,' Sorcha replied. I guess as a means to justify how depressing it was.

There was something small and scrappy running under the fronds of a desiccated fern; I could hear manic scuttling and I braced myself, then a small dog emerged, hoisting itself on to its hind legs with a loud grunt.

No, not a dog – a monkey in what looked like a nappy.

We all stared at the monkey, and it looked at us, aghast, with squinted eyes, scratching its head where great tufts of fur were missing and the skin was pink and scabby. Then it bared its pointy little teeth and hissed. When we didn't respond, it ran back under a plant.

I could hear it slurping on something.

'A monkey,' Tabitha declared loudly, with zero judgement.

'My father likes to keep him here. It's very old-fashioned, I know, to keep a monkey. Don't go near him,' Sorcha said.

Ava and I exchanged a look. There was no chance at all of me going anywhere near the monkey.

Before we sat down, Tabitha embraced Sorcha in a hug for some reason, and the embrace looked very tight.

'Thank you so much for having us,' Tabitha said.

Sorcha extricated herself from the hug, her face red, and she shuffled back looking shell-shocked. 'That's OK,' she said.

'We're so excited to learn to shoot tomorrow, if you'll take us,' Tabitha said. 'Honestly, it's something we've wanted to do, well, forever really, so it means the world to us, you letting us come and learn, and in this truly *stunning* home. Do you live here all the time or are you just visiting? Are you studying nearby?'

Sorcha sat down. We all did. She looked taken aback at the onslaught, and I felt for her. Tabitha had a tendency to purposely pile on questions when she met strangers, so they found themselves twisted up in her interrogation.

'Just visiting from St Andrews for Christmas.' Sorcha smiled wanly.

Ava gave Sorcha a look of solidarity that said, *I know, I think this is as odd as you think it is.* I remembered how Ava had calmed me at that first dinner party. She was good at it. Sorcha seemed reassured.

Limp clouds hung over the orangery outside. The same silver skies that I was used to in Edinburgh.

'The plants don't last long here,' Sorcha said.

I wondered why you would have all these plants and then let them wilt away through lack of care, but I didn't ask.

'They just die and no one really knows why,' she continued, staring out over them into the distance.

For some reason, her explanation made sense to me. The rules of normal life didn't seem to apply.

48.

Finally, after drinking our cups of weak tea, we were allowed out of the orangery and Sorcha took us upstairs to our rooms so we could get ready for the evening. On the first floor, there was a line of doors, like a hotel corridor. The house must have had at least a dozen bedrooms based on how big the place looked from the front. I was a little surprised as I'd assumed we'd be sharing, put up on a sofa or an airbed.

We went to my room last, which was traditionally styled with a single bed and heavy wooden furniture. I put my bag down on the bed and rifled through to see what I'd change into. Tabitha disappeared, leaving Ava and me alone.

Ava hung about, unwilling to leave.

'That was weird, right?' she said. I wondered if she was talking about the interaction with the group of men, or the monkey. I decided on the latter.

'That monkey . . .' I said.

She grimaced and nodded in agreement. 'Are you sure you're ready for this?' she asked me, her voice only slightly less level than usual.

'I'm fine. I mean, Sorcha seems a bit odd. And this whole thing, it's much more than what we were doing before, more involved. But I still feel fine so far.'

'If I can be honest with you, I'm looking forward to this weekend being over,' she said, sighing.

I held up a red dress to the mirror, one of a few outfits I'd brought along. It was too much against my skin in the light. I'd opt for something darker, maybe.

'Hopefully Tabitha doesn't go wild like she did before,'

I said. Hardly even thinking before the words came out. I hadn't meant to bring it up.

'What do you mean?' Ava asked sharply.

'Tabitha. She threw fake acid in a man's face on one of the other jobs we did.'

For a second, I thought she might be surprised, but she wasn't at all – of course she wasn't, there was nothing Ava didn't know. However, she did look slightly pained. She shrugged, and I guessed Tabitha had spun the story in her favour.

Tabitha had probably made it all sound like *such fun*.

'Yes, I did know about that,' Ava said. 'Remember, it wasn't acid, though, was it? It wasn't that different to what you did.'

'What do you mean?'

'Périgueux.'

I felt my jaw clench. The way she said it annoyed me. Like it belonged to her too. Perhaps the two things were similar, but that wasn't a good thing. I shook my head. 'It was risky. She's mixing in some kind of desire for justice,' I said.

A crease in Ava's brow. I knew she was thinking about how best to manage me.

'You're right,' she agreed. 'I wasn't too happy about it either. It was too far, probably. She didn't need to do it. I'll have a word with her. It won't happen again, but don't get *upset* over it. His wife was happy. He was fine – it was all . . . fine.'

'I'm not upset. It was just unexpected.'

It had been, and the more I'd thought about it, the more it seemed like Tabitha had taken me along with her because I was more disposable than the rest of them.

The whole conversation was feeling off. I'd expected us to be excited, to be ready to go and take on whatever the evening threw at us, but Ava was anxious, and I wanted to reassure her, which was a complete role reversal.

'We'll be fine this weekend too,' I said. 'It'll fly by – I'm sure of it.'

'Just be careful?' she said, as a question.

She seemed to be giving me an opt-out, waiting for me to say something, but what could I possibly say? She turned and stared out of the window.

It was so very dark out there. Nothing around us for miles.

49.

The ballroom was a dim and cavernous space, and Ava and Tabitha split away from me straight away without explaining why, leaving me to absorb it all on my own.

There was a parquet floor warped with age. The walls were papered in red to suck out what little light there was, and it made you focus on the paintings with their thick, highly decorated frames. I took the time to steady myself and look at them, walking around the perimeter of the room. In the main, there was artwork that felt fitting – portraits of stern-faced mistresses and generals looking down on us haughtily, their names and dates engraved at the bottom – but there were also some large, modern abstracts that I recognized. A real Kandinsky, perhaps. A Picasso that looked to be genuine, although I knew you could get a Picasso sketch cheaply – it was something Tabitha talked about all the time.

Nerves steeled as I'd scoped the layout, I looked to the guests. There were various small groups of men and they were indistinguishable in similar types of suits. All the signifiers of wealth were there as expected, and I noticed the rings – heavy gold pinky rings, some with jewels. I'd always loved the term 'dripping with diamonds'. It was one of the first idioms I learned when I moved to England, and the phrase doesn't translate to French particularly nicely. In any case, this jewellery didn't drip, it was lodged in place firmly. Flesh and gold.

Staff circled with platters of canapés and topped up our glasses. I took a sagging square of something greasy, not even looking down to see what it was. The first bite delivered a hit of fat and some kind of rich meat, like foie gras. It didn't feel like a good sign, but I chose to push the thought to one side.

I sipped champagne to clear my mouth of the taste of the food, and I looked for them. I saw Ava steering Tabitha through the crowd as they moved from one group of men to another. I had a good view of the room, from the side, and the way they were behaving seemed . . . obvious. Body language that spoke of easy availability. Tabitha's voice rang clear as a bell above the background murmur – so confident and so sure that the whole world would want to hear what she had to say. She was right. The men were listening, taking in and assessing this precocious young woman.

I went over to them and met his eye as I approached – The Pig, finally. He was a big man, towering even above the three of us. I extended one hand directly to him and introduced myself with a name, one chosen by someone else.

So many names by then. Sometimes if someone called out 'Clare', I'd have to jolt myself to remember to reply. *Yes, I'm Clare.*

I was transported back to Périgueux immediately as I took in his body shape (round) and his face (red with veins broken in the cheeks). He looked like a man who ate and drank a lot. More of a boar than a pig. Thick bristles of black hair and greasy skin.

Honestly, although seeing him made me think of things I'd rather have forgotten, surprisingly, I felt . . . good, like everything had led me to this specific moment.

When our hands touched, power buzzed through my body like an electric shock.

'So, shooting tomorrow, friends of Sorcha?' he said, letting the words run long and comfortable. He had the room's attention, there was no need to rush. It seemed that even Tabitha wasn't bursting for her turn to speak, and the group of men leaned in to hear what he had to say, nodding away, deferring to him.

'Yes,' I said, 'we're so excited.'

I was adept at speaking like this. Kind of breathy while I worked out a strategy.

He looked at me, faintly amused. 'Not squeamish at all?'

'Not at all. I think there's something right about knowing where your food comes from, killing it yourself.' A brilliant lie.

'Do you now?' He appraised me with new interest, for just a second, then he turned away and started speaking to a man who straddled the group on the periphery.

My face flushed with colour at the snub. A man who stood to my left took pity on me, picking up the conversation where it had faltered.

'And what did you say you were studying, dear?' he asked, keen to smooth over the moment and keep the group chatting, but I stuttered and excused myself.

I was embarrassed, far more than the situation warranted, and I gave myself a pinch on my arm, something to keep me focused. A hard pinch to stay on track.

Time to reassess. I'd drunk precisely two glasses of champagne with purpose – monitoring the pace so the flute wouldn't get filled up again. It had taken some time, but we never used alcohol as a crutch for confidence, none of us did. A few glasses maybe, nothing excessive, and especially in these situations, we watched what we drank with obsessive detail. I felt like I'd been drinking slowly. Usually, that amount wouldn't have affected me, but I was unsteady and I'd noticed the room getting hot. That deep red room, like peering down a throat.

We'd been in there for forty-five minutes or so (I had become very good at assessing time passed) and I wondered if I could get away with leaving for ten minutes, just to clear my head. I decided I could; I went out to the front of the house and stood there in the freezing cold in my sleeveless dress.

Going outside meant I could gather my thoughts.

I hadn't believed that anything much would happen with

Jack the Pig, that I'd manage to steal a kiss during the weekend. The whole thing was bordering on madness – we had barely forty-eight hours with him, so it would probably have relied on him getting completely drunk. Plus, there were far too many other people there.

In the past, the men had taken either weeks of sustained attempts or else the setting had been . . . right. One that we'd had complete control over. At that moment, we had no control over any of it.

It was very cold. Then I felt that there was someone behind me. I smelt it. Whoever it was, they were smoking a cigar.

Him. He didn't touch me.

'So, you care about where your food comes from?' he asked. I turned to meet his gaze, this man who apparently droned on about the benefits of a plant-based diet but saw no problem with hunting pheasants.

He was even more boar-like up that close.

Then, I didn't answer quickly enough because he was walking away. He called back to me over his shoulder: 'Follow me.' With complete confidence that I'd obey.

Back into the house, cigar still in hand, through the hall and then down, into a cellar, as if the whole chain of events was perfectly natural. I followed and my feet seemed to move of their own accord, down the steps, until the noise of the party above became a soft buzz.

At first, I couldn't quite see the contents of the cellar. There were these things, hanging up, and as my sight adjusted to the lack of light, I realized what they were. Pheasants – their eyes dead and their bodies dark. Their feathers were shiny with oil and they gave off a noticeable smell; it wasn't exactly unpleasant and it mixed with the other smells in the basement. Dampness and a waft of something that could have been chlorine.

He stood next to them. He didn't blink enough. That was disconcerting.

'They need at least twenty-four hours,' he said.

'Why?' I asked.

'Well, you need to let the rigor mortis set in. Then you need to leave them for long enough to get tender, but not so long that the maggots find them.'

I was envisaging a maggot worming through the feathers when he reached out.

It was hard to assess how close he was, but then his hands were on me before I could gauge where the rest of him was.

Instinctively, I moved back. My head hit the musty body of a pheasant and I jerked forwards, into him.

He caught me and pushed me past the pheasants, hard against the wall of the cellar; my back slammed against stone.

Searing pain in the form of a hard, quick punch to my stomach, and I was glued to the wall in agony.

His mouth was against my ear. 'This is what you want, isn't it.' It wasn't a question.

Then his hands were around my neck, squeezing until I was panting and pushing him away, but I couldn't, I was weakening and my face burned. Pressure all over my head. I started to lose vision as cloudiness began to creep in on either side.

His breath. Hot on the side of my neck as his face was pushed into me, like he was inhaling my skin. I could feel him drive the hardness of his crotch against me.

The thought passed through my head that this was a fitting end for me.

There had been *the episode* in Périgueux, and my death in the Highlands would be the same. Reported on, but the details glossed over and buried because they were so unpalatable.

Instead of tightening for a final squeeze, his hands loosened and I pulled away, coughing. I could see again; I could see behind him very faintly – there was someone standing on the stairs.

It was Sorcha.

The Pig pushed past me, walking away as if nothing had happened, straightening his tie around his neck, staggering but with a swagger, his face almost jubilant, as if he'd been caught but didn't really care. No proper acknowledgement of Sorcha, he just jabbed his shoulder against her, hard, as he moved past.

Once he'd left, she came forward, and she held me for a moment, supporting my body so I didn't fall, seemingly waiting until we heard his footsteps going back into the ballroom. How long had she been there, I wondered?

'Come with me,' she said.

Any shyness I'd seen in her had disappeared; instead, there was a strong sense of urgency. She took me upstairs, but not to my bedroom. We were in what might have been her room.

'They're all about to eat. You should stay here,' she said.

'I can't. I need to leave.'

'That's not a good idea,' she said calmly. 'Stay. Rest. I don't think you need to go to the hospital, but it's going to be visible.'

What on earth had happened to that girl, the one who'd greeted us? Who'd been so intimidated by us? We'd pitied her because she was so shyly accommodating, but I should have given her more credit – she had known what was coming. She hadn't known what we had planned, I don't think, but she certainly knew what happened in this terrible house. She hadn't been scared *of* us, she had been scared *for* us.

I wanted to ask her more about the men and what they did.

How did the parties usually play out?

How many times had this happened before?

But she was already gone, shutting the door behind her. I sensed her self-preservation as she placed distance between us. She was willing to help me as best she could without sacrificing herself, which seemed fair. I'd need to rescue myself, but I couldn't move, not yet.

The air was full of the fumes of meat that signalled dinner

was being served, and Ava and Tabitha wouldn't know where I was; they would be wondering what had happened to me. I lay and felt my breaths, tried to slow them and focus. There was a lot of pain.

I couldn't have said how much time passed. It was long enough that I must have fallen into a light sleep, and I woke up to something licking my hand gently.

That disgusting monkey with tiny fingers clutching my wrist to steady itself; my arm was clammy with its spit. I almost screamed out, almost thrust the tight little body away from me so it would fly across the room. I managed to restrain myself. Instead, I got up and backed away from it and out of the room.

I couldn't hear as much from downstairs, but I knew that I needed to find them. I could vaguely assess where I was and, although I was shaky, I half ran along the corridor.

So many doors. I tried to recall which one was Tabitha's room. When I found it, I went straight in without knocking.

It was similar to mine: a simple single bed in the centre of the room. A fire at the side was lit.

The thicker covers had been tossed off into a pile on the floor, and there was a sheet twisted around the two of them.

Tabitha's head was flung back and her hair was spread about her, more mane-like than ever. Her mouth was open in a silent moan and, between her legs, her hands gripped on to Tabitha's thighs, was Ava. Tabitha's eyes opened to meet mine, but I could barely look past her body. Laid out in the light, she looked almost like one of Klimt's ornamental women, the warm glow of the room transforming her, and her skin seemed to move in quivering folds like a piece of satin. She became a writhing, gilded dress that night. A piece of art. Her face was flushed, but she didn't say anything. She gave me what I thought was a lazy smile. But it might not even have been for me.

Ava didn't turn at all. Tabitha closed her eyes again, and I backed out of the room, pulling the door shut.

The house hadn't settled for the night. I could hear the faint buzz of people moving around, the intermittent crack of a frame broken in a game of snooker several floors down, which felt like another world. It was like the parties my parents had held when I was very young. With so many guests, they went on late into the night, and the house never truly slept.

The logistics of what happened next are a blur. I know I got dressed and managed to book a taxi somehow. Then there are fragments that I can recall: harsh bluish light in the early morning; sitting at the end of the drive of that vast house where I waited and waited for the taxi, and then the driver's blank face when he saw the mess I was in. He just clarified where we were going, and I wondered if he'd done this journey before with someone like me. I wondered how many incidents like this had taken place in this very location. It was, of course, best for him not to ask any questions.

We stopped at a cashpoint when we reached central Edinburgh, and I walked back to the cab stiffly with a wad of notes to pay for the journey, my neck so painful that if I moved even an inch it would snap and my untethered head might float away like some monstrous helium balloon.

I got back to the flat and sat on my bed – all I could hear was a dull ringing sound, and it was like someone had poured a stream of boiling water down either side of my spine then thrown ice at me, a crushing state of hot and cold sweat. I couldn't stop shaking, and I remember focusing more than usual on the flat. The curtains were drawn, and the room was cold and grubbier than usual. The bedding was unwashed and balled up at the bottom of the bed where I'd flung it off at some point. My carefully arranged wardrobe that Imogen had helped me with had been abandoned, and there were clothes piled all over the floor, dirty and clean mixed together. I'd been so busy – so delighted with my control over everything – that I hadn't even noticed.

That was the end of it. The end of that perfect slice of life, of jumping higher and higher, achieving more and more. Of everything always working out because we were blessed.

Nothing would be the same after that night, however hard we tried to piece it all back together.

50.

A tall drink of water. Those are not my words. It's a phrase someone old, a relative of my husband's, once used about me behind my back. It was apparently a compliment. Now, people certainly remark how *composed* I seem, and this does not usually feel like praise.

I am capable, but also different, and I cannot be fixed by anyone or anything however hard they might try.

Behind closed doors, you see the cracks if you care to look. When I think about that night up in the Highlands, I remember the sense of everything that we'd worked so hard for gone in a flash, and it wasn't just the group that fractured after the attack – I broke too, not for the first time, and I've broken again and again since, in so many ways. Tiny fissures. A prized vase glued together then shattered once more. You can't believe how many times it can stand to be patched up. My sour contents all milky and spilling out, leaking and bubbling every time, then mended until I become presentable.

I can be violent with him sometimes, with my husband, in a way that is painful and secretive. Our bodies are hard and strangely solid against each other in a brutal clash like a fight which he enjoys. He would never say so, and he doesn't see the full extent of it, not really. If I am wild, then he is submissive to it all, to my bites, my scratches, to the way I pin him down.

I do not see myself as a *drink of water.* I am surrounded by fire, and the flames lick close to me over the years, hotter sometimes, dying down to embers at other times. Is it a good or a bad thing? It is welcome sometimes, but it can also be uncontrollable.

He is a man who looks crisp, always. He does not like to be dirty or unshaven. He does not like me to be dirty or unshaven either and, on the surface, I oblige. I am freshly folded – take me out and put me away.

Clean sheets on the bed, starched and white, the highest thread count, and then my limbs are hot and I burn and burn.

51.

Back to where it all began. Back to Périgueux.

My parents worked a lot when I was very young. That was how they met. Maybe it was love at first sight or maybe it wasn't like that at all, but I like to think it was. I felt sure that their eyes met in an overcrowded office. Seeing each other for the first time: her – impossibly beautiful in a sallow and interesting way, like a dying princess; him – working class, British, a bit of a lad perhaps, before he calmed down and mellowed out to suit her. He'd worked hard to get where he was, which was why the fall later was so difficult.

They met, and they chose Périgueux, with its winding streets and leafy squares. They bought a huge house, lived in the countryside and travelled far and wide for work. I know that.

Then I was born and it all started to go wrong. My mother stopped working because of her migraines. I could have been what was causing them; each time I came near, her hand would dart to her forehead as my father shook his head at me, batting me away.

When I played, I was rough 'like a boy', my mother would bemoan, but I was strategic in my attacks. When little girls fight there's a particular brand of planned cruelty. I waited and retreated, then I'd spring into action, go for a jab in the eyes. Boisterous and unsuited to the cool, quiet house my parents flitted in and out of. They would catch my eye as you would with a casual acquaintance in the street, as if they were scared of what I'd do if they turned from me, as if I'd hurt them. I can't remember ever actually doing anything too bad in those early years. But if you listened to their muddled accounts, I was terrible.

My granny never corroborated this. I remember her visiting, and her reaction: 'She's a child!' she said. 'Of course she's noisy.' She wasn't scared of me in the slightest; she'd just shout at me to shut up.

For that reason, it worked for me to spend most summers in Hull at my granny's house and I became a little more stable. Not happier, I don't think, it wasn't home. Things were easier, though. My English got better. *Caught between a rock and a hard place. I've put my foot in it.* Phrases where the intonation fell wrong at first.

Despite my granny's protestations, my parents were convinced something was wrong with me. I went to many doctors' offices in France. No clinical waiting rooms in a city hospital where they take your temperature and give you a proper diagnosis full of hyphens. No, they took me to the alternative kind of specialists, who held afternoon clinics in home offices at the bottom of their gardens. The specialists never diagnosed me with anything in particular: the consensus was that I was an ordinary child. But my parents thought differently.

The therapies were expensive and over time the money drained away, slowly at first, and I was too young to notice. Then my father lost his job. Just like that, the big house, the fancy cars, the tropical holidays, they were all gone.

We moved from the vast house to a tiny apartment where we were packed in tightly like sardines and all noise was an irritant to my mother. No new clothes, no things to hide the fact we were unhappy. Both of them found it difficult. My mother because she couldn't bear my closeness and my father because he couldn't bear her sadness, and her illness was *everywhere* – in the curtains that were always closed, in the air that smelt stale and old. Still, he loved her a lot, that was always clear.

Then there was the final attempt. A doctor who had trained

in Paris and was highly respected. He was a big advocate of seclusion therapy. The idea was that I'd be locked away on my own and it would help my emotional development for some reason. My parents took to the concept well, it was certainly convenient.

They locked me in my room. The room had very little in it. Nothing to do (so nothing to damage). At first, I remember being so angry with them, but screaming and shouting didn't work; it didn't make them unlock the door, so I started to plan different ways to punish them.

When I was allowed out, I'd always go back downstairs and watch them edge around me like I was about to explode. A week later I would slip a piece of glass into my mother's food. A long and slender shard, glistening in the sauce around her pasta. Not to hurt her, just so she had to fish it out. She would see something like that before she ate it, and she would know it was me. I would be sweetness and light, and then she'd come downstairs, hand pressed to her head with a cold compress, questioning me about a silk top slashed in half, the pieces laid out on her bed for her to see.

There was a theatre to it. A show.

I became used to letting the anger settle, to waiting it out and performing a kind of delayed justice.

When you're locked away like I was, you start to go mad, I think, but you also learn patience.

You think it's all your fault, and time passes too slowly and then too fast. It made me realize that I wasn't going to get what I needed from my parents.

I wanted friends.

52.

I met them at school.

School was a fresh start. I was smart – I had always been smart, started speaking early, learned to read young, good at languages.

The first few schools didn't work out, then I got into an exclusive school on a scholarship, located around the ruins of a Roman fortress, up in the hills where most students were boarders. That fresh feeling of September: new books, new uniform, new life. Not as fancy as Tabitha and The Shiver's school, but not far off.

Pulling up on that first day, I knew my mother had been in touch with the school in advance. I'd heard her on the phone, her words quick and shrill: 'I need to warn you, she can be difficult . . . She might not get on with the other pupils . . . She's had problems in the past.'

My mother was wrong. I don't remember it being hard at all. I was worried that I wouldn't be accepted but I was careful to sit back at first and work out a plan of how I'd behave. And I was selective too, of course. I couldn't be friends with just anyone, they needed to be special.

I didn't really think I had anything to offer, but when I met Dina and Adrienne, I made myself appealing for them – just the right blend of enthusiastic and admiring and fun. They welcomed me in, and they were exactly who I wanted to meet – carefree in a way only lovely little rich girls can be. I needed to find friends who were going to make me the best version of myself, and they already had that ease with each other that felt so natural. I slotted in.

Me. Dina. Adrienne. Those aren't their names any more. I have no idea what they're called now.

'Three is a good number,' Dina had said firmly.

And at the time I agreed. Now, I know threes can be tricky and sometimes it helps to diffuse the intensity with larger numbers, but for a while it really was good. We balanced each other out. Adrienne was so serious, she seemed anxious all the time, but she managed to hide it behind the most beautiful gravelly voice so that when she spoke you wanted to listen to her all day. You hoped she'd never stop talking no matter what it was about. Dina was smaller and more animated. She laughed a lot and did cartwheels, so her T-shirt rose over her head and she'd pull it down self-consciously.

Then there was me. I was different then. I was loud and I was prone to shout if I thought no one was listening to me. I had worked to make them like me, but I was still working on being calmer. That was going well up to a point. There were no vengeful acts. There was no need to plot and plan. But things changed over the year.

We were always looking for ways to relieve the boredom of being teenagers in the countryside. Hot days down by the lake where the light cast dancing shadows over the water. Drinking warm beer with *sirop* and smoking weed in the summer. Boredom, of course, and food.

Food was the catalyst. They talked about it all the time. I think it could have been something like an eating disorder perhaps, at least for Adrienne. Both of them had been vegetarian for a while, which back then meant they lived on cheese. Still, it just made them seem more exotic and exciting to me.

I loved rare steak on the bone; I still do to this day. Slithers of beef, fibrous between my teeth. When we were rich, we ate food like that at home all the time. But I was happy to pretend to be vegetarian around them.

Their enduring fixation was with foie gras, which made

sense because where we lived in France was infamous for the production of the stuff, and it was exported all over the world in old-fashioned bevelled glass jars, an illustration of a jolly-looking goose or a duck on the side. It was a practice both girls talked about constantly.

I considered it myself a fair bit – an entire industry based around the ability that some waterfowl have to expand their oesophagus. A food where sustained and methodical torture correlates to how delicious it tastes, and when you eat it, the fat sticks at the back of your mouth and it is glorious and disgusting at the same time. Their opinions were less lenient.

'It's unforgivable,' said Adrienne.

'So cruel,' Dina agreed, nodding.

Adrienne and Dina were very interested in a man we met down by the lake. His daughters were a few years younger than us, and he was known in the area – he was a foie gras producer, a wealthy one with farms across the region. Adrienne and Dina homed in on him because we were obsessed with having a cause. The cause could have been anything, I think, but foie gras production struck a particular note. He was a brilliantly vile target whose depraved acts mainly took place in our heads.

We dived deep into the world of foie gras production.

'What do you think he has for dinner?' Adrienne said. 'I bet he only eats foie gras. Gorges and stuffs it in his mouth on its own. Disgusting. Don't you think so?' she asked, because we were always seeking speedy validation from each other. That's the way we spoke, in a questioning circuit – *What do you think? No, what do you think?* – until we became far too wrapped up in our own uncertainty. That was how it always was until they stopped trusting me and consulting me on things.

I didn't reply, I just sucked on a strawberry. We were scavengers that year. Because we didn't board, we were regularly forgotten, living at the ragged edges of the school population, not accounted for by anyone, let alone our parents, piecing together meals where we could from old baguettes, scraping the remnants from a jar of jam. Eating with our fingers because we could and stealing beer and wine because we wanted to. Opening it too fast, so it fizzed over on to our palms.

I finished my strawberry, popped in two pieces of gum at once.

'Don't you think?' she said again. Adrienne's voice was low and persistent.

At that point I felt sure they were beginning to distance themselves from me a little. I was too intense. They were leaving me out sometimes, which I hated. But I tried to ignore the sharp bolt of pain of being excluded. I didn't push it as that would make things worse.

I think that was why I said it. To win them back.

'There are things we could do,' I said. An impulsive comment. I hadn't thought anything through. I blew a final bubble with my gum, then took it out and stuck it underneath the picnic bench.

I remember the way they waited expectantly while I secured the gum, taking my time because I had their full attention. They looked intrigued. It was the first time I'd been the centre of our threesome and in charge. I swelled in their gaze.

'We could make him pay for it,' I said.

'What do you mean?' Dina asked.

'Imagine if we could do something to scare him,' I said.

'Scare him?'

'Yes. Something exciting.'

I explained my idea, which wasn't fully formed. We could do something to shock him.

Dina squealed with laughter. Adrienne smiled. We all dwelled on our shared hatred, a perfect three again. Luxuriated in the discussion as we thought about the things he did when he was alone.

He was all we talked about.

For a while, it was fine to plan, and they both seemed into the idea, until gradually the full horror of what I had in mind dawned on them. We discussed buying the food and I described how we'd force-feed him. The whole thing became something very elaborate, almost ceremonial.

They were nervous. I went the other way; I was excited by the detail. And then, the more excited I became by it, the more they pulled back from me. It would have been subtle to an observer, but I knew them well. Recognized the furtive look from one to the other and the edging away from me at lunch. 'Ties! Are you sure?' or 'Won't that hurt him?' But although they were scared, I knew they were also intrigued.

It had been my idea that we would have the tube they used to feed the ducks and geese, a nod to the process of *gavage* – to show him why we were doing it. That wasn't so difficult to find in the end. He would be confused and scared when he saw it. Looking back, it seems like a particularly odd touch, and even thinking about it now, the effort we went to was excessive, but we wanted to scare him, to make him see the sense of theatre.

Then things started to fall apart. Dina and Adrienne weren't sure about any of it. They weren't sure if it was a good idea to go through with our plan, and I worried that they weren't sure about me either.

What you must understand is that, despite how it ended up, it was their issues with foie gras that started it all, not me. That part was all them, and I did it for them and because of them.

53.

My family weren't rich; they had been once, but the memories of when we had money are frustratingly insubstantial. When I try to grasp them, they fade away. Wispy fragments of slight pinks and sunny yellows – the colour of a straw hat on holiday or the pressed linen of a restaurant napkin with iron marks when you unfold it. I'm not sure they are true or if they've become stuck in my mind from somewhere else.

Clearer is the memory of my mother in a squalid little room with her hand to her forehead. Her complaints were vast, but many of them revolved round her claims of mould, in the air, on the walls, and she had me searching for the shifting substance – the presumed root of her physical maladies – while she rested close by.

The insects buzzing around her, I remember those, and they came closer than you would expect, sat on her for longer, because she lay there so still.

By the time I was sixteen, there was no more seclusion therapy, technically, but when I wasn't at school it had become normal for me to be locked in my room. I'd become used to it there. Sometimes I hated it and sometimes I craved it. It forced me to practise conversations, and then when I went to speak, my words were forced and unnatural.

Things weren't working any more with Dina and Adrienne. One day, outside school, feeling hot and tired, I told a complicated, repetitive story because I craved their attention.

My voice was too loud and the story was too long. The words kept falling on top of each other. My movements were getting bigger, my hand gestures more extreme, as the two of them stood there listening to me. I remember Dina looked to Adrienne, and Adrienne rolled her eyes. A small movement, but I still saw and felt chastised. I wanted to get my point across.

I was so *angry* that they were laughing at me. I leaned over, physically towering over them, trying to make them stay so I could finish my story. Still, at the same time, there was that thick choking wave of embarrassment.

I wished I could stop speaking; I wished I'd never started it. I could imagine what they were thinking: *We thought three would work, but it hasn't, not really – how do we get rid of her?*

My father was picking me up from school that day – a rare occurrence. He arrived in what he called his old banger; it wasn't as fancy as any of the other parents' cars. He watched the exchange and beeped the horn – a sign for me to get in. For a minute, I was grateful to him for saving me from the end of my story, and not embarrassed like I'd usually be; I stopped speaking and slid into the back seat.

He stared straight ahead. 'Those friends of yours. Be careful,' he said, pulling away. He spoke to me in English, as always.

'Why be careful?' I asked, anxious disdain dripping from the words. I was calmer already, sitting in the car away from them.

'They're scared of you,' he said, quite simply.

We arrived back at the apartment.

'Your mother has a migraine so it's best not to bother her,' he said.

My father still lowered his voice like he did when we'd lived in our old house, where we'd led a muted existence, the rooms stuffed to the brim with soft furnishings: thick carpets and heavy curtains. I strained to hear him – I was always asking my father to repeat himself.

I ignored his instruction and went to her room. There she was, laid out on her bed as if she'd melted into the sheets. Blinds shut. Everything was dusty.

I didn't tell her about the plan. I just told her about how I felt. That my friends didn't like me any more, that they glanced at each other when I spoke, thinking I was too much. Leaving me out.

She pulled the towel from her eyes and looked at me.

'That's a shame,' she said. She placed the towel back.

I expected her to say something more. She didn't, though. She lay with her palm pressed to her forehead. A low, dull sound came out through her teeth, almost a hiss. I knew that she did this to distract herself from the pain in her head.

'Sit here,' she said, pointing to the chair next to her. We didn't often sit together in her room, but I obliged and sat down.

'You know, it doesn't need to be like this,' she said.

I leaned in closer because this was unusual. My mother didn't impart knowledge or wisdom to me often. *'Tu as tes règles?'* she'd asked me, quite matter-of-factly, when I first saw that reddish stain of blood in my knickers, but she didn't offer any other advice.

I waited for her to continue, and she did, towel on her face so I couldn't make out her expression.

'You're far too invested in them,' she said. 'You'll see when you get older. You'll have friends for different purposes in life. Some friends make you laugh, and then there are friends who help you climb to get to where you want to be, friends from work too. Friends of your husband and friends you play tennis with. So many friends. This attachment to these girls, it won't always be like this, I promise. It won't always feel like everything.'

'I don't know how not to care,' I said.

'I know,' she sighed. 'You just need to try harder. This is far too much.'

She meant I was too much, so I sat and tried not to make a noise while she rested.

Before Adrienne and Dina, while my mother was having

one of her migraines, I'd gone into the kitchen and taken each plate out of the cupboard, thrown every single one to the floor, watching them smash against the tiles and delighting in the sound they made, cutting through the silence in the apartment. It'd been a long time since I'd done something like that – that wouldn't be enough any more.

I knew that what we had planned would make them notice me. Punish them for the whispers. Punish him too. Impress everyone.

I was excited. Attention all on me as I executed the plan for us. All of it was for them.

54.

The first part was the drugs.

My mother was like Minta. When I was younger, she had a whole range of potions crammed on the bathroom shelves. Included in the mix of the hard medicinal and the shiny supplements, there was an anxiety medication. A jar of pills sat amongst the usual detritus of cotton buds and old creams.

A day or so before *the episode*, I took the anxiety pills from the bathroom at home. Dina had advised that we would just need two or three; she had questioned why we even needed to drug him at all when we were only meaning to scare him.

I counted eight.

Eight round white tablets.

So big I couldn't believe anyone could swallow them whole, and I thought I might grind them into a powder and mix them into a glass of water.

'Are you sure?' Dina exclaimed when I told her what we were going to do. Eyes wide, expression fearful.

She wasn't with me any more, but I had a plan.

PART 3

55.

I would never have said so. I didn't even like to think about it, but I couldn't help but wonder if I had deserved what had happened in the cellar. As night became day after the attack, it was hard not to think that it was all my fault. What he did to me. We'd set it up in that way, hadn't we? We'd asked for it? *I'd* asked for it?

Maybe this was my punishment. And it would be an appropriate one. Those jilting, half-formed thoughts, all the *ifs* and *whys* and *buts*, crowded my head like crows circling.

The next day I wrapped a scarf tight around my neck. I felt as stiff as a board that morning, a croaking invalid. I avoided questions from Ashley and Georgia, who tiptoed around me. Shot them a look they knew well, a look that said *don't ask*.

Then The Shiver turned up without even letting me know in advance. All four of them. They filed in, a line of them like they were on a school trip, and I could see immediately how wary they were, painfully bright and cheerful all of them, tiptoeing around me as if I might bite.

Tabitha reacted to my cheap things exactly how I'd expected her to. 'Oh, this is just lovely, Clare!' she said with deep sincerity about a chipped yellow mug I'd bought from a pound shop, as she held it up and pretended to take a sip from it.

I was seething under it all. Just about managing not to shout at them. So angry at Ava and Tabitha, who hadn't bothered to follow me – they'd let me be all alone that night.

I pulled away my scarf slowly, delighting in the act of it. A show. It was always a show with them.

My neck was sore, and I could still feel the hands wrapped

around it. Overnight, the bruises had blossomed into a marbled purple, like leaking ink on water – the first colour of many before they faded away. Beautiful bruises that I wanted to show off because they were my evidence, and they all looked suitably shocked.

Tabitha cleared her throat and looked so sad, so very sympathetic. 'Oh, Clare. Darling, darling Clare. Whatever happened to you?'

'He attacked me,' I said, louder than I intended.

I pulled myself back in a little as I saw them all recoil.

Be quieter. Be meek.

Don't make a fuss because people don't like that. It makes them uncomfortable, and they squirm and look away, and it's your fault.

Don't try and be the centre of attention – the star – as that can only end badly. Try to blend in because that's what everyone wants.

Don't care so much what people think.

And most of all, above all else, don't be angry.

To my surprise, it was Imogen who seemed the most concerned, her forehead a knot, but not of irritation for a change, it was worry, I was sure of it, and her voice was shaky. 'That's so awful. Why don't you talk us through what happened? For Samuel and me, as we weren't there,' she asked carefully.

Samuel had barely said a word, he just stared at me. Then Tabitha jumped in before I could start. 'Yes, do take us through it all, Clare. You disappeared! It was unexpected.'

I took a deep breath. 'In the cellar, he led me down there, he did this to me before I could get away.'

They all looked horrified, and I thought of Ava and Tabitha wrapped between the sheets. Me standing away from them at the door, watching them.

'So, what happened?' Imogen asked.

'Tell us, Clare, we want to help you!' Tabitha said.

And despite everything, the feeling of having them all listening to me was so good. I couldn't help continuing. 'Once we got down there, he went for me; he tried to strangle me . . .'

'Strangle you!' Tabitha shrieked.

All of the rest of them were listening silently, but I knew they would take the lead from Tabitha when it came down to it.

I changed tack. I tried to speak calmly. 'There's no need for this at all. For you all to be here. I don't need to sit down and go through it all again. I just need to know how this happened. I thought we researched them? All of them? But this wasn't a one-off. Sorcha knew about that man; she knew he was violent.'

'What do you mean?' Ava interjected.

'It felt like a trap. He's a predator. Whatever we thought we were doing, he planned it.'

'A trap!' Tabitha said. 'No, no, nothing like that. Honestly, your neck! I feel *terrible* for you.'

Standing to one side of her, Imogen winced at my injuries.

Ava and Samuel were in the background, but they were more of a blur because I was wholly concentrated on Tabitha, her eyes so wide. Her hand had somehow managed to land on mine, consoling me, stroking my wrist.

I spoke before I'd properly considered my words: 'I can't do this again. I'm out.'

Tabitha pulled her hand back as if I'd electrocuted her, and even as the words left my mouth, I knew it was more complicated than just saying *that's it* and walking away.

What did I really think was going to happen? That I could stop what we were doing but still be friends with them?

Then Tabitha was begging me, jabbering away. 'No, no, Clare. You just *can't*! We're doing so well. I know what happened was awful, but you can rest, fully recover, then we'll get back to it? You do trust me, don't you? You've seen how much we can achieve, and we can't do any of it without you. You're vital to the whole thing. This – this just got . . . out of hand.'

A rush of words and excuses. A most un-Tabitha-like panic.

'I agree. I just think this is where it ends for me,' I said.

And the idea of what that end would be like solidified.

It was the first time I'd thought of a swift escape, of leaving them and starting somewhere new, and I let it sit there, not expanding upon it, but still allowing the thought to form for us all.

There was silence. You could almost see Tabitha working out where to go next, tactically.

'Give me a few days, Clare,' she said. 'I can make this right; I *know* I can.'

I should have said no, but seeing her there, the person I had thought I'd do anything for, hearing her make that promise, I can only say that it was impossible in that moment to pull away from her.

I said 'OK' in a quiet voice. Agreed, even though I didn't know what I was agreeing to. I had no idea what *making it right* meant. I thought sorting it out was about me – about looking after me.

'I want to know what's going on up there at that house, what Sorcha knew,' I said, trying to lay down my own terms, but she was hardly listening because they were all around me, reaching for me, and it was lovely, in that moment, having them all on my side. That could be enough to banish the dark thought crows.

Not since some of those early dinner parties, since France, had I enjoyed them as a tactile swarm. Imogen's arms on me, Samuel cuddling me too, their combined glow dousing me in something warm. Tabitha pressing her powdered cheek to mine and Ava's collarbone hard against my back. Us moving together as one beast. When I stepped back from them all, I couldn't work out Tabitha's face exactly, but she was happy, certainly, with a faint smile.

I think all I needed was for them to acknowledge what had happened to me. I got it in that moment, but then Tabitha looked past that, needed to do something else. Thought I wanted more.

'The things we do for our friends,' Tabitha said to no one in particular. 'We help them. We *have* to. Anyway, we'll tell Finn you're sick. You don't need to worry about anything. Come back and stay at ours for a few days.'

And, of course, as we left together, I realized how little we'd actually discussed of what would come next. Tabitha steering and shrieking and taking up so much room, as always, while the rest of them had stayed in the shadows.

56.

I slept in Imogen's bed – she'd been relegated to the drawing room.

There was a new addition: a huge print at the bottom of the bed, pinned up to the wall.

Caravaggio's Judith.

His version was unlike Klimt's. Imogen would have described it better, but to me, it was a measured kind of horror. Their expressions were realistic, but also too restrained. Holofernes's darkened eyes bulged a little as the blood spurted from his neck in an extremely tidy arc, and Judith was tentative as she guided the sword into the skin.

Tabitha and Ava were absent some days, and Imogen and Samuel weren't around. Later, when everything had come to an end, Ava assured me that there were no drugs involved during those days spent at Tabitha's flat. But why, then, did the rest of the week take on a euphoric blur of feverish sleep and hazy waking hours? Dreams of Judith with her sword, of Tabitha's hair plaited and wrapped around my neck in a flaxen rope, of ducks running about squawking in my face, and then their guts spilled and mixed with plucked feathers. Meaningful or meaningless images.

In England, they seemed very fond of Calpol – the silky sweetness of it coating my mouth as a child at my granny's – and I think of that taste when I remember those days in bed at Tabitha's.

It is no matter though, because despite how it sounds, they were not bad days.

In many ways they were some of the best.

When Tabitha was around it was as sweet as it had ever been, and she nursed me in a lair of screwed-up tissues, my legs wrapped in knotted sheets and my hair matted. Her T-shirt, which I wore for days, became rank with sweat. I lay there and let Tabitha and Ava bring me trays of plain biscuits and tea and bowls of watery soup, as if I was too ill to have any kind of real food. My mind emptied as Tabitha's long, cool fingers tucked me into bed. We didn't discuss anything much, but there was such joy in her curling up with me and pressing her body tight against mine until I fell asleep. She treated me like her favourite pet – all the attention from her that I could possibly want, I got.

When I told my husband that Tabitha was *like a mother*, it was those precious days that I was recalling. When I was cared for like I've never been cared for before or since, really.

After a few days I emerged, my bruises faded, my body feeling a little better. I needed to forget what had happened in the Highlands, and there was enough to distract me with a return to routine.

Tabitha had been excited to start sharing some of her plans about the Advocate – our newest target. She'd bought an expensive-looking barrister wig to 'get into character'. It was confusing to me why she'd need to, but I couldn't bring myself to ask much more.

When I finally left to go back to my flat, she presented me with a sprawling bunch of red roses and freesias. She said, 'I'll make it all better, I promise,' and what a treat it was to just . . . let her, without considering what that even meant.

In the days afterwards, my mobile rang late at night. So late it was almost morning, but I was awake anyway. The number was withheld. When it first buzzed against the table, I thought instinctively of my granny – some accident perhaps – and I jumped to answer it. The caller didn't speak. They just . . . waited, and I tried to somehow work out who it was from the soft breathing.

Perhaps it was Tabitha, or maybe Finn? The more I pulled away from him, the more he clung to me with his stories and mild concern. It didn't seem like the kind of thing either of them would do, though. A journalist then? Something to do with my past? But why would they stay silent?

Like a slap to the face, the sudden realization came that perhaps it was Sorcha trying to get through to me. Quiet Sorcha with the eyes like a winter's puddle, who knew more than we had thought.

I hung up.

They rang again. Then *they* hung up.

Then again, and I answered, and neither of us hung up, and I waited and waited for them to speak, but instead their breathing grew more and more rushed and throaty, and I could hear the forcible attempt to hold back a gush of tears.

'Who is it?' I asked, first in English, then eventually, reluctantly, in French; regardless, they didn't respond. Every night they called. And I listened.

A woman. I was sure of it, from the pitch of her moan as she started to say something, then pulled back.

Call after call, and I was so tired. The flowers from Tabitha withered straight away next to the window. The petals dried out, crisped up and fell on to the floor. I didn't bother to clean them up and I ended up standing on them, so they pressed into the rug in red little welts.

At first, the reason I didn't put my phone on silent or turn it off was completely irrational, but in my long list of people it could be, there was the secret thought that it might be my mother. Even though I hadn't heard from her for years, there was still a small chance. I knew it was unlikely. It would have been out of character for her to call like that.

And then, as the next few days passed, I didn't hang up because it became a comforting presence. I found it less threatening, and I listened. Just when I felt like the mystery caller was about to reveal themselves, they would suddenly put the phone down. Whoever was on the other end of the line sounded unbearably sad, and we lay there at night together, her crying and me listening. We shared her sadness between us.

Each night, when I drifted off between the calls, I began to dream in distorted Technicolor, like I was watching an old television with a broken aerial. I dreamed of us all. They were more alive than ever and conjoined in the most grotesque forms. Georgia and Ashley, their arms joined together gawkishly, Dina and Adrienne, frozen at the age of sixteen and fixed to each other at the cheeks with roughly sewn stitches. Tabitha and Ava were almost one person. Their shared spine twisted horribly into a ragged S. They danced around, and their movements were stilted, like puppets in a circus top.

The audience were hysterical with silent laughter, tears rolling down their cheeks.

Encore, they mouthed.

And the girls danced again, and again, and again.

57.

It was two days before Christmas, and I welcomed the cold. Hoped for snow on the streets so my boots could break through the white sheet of it and leave a trail of footprints. But there wasn't any proper snow outside, just slush churned by mess and movement in the city. Dirty slush that soaked through my shoes and stained the leather. The cold meant the rats moved inside. I heard them scurrying. Saw one chasing a cat.

Tabitha had told me I needed to come over to hers. Inside, she stood next to the Christmas tree. She looked like she might at any moment transform into an angel and her wings would rise and tear through the skin, puncturing her back and pushing up so she could take off, and I'm not sure why that thought came to me in a flash.

She displayed her wares proudly. Laid out to the side of the room, I saw a fussy spread, like a dolls' tea party. A vast feast lying there untouched. Cocktail sticks with sweet chunks of pineapple skewered next to greasy cubes of Cheddar.

She passed me a plate from the table, and I thought she was about to pick some pieces of food for me, like I was an invalid, but she didn't.

'I'm not hungry,' I said.

Her smile faltered only for a second. 'No problem! No worries at all!'

I was expecting the others to be there. To see Imogen scurrying around with napkins, laying them out for us, brandishing coasters, hissing at me to use one. To let my eyes wander and savour the slow dance of Ava as she stretched her spine out by folding it down vertebra by vertebra along the window seat.

But when I walked in, I knew it was not to be. I felt the silence in their absence. I was quite sure that it was just Tabitha and me.

'Thanks for coming round.' She beamed at me.

I was transported back to when I'd been summoned here for the haircut. It was the same sense of tingly anticipation that wasn't unpleasant.

We sat, and I saw there was something that wasn't usually there just to the side of the room. A television on one of those old-fashioned stands with wheels on.

I had no idea where it had come from. I had never seen Tabitha watch television before, or known her to show any interest.

'This is something for you,' Tabitha said.

'What is it?' I asked, excited that she'd done something for me, wondering what it could be.

'I "did" a present for you. And I hope that will mean you'll stay. Now I'll show you.'

A present.

Tabitha loved to dish out presents as a means of control; generally, she'd tease it out with more of a preamble, but then and there, she was brisk.

She handed me a small bowl of popcorn and pointed the remote at the screen.

It crackled to life.

The footage was rough, and I struggled to work it out, but the basics were clear enough. It must have been shot on a camcorder; the picture darted about like an amateur recording. The colours were strange, perhaps because of the lighting, although I could tell it was outside, and the scene opened on the back of a head and then panned away so you could see the road. Somewhere remote.

A car in the middle of the road, blocking it completely, and the back of the head was clearer as the person filming moved away. The head had long blonde hair in a French plait. I wore my hair like that quite a lot.

The person holding the camera moved back. Whoever was filming seemed to be stepping away so they were hidden.

And there was a pause.

Another car pulled up. A far fancier one, and they had to stop because the road was blocked by the first car. A man got out and my blood ran cold.

Jack the Pig got out of the car. He went up to the blonde head, to the girl, to Tabitha.

Her voice – you could just about hear it as she spoke.

I heard the breathy words 'broken down', but it was strange. When she spoke, I could hear it didn't sound like her. She was altering her voice, and Tabitha had always been an excellent mimic.

Then the scene changed.

Blackness first, then a bright strip light. The action had moved inside, and the person filming panned out so I could see they were somewhere else. I wasn't entirely sure where, but there was a lot of metal everywhere, sheets of it, and hooks hanging and then flesh.

Dead pigs.

A slaughterhouse.

Jack the Pig close to a large, shiny hook as the camera pulled away, and I could see he was tied up. Was he naked? It was hard to say for sure, the camera was jerky, but he certainly wasn't wearing much. You could see a lot of his body, and his shoulders were peppered with an angry rash.

Tabitha came into the frame. She had her back to the camera, but she was holding what looked like a cattle prod and she jabbed it in the small of his back, pushing him towards the hook.

He swayed. He turned to face her by twisting his head over his shoulder and peering closely.

I heard him almost growl at Tabitha. She steered him away from the hook now. Most of the pig carcasses were hung up in the background – I could see them clearly because they were longer and pinker than I had expected – and with Jack the Pig in the frame there was an overwhelming amount of the colour pink so it was hard to work out what was going on and what skin belonged to whom.

One carcass lay there on the floor, severed from the snout downwards to create something like a fleshy sleeping bag for him.

He kind of stepped in, shuffling in his restraints, even though he didn't fit, prodded by a relaxed-seeming Tabitha, his body shaking. It wasn't fear, it was the same fizz of rage he'd had in the cellar, but then it had all been directed at me.

'I hardly touched you,' he spat at her.

It didn't make sense until it did.

I could hear her instructions as she asked him calmly to lower himself into the carcass. She had made her voice sound like mine, with that slight awkwardness. The halting way she finished each sentence.

You know the way the sound of your own voice is excruciating when you hear it played back to you? The sound of someone else 'doing' your voice is even worse, I can assure you of that.

The plait too. I reached to my own plait, and at that point I looked to her. I wanted to rip the remote control out of her hands and throw it to the floor. Smash her to the floor too. Pull at her lips with my hands and rip the smile from her face.

The screen went blank.

'He thinks it's me, doesn't he?' I said, although I knew the answer.

And *of course* he would.

She'd done it so slowly, taken all the pieces of me she cared to use and stitched them on to herself.

She turned to me, smiled at me, as pure as an angel, and she was about to reply but I spoke first. Only just managed to lower my voice, managed to control myself in order to produce more of a low snarl than a shout. 'What the fuck have you done?'

Tabitha didn't even respond properly, just pressed a finger to my lips, tasting of corn and salt, before she drew it back and switched the television off.

'What on earth is the matter?' she asked finally, and I think she genuinely didn't understand. She wanted to know what was wrong because she couldn't believe that I was upset about it. It was so ungracious of me not to like my present.

I was frozen to the sofa, unable to speak for a second, then I regained the ability and asked her again. 'What did you do?'

'We helped you.'

'Who was filming?'

'Why does it matter!'

It mattered because I needed to work out who my allies were.

She continued. 'Clare, we did this for *you*. This is all for you. To punish him. What did you think we were going to do? It was a lot of effort, you're being very –'

She managed to cut herself off, but I knew she wanted to say 'ungrateful'.

'You knew what you were doing! You made it so he would think that it was me?' I asked.

She seemed confused. 'But that means *you* got revenge? Because it came from *you*!' she said as if I was stupid and just needed it spelling out slowly.

I couldn't be involved in something like this. I could hardly breathe, ran through the scenarios in my head, replayed the video. 'Is he even alive? What did you do to him?' I asked.

She shook her head.

'Clare, *do* calm down,' she said as if I was a child having a tantrum.

'But how could you?' I said, hearing how I sounded, my voice breaking in frustration.

She had stamped on my fresh start with ease, didn't care, and she'd done it in the showiest way imaginable.

Theatre.

It made me sick, the more I let it sit there. So similar in design to what had happened in Périgueux.

She looked at me as if I'd lost my mind completely, and she reached out to placate me like she always did, but I pulled away for good.

And the decision was made quite suddenly, more decisive this time.

'I'm out,' I said. 'Don't contact me again.'

58.

Ashley and Georgia tiptoed around me like I might attack them when I got back that night, even more than they usually did. It was a strong indication that I was not behaving normally.

I had left.

I was on my own, which seemed like a crazy thing to do with the video out, and perhaps circulating in the world.

Once I had shut myself away in my bedroom, I started to think more rationally about it all.

The first question was what would they do with the video? It looked and sounded so like me. What would The Pig do? Was he the one calling me? Would he try to track me down? I imagined the press linking me and the crimes together, the girl who did these things. Who knew about the video, about my past?

I went to Hull on Christmas Eve, the next day, a journey I'd already had planned, and so it was time to leave Edinburgh anyway. Get away from Tabitha and the phone calls, which I had now become convinced were coming from The Pig's wife.

I went back to Hull with the main goal of seeing if I could get money from my granny, because the only solution I could think of was to start afresh.

She was there waiting, at the station, even though I'd told her not to bother. It was the first time I'd seen her in a year. I hadn't gone back at all during the summer. I'd kidded myself that the reason I'd stayed in Edinburgh was because we were so busy, but that was half the truth. I hadn't wanted to leave.

'You're very blonde. You look thin,' she said into my hair as she hugged me.

I made a note to cut it all off as soon as I could.

'I know. I think I'm sick.' I summoned a feeble cough, and she looked at me sceptically, but she didn't say anything else.

We walked back to the house, speaking very little.

'Tea?'

'Please.'

The tea was hot and milky. It was comforting to sip on, sitting in that cramped living room on the sofa. I could tell that she was waiting to ask me something.

Finally, she blurted out, 'You're not pregnant, are you?'

I almost laughed. 'I promise, I'm not pregnant.' And as soon as I said it I wondered if I should have lied, got money from her by claiming it in that way.

'Thank God.'

'What do you mean?'

'I don't mean anything by it, it's just, you know, I worry about you. If you got pregnant . . .' She left the words hanging there for us.

'How are they?' I asked.

'Love, I don't think it's a good idea to talk about them.'

'You've heard from them?'

'A bit. They're doing OK. Your dad might come over next year.'

We both knew he wouldn't be coming over.

'So, they're still in France?'

She had that look on her face. She felt sorry for me. 'Yes, not that I've been out there for a long time. Can't stand the food.' She wrinkled her nose. 'Don't think about them. It's all been difficult for them, and you know that.'

'I'm just supposed to pretend they don't exist?' I asked.

'You've been doing OK so far.'

'I don't think I'm doing so well now.'

She gave me a weak smile. She must have thought of her son who never left France any more, a French daughter-in-law who she'd never liked and a granddaughter who was cold and closed off. I was a flesh-and-blood relative; I was part of her, and I'd done something that she'd heard about in whispers, something no one could fully understand.

I owed her, and I felt like the only way I could pay her back was to make sure she didn't have to think about what I'd done, to not worry her at all. Then we could just sit and drink tea together, watch TV and pretend everything was normal.

She put her arm around me and squeezed me. She could have asked me why I wasn't doing so well, but she didn't. She spoke softly. 'What they did to you. The way they treated you. That wasn't your fault, you know. No child should ever be treated like that.'

There was a lump in my throat. I wouldn't cry. I wasn't a crier. I just nodded.

She snapped back into business mode.

'I didn't get you a present,' she said. 'I didn't want to get something you didn't want. We can go choose something for you after Christmas if you want.'

'It's fine; there's nothing I need.'

I took my bag upstairs and noticed the single paper garland that had been threaded around the banister. A depressing attempt. I rubbed it between two fingers. Flimsy, made of cheap red paper and put up hastily, so it half fell and grazed the floor. I let it sit in my hand, then I pulled at it, wrenching the paper down and stuffing it in the bin in my room.

That Christmas was worse than the last. The pains that I had felt in that week before magnified in my stomach, in my neck. I didn't sleep, didn't eat.

Then I realized that the phone calls had stopped. I didn't know what that meant.

I got up each day but just to shuffle down the stairs and col-lapse on to the sofa in front of the TV. I found that if I put it on loudly enough, the sounds blocked out all the thoughts in my head, and I could almost ignore them. Only then was I able to sleep, although my granny would come downstairs, shocked, and shake me to, and every time she did I jumped to a start, thinking the police were at the door, or The Pig, or Tabitha had somehow managed to track me down.

'You really are sick,' my granny commented as I lay on the sofa. 'I think it's best that you rest, you've obviously been working far too hard. Do you have friends to keep an eye on you while you're up there? Have you thought about going to the doctor?'

I ignored her and waited until I had to go back to Scotland.

59.

The beginning of January was bleak when I arrived back in Edinburgh. The twinkly Christmas lights came down and the city was plunged into darkness, as the sun hardly rose. The tourists vanished and their absence made the divide in the streets even keener. I saw things out of my window that I'd never noticed before. A woman begged on the street, her thin arms lined with scars. I heard about a man who threw himself off the Forth Bridge, plunged into the icy water and somehow survived, which was surprising enough to be reported in the papers.

My city had played at being charming for a while. That came to an end, and in January it was catty and combative, slapping me around happily in a gale, and even when the wind died down, the sweet malty smell from the breweries that sat in the air some days gathered in my mouth and made me want to be sick.

The fact that Edinburgh seemed to have turned her back on me – the city I'd loved so much right from the very beginning as my fresh start – made me more inclined to leave, but I hadn't been able to bring myself to ask my granny for money.

Time to plan my escape.

I didn't believe they'd show the video to anyone, but I also felt that I could maybe convince Ava to hand it over to me. One of the key questions was, did Ava even know about it? I had assumed she'd been the person filming. Notably, the car in the video hadn't been Samuel's. They must have gone back up to the Highlands while I had lain there in a dreamlike state, not quite knowing where they were, but they'd tracked The Pig down only a few days after he'd attacked me. I was sure that someone with Ava's access to money would have been able to orchestrate what I'd seen on that video.

It was worryingly like Périgueux. I couldn't deny that. If I left, left Edinburgh completely, I wondered what would happen. Would they bring me back? How far would they go and what would they do with the video?

Tabitha turned up on my doorstep after I got back. I watched her out of the window looking ruffled, so unused to me being disobedient. She rang the buzzer again and again.

Georgia peered out. 'Are you not going to let your friend in?' she asked.

'No. Ignore her,' I said.

I couldn't ignore them forever, but I had to focus on my new start and the only way to do that was to get money.

I would go to work and take on more shifts at the bar. I'd be nicer to Finn because I needed the job if I was going to save enough to leave; I'd listen to his stories properly and respond appropriately. I would pound my body into submission with exercise that would also help me relax and clear my head. I would run, because having a hobby might help. I'd stand under a cold shower in the morning to wake me up and get rid of the grit in my eyes. Most importantly, I'd establish who had seen that video.

If I could just get some sleep, the whole plan would be easier.

January. Traditionally, a new beginning, but in the back of my mind, I heard my granny: *I don't know why you'd expect it to be different.* She always said that, and she was right. I pictured my escape, but I knew that even if I left they could still ruin me.

I went back to work, wrung out like a dishcloth squeezed dry. Finn enveloped me in a huge hug on my first shift, and he smelt like laundry detergent and chip fat. I was so relieved I almost burst into tears because his smell was familiar, and I wished he'd launch into some long repetitive story because that would be most soothing for me.

I nearly told him everything that had happened that night, just to tell someone, then I had to pull back. He didn't know who I was at all.

Sleep was still elusive. I lay there and watched the minutes pass. If I fell asleep even for a second, vivid nightmares woke me. There were invisible hands running up and down my body.

Other people's dreams are very boring, aren't they? But we cannot help spluttering out our jumbled narratives, and I dreamed of an array of cutlery from the drawer stabbing into my back; the metal became melted and the pieces curled like bent spoons from a magician's trick cradling my lungs, wrapped around my heart. Forks twisted into hooks to hang me up from the inside.

60.

It started with a noise. The sound of a break-in.

The bar was closed and we were in full cleaning mode. I'd been hearing strange sounds for the past few hours, and when I heard something too loud to ignore below us, Finn didn't believe me.

'Go check it out, then,' he said, indulging me.

I went downstairs. The fire exit was open, just slightly, the door gaping in the wind. I peered out. There was no one. As I came back inside, I moved to close the door, but the wind slammed it shut, almost trapping my hand, and it locked behind me with a loud click.

'See? Nothing to it,' Finn said when I told him.

'I guess.'

He smirked. 'No one's been in here. They would have gone for the cash register. If you're worried, I can check the cameras.'

That was a small joke. There were cameras, but they were fake.

'No, it's fine,' I said.

He persisted with a chuckle. 'Unless you think there really are ghosties and ghouls here. You know the body snatchers Burke and Hare lured their customers in these bars?'

'Really?'

'Yup. Found them here and all along the Grassmarket, managed to get the poor buggers back to theirs, and then . . .' He ran his thumb across his throat in a slow cutting motion. 'Then they were sold on for dissection at the medical school.'

Of course, I knew the story. Tabitha had told me, less to scare me and more because she'd wanted to impress upon me that it was a *brilliant example of supply and demand.*

I shuddered at the idea. Malevolent spirits moving through the bar, knocking glasses and slamming doors.

Finn took a long sip of water. 'That's why I had to ban all those ghost tours from sniffing around in here, standing in their anoraks then ordering a pint of tap water.'

He toasted me with his own pint of tap water that had been sitting on the side for hours, then told me a long and tedious story about the traffic in Shetland (or the lack of). The change of subject was irritating. Although I tried to pay attention to his tale, I kept zoning out, then having to force myself to concentrate with the reminder that part of my new plan was to *be kinder to Finn.*

Get shifts.

Earn enough money to at least think about the details of an escape.

Despite my resolutions, I was struggling with Finn in particular. I so wanted to be distracted by him, to lose myself in his stories, and he was behaving sympathetically in that he hadn't mentioned my sudden disappearance over Christmas – one of our busiest times. I didn't know what Ava had said to him, but it seemed unspoken that something bad had happened.

The idea of being nice was easier than the reality of it. He was a sharp stone in the shoe and lack of sleep was only making that worse.

He stopped speaking. He held an ice bucket in one hand and a scoop in the other, but he wasn't moving.

'Are you drunk?' I asked him, almost joking. Not like Finn to get ill or feel faint.

'I'm not sure.' He sat down on a bar stool, his face very white, and his expression was pained. 'It's bizarre, I–I'm not sure I can swallow?'

He looked terrible.

'I should take you to the hospital. It might be anaphylactic shock or something – are you allergic to anything?'

'I don't want to,' he said, reaching out to me to steady himself. His hands were shaky.

I ran through what to do in my head. There were a few options, but I knew the person who would help – someone who always had a contact for everything. I hadn't spoken to him since before Christmas.

'Samuel,' I said into my phone.

He didn't exactly sound happy to hear from me, but he didn't sound unhappy. I was filled with an excruciating pang of longing for them as I heard him stretch my name like he was chewing the vowels up, like they all did – *Clareeeeee*.

'I need your help. You have a doctor friend?' I asked.

'Yes, he's a registrar down at the Royal. Why?' He couldn't help but sound a little smug that I needed his assistance. While Samuel loved to dish out acts of kindness, I knew he didn't do it for nothing. He never forgot what was owed.

'Do you think he'd do us a huge favour and come out to the bar?' I asked.

'I'm sure he would. To be honest, he owes me one. What's happened? Are you OK?'

'I'm fine. If you could get him to come out here. It's Finn, and he won't go to the hospital.' I thought I could sense him cool at the mention of Finn.

He recovered. 'On it. I'll call him right now. Have you spoken to Tabitha?'

I wondered why he was asking about Tabitha. 'No,' I said. 'Is there something I need to know?'

He let out a kind of cough. He seemed a little lost for words and I didn't have time to push him to speak sense.

'Look, I have to go,' I said, because Finn was slumped on the stool like a sack. He was blinking fast and he seemed to be using all his energy to keep himself from toppling to the floor.

'Right, why don't you tell me about your cousin again?' I said.

Finn started to go through the story as we waited for the doctor to arrive. He turned out to be an amiable man in his late twenties. He took Finn's blood pressure and temperature and sat next to him on a stool, then shone a torch in both his eyes. How odd to see them together, because they were about the same age, and I was like a child watching two grown-ups.

'OK. I need to ask you, have you taken anything?' he asked Finn.

Finn shook his head and the movement was shuddery.

'No, I swear, nothing.' His words came out slurred.

The doctor turned to me. 'I think he'll be OK. Whatever it is, it looks like it's wearing off. His blood pressure is fine and his breathing's pretty regular. I don't think there's any real imminent danger, but I would suggest going to the hospital to get fully checked out. And, even if you're not going to do that, keep an eye on him for the next few hours.'

'Absolutely, and thank you so much for coming out so late.' I nodded, played the sweet, concerned girlfriend and co-worker.

The doctor smiled at me. He looked tired. 'Really, it's not a big deal. Any chance you could call me a taxi?'

I went to my bag in the staffroom and was rummaging through for a battered card with the details of a taxi firm when my hand brushed against something. Pulling it out, my whole body went cold as I read the label. It was faded, but the brand on the bottle was still identifiable.

It was the medication we'd used that night in Périgueux.

I could feel something high in my throat about to spill out – a scream or howl or something – and I covered my mouth; a knuckled fist pushed against my lips to stop myself making a sound.

My first thought was Tabitha.

It must be.

Reminding me of how much she knew, showing me that I couldn't just walk away.

She knew what we'd used, which would have taken some digging. I'd suspected that she had some contacts out there. And she'd managed to get a French prescription for it. Maybe the others had helped?

I thought of the fire escape door flailing in the wind. It would have been easy to do, to creep in. Whoever had done this couldn't have known that it was his drink they were spiking, and they likely knew that it didn't matter. If *I'd* been drugged, I would have been equally shaken by the whole thing. It was clever in that way.

I managed to pull myself together enough to call a taxi for the doctor and pushed the pill bottle deep down into my bag. I tried to concentrate on Finn, who sat there, looking forlorn.

We ended up back at his flat. He had little curiosity for what had happened: *It's just one of those things! An unexplainable turn.*

His breaths became heavier and slower as he drifted into sleep. I lay next to him, without moving my body an inch.

I thought back to my turret room at Minta's house in France, and I remembered the familiar sensation that I was staying awake to monitor things. If I dared to close my eyes, everything would fall apart and tumble down around me.

Nothing bad could happen if I kept watch.

61.

The next day, I lay on my side staring at his face until, after a while, he woke up and blinked at me.

'Jesus, how long have you been staring at me? You're creeping me out.'

'Why do you like me?'

He sighed. 'Really? That's what we're doing now?'

He rolled away from me and took a big gulp of water, then sat up in bed. Through the haze of sleep, he looked as though he was genuinely considering the question, adjusting to having a *serious conversation* so early in the morning. 'I guess I thought you were hardworking. Shy. I thought there was something behind the shyness and that you'd open up. I mean, I still haven't worked out quite who you are. What do you even *like*? What even makes you happy, Clare?'

I considered it.

I liked the second before I knew I was going to drift off to sleep, when sleep was inevitable and I could relish the thought of falling into it and forgetting who I was. I liked lying in the sun for hours, avoiding the shade, getting as hot as possible so my skin fizzed and burned. I liked Edinburgh when the streets were dark and quiet, before the city had turned on me. My favourite thing had been Tabitha and the way she made me feel that we were powerful, but I also liked it when she cared for me like a sick child. I liked the world we'd created until it had all gone wrong.

Then there were the things I didn't like. I hated being out on the edge of it all sometimes, being left out and having so little control. I hated not being able to trust my body as it fell apart at the seams, my mind broken. I took it out on Georgia and Ashley, and I was filled with an almost uncontrollable rage at them; I would put salt in the sugar bowl, rip through cereal packets so that the grains spilled out when they took the box down from a cupboard. They either didn't notice or chose to ignore it.

'I'm not who you think I am.' The words sounded dramatic as I said them.

He nodded slowly, still confused. There was a brief silence before he spoke again, and his voice was softer. 'What do you mean?'

'It means I think we should end things.'

'What the *fuck*, Clare?' He looked at me in confusion.

'I don't think I'm the person you think I am,' I said.

He sighed again, calming down. 'Yes, you've said that,' he said, as if I was very fragile.

Patient Finn.

He was sad, of course, Finn with the puppy-dog eyes, but I'd played the scene out in my head all night. I had come to terms with it.

Looking back now, I'm proud of myself because I have never been drawn to kind acts, but it was a kind thing to do, one of the kindest things I've ever done.

The safest thing for Finn was if he was cut out entirely, and if that meant I had to give up the comfort, the predictability he had dosed out to me for so long, then that was what had to happen.

Cut away the fat to get to the meat, Tabitha had always said.

I didn't want any harm to come to him, and he didn't belong to whatever was sure to come next.

62.

There were still no more silent calls. All the same, it was easy to catastrophize. A newspaper article about it perhaps. Eyes on me as I walked down the street. If it came out, I would be stripped bare. It was painful to consider the possibility.

I was on a mission to understand how many of them had been involved in making the video. That would help me work out what the repercussions might be. To remove myself cleanly from them, I knew that I needed more information.

My first port of call was Ava because she was the one I was closest to. My calm and collected friend who had generally always been on my side. Right at the beginning, we'd stood outside on the street and smoked, and she'd promised me it would be everything I could ever hope for.

She agreed to meet, and I chose a tiny pub located on the Royal Mile, all dark chipped wood and fussy oil paintings of grazing cattle.

I smelt something in the pub when I sat down. The scent was earthy, with a moist heaviness in the air that hit the back of my throat with each intake of breath. I peered down and it was there under the table, behind old pieces of chewing gum stuck to the underside. A faint line of mould, black and furry, just peeking out.

I felt sick, but I pulled back and sat up when I saw Ava come in. She didn't look uncomfortable, even though by all rights she should have been, dressed up, as usual, in the strangest combination of garments: leather trousers and a suede coat that looked as soft as a baby rabbit, dyed the colour of a hi-vis vest.

Three old men hunched over, almost welded to the bar top like they'd been there for years, and they all turned and watched her duck to avoid bashing her head on the low beams. She didn't notice their stares. That was just like Ava; she was good at being focused on the matter at hand.

She sat in the nook next to me. Taking in everything to work out how best to handle me, pulling her hair forward so that it fell over the table and pooled softly like a kitten curled into a ball.

'What's the matter?' she asked, taking a sip from the glass of wine I'd bought for her.

'The video.'

'What video?' she asked.

Like chess. Where to go from there and what to say? Instead of pushing her, I went in another direction.

'She poisoned Finn.'

She listened to my story without interruption, letting me explain the full thing: the fire exit, the drug that was the same as the one from *the episode*, from Périgueux. I didn't go into detail about Périgueux, just the bones of the story. I also wasn't about to tell her I was planning on leaving Edinburgh for good.

'Well, that's quite a tale,' she said.

'He could have died!'

'Could have. He didn't.' She sounded so unfazed.

'No, but he was very unwell,' I said, hearing how prim I sounded. 'So, what do you think?'

She softened a little. 'I think it sounds . . . stressful for you, and horrible,' she said kindly. 'I guess if you're asking me what you should do, I think that you should come back.'

'I'm not sure I can.'

'Of course you can! This was always going to be hard, but it will pass. These things will feel easier with time. Come back to us. It sounds like Finn has his own stuff going on; maybe your theory's wrong, maybe he's on something?'

'I really don't think so. I've ended it with him anyway. I don't want him being brought into all this. How do I make her leave me alone? For good. I was wondering if I should speak to her?' I said.

She shook her head. 'I wouldn't.'

'Why?'

'What would you say? If she did do it, it's about you coming back. That's what she wants. It's all she wants. She talks about you all the time.'

Despite myself, there was a dizzying rush of satisfaction at the idea of Tabitha talking about me.

'There are two options here,' she said. 'You come back or you don't. You can try to forget about everything that happened and we can keep going with what we were doing. Before that night, we were fine, weren't we? Maybe it can all be fine again.'

'I'm not sure. I can't go back because I'm not sleeping or eating –'

'None of that.' She cut me off. 'We'll sleep when we're dead.'

It was harsh, but she softened the words with a smile and gave my arm a comforting squeeze. 'Look on the bright side. Finn's OK.'

I thought back to the two of them: Tabitha and Ava. Their bodies entwined on that bed. I wasn't even sure why I trusted Ava or wanted her advice, but I did.

'I can't go back,' I said.

She smiled. 'I understand, but I don't think there is an out for you.'

'I guess I just don't get why it's so important that I'm part of it.'

'Because you're good at it.'

'Surely that's not enough?'

'It's enough for now.'

We both sipped on our drinks, and I thought we might stay and chat more. I asked her about Imogen and Samuel.

'They're not involved any more,' she said, sighing.

'Not involved? What do you mean? They're not in the group?'

Even as I said it I realized how hard it was to sum up what Imogen and Samuel . . . were. Friends, colleagues, enemies, advisers? Flailing legs of The Shiver cut off?

'They just left.' She closed down that topic of conversation promptly.

Interesting. So that was what Samuel had been trying to spit out. And the fact they'd left was maddening. I wanted to scream, because it was so unfair that *they* were allowed to leave. It hurt much more than I would have ever thought, and I knew it was because I wasn't permitted to. I was trapped, but also fully disposable.

'Why have they left?' I persisted.

But she just shrugged and changed the subject. 'It's funny, when you think of Finn being poisoned, because we're always careful with that kind of thing. This drink,' she said, holding it towards me. 'You saw them pour it, I assume?'

'Sure,' I said. I was pretty certain I'd been the first person to order wine in a long time. The barman had had to root around for a while to find something to give me.

'That's good. You know I saved Tabitha once.' She said it so offhandedly, as if it was perfectly natural. That thing she did, that they all did, changing the subject so quickly, and then forcing me to be the one to ask the questions.

'In what way?'

'Her drink. It was spiked. Back in London just before we came to Edinburgh for the first time. I didn't see who had done it.' She shook her head at her own stupidity.

'I'm sorry,' I said.

Her face was quite blank. 'Don't be. It was fine in the

end – you should have seen her, though. It was so strange for Tabitha to be out of control, stumbling,' she said.

'You saved her,' I stated.

She just took another large gulp from her glass. Because of her silence, I did what I always did, and filled in the scenes myself. Tabitha's limbs loose, her hair in her face, unable to speak, with predators circling her. I was angry for her, of course, but it didn't take away from what she was doing.

Ava shrugged, and I pressed for more, but she wouldn't say another word on it. And I could tell there was to be no more talking about Samuel or Imogen, or even about Tabitha. About any of it.

Ava stood up. 'Stay in touch. This isn't the end.' But she was less confident than usual.

Final words, and then she was gone, out into the night. The men at the bar all surveyed her as she left, and she didn't look back even though she must have felt all our eyes boring into her.

63.

I found traces of fungus everywhere, and I was sure that the mould was a contributing factor to my illness. I saw it in my bedroom next. The path was visible, like the trail from a snail, up from the skirting boards, seeping across the wall then settling in a greenish cloud, and it wouldn't stay there, cowardly and confined to the wall; the naked spores would gravitate towards the warm moisture of my breath, and then, of course, they'd make their way into my lungs.

It didn't look the same as in the pub. It was mossier, more like forest lichen with hard, defined edges on the patches that had formed. Thinking about it growing away, larger and thicker every minute, made sleep impossible. My limbs were filled with cement. I almost felt like I might never sleep again. Spores in my lungs and hands around my neck. And the mould reminded me so much of my mother, ill in her room, lying there without a cure, and of Samuel in a mock-seizure on the floor.

I scrubbed the room for hours to try and get rid of it, then sought refuge outside, but when I went out, it was freezing. I'd end up hiding away down a piss-stinking wynd, desperate to be back inside in the warmth. I couldn't win. As soon as I was back in my flat, the mould was in my lungs again, making me cough and my head ache. The skin around my nails in particular became so dry and cracked that it bled and bled.

My room that I had loved so much had betrayed me, it had stopped being a sanctuary. I had a solution, though. There was an attic – a tiny crawl space. It was only a few feet wide, but I could climb up via the radiator, open up the little hatch and just about clamber in.

It was ideal, because I recognized that lack of sleep made me prone to snap and react in a way I wasn't sure I'd be able to control. I had less of a hold on myself, which was frustrating when I'd been doing quite well with that side of things. So, I hid away.

The ceiling practically touched my nose and the walls just about grazed the sides of my body. It wasn't some cosy nook, more of a halfway space between indoor and outdoor where gusts came in strong through holes in the roof. There was a smell that could have been mouse droppings and sometimes cold splashes of rain leaked on to my legs. I liked it, though. The space was dark, no light at all, and of course, importantly, no mould that I could see. Once I was there, nothing could find me, and sometimes, if I lay there long enough, I finally managed to get a few hours of sleep. It was safe.

Not much longer. I would be leaving soon to somewhere new, although I hadn't decided where. I couldn't let myself plan too much.

I researched my maladies at night before I climbed up, becoming preoccupied with them ever since I'd heard about someone spiking Tabitha's drink, which almost certainly hadn't been the point of that story. I thought of Tabitha a lot. Drugged and staggering around a club. Saved by Ava. And as much as I slid pieces around in my mind, I still didn't know exactly what I was going to do.

I looked to times when the inexplicable had been solved with time and careful logic. Read about children who thought they were haunted by ghosts, who writhed in pain and hot madness, but it turned out to be carbon monoxide poisoning. Witches in the past whose splendid strangeness could be attributed not to magical trickery, but to the seemingly innocuous ingestion of a common parasitic fungus.

The lack of sleep, the aching limbs and fuzz in my head, the feeling of hands around my neck as vivid as if it had happened hours ago, my inability to properly plan my escape: it might be a diagnosable, physiological condition, perhaps related to the mould.

I ended up in the doctor's surgery at the university even though I didn't trust doctors.

The GP didn't ask many questions. He didn't question my appearance. He ran some tests; he took various vials of blood to check on a lot of things I'd never heard of, then he called me back into the surgery to talk over the results.

'So, the issue is sleep?' he asked again.

'I'm hardly sleeping at all,' I answered.

He turned back to his computer screen. He didn't have my medical records from France, or the name associated with them. My slate was clean.

'Mood?'

'Mood is . . . variable,' I replied.

He nodded, tapping away.

I wanted to tell him that sometimes I got so angry that I wanted to smash everything in sight. I needed to lash out – it was the only thing that relieved it. And then the rage left, and I was fine.

That would have been the moment to do it. But I didn't, because how could I possibly explain it? He was only marginally interested. I don't think I represented a diagnostic quandary worth investigating. I looked like all the students he saw: young, rich and unduly anxious.

'Working?' he asked.

I didn't reply. *Oh yes, I work as a honey trapper, and I'm scared that the girl I work with poisoned my boyfriend (maybe she meant to poison me!). Although the reason she did it is because I actually tried to poison someone myself. Oh, and she also pretended to be me and she may or may not have used a cattle prod and forced a man to climb into a carcass of a pig . . .*

I smiled faintly at the idea of even trying to explain it.

'I'm a student,' I said.

'Drugs and alcohol?'

'Rarely.'

'OK, well you do seem a little peaky.' He took his glasses off and rubbed his nose where they'd sat, before placing them on his desk. He gave me a long, hard look. 'Why don't we try to get your sleep sorted first, that often helps. Just a little kick-start. You can take these for a week, and we'll see how it goes.'

He wrote out a prescription for me.

I didn't turn back. I hadn't even mentioned the mould.

64.

Just like that, I was medicated again. It had been a long time since I'd been medicated. Two round white tablets every day. With water and not on an empty stomach. *Make sure your prescription stays filled because you don't want to run out and go through withdrawal.*

I was back studying, and Tabitha kept leaving me voice-mails. *'Come on, Clare; we need you for this. All the wives love you; you're the prettiest,'* she sang into the phone, like a lullaby. I hated the term 'the wives', like some flock of sheep. Or, *'Clare, let's not end it like this – we can make it work again. I know we can.'*

I very nearly picked up the phone because, despite everything, hearing her voice made me want to speak to her badly, an instinctive thought before my mind could catch up and remember what she'd done.

And then there was the strong desire for someone to save me if I couldn't save myself. I craved the simplicity of Imogen. She'd scrub away any mould or say *Don't be so silly.* She had more information as well, I was sure of it. And if not Imogen, just someone who would hold their palm to my forehead and take my temperature and tell me I was fine and that I was worrying over nothing, that my world wasn't falling apart, that one day I would stop feeling those hands on my neck and the sensation that I was going to die would go away. Tell me I would stop seeing the mould and scratching off the skin around my fingers. That I would stop dreaming of a hook in my back, and thinking about what Tabitha might do with the video.

I needed to understand why Imogen and Samuel had left.

I thought of Imogen's face, the pained expression when

she'd realized what had happened to me in the Highlands. Had she been exiled or had she left of her own accord?

I picked up the phone and called her.

'Hello?' She answered on the first ring.

'Imogen, it's Clare.'

'What do you want?' She sounded wary. Although I had her number, she was like Tabitha and rarely used a mobile, so I was surprised she'd answered at all.

'You're out, you and Samuel. I just wanted to speak to you again. Understand more about why you left.'

She cut me off. 'Clare, I can't talk to you. Not about any of this. I'm sorry.'

She hung up.

A day later, and Imogen was still on my mind. I needed to work out how to get her to talk to me and to understand exactly what she knew and why she'd left. Maybe she had something on Tabitha that I could use?

'Clare,' Ashley called through the flat to me. 'Someone for you.'

I got up, running through the options of who it could be.

In the living room, I saw her, and I thought I might be sick. A girl a little younger than me sat on the sofa waiting, with her hands clasped together on her lap. She was dressed simply in trousers and a loose top. I recognized her, of course, although she looked different from how I remembered her, and different still to how I had thought she would grow up back when we'd been deep in the throes of it all. When I moved closer to her, I could see that she was washed out, and fatigue sat on her face like someone had pressed charcoal under her eyes.

She greeted me. If she looked shocked at my appearance, she didn't say anything. I hardly recognized myself in the mirror by that point. My face looked like a chunk of fatty meat – white like gristle in some places, red and raw in others.

'Hello,' I said, feeling sick at the sight of the girl.

Ashley stood up as if she might leave, then, desperate to be involved, she sat back down and jiggled on the edge of the sofa.

'So, who's this?' Ashley asked me, smiling at the girl as she spoke.

I turned to her and channelled my most Tabitha-like commanding voice. 'Could you give us a minute?'

Ashley looked a bit confused. She nodded. 'Sure, sure.'

She left, so it was just the two of us, and I took a seat opposite the girl.

'Would you prefer we spoke in French?' she asked, after greeting me with my old name.

'No, I never speak French any more, and you can call me Clare now.' I didn't use her name. To use her name would be accepting that we could go back so easily, as if it was fine to discuss, so I avoided calling her anything at all.

'What are you doing here?' I asked.

'What a welcome!' she replied.

'I'm just surprised to see you. Would you like a drink?' I sounded like a robot.

'No, I would not like a drink. You mean you're surprised I found you, you are able to just say it.' Her English was good but not great. The phrasing was a bit clunky, and I was relieved. I was hopeful she was just visiting and that she hadn't moved to Scotland.

'OK, yes, I'm surprised.'

'Your voice, it sounds strange,' she said.

'Maybe just hearing me speak English.'

'Maybe.'

'What do you want?' I asked.

She fidgeted a little before speaking. 'I don't want much. I just need you to tell me about that night. Everything exactly how it happened.'

'You know what happened.' I tried to sound convincing.

She seemed unmoved. 'That's the thing. I don't believe you. You're a liar.' She paused, to let it sink in. 'What you said back then, we all know it doesn't stand up at all. It doesn't make sense. I'm not trying to make trouble. I'm not going to go to the police. I just want to go back home, to see my mother and to be able to tell her what happened.'

I shrugged.

She tried again. 'Come on! I don't even care about telling anyone else; I just want her to be able to go to sleep at night without it hanging over her that my papa had some kind of "thing" for young girls.'

There it was.

We had danced around it, but she wasn't embarrassed or ashamed that she was his daughter. She suspected things, had interrogated the facts.

I had thought of her from time to time over the years. The few memories I had of her were of her smiling as she ran around the lake, throwing herself in, running up to the car afterwards, dripping with water. Her body, all shiny like a wet fish in her swimming costume.

And that was how it had happened. We had called my father afterwards, and he presented it to the police. And we told them what had happened. He was a predator. *A violent man who'd attacked us out of nowhere, picked us up and dropped us off as a favour, then stayed on without invitation. Mauled us with fat hands. It was disgusting – we were practically the same age as his own daughters and, fighting for our lives, we'd managed to slip him something. To drug him. After all, there were three of us. Why would three teenage girls abduct a grown man?* Well, this girl's mother had corroborated our tale when she stood up in court looking haggard, her clothes hanging on her tiny frame, and her hair scraped back so you could see dandruff on her shoulders. She was sorry, she said, so sorry for those poor girls who he'd abducted (because by then the idea he'd abducted us was firmly established), and yes, she had perhaps seen something in him, something dark when they'd been sitting together in a restaurant. His hand inching up her leg to the top of her thigh and then pinching her hard and twisting the flesh, enjoying her wince. At the time maybe she'd convinced herself she'd enjoyed it. She hadn't really, and there was that time at a dinner party when he'd accused her of being too loud in front of his colleagues, saying she sounded like a whore, and he'd laughed and said he was glad he wasn't paying for it. She said she was *terribly sorry* for those girls, especially considering her own daughters, so young now, but if he was that type of man then who knows what could have happened, or what had already happened.

The court case had been difficult. All three sets of parents were heavily involved, and the publicity caused the man's business to fail, so the family was left with virtually nothing.

The girl had to withdraw from school along with her sister. As for us, we withdrew too.

I looked hard at the girl, couldn't stop myself, but it wasn't her I was seeing. It was her mother. I felt bad for them all.

'I can't help you,' I said.

That was what did it, and her face broke. Everything she had been holding in came out, and she looked so ugly.

'You're disgusting,' she spat.

Time for it to end.

'I'm sorry. I think you should leave,' I said as authoritatively as I could.

'Fine.' She stood up.

'Can I ask you how you found me?' I asked.

She sneered. 'A friend of yours called me up and said she thought I might be interested in speaking to you. I wasn't looking for you before.'

'When did she call you?'

She seemed insulted at my question. 'Why would I tell you anything else?' she said. 'I wanted to give you a chance to tell the truth and to let my family have some peace. I know it didn't happen like you said it did, but you obviously don't care about any of that.'

I stood up to match her. 'Have you been calling me? At night?' I asked her.

'Calling you? No.' She barked the 'no'. I could tell that she was clinging on to the faint hope that I might say something to help her.

'I'm sorry,' I said. 'You can go back and tell your mother that I'm sorry about the way it all panned out.'

She didn't have anything with her, no bag or coat, and it looked like she could have appeared from anywhere. She nodded, no crying or shouting, and I admired her self-restraint.

Did I want to tell her about that night? I couldn't. What would I have said?

She was stiff like she didn't quite know how to cut the exchange off. She didn't even seem angry any more, just tired, and I thought she was about to walk out.

Then I saw there was a problem. I couldn't just let her leave.

She'd found me, and there was no way that was going to be enough. How could it be? Who knew which one of them had given her my details.

I'd learned so much about self-control since Dina and Adrienne. I didn't shout or even raise my voice, but I knew I needed to handle her. Nip it in the bud.

'You should leave, and you can't come back here,' I said.

She pursed her lips. 'And why is that?'

'If you come back, if you get in contact with me, I'll find your mother and tell her stories about your father. I'll find her and tell her things that will mean she'll never be able to sleep again.'

She went to speak and I interrupted her. 'It'll be your worst nightmare. Like you said, I'm a liar. Even if she doesn't believe me, it doesn't matter.'

The girl was braver than I would have thought. I could see her rooting around, trying to think of what she could say. A million thoughts and options: she weighed them up. 'I won't come back here,' she said mechanically.

Once she'd left, I collapsed on to the sofa and Ashley came out of her bedroom.

'That was quick. What was all that about? Where was that girl from? She sounded foreign.'

'Foreign' was said with a nervous tremor.

'Just someone I used to know,' I replied.

'Oh, fun!' She smiled, waiting for more.

'I have a migraine coming on. I think I'm going to lie down. Don't disturb me.'

'Of course! You need to look after yourself,' she said soothingly. Ashley loved it when I was incapacitated.

As I walked from the room, I saw something out of the corner of my eye. 'Come here!' I called to Ashley. 'Do you see it?'

'See what?' she asked.

'Mould.' I pointed at the wall near the door.

Ashley came rushing back and bent down, looking at the wall with deep interest, her bottom high in the air, her face almost touching the floor.

She turned back to me. 'I don't know, Clare. I'm not sure that I can see anything really, just a stain. Honestly, I wish I could help!' She gave me an apologetic smile like I was a crazy person. 'Maybe you should get some more rest. And we can open the windows too – let the air in.'

I went to my bedroom as directed, and I pulled the cover over my head to block out the world. The feeling of remembering and even the idea of dreaming was far too much to bear, so I ignored them all, popped a pill and welcomed the blackness.

65.

Imagine the mess of it all. The mess of me.

Bleeding nails that left crusty crescents of blood on my sheets. Very little sleep. I was far from well enough to socialize, but I was set on convincing Imogen to meet up with me, and finally I managed it.

Imogen had said she'd pick me up, claimed she had something to show me, to explain things, and she arrived in a smart little Mini, beeping her horn outside my flat and leaning over to open the door so I could get in, with a look that wasn't particularly kind. She was all bundled up in a duffel coat and a pair of mittens, and the effect was unappealing, like an overgrown toddler.

'You look awful!' she said happily.

How refreshingly Imogen.

'I didn't know you had a car,' I said.

She gave me a smug smile. 'Well, I do.'

I had examined the car before I got in. It definitely wasn't the one from Tabitha's video, which was something at least.

'Where are we going?' I asked.

'To the beach.'

I came out with it as we set off; it had niggled at me for a while. 'Servants' Christmas. You never told me.'

'Oh my God, I literally can't believe we're going to talk about that. I will tell you. It's why I stuck around as long as I did.'

I waited until she spoke again, and finally she did. 'You're very good at that thing where you just don't talk, aren't you? I think you've picked it up from Tabitha. They do have something on me, if you can forgive that ridiculous expression, but I'm sure it's not as sinister as you seem to think it is.'

'You may as well tell me.'

'If you want. Be warned, it doesn't exactly paint me in the best of lights. My present for Tabitha – it was what I did for her.'

'Which was?'

She sighed. 'The whole Servants' Christmas thing. I think she only set it up because she knew what she wanted from me. She basically told me what I needed to do. She wanted me to write her essays.'

'All of them?'

'Well, it didn't start like that, but yes, pretty much by the end. You must have been surprised she wasn't failing? She's shockingly bad at writing, isn't she? Even your essays are better than hers.'

'That's so much work!' I exclaimed, ignoring the dig.

'Yup. It was. But she'd have failed if I hadn't helped her. I didn't mind that much at first. I did a fair bit for her at school too, you see. She stuck up for me when I was bullied. I owed her. That's what she does. She makes it so you feel like you owe her so much. That you should do anything she asks.'

'So, what went wrong?' I asked.

'When I said I was going to stop, she said she'd report me to the university. She'd say I'd written everything. She's been holding it against me for ages. I wouldn't be surprised if she'd written that bloody fortune cookie herself. *Your intelligence is an asset to be shared* . . . Fuck. Off,' she spat.

I couldn't picture Tabitha creating custom fortune cookies. For some reason the only person I could think of who had the patience for that was Ava. I remembered Imogen's vehement reaction at the Chinese restaurant.

'Really?' I asked. 'That's a lot of effort to make a point, and if you were writing her essays for her, it's a deadlock. She'd get thrown out as well.'

'She wouldn't care. She knows studying here means a lot more to me than to her. Anyway, she won't now.'

'Why won't she now?' I asked.

'I know too much. She'll never tell anyone about me now,' she said.

'What do you know?'

'You'll see.' Her focus didn't leave the road. She was a very slow and careful driver.

'Now, tell me what she's doing to you?' she asked. Keen to turn the focus away from herself.

'It's hard to explain. Odd things are happening. Things I don't understand,' I said.

She was interested, suddenly brightening. 'What?'

How could I tell her? Where to even begin?

'I want to. I just . . . can't, not at the moment.'

She snorted, and still she didn't look over at me. 'Fine. I don't know what I expected. You never opened up, not really to any of them. I think it was why they all liked you so much. Then again, you probably knew that. Mysterious Clare. But *I* knew it was just because you didn't want to say the wrong thing, embarrass yourself. Because you're weird.'

There wasn't much else to say. She was right, and we sat in silence until we arrived at a town I didn't know. Imogen shooed me out of the car and we started walking through the high street, a few women greeting me as I passed. At first, I felt nervous that these women might have been our clients, ones I'd forgotten. Of course, that wasn't the case. They were just friendly because it was all softer out of the city.

'Where are you living now?' I asked her as we trudged along in the wind. It was a miserable day out, but I didn't want to complain in case she refused to talk to me.

'I think it's better if you don't know that,' she clucked. 'I'm glad to be out of there in some ways, even though that flat was fantastic, wasn't it? By the end, though, everything was awful, waiting on the two of them.'

'Where are you taking me?' I asked.

She turned and faced me, and her hair was knotty from the wind, her nose and cheeks shot with red. I hadn't had a proper conversation with her, like this, for so long. Dark hair, dark eyes. She was pretty when she wasn't frowning so much, or looking haughty about something or other.

'You'll see,' she said.

We carried on, and we reached the beach. The houses were a mix of faded pastels with views of frothy waves. We were virtually the only people there on that cold afternoon. The sand licked by the tides, so the shore looked gritty and black.

There he was, standing close to the water.

'What's he doing here?' I asked, but I was glad to see him.

'I invited him,' she said.

Samuel nodded his head at us awkwardly. 'Clare. Imogen,' he said quite formally. No raffish smile. It was unlike Samuel to look so dishevelled and to be wearing creased clothes, and his face was a bit green. He had a coffee cup in one hand.

The three of us stood in a rough triangle on the beach. A splintery gale whipped up around us.

'I invited him because there are bits I know and bits *he* knows,' she said.

It made sense. She regarded Samuel with a complete lack of interest, and I knew in an instant that her crush on him, that girlish, blushing, tongue-tied crush that we'd all known about and ignored, had well and truly gone, in an explosive bang perhaps, or maybe it had just faded away. There was nothing there at all any more; it was hard to believe they even knew each other.

'I'll start,' she said.

Samuel nodded.

'I was never *fully* into it,' Imogen said carefully, watching the sea as if she was telling the waves her story instead of reciting it to me.

I had known that. I'd always felt Imogen had other reasons for hanging around.

'You were involved from the beginning,' I said.

'Yes, because Tabitha wanted it all so much. She was obsessed from the outset; you should have heard her. Then Ava went along with everything, of course. Anyway, in the end, it wasn't Tabitha's decision; it was mine. I moved out of that flat, which was a shame, it was a very nice flat.'

I wished we could move away from discussing the flat.

'What made you move out?' I asked.

'Well, firstly, I didn't like what happened with that man, what he did to you, and how we couldn't report it –'

Samuel jumped in. 'Me neither, Clare. I was nothing to do with the planning there. You know that Ava and Tabitha kept that entirely to themselves. They must have known.'

Imogen rolled her eyes and continued. 'I was unhappy for *ages*, before Christmas. But that wasn't why I left. Or why he left.'

She was so dismissive of Samuel and it was so odd to see her behave so coldly towards him.

'Why then? Was it the video?' I asked.

She looked at me, confused. 'What video?'

I looked to Samuel.

'I don't know what video you mean,' he said, and I believed him.

They both waited for me to explain more but I knew enough. Neither of them had seen or been involved, I was sure of it.

That was something, at least.

It hit me that they had their own things going on with Tabitha, in general, and I needed to ask outright.

'Why did you leave? Why did they let you leave?' I just wanted clarity – for them to tell me what was going on.

They looked at each other for a split second.

'I'll show you,' Imogen said.

66.

Heavy footsteps on wet sand as we turned a corner and looked out. The coastline became rockier, and then there was a house, like a box on a hill, teetering. The reflections from the sea moved on the glass.

I realized where we were. We must have approached this place from a different way last time, because I hadn't recognized it at all.

The Landores' house.

'And *that* is why I left,' she said.

'Because of the Landores?' I asked. I had barely given them a thought since the ceilidh.

'Because of the Landores,' she repeated. She turned to Samuel sharply. 'It's why he left too. Although he knows more than me.'

He didn't respond. Looked up at the house, letting her take centre stage.

'Eve Landore is dead,' Imogen said.

Samuel let out something close to a moan.

'She killed herself,' Imogen finished, grimly.

I didn't know what to say. I looked to the cliffs.

A body. I pictured it tumbling down the crags and falling into the sea where it would be ripped apart on the rocks. You might not even find her after the sea was finished.

'When?' I asked.

'Not long ago.'

'Why did no one tell me?'

'We kept it from you, Tabitha insisted on it,' Imogen said. 'She did it on Boxing Day. She took a load of pills. Downed a

327

bottle of wine. We knew things were getting out of control before then though, when you came back and told us about what had happened with The Pig.'

Not what I had imagined. Eve Landore in her beautiful house with the marble floors polished like a gallery. I couldn't reconcile that with a body lying there splayed out, vomit on the floor and speckling her lips. Glassy eyes.

The image was so messy, it just didn't feel like her. But then again, we'd only met her once – that half-hour I'd spent with her and all that research on her and her husband. None of it meant we knew them. All we had was a snapshot. We'd just gone in and stampeded through their lives.

It was tough to tell if Imogen was in any way sad about it. She shared this information with a certain haughtiness.

'We didn't care whose lives we were fucking up. Children playing at being grown-ups, really,' Imogen said.

'I think we still are,' I replied.

She looked at me, amused. 'Ummmm, no. *You* are. Anyway, that's why I left. Fuck being involved in all that.' She switched to Samuel. '*You* left then too. They were your family friends, after all. You know more, do tell us.' Hands on hips, a glimpse of fussiness.

A pained smile from Samuel. 'You don't understand why she did it, do you?' he said to her. A bit of whatever was in his coffee cup dribbled down the side of his mouth. There was a robust aroma coming off him that the sea breeze couldn't sweep away – sweet and musty, something unfashionable like brandy.

'You're drunk,' I said.

He looked contrite. He flicked his tongue down over his chin and lips, loving how uncomfortable I was at the action – a small hint of the old Samuel.

Definitely drunk.

'There, there, Clarey. No need to be a spoilsport.'

'Don't call me Clarey. So they told Eve Landore that he'd cheated on her?' I asked.

'Yes, but that wasn't the problem. They told her what had happened, and it upset her, of course. Eve was pretty pragmatic, though. She spoke to Tom, and he said it had just been this silly flirtation. She could understand it. If anything, she was relieved it was all out in the open. A whole new beginning. But Tabitha wasn't happy at all.'

Imogen let out a mirthless laugh. She was used to Tabitha being *not happy*.

'Why?' I asked. This was news to me. It had all gone well as far as I was concerned.

'Because she wanted Eve to leave him,' Samuel continued. 'She couldn't understand how she could stay with him. It was the first proper success, if you remember, the blueprint for the whole thing, and she'd planned that all these wives would leave their husbands. This is where the story gets crazy. Tabitha levels of crazy. She said that if Eve didn't leave him, she'd tell his firm.'

'What was there to tell them?' I asked. 'A few grainy photos of him kissing some woman?'

'Ah, but that's the point, it wasn't just some woman,' Samuel replied.

'What do you mean?'

'She was going to tell the world that you were fifteen. She was going to somehow engineer her fucking narrative so that he'd shagged a fifteen-year-old.'

'Why? And I didn't sleep with him! Why would she do that?'

'I've told you. She couldn't believe that Eve Landore was staying with him. She saw it as a betrayal of the whole thing. Absolutely going against the ethos of what we were trying to achieve. Anyway, she had this idea, she didn't even run what she wanted to do past any of us. It was clever, she didn't outright say you were underage. She implied it in so many ways. It's hard to describe, but you can imagine.'

I could imagine that very easily. Remembered some of the strain in the group before Christmas at the Chinese restaurant. The absence of Samuel and Imogen afterwards.

'I found out because Eve called me, she was just so upset,' he said.

'So why didn't you tell her the truth?' I asked.

He looked at me like I was mad. 'I couldn't do that to *Tabitha*. Not then. I owe her so much. It all got out of control – you know what it's like when you're involved in something with her. I had no idea quite how far Tabs would push it all. Anyway, Eve didn't see a way out. She didn't want to leave him. To sell the house. You saw how she was about that bloody house.'

'Yes, I saw.'

He looked at me closer this time, like he was seeing me properly for the first time that day. 'Remember how you saw Tom Landore at that ceilidh? Tabitha was absolutely shitting herself thinking that he'd said something to you, because that was right when it was all going down, when things were getting tricky.'

I shook my head. Remembered Tom Landore's look with so many things mixed in, and how I'd run away from him.

A quick calculation – that would have been about two weeks before she did it, and things must have been bad. He'd wanted to speak to me that night.

'That's awful,' I said.

'By the way, this is *all* news to me,' Imogen piped up.

Samuel and I ignored her, and he continued. 'Eve was so upset. But I never thought she'd do anything so final. You're sure you didn't know any of this?' he asked me, as if it was impossible that so many things could have been going on that I hadn't been aware of.

How oblivious I'd been to what was happening around me even though the signs of discontent from the two of them had been there for a while. When things had been going well, I'd been more than happy to ignore anything that felt wrong, and even then and there on the beach, I wanted to run away from it all. Wished I could go back in time to when we were all a group.

'I only ask because right at the end, before Christmas, I gave Eve your number,' he said.

'What!' A sudden sickness as a thought bubbled. 'Why on earth would you do that?' I asked.

'I just thought it might straighten some things out. It was all such a mess. God, the whole thing's such a fucking mess still, really. I don't know what I was doing, to be honest. Did she call you? Did you speak to her before she did it?'

The calls.

I thought of the breaths, catching and weepy. So late at night that they barely felt real. Nights so long and desperate and cold that I was sure no one else in the world could have possibly been awake apart from me and the person on the other end of the line. Then they had just stopped.

'No. No calls,' I said, because I couldn't bring myself to go into it with him.

'I know there are things Tabitha has on you,' he said. 'You can tell me.'

'I really can't.'

He rubbed his eyes, wearily. 'Fine,' he said.

'So, what now?' I asked.

He considered it. 'I doubt they'd let you go so easily. You hold the whole thing together, far more than Tabitha. Who would have thought you'd be so good at it?'

Imogen nodded in bored agreement. 'You *are* good at it.'

I didn't respond.

'The boys found Eve,' Samuel continued. Now he'd started, he seemed to be unable to stop. 'They called me. Everyone always calls me. After that, there was no way I could be part of any of this.'

Imogen stared at the house. 'You should get out too. Stay away from them and stick to that boring boyfriend of yours,' she said.

Samuel smiled properly for the first time that afternoon. He reached out, and I thought he might touch my cheek, but he didn't even though I think he wanted to. I would have let his fingers run over my face just to feel warmth on that cold afternoon.

'Look at you! You wouldn't say boo to a goose before and now you're so . . . spiky! It's good. I like it,' he said.

Imogen's eyes were rolling almost out of her head again, and I wanted to scream and shout – *Do you know how hard I worked to be a better person? How hard I worked to be good and kind and quiet, to speak correctly like everyone else, to not cause any trouble, and to never let things spiral out of control? To not be the centre of attention? To not be spiky?*

What had it all been for? I was trapped.

He tried again. 'I stuck around for longer than I should because I owed Tabitha so much. I always have. I never felt like I'd paid her back for helping me get off the booze, and things just got out of hand, and then at some point, me and Imogen realized it had all gone too far. What Tabitha wants to do, it's about something else. She likes it when we hurt people, but what were we supposed to do?' he asked me. 'We've known Tabs forever. And you know how good it feels.' He looked at me, almost pleadingly. Then we both turned to Imogen, who was coughing away for attention.

'You don't need to speak for me,' she snapped at him.

67.

We walked without speaking, which was made easier because of the wind; it forced us to pull our hoods up around our ears. When we got back to the town centre, I bought chips to share because I thought it might perk Samuel up and he might stay to discuss things more, but he said his goodbyes swiftly and disappeared in his car. I also bought a battered sausage, picked off the batter and ate the reconstituted meat; the grease hardened and became thick and yellow when it met my frozen hands. Imogen watched with unconcealed revulsion. I didn't care.

Nothing worked any more. Seeing Samuel and Imogen together, they didn't seem interested in each other at all. I knew if I tried hard enough, I could remember how we used to glow and dance around each other – *whisky in the kitchen, the night at the casino*. But the magic had never come from the two of them and I suspected it had gone forever. Even as Imogen had laid out the story, there was none of the dramatic choreography I'd grown to expect.

How Samuel was with me was so formal too, which made it easy to think about how things might have been constructed. I could see it now, Tabitha sidling up to him, her hands all over him: *Flirt with Clare, make out you're interested, just a little. She'd like that! You're such a bloody catch. It'll keep her closer to us all . . . One for the team . . .*

There was nothing special about either of them in the slightest. Perhaps there never had been. Imogen, who liked her neat hobbies and claimed to want to research our targets, and Samuel, who presented himself as a fixer dishing out favours, with his shark smile, but it was all a lie. When you stripped away the layers, both of them were so completely ordinary, elevated only by their association with Tabitha. They'd stuck around for so long because of childish ties and threats.

A dry bit of skin on Samuel's cheek that he kept picking at.

A tear down Imogen's face from the wind.

I kept those images to the forefront of my mind, so I wouldn't have to remember Eve Landore's tears down the phone to me late at night.

68.

Surely, I was that girl from the video who attacked a man and forced him to climb into the carcass of a pig.

Certainly, I was a 'fifteen-year-old' whose actions caused a woman to kill herself.

Whoever I was, Tabitha had done this to me.

My bag was packed in the flat. I'd been gathering things together for weeks in preparation, trying not to make it obvious, but they still noticed.

'What are you doing?' Ashley asked. 'Why are you packing?' She looked shocked.

'Just leave me alone.'

'No! Tell us what's going on, you owe us that . . .' Her voice was whiny and insistent.

I had never felt like I owed her at all.

She continued pouring her concerns on to me: 'Clare, your nails, they're bleeding! You're going somewhere? Are you . . . dropping out?'

I went up to her, and she took a step back like she thought I might hit her, but instead I reached out and put my fingers to her hair, just to the very tips.

She froze, like an animal playing dead. If I tugged it hard enough, I could have pulled a chunk out. I didn't. I released it and her body seemed to relax, a strong exhale, her fear easing.

'I don't owe you anything.'

'But we're your *friends*.'

'We're not friends.'

I thought back to those first days. Ashley's aged dog had

looked so pathetic. It had ambled from room to room and, that day, I hadn't held back. I'd let my anger come out at the boxy little flat and I'd given it a sharp kick. It had wheezed and retreated, settling away from me warily.

Ashley didn't stay meek. It was fascinating to see her transform. Her whole face, which never usually had much expression, started to twist – it reminded me a little of Imogen's scowl. It was hatred, I think.

'Fine. Leave. We're better off without you. You're disgusting.'

I was surprised (and slightly impressed) that she had it in her – I'd clearly underestimated her. But, like when I'd ended things with Finn, none of it mattered any more.

I left the flat before I could do anything to Ashley, and I went round to Tabitha's.

69.

The only thing worse than hearing other people's dreams is hearing their nightmares, but it's important to me to express the sheer helplessness of it all. You see, it really was like one of those nightmares where you can't quite grasp what you're doing or where you're going. There's a low-level buzz of frustration, and however you try to divert the chain of events and drag it back to the path you want to take, the outcome evades you, it is forever the same. All roads ended with me turning up at Tabitha's. She would open the door again and again, and she always let me in.

I felt so many things when I saw her that night, but what I remember most is the pure joy when our eyes met, before I made myself recall everything she'd done.

She wore a green knitted dress that I'd never seen before and it gave her the appearance of an emaciated nymph because the skirt was tight, so her hip bones poked against the ribbing. Green wasn't her colour, and the skin on her chest looked almost translucent. She seemed diminished in some way; usually she took up so much space, but that night she was less of herself than ever. I didn't want to contemplate my appearance (and she didn't comment on it) but my demeanour was fine. I was calm.

'Oh, you're wearing my skirt.' She reached out and gave my upper thigh an appreciative little stroke.

'I'm sorry. Do you want it back?' I said, with no intention of actually returning it. The words were stiff and flat.

She didn't notice any awkwardness between us. 'No, no. It's just perfect on you!'

Ava emerged from her bedroom to the sound of me coming into the flat, and I wondered what domestic scene I was disturbing. There was a towel wrapped around her head and she wore a pair of silky, peach-coloured pyjamas. She whipped the towel away almost guiltily, the hair falling in a thick wet braid and slapping against her back with a thud. We hugged, so my face pressed against her shoulder, and she smelt of herself – orange rind and salt. She was fresh and damp. But tired. Something wasn't right, I sensed it as I looked from one of them to the other. The aftermath of an argument. A chilly hostility that I'd never known before with Tabitha and Ava. It hovered there just under the surface.

Tabitha saw my bag, and her face lit up with a smile. 'And you're staying! Brilliant news!'

'I couldn't stay there with them any more,' I said simply, hoping for no further questions.

Tabitha looked delighted, shifting her weight from one leg to the other, running her hands down the side of her legs and pulling the dress down over her hips. 'Of course, of course. A new flatmate for us! You've always been our *favourite*! This is where you belong.'

Ava raised an eyebrow at me with interest, as if to say, *Let's discuss this further later.*

'Anyway, so good to have you back,' Tabitha said. A very minimal statement for her. No mention of why I'd left in the first place.

I pictured her sneaking around, bold and brash. So many questions. How had she managed to get those drugs to Finn? How had she found that girl and convinced her to come over from France?

Who else had seen the video and what had she ended up doing to Jack the Pig? Was he coming after us?

She was clingy that night; she pulled me in, hugged me again. 'It's so good to have you here,' she whispered in my ear.

70.

We ate – a feast of artichokes. Then, some restrained conversation about nothing much at all. We avoided the obvious topics.

I wanted to get to Tabitha's room, but the rules had changed. The doors to the other rooms in the flat were closed to me again – Ava had shut them all shortly after I'd arrived. I excused myself to go to the toilet, and decided to look into Tabitha's bedroom, because it felt like home.

I opened the door.

It wasn't like that any more. I was shocked at the state. I'd always found Tabitha's mess comforting and romanticized it. That night, it was far beyond simple youthful chaos. Her things were everywhere and when I looked closer, I could locate the source of a smell – something that lived in the corner. It made me turn up my nose instinctively. Dust and body fluids dried and left too long; rising musk from a heap of clothes, or stock as it appeared to be. You could tell it was cheap, and someone had attempted to package some of it up roughly in paper and plastic.

Perfect Pieces.

When I got closer, I could see that the items were in far worse condition than Samuel would have allowed. They were ripped and dirty. Some looked stained with blackish substances – dried-on blood perhaps or who knows what else? And then the accompaniments: what looked to be letters, torn from a pad and left on the floor, stuffed in with the foul-smelling items. Letters with messy handwriting and featuring her imaginative spelling. They were scrawled, and it reminded me of those first few days when we'd met and Tabitha had stabbed her pen against the desks.

Abstract, disjointed tales and a complete change in direction to the easy smut we usually wrote. Her speciality seemed to be sparks of vitriol and secret promises of acts performed with barbed wire, or hot metal implements on soft skin and lips, then hard surfaces and pain to create images that left me hot in a shameful way, then so much talk of death and of torture. They were clearly real letters, addressed to real people who were buying those scrappy clothes. She'd become a violent pen pal without Samuel's commercial steer. Perfect Pieces had lost any semblance of structure and descended into something else.

The mess meant it was fine to dive into it all and I moved the top of a pile to one side. First some of Tabitha's little sketches, a self-portrait by Schiele copied, the rangy limbs well captured in pencil but with the head hacked off. Van Gogh with his auburn beard consumed in a red oil pastel attack.

I saw the printouts of chat rooms mixed in the pile, of the women tentative at first, and then adamant, describing what Jack the Pig had done to them with details and places, talking about how they'd walked away with injuries because he liked to hurt them. He'd taken pleasure in it; he could only enjoy it when pain was involved. Extreme acts. It made my encounter seem like nothing at all, but it had been something. They were anonymous – all tightly bound up in NDAs. I could perhaps recognize him from some of the more telling physical descriptions, but I couldn't have proved anything – I wasn't even a hundred per cent sure what they were saying was about him. And the fact they were here printed out in Tabitha's room, again, it didn't mean she'd known what would happen to me in the cellar, not conclusively. But she would have suspected it, surely? Decided that if it happened she could punish later and that would be enough.

The fee had been so high. Far higher even than Tabitha had

expected, I think. It was the kind of money where some collateral damage was to be expected. *Move fast and deal with it afterwards* had been Tabitha's tactic. Punish him once everything was paid up.

The photos of me were still there from before and I couldn't resist looking. It felt like a lifetime ago, but I wasn't happy or smug to see them any more. They signalled, above all else, that I was the chosen one, that I wouldn't be allowed to leave. Far too useful to be set free, unlike Imogen and Samuel who had both been permitted their respective exits.

Ava poked her head around the door and grimaced when she saw me in the centre of it all. 'What are you doing in here? Come on.'

I knew what would happen.

My bag was in the corridor, sitting ready for wherever I was going to go, the next part of life, the next big escape. And even though I was ready, it was almost comical that I'd thought I could just leave Edinburgh and that would be enough for them. I let out a high laugh at the audacity and Ava looked at me like I'd lost my mind; she led me back through to the kitchen.

I'd brought two bottles of champagne with me.

'Let's drink it on the roof,' I suggested. It was cold outside, but we liked the roof – we always had.

Tabitha nodded eagerly, and Ava seemed willing enough.

We climbed up the ladder in our scarves and coats, shivering as we ascended. Ava, Tabitha and I.

Up high so we could see the spread of the New Town around us, glittering on demand, like we'd turned it on at the plug for our own evening enjoyment. The air was crisp and it was quiet. We took our glasses and we lay out.

I thought back to Jack, champagne and his hands on my neck, the drink coming back up my throat. The memory of drinking champagne for the first time during *the episode*. I had that same feeling of electricity, that acidic buzz. Although maybe I'm conflating these feelings in my mind now as I look back, because the whole night took on a strange aura of other-worldliness.

We drank. Not much time passed; we were ravenous though, filled our glasses again and again, raced like there was a deadline to finish the bottles. In retrospect, I was the one pushing the drinking.

Tabitha got up and pulled me with her, and then we were dancing disjointedly, drunkenly. Ava lay watching us on an old rug.

Tabitha looked so beautiful. Maybe it was coming outside that had reinvigorated her. Alert in the way her gaze moved between Ava and me, and also relaxed – like her limbs were made of jelly – and when she danced she threw her head back in wild laughter at the delight of it, of seeing me, of being up on the roof.

It happened in a second. I reached out and I think she thought I was going to hug her; she leaned forward, smiling slightly, swaying a little.

At first, maybe I did plan to hug her; we so often touched – our hands, our arms, grazing, clawing, exploring each other all the time as if it was the only way to be close. It wouldn't have been out of character.

In that moment, as my cold hands met her shoulders, I didn't draw her closer.

How I felt about Tabitha was painful and hot and swirling. The cleanest of feelings, and an excruciating cocktail of love and hate and joy all at once.

Both hands, and one met each of her shoulders.

I gave her a push.

One quick, final push.

She reached out to steady herself – to hold on to me – but I stepped back as quickly as I'd done it.

She fell.

There was no other outcome. Stopping had been impossible, even if I'd wanted to, because, like Tabitha, I have always believed in punishment.

Tabitha had taken so much from me. Instead of protecting me, she'd brought *the episode* back. Dragged it out into the light – dirty and disgusting – and thrown it at me. Everything she'd done and everything she'd promised me had been a lie. She'd forced me to join her in something twisted, and I was the one who'd never be allowed to break free. She'd provoked me until it happened, created me, broken me, made me sick, mimicked me, bent it all, and by the time we reached that point on the roof, it was almost inevitable because I could do bold things like her.

It could have tied everything up well, because after the mourning, after the disbelief and the reminiscence, death can be very tidy.

That is not how it ended, though, because Tabitha didn't die.

71.

After Tabitha fell, I didn't have my father to call. I did have Ava, who sprang to life, scrambling up, and suddenly she was next to me because I was frozen, and then she was pulling me back as I tried to step towards the edge of the roof; I think maybe she thought I might jump and follow Tabitha in a grand gesture.

'I didn't mean to push her –' I started, even though it clearly wasn't true. Ava was close to me, and I wondered if she'd hit me or shake me or something. She was kinder than that, and she turned me around, put both hands on my shoulders instead, so we were standing there on the roof facing each other.

'I'm calling the ambulance, Clare. Just be calm. You don't have to do anything at all.'

We were close enough to the edge, and I found it impossible not to peek over; I couldn't help but look. Scaffolding had broken her fall and presumably saved her life. She was laid out on the boards, framed by steel posts, and she stared up at me, but she was too far down for me to see her true expression. The path of her fall had been bumpy and her body must have ricocheted off the side of the building. I saw that her hips were crooked, and it seemed inconceivable that a body could be so mangled, with her curved neck almost swanlike, or like the goose's neck as it takes *gavage*.

Such an unnatural angle for a person.

She twitched.

Then everything happened quickly. The ambulance arrived and we were whisked off to the hospital. Samuel turned up and Imogen too. Ava must have told them.

We sat in the waiting room in a row. None of it fit any more without Tabitha. How odd it was for us all to be there, under those unforgiving strip lights. No more casino nights or candle-lit dinners.

'What happened?' Samuel asked Ava.

'She fell,' Ava said.

'She fell?' Imogen asked, brushing tears from her face. After all the animosity between Imogen and Tabitha, she was still genuinely upset.

'Yes, she fell,' Ava said quietly. 'We were drinking up there, drinking far too much, and then we danced, and you know what she's like, she took it too far and it was dark. She slipped.'

She seemed so calm, lying for me with ease.

'I can't believe it!' Imogen said. 'What did the doctor say?'

'We don't know; she's not responsive at the moment.' Ava reached out and put her arm around Imogen, whose crying had become noisy.

Samuel looked to me. 'You were there,' he said unsteadily. 'You saw it all. How are you?'

'I'm fine,' I said.

We waited to see who would lead.

'We need to call her parents,' he said.

'We need to do no such thing,' Ava replied. 'The doctors will do that, or the police if they come. Just calm down and wait. Actually, Imogen, Samuel, why don't you leave? I'll stay in touch – I promise.'

Eventually, she was able to persuade them that it was fine to go.

We sat there in the hospital, sat so stiffly on those awful plastic hospital seats. I realized it was nearly morning. I wished I could take one of my pills and go back to my flat, pull up the covers over my head and sleep until everything ended.

The consultant came out and looked at us kindly. I'd always thought we must have seemed so unusual-looking, so impressive, but we probably just looked like two drunk, tired students.

'Could I have a word?' She took Ava through to a consulting room.

Ava was only in there for about ten minutes, then she returned and sat down next to me. She was still, and I could barely even hear her breathing, then she turned to me, eyes bloodshot like a hound. I noticed the blush of her pyjama top that she hadn't bothered to change out of, so you could see it poking from underneath her coat.

Looking straight at me, she might have said something about what had happened. The two of us were in our own bubble in the hospital waiting room. She could have said something, surely, but she chose to stay silent, and all I could think of was how much she might have revealed in private with the consultant about what had actually happened.

I wanted to shake her and say, *What are you doing? Why aren't you screaming at me, telling the world what I did?*

'What did they say?' I asked.

'You need to give me a minute,' she replied. It was more than a minute. We sat together and she didn't speak at all.

72.

And then the police arrived, and I was shocked even though of course the police were bound to show up. There were two of them. One was in uniform – a man who looked barely older than us – and then a woman who seemed more senior, but didn't speak.

'Hi, girls,' the male officer said slowly as if we might have trouble understanding. 'I'm sure you're very upset about your friend, but we need to talk to you about what happened last night.'

Last night. It was already last night.

'We're going to take you over to the police station, which is close by, and then we'll bring you back here.'

'Do I have to go?' My voice sounded weak. I looked at Ava for guidance.

'We've been up for a long time,' she said to the man, and I wondered how he might perceive her, this girl who spoke to him like a complete equal and who didn't see him as an authority figure at all. The police officer nodded but took little notice.

'It's important we speak to you now while everything's still fresh. I know you've spoken to the doctors already, so you're aware of the seriousness of the situation – you're aware your friend might not make it.'

I wasn't aware. I looked to Ava again, but she was impossible to reach. There was a blankness to her that scared me.

He gestured to us again. 'Come on, both of you.' He steered us through the brightly lit corridor; at first it looked like he was going to put one hand on my back, then he seemed to think better of it, and he walked behind us, escorting us out of the hospital and into a police car that sat waiting at the entrance. A few people skulked around the doors. There was a mix of hospital staff and patients smoking, and they stared, then looked away, surely imagining what we'd done.

We sat in silence in the back of the police car and looked out of the window. I had hoped it would take longer, but the station was close by.

At the police station, Ava went in first, and she gave me a quick smile before standing up – the first time she'd interacted with me since the hospital.

I sat in the corridor, forcing myself to read the posters stuck up on the wall to take my mind off what was about to happen.

A woman brought me a weak cup of tea, a gesture that seemed to signify that it was officially morning, as shortly after I started to drink, light began to flood in through the window.

Ava emerged. She was as calm as ever. She sat down, but she didn't look at me.

I was certain she would have told them. I waited for the inevitable, and the police officer popped his head around the door and beckoned me forward.

'Right, you can come in now. Clare, is it?'

The end had come. I went in; he and his colleague sat across from me.

'Take a seat,' he said.

They introduced themselves.

'I think I should get a solicitor?' I said. I didn't know if I was even allowed one. When I thought back to Périgueux, so much of what had happened had been obscured from me. I was protected from it all because we'd been so young. *You won't understand. Just leave it to the grown-ups.* But I was alone now and asking for a solicitor seemed like the right thing to do.

'You're within your rights to have access to a solicitor,' he said. 'This is just a chat, though. You're not being charged with anything. We just want to understand what happened last night.' He checked his watch; he was a lot more confident than he'd been in the hospital.

'So, Clare, we're up to here. You're all on the roof, drinking no doubt, maybe something other than booze too?' He gave me a conspiratorial wink and rechecked his notes.

I didn't respond.

His colleague looked irritated.

'This is all a lot for you, I'm sure.' He changed tack. 'Anyway, Tabitha ends up on the scaffolding below at about one a.m.? She's fallen from multiple storeys, bashed around a bit on the way down.'

Bashed around. Horrible.

'She hit some obstacles,' he corrected himself quickly. 'So, from our perspective, the question is simply, what happened up there? I'm struggling to work out how she gets from being on the roof to being on the scaffolding. Let's go back to the beginning: what were you doing outside to start with?'

'We go up there all the time. The flat has these amazing views.'

'Yes. A very nice address, your pal's place.'

I nodded, not sure what to say.

'So, why don't you talk through the fall. What happened right before she fell?' he asked.

'I don't know,' I replied. 'We were dancing, and it was so dark up there; we'd been drinking. We were close to the edge, and she just . . . fell, I guess.'

'How? Did she slip on something?' He tapped his pen on the table, waiting.

The woman leaned in, coming closer towards me. 'It's funny, Clare,' she said. 'People respond to trauma in different ways. For some folk we see, it seems to almost go into slow motion. The world stops, time stops. For some, it speeds up; everything goes a hundred miles an hour – it's the adrenaline. Despite what you see in films or what you might read, it's incredibly rare for someone just to block it out, to actually not remember what happened. Do you understand what I'm saying?'

'I understand.'

'OK,' she sighed. 'To be completely clear, I think you remember. And I want to understand, from you, exactly what happened on the roof that led to your friend falling, your friend who might die. That's why it's so important you tell us now.'

Silence.

She sighed. Her lipstick was smudged around her mouth. 'I'm going to ask you another question. Did your friend Ava push Tabitha off that roof?'

My eyes widened. 'No, of course not, she'd never do that. Tabitha fell.'

The policewoman looked very tired of the whole thing. 'Tabitha slipped off that roof? Because she was drunk? Because she'd taken drugs?'

'No, I mean we'd drunk a bit.'

'And what were you drinking?' the man asked.

'Champagne,' I replied.

He gave me such an ugly smile. It reminded me of the way Imogen sometimes smiled. I could feel his contempt.

'Drinking champagne on the roof? OK, then.'

They both looked at me expectantly as if I might jump in and start speaking. I didn't.

Then there were more questions, but nothing from me. I'd reached the end. I was spent. They never actually accused me of doing anything and I spent a lot of time nodding, agreeing – *Yes, we were good friends; yes, I was happy to be there* – or shaking my head emphatically – *No, I wasn't taking any hallucinogens* – until it stopped, slowly grinding to an unsatisfying end.

Eventually, the woman said, 'OK. Let's leave it there for today, we're not charging either of you with anything, but we probably will want to speak to you again. I'll take you both back to the hospital.' She stood up and then, almost as an after-thought, added, 'Do either of you have parents you want us to call? The university will have a duty of care over you both, but it might be worth speaking to your parents?'

I shook my head. My granny would've hated to get involved. 'There isn't anyone.'

I walked out, and Ava sat there in the chair in front of me. And it was hard even to look at her, hard not to ask her, to scream out and demand to know why she was protecting me.

73.

At the hospital, away from the police, we went outside. Ava led me further away from the building until we reached a housing estate. The place was bleak, with some teenagers milling around doing tricks on bikes, and a group of men leaning against a parked car, looking like they might suddenly smash the windows in. It was so early in the morning, and everyone should have been in bed. People were up though; they were still in the night before. It didn't seem like a safe place to discuss anything.

We reached a bus stop crowded with broken glass. Ava stepped over it and perched on the bench, patting the seat, but I didn't want to sit next to her, to relax, so she stood up next to me instead and offered me a cigarette.

I got right to the point. 'Why are you saying she fell?' I asked.

She shushed me with a flick of the wrist, lit her cigarette and inhaled deeply. 'I needed that. Right, there are people around here, and I don't want them to hear this. *On parle en français?*'

'I never speak in French any more.'

'Oh, I'm sure you can manage it now,' she replied mildly in perfect French.

I hadn't known about her language skills then. But it didn't surprise me.

'Locked-in syndrome,' she said. 'At least, that's what the consultant thinks; they're not sure about the full extent of any of it yet. It's worked out well for you.'

'What do you mean?'

'Oh, you know. Everything locked in there, in her head, what happened.'

'I didn't mean for her to die.'

She smiled at me faintly. 'I don't think that's true at all. Anyway, things have worked out very differently than I could have expected at the beginning. There are things you might have . . . assumed.'

'Might have assumed?'

She sighed. 'Tabitha never knew about what you did in Périgueux, about any of it.' She laughed, a short, sharp yelp of a noise that had no humour to it.

I didn't understand at all; I tried to think back, replay the last year quickly, all the things that had happened. It didn't make sense.

'But she *must* have. The video she made, or whoever made. The things that happened afterwards . . .' I said.

'The things that happened over the last few months were so that you didn't quit for good. That was all me. I've never known *exactly* what went on with you and that man when you were at school. The parts I did know were enough to use. Anyway, Tabitha couldn't have coordinated any of that – too busy tormenting Imogen most of the time.'

She took a deep breath and sighed before continuing. 'Yes, anyway, the video. She did rope me into that, and I saw the parallels at the time. I should have known how much it would upset you. It was . . . misjudged.'

She shrugged, then pressed further as if something had occurred to her. 'You were worried about the footage, weren't you? That he'd track you down? You needn't have been. He paid more to get that footage back in the end. He doesn't want anyone to see that! Of course he doesn't. She knew he'd pay up.'

Clever. How naive of me not to consider that, when it came down to it, money sat alongside vengeance – equally important – two sides of a coin in the violent currency The Shiver had chosen.

I thought of his body, flabby and pink as he climbed inside the carcass.

Then there had been the graveyard. Tabitha's confusion when I'd spoken a single word of French.

'I don't understand?' I said. 'She never asked me about my family, about my background, not once, not one question. I thought it was because she knew. That she was *helping* me by not asking. By not bringing it up.'

'She didn't know. She certainly wasn't helping you. It's just what Tabitha's like. She didn't care. She said she needed to understand you, of course she did, but think harder. Did she really? Did she ever ask you a proper question about anything much? One that wasn't linked to something she wanted or to something helpful for her? She wasn't ever curious, was she? Don't be offended – she's always been like that.'

I thought back to Tabitha and her twisty stories. The words spilling over each other like she'd die if her thoughts were trapped inside for too long.

'All you?' I repeated.

She didn't reply directly. 'I would have done anything for her, and in this case, keeping you was what she wanted. I knew how this would seem when I explained it all to you. It's like I'm the villain. I set all these traps to make you come back. I had suspicions beforehand of what that man might do to you in the Highlands.'

She ran through a list. 'And giving Finn those drugs, and chasing down that girl from your school. I didn't *enjoy* doing any of that. Truly now when I look back, I am sorry. You've done some awful things, Clare, and so have I, but pushing Tabitha was verging on the inevitable. It brings this all to an end because the whole thing was getting silly, wasn't it?'

She watched me expectantly. The way she spoke was so light-hearted and sing-song, it felt like we'd been through a series of wacky dares. It was disconnected from the gravity of everything we'd done, and I think it allowed her to get through her explanation.

She continued. 'Is it a relief that you're not losing your mind? My intention wasn't to make you . . . unhinged. It was just to hold it all together, make you come back, and somehow I failed and things just fell apart. Too many moving cogs.'

I didn't answer.

'They're all gone,' she said. 'Imogen, Samuel. Then you know what happened with the Landores?'

I nodded. 'They told me.'

'They didn't like that, and who can blame them? Too seedy, too much for most of us, but not for Tabitha,' she continued. 'The odder it got, the more she liked it. The attack up north with Jack the Pig – I researched him, I wasn't sure at all about it, but she delighted in that, she knew what could happen. She said people like him were a whole "new market". Yup, those were the words she used. Because violence didn't faze her – it never has. Of course, she enjoyed the way we punished him, even though she maintains that was a present for you when you were so upset by the whole thing. And then you saw the direction she planned to take Perfect Pieces in?'

She sighed. 'She wasn't so interested in the actual honey trapping by the end. You know how the clients always "seemed" to choose you? She didn't really give them the option to choose her because she had bigger plans. Once you looked and acted how she wanted you to, she was absolutely fine with you taking it all on. It was why I was under such pressure to keep you.'

There was so much to take in, forcing me to examine everything between Tabitha and me, to cast her in a new light, but deep down I knew she hadn't hidden any of this. She had never really been anything other than her own glorious, terrible self, but to see her true colours would have been like staring into the sun – painful. It had always been easier to just enjoy the warmth.

'You were together that night in the Highlands?' I asked.

'We'd been together for a while in a sense,' she said sadly.

'Not properly. There's always been something, though. You know, the funny thing is, she wouldn't have minded about what you did to that man in Périgueux – whatever exactly it was you did – but I kept it from her because my job was to sort you out and knowing more would have excited her, made her use you in ways that would have been even riskier for you. Sometimes I considered telling her, but I never managed to. She would have been far worse than me, you know. I was protecting you from her. She'd take you and cut you with it in a second.'

She could have been right. If anything, history had shown that Ava was fair. She used her power only when strictly necessary. I thought of how unsure she'd been about the Highlands, and how the knowledge had pained her. She didn't seem keen to dwell on it, and I never did find out exactly what the set-up was with those men. I never went back to save Sorcha from them.

She kept speaking. 'When she came up with the idea for the whole thing, I knew you'd probably go along with what we had planned, but it was safer to have that in the background. You never seemed especially concerned with wealth, and we needed you so much. You always held the whole thing together, right from the start, so if the carrot was the money, then what was the stick? I thought it would be good to have both.'

'Something on me.'

She looked at me fondly. 'You were perfect. The best of a solid bunch. Tabitha and I found you, back then, right at the beginning. Then she backed off, and I did some digging, and I couldn't believe it. To be honest, I never thought the skeletons in your closet would be so juicy, such an *odd* story, and I also questioned whether you'd really even care if it "came out" as such, but you would have, I think. You've reinvented yourself so well. And it showed that you had an appetite for what we wanted to do. Your past – it was just *so* suited to our plan, like it was meant to be, blew the other candidates out of the water. It's funny, though, I don't think you have the same level of viciousness as her. Close, but not quite.'

I didn't feel that Tabitha and I were the same. I'd only ever felt that fleetingly when it had all been going well.

The question sat there on my tongue, burning. 'Why don't you hate me?'

She gripped my hands tightly. 'I was relieved when you did it. I've been thinking about when she watched The Pig take you down the stairs – she didn't care much at the time. I've seen the way she wants to do it and it's not what I want. Naively, I thought it would be a proper business, and then it spiralled out of control. It took a while for me, but now I can see how awful it had all become. How awful *I'd* become.

'I didn't realize properly for too long, I was so busy doing what I'd always done – trying to please her, trying to make sure you stayed – then when you pushed her, it made me see how unhappy I was. I'd always thought the two of us living together would be perfect, but it hasn't been. Not at all.'

Her relationship to Tabitha was different to the others. I thought of Imogen and her essays; Samuel's debts to Tabitha for the drinking. If anything, Tabitha had owed Ava.

'She trusted you,' I said. 'She never had anything over you like with the rest of them.'

'Kind of. There are aspects of my family business that I'd rather were kept separate and, credit to her, she didn't ask me for money after the initial capital injection, or even mention it – nothing like that – but you're right, I think she would have trusted me with it all forever. She shouldn't have. If you hadn't done what you did last night, I would have ended it in another way eventually. When you did it, when you pushed her, I felt it. Like I was pushing her myself.'

She put one hand on my shoulder, the other still holding a cigarette where the ash hung in a teetering link and then fell to the pavement. She gave me a firm shove, right in the centre of my chest, so I stumbled back, not so I lost my footing entirely, but hard enough to display how much strength was locked up inside of her.

'Like that, that's what you did,' she said. 'That's what I saw you do. But we made you into this, not just me, or even me and Tabitha, all of us. We found you and we turned you into everything we wanted. I've saved her once, but I won't do it again. Now it's you and me, and you can be the star.' She came close with her lips right up to my ear so I could almost feel her tongue on my skin, soft and wet.

'I'll never tell.' She almost spat it.

And she stepped back away from me. Hands clenched like claws. Hair blowing in the wind.

She was so spectacular lurching towards me on that cold morning. It was one of the only times that the veneer of calm I always associated with her melted away and she had a bit of Tabitha's wildness.

'What now?' I asked.

'Now, we do things differently,' she said.

74.

Many years have passed.

If we have *the episode* for what happened in France, what happened with Tabitha became known as *the accident* between Ava and me.

I am different now.

I look similar, but so much of someone is in how they move and how they speak. Before, I asked questions. I was odd. My words were stilted and my remarks carefully constructed. Now, I speak confidently, and people often comment on how I sound, say they can't quite place where I'm from, and I don't elaborate. I'm happy to let them wonder.

So where did everyone end up? Imogen graduated and married a banker. Although I tried to reach out to her after Tabitha's fall, she didn't return my calls and finally she got in touch to say that she wanted nothing to do with me, ever again. This struck me as fair; there was no love lost there.

Samuel enjoyed working for himself, and he started something similar to Perfect Pieces (I'd always thought he'd found Perfect Pieces genuinely enjoyable) but a little more vanilla, which was a better fit for him. Looking at the new listings was an excellent way to keep tabs on him for a while; I'd scroll through the knickers and camisoles, watching the stories become more elaborate and less tasteful, and it was like I was talking to him. As with Imogen, he said he would prefer not to stay in touch. He said it was *too difficult* considering what had happened.

There was never much of a follow-up from the police after the accident; our stories must have been convincing enough.

Still, there was a fair bit of coverage in the press. Beautiful young student topples with catastrophic injuries – who can blame them? My parents contacted me through my granny, they said under no circumstances was I to get in touch with them, not ever. I've respected their wishes and I haven't contacted them since.

And Tabitha? I can say in all honesty that I wish Tabitha had died. How final that sounds! When I saw her body lying there after having fallen so far down, so battered, I thought it was over.

Ava steers away from the question. She has never asked me if I feel any guilt. Perhaps because she'd rather not hear the answer. But I have asked myself that, and although I wish everything had worked out differently, I'm not sure how it could have. For some people, when they get very close to the edge of doing something bad, they draw back. When that happens to me, when I get that close, it has to happen and there is no other option. What I will say is that I've gained the clarity that comes with the passing of time, and I can recognize some of my flaws. I see how I scrutinized The Shiver, how I made them my entire world and relied on them for excitement, for joy, for everything.

I visit Tabitha often. Usually, I have the radio on in the car, but on those trips I drive out in silence, thinking about what to say to her and what she'd like to hear. I often think about what would impress her.

It hasn't always been like that. In the beginning, I would go every day, then hardly at all, maybe once a year. She lives in a residential home outside the city. A place where the doors are locked at night and visitors sign in and out. I could have gone as much as I wanted, but I struggled with it eventually. What was too much? If I went every week, surely it would look like I had something to hide, like I was too attached to her?

Now, I'm less concerned with what people might think of me, and I go there often again. I sit there and watch her; she's mostly awake – staring, locked in. I like to think she understands and that she's listening.

Her eyes are glassy, and she doesn't blink much. They suspected she could communicate with flickering eye movements at the beginning, but she never managed to get very far, and I wonder if that was because of my presence in those early days.

I feel very protective over her, which is nice; I'm the one in charge, and she has no choice but to sit there listening to my stories. I tell her about the business, about what's working and what's not because I always think she'd enjoy that. I tell her about my marriage, about what it's like to be married, about the freedom I miss sometimes, about the plans I have next. And I always speak to her about Ava, about how beautiful she is, still. Ava likes someone else to be in charge, someone else to ultimately defer to. First she had Tabitha and now she has me.

The things that keep her alive beep companionably as I talk, and she's kept presentable by the staff. I researched her condition more in the years after it happened. It was a rare condition to be brought on by a fall, and it would be even rarer for her to ever emerge to anything like her old self. At this point, the consensus from the medical team is that too much time has elapsed for any improvement to be expected.

I digress. Tabitha represents a tiny part of my life; a scheduled, regular visit. For a long time she hardly occupied my thoughts at all, not until Minta asked me to write down my memories of her.

Tonight, for example, I'm sitting in my dining room; it's spacious with large windows and views out on to the park. I've decorated the place quite a few times over the years, no doubt helped by the many tips I picked up from them all. The rugs and artwork are old, most of them sourced at auction, and they speak of excellent taste, I think. Of heirlooms. If someone assumes that I've inherited these items, I don't contradict them – I let people think they're pieces that have been kept in the family because that works for the story many craft about me in their heads. I even have some of the furniture from Tabitha's flat in Edinburgh, but I'm no Luddite. I also welcome modernity with a speaker system that cost several times more than the average car. And the decoration helps keep certain things at bay. If I ever see the suggestion of a furry little trail of mould, I tend to repaint. That serves to eradicate it from the walls, or just from my head.

There's a fire in the fireplace. I've lit it even though it's relatively mild outside because people are always drawn to it. They slink over and warm their hands. To cater to my guests, I've also placed a tray of hors d'oeuvres and a bottle of decent red there, at an easy reaching distance.

This set-up, the decorum, is something well practised over the years, so now in our small, rather elite circle of friends I have no doubt what they say about me when I'm not there: 'Clare, she's a fantastic cook,' or 'Always such a fun night at Clare's house.'

If you asked them more about me, where I'm from, what I do for work, they'd tip their heads and say, 'Oh, I'm not sure about that, she keeps herself to herself. Maybe something in finance.'

Even if they do ask me outright, I'll often say, 'It's so boring, you must tell me about that project you're working on. It sounds so interesting, but I do remember your boss was a total micromanager . . .' Because one of the things I learned from Tabitha is that most people love speaking about themselves. Those who don't, who want to know more about me, usually don't last too long as friends, and I'm able to shed them with relative ease.

Beside me is my husband, the advocate for the expensive speaker system, whose hand rests firmly on mine. In front of me, friends from his work. The wife sits with her back to the fire, her shoes kicked off as she luxuriates in the heat. I can hear her congratulating me on my tarte Tatin, and I thank her and offer her another slice, even though she hasn't finished the first, extricating myself from my husband's grip as I plan to go and fetch coffee and whiskies. In essence, he prefers to keep it traditional in terms of what's served when, and I'm happy to cater to his preferences. Throwing a dinner party like this is like sleepwalking for me, and I'll go through the motions as many times as I need to.

'Did you say you made it yourself?' She licks her lips and places her spoon on the side of the plate to show she's finished. There is one tiny slither of the pastry left on her plate, a lank little slice where the apple has flopped away from the crust. She's pushed it to one side, as though it offends her. A smear of crème anglaise is set in a thin film. For some reason, this niggles at me irrationally, and I want to pick up the plate and shove it under her mouth, pushing her face into it and forcing her to eat the last bit. I want to tell her there's one mouthful left and who doesn't eat the final morsel from their dessert to save the hostess from scraping it into the bin? But I don't.

'I did, I'm so glad you liked it. It's effortless to make, a real cheat's recipe!' I say pleasantly.

'I love it, really well done, you, and thanks so much for having us round,' she responds.

'It's the least I can do.' I catch my reflection in the window across the room. There is a fleeting smile that just lifts from the mouth and touches my cheeks to show the slightest hint of gracious humour.

My husband looks up at me appreciatively, the skin around his temples crinkling. When it comes to the couple across from us, I don't know them well enough to be sarcastic or to put down my husband in front of them, not that it's something I do so much – he seems to prefer a quiet deference anyway. Instead,

I'm sincere and appreciative. We've only been married just over a year, so the glow hasn't worn off yet for him.

Ava had suggested we might want to try one of our girls on him at some point to see if he bites, to see how loyal he really is, because over this past year we've both come to the silent agreement that it probably won't last, and then it's just a case of how it ends.

Of course, one of the problems there is how we trained those girls, how they ask questions, how they engage. It's all us, so I find it hard to believe that he wouldn't recognize my words and my inflections as Ava and I have been a little more structured in how we run it.

We would never expect a girl to speak about Napoleon at length because we know that's not what's required. Instead, it's preferable to listen and purr in agreement. It's all online now, which is so much easier. All chat rooms and smartphones and apps, and a level of technical ingenuity you wouldn't believe. Oh, how Tabitha would despair at that, but you can't halt progress.

Ava and I have worked well together so far. She knows that there might be changes afoot. One of the ways I'm able to stay so calm, so very perfectly calm, and one of the reasons I don't take that woman's head and smash it against the table, is that this is not the final act. I don't know quite how it will end, but I have some plans in place.

I've bought a little house up north. Inside, the walls are blue like the morning sky. It's high up, and the windows look out over the sea where the waves lap in and out, over a pebbled beach.

It's not for me to live in; it's not some kind of escape. I have learned that escaping is not the way to do it, and I have no intention of moving out to the coast at this stage. My husband thinks I chose the house because it's close to a place he mentioned holidaying in as a child. He thinks there's some sentimental reason, and I took him there and we lay naked outside under the sky at night. He is right in a way, I did choose it because of the location. It has a specific set of advantages: remote, few passers-by, and the coastal weather changes in an instant.

When I went for the first time after we'd bought it, I did a proper survey of the surrounding shores. I left him in bed and I walked along the path that curves high across the cliffs through the wild grasses. Right at the edge there's a small clearing, and if I sense that he's getting too close to what Ava and I do, who we are, perhaps I'll take him for a walk.

There's something to be said for my years with Ava; she's such a natural planner and some of those skills have rubbed off on me. I understand the angles better now. I tossed a pebble down there while my husband was gripped by his emails back at the cottage and saw how it cut through the water in a second. I threw an armchair over in a rage when I first visited alone, the old one from Tabitha's where the innards seeped out through the holes. I have pictured the bulky thing, pictured where it would fall and how the waves would consume it.

One of the only people I've told about my little house near the cliffs is Tabitha. I ran some thoughts past her, and she may have twitched.

I think she approves.

In my dining room, I open the sliding door and I gesture to my guests to come through to the library for coffee. I've already brewed a pot just how I like it, so strong that it's almost a punishment to force it down.

Epilogue

A final night in Périgueux before I moved to England to stay with my granny.

My parents were not speaking to me.

I heard the word.

Psychopathe

They whispered it to each other.

'Do you feel guilty that he died?' my mother asked me.

One of her final questions before I left France because we'd hardly discussed it at all. But she knew there was more to it. I didn't answer her straight away; I wanted her to see that I was considering her words.

Dina and Adrienne and I drank champagne because it felt like an occasion.

It was the first time I'd ever drunk it, and it was delicious; I swilled it around my mouth to make the taste last longer. Nothing I've ever tasted since has evoked the same bliss as that first glass. I didn't know words like 'rounded' or 'full-bodied'. Back then, I just thought it was some kind of magical elixir that made the world brighter. The bottle had been from Dina's father's cellar and we brought it into the house that night. We drank out of plastic cups in the kitchen – we hadn't even bothered to chill it. We screamed in delirium as the cork fired into the air, and I remember how we finished the bottle and the giddiness turned into a vague sort of indeterminable nausea.

It was fun at first and they enjoyed it, we all did. Their reticence seemed quelled. Maybe everything would be fine. In its essence, the plan was simple. We force-fed him in the most fitting way – punished him with vegetarian food – and it was perfect. They joined in in a way that was nearly willing.

The night didn't stay fun. Dina was worried about him. She kept disappearing off to the toilet with Adrienne and they edged away from me.

They wouldn't go near him after a while.

We played music – the same songs on repeat again and again. He'd been tied up for most of the night, and we'd stopped feeding him hours before. I poured the water for him. He dribbled as if he'd lost some of the ability to control his mouth, and his eyes were bulging, like if you were to squeeze a fish. He gulped at us.

The girls had both been crying, but they had tried to hide their tears. They were trying to be assertive.

'We could leave now,' Adrienne said, her voice unsteady, almost pleading. 'If we left, no one would ever know. Maybe he wouldn't tell anyone.'

'It's too late to leave,' I said. I had a plan.

'Why are you laughing?' Dina asked softly, looking at me like I was insane. I had hardly even noticed, but she was right, I was laughing, just a little.

They were so *nervous*, and I could see Adrienne backing away. The two of them looked petrified.

Dina was brave enough to speak up. 'Why are you doing this?' she asked me.

'This is your fault,' I replied. I didn't explain it to them fully, but I needed them to know. 'You made me do this,' I said.

I walked over to him where he sat, just slightly away from the house, ever so quiet and hardly moving. The drugs from earlier were probably causing the gulping. The veins on his neck stuck out, and he tried to swallow and get more air into his body.

Bright moonlight, and you could still see the mess of it all. Stickiness on the ground, on our hands and on the table. Food everywhere with a slimy film setting on the remains. I could see he'd spat some of the meal out and that would need to be cleaned up later.

Dina was pulling at me, breathing fast. 'We should get him to a hospital.'

I turned to her slowly, feeling light, like I was made of air, and I put both hands on her shoulders. Her eyes were wide open in terror and she pulled at me to hold me back, and keep me with her, but I pushed her away.

A plastic bag lay to the side of him, just at his elbow.

I took it in both hands and placed it hard against his mouth, so the skin became a taut bulge. His breath made it expand and contract, and the bag itself looked like a shiny branded organ. A Carrefour lung. Those are the kind of thoughts I had as I pushed harder and harder.

He wheezed heavily, so laboured, but he was alive. When I pressed down (because the other two wouldn't help), he was grateful, I'm sure of it.

He didn't struggle, although I knew that was because of the drugs in his system. He wouldn't have been able to stop struggling otherwise, even though he was ready for it all to be over – it's part of the human condition to want to stay alive, to grasp and pull at that final stretch of life even if you realize it's for the best.

I'm sure I didn't know at the time that smothering was hard to detect under autopsy. I was just lucky.

A final breath and then nothing.

Dina and Adrienne watched, and I could see they were both crying.

I said we needed to call someone. An adult needed to sort the whole thing out for us because there was nothing more we could do.

More crying, but it was confusion and exhaustion at this point. They asked me why I'd done it, although they could barely get the words out through their tears. My anger hadn't gone away at this point. It was still there – hot and black, sticky like treacle, ready for me to inflict on them.

I told them both: 'I did it for you.'

It was always for them, to punish them, to show them, to finish what we started.

'*Tu es folle*,' Adrienne said simply. You're crazy.

They didn't really understand. Said they were going to 'tell on me'. How childish it sounds, to tell on someone. Those were the words they used. It was Adrienne who said it, and I grabbed her wrist and bent it back, not enough to break a bone, but enough so she screamed out in pain. She pulled away from me and I saw how scared she was.

I wanted to explain to them that they'd caused it all, that there was really nothing I could have done about it. Not once the wheels were in motion. The need to show them, to impress them, to stay part of their threesome, and finally to scare them. Everything had come together in a singularly perfect event. I wasn't nervous, and I wasn't out of it that night in France, not drunk or messy. At the time, I felt all the nerve endings, mind and body perfectly in tune.

'No. It was their fault,' I said to my mother.

She moved away from me to create more distance between us.

My mother in her cramped little room, with the damp seeping up the walls. That night she locked me away, and it was very dark and very cold. I had realized by then that my parents felt much safer when there was a locked door between us.

My final night before I moved to England.

I slept well.

Acknowledgements

Firstly, thank you to my wonderful agent, Emily Glenister, for believing in this book right from the very start. I am also eternally thankful to my brilliant editors, Victoria Moynes and Jesse Shuman.

Thank you to the rest of the team: Lydia Fried, Harriet Bourton, Ellie Hudson, Hayley Cox, Olivia Mead, Amelia Evans, Monique Corless, Catherine Turner, Annie Underwood, Emma Brown, Charlotte Daniels, Meredith Benson, Sam Fanaken, Rachel Myers, Eleanor Rhodes Davies, Kyla Dean, Tineke Mollemans, Riannah Donald, Linda Viberg and Maddy Bennett, Karen Whitlock, Bela Cunha and Anne Cook. In the US, thank you to Anne Speyer and Elana Seplow-Jolley for their sage editorial contributions. Also, thanks to Jennifer Hershey, Kim Hovey, Kara Welsh, Maya Franson, Kathleen Quinlan and Corina Diez.

The following people helped enormously along the way. In Edinburgh, I am indebted to Louise, Sarah, Lucie, Natasha, Rose, Georgie. Also, Graham for the photographs, everyone at Mallzee and in particular Mel, Cally, Catriona and Rachelle. Thank you to Cathy and the Pyes for weekends spent at Rednock over the years and thank you early readers Richard Wilson and Barbara Wray. Thank you also to Alice Green, Graham Bartlett, Sarah Lansley, Richard Howell and Raymond Wray.

I've met so many new friends who have always been around to generously answer questions and quell anxiety, like Niamh Hargan, as well as the CBC Creative gang and the incredible Debut '22 and '23 communities – too many deeply supportive people to name but you know who you are.

Finally, massive thanks to Liv, Sonia, Vicky, James and Andy, who made my time in Edinburgh worth remembering.

Noelle Darwent, Melissa Darwent, Neil Darwent for their ongoing support, love and care.

And Daniel, who helped so much with plot and character and *speaker systems*. You built a house around me while I wrote this book from the sofa – I appreciate it and you.

Reading Group Questions

1. Do you think Clare is an inherently 'bad' person, or a product of her upbringing?
2. How do you think Clare's parents have shaped her? Do you agree with how they acted?
3. How do Clare's parents compare to Tabitha's parents?
4. What is the significance of the Edinburgh setting?
5. What do you think of the relationship between Clare and Tabitha? Do the two women mirror each other at all?
6. What do you think of Samuel? What is his role within the shiver?
7. How did your impressions of Imogen and Ava develop as the plot unfolded?
8. Do you think class plays a role in Clare's fixation on the shiver?
9. Is Tabitha's honeypot scheme a feminist act?
10. Does this book accurately represent female rage?
11. Do you think the men in this book deserve the treatment they receive?